THE AVEROIGNE LEGACY

TRIBUTE TALES IN THE WORLD OF

CLARK ASHTON SMITH

Edited by Edward Stasheff

eBook available at:

Amazon Kindle Store:	http://tinyurl.com/AveroigneLegacy-amazon
Barnes & Noble Nook:	http://tinyurl.com/AveroigneLegacy-nook
Google Play:	http://tinyurl.com/AveroigneLegacy-google
Apple iBooks:	http://tinyurl.com/AveroigneLegacy-apple
Kobo eBookstore:	http://tinyurl.com/AveroigneLegacy–kobo

COPYRIGHT INFORMATION

TABLE OF CONTENTS
Titles in italics are poetry

PRONUNCIATION GUIDE

PLACES

Averoigne	ah-ver-OWN *or* ah-veh-ROIN
Bonne Jouissance	bun jeu-ee-SAWNS
Conflans	kohn-FLOHN
Cordeliers	KOR-doo-lee-ay
Château Faussesflammes	shah-TOW foss-FLAHM
Grémoire-en-Chaux	gray-MWAH-on-SHOW
Hameu de Malinbois	AH-moo duh mal-in-BWAH
Isoile	eez-WAHL
La Frênaie	la freh-NAY
Les Hiboux	lay ee-BOO
Morraine	MOHR-en
Périgon	pay-ree-GONE
Ste. Zénobie	sant zay-no-BEE
Sylaire	see-LAIR
Vyônes	vee-OWN
Ximes	zeem
Ylourgne	ee-LOORN

PEOPLE

Azédarac	uh-ZAY-dah-rak
Chantillion	SHAT-ee-YOHN
François	fron-SWAH
Gasquet	GAHS-kay
Gérard Dhuyne	zheh-RARD doo-EEN
Guy Broche	GEE brosh
Habile	ah-BEEL
Henri Giroux	on-REE ZHEER-roo
Iog-Sotôt	ee-OG suh-TOWT
Jehan Mauvaissoir	ZHEE-own mow-vay-SWAH
Luc le Chaudronnier	LUKE luh SHOWD-ron-yay
Maurice Daumard	MOW-rees DOO-mah
Marguet	MAR-gay
Matois	mah-TWAH
Moïse ben Belzévuthe	moyz ben bel-zay-VOOT
Nathaire	na-TAIR
Pierre Udon	pee-AIR oo-DOHN
Raquel D'Hubert	RAH-kehl doo-BEHR
Salfuyche	sal-foo-EESH
Séphora	say-fo-RAH

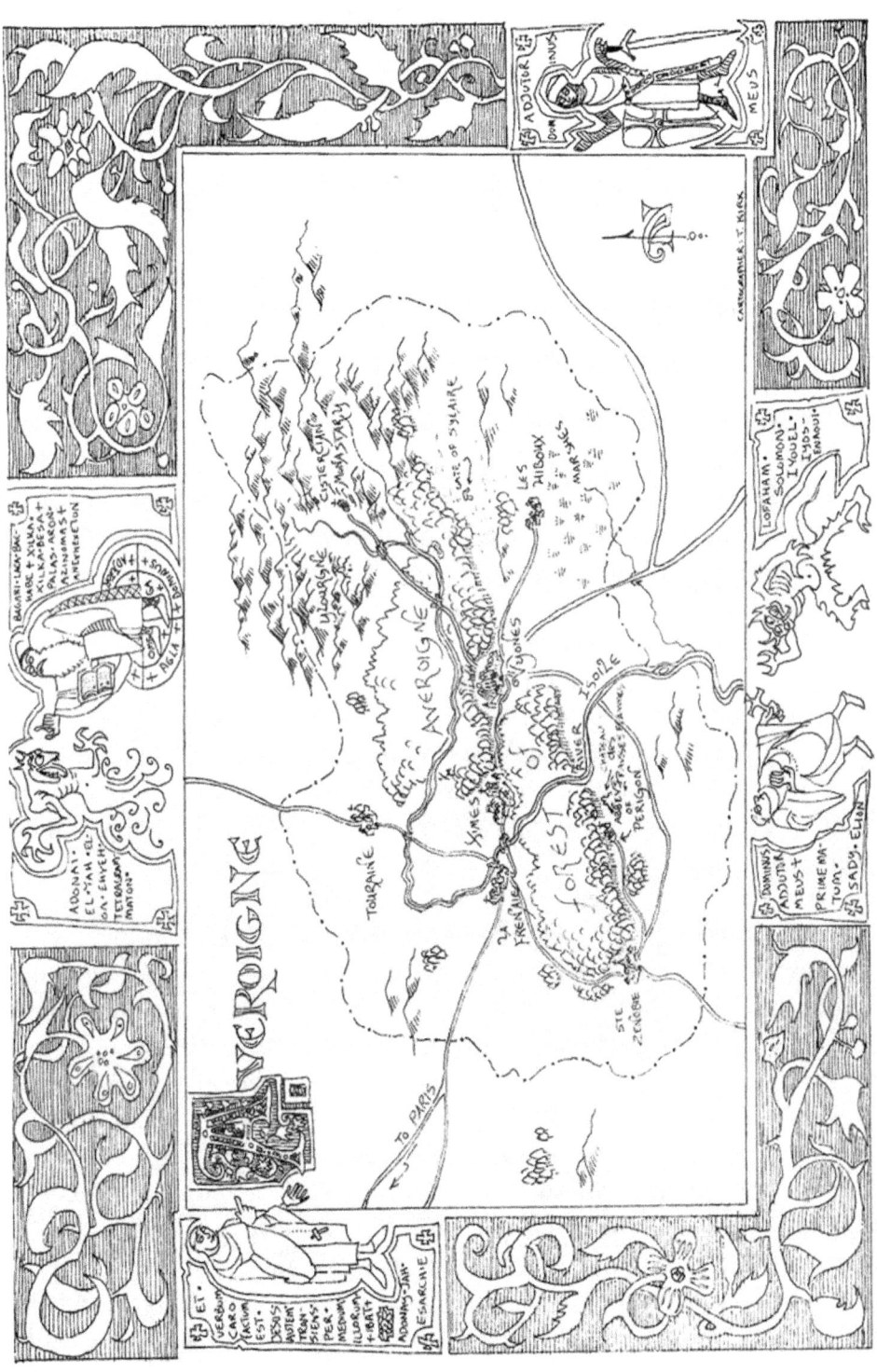

NOT THE END OF THE STORY

Introduction to *The Averoigne Legacy*

The world of Averoigne, much like its vampires and necromancers, just won't die. The fact that new generations are still reading and enjoying Clark Ashton Smith's dark fantasy tales of the monster-haunted province of medieval France—nearly a century after the first Averoigne tale was published—attests to their longevity and timeless appeal. Moreover, more and more authors writing new stories set in Averoigne demonstrates how the depth and mystique of this imaginary world hooks the imagination and won't let go.

It has been a long and bumpy road, however, and Averoigne has been in danger of fading into obscurity several times in its long history—yet it always managed to hang on, and even stage a comeback.

The heyday of Averoigne, of course, was the early 1930s, where one or more stories appeared every year in the legendary pulp magazine *Weird Tales*. The cursed medieval province was popular enough with readers that one fan, Grace Stillman, was inspired to write the poem *The Woods of Averoigne* and submit it to *Weird Tales*, where it was published alongside *The Colossus of Ylourgne* in the June 1934 issue. After H.P. Lovecraft's untimely death in 1937, the poem *To Klarkash-Ton, Lord of Averoigne* was found on his desk, quite possibly the last poem he ever wrote.

After the final Averoigne tale (*The Enchantress of Sylaire*) was published in *Weird Tales* in 1941, the world of Averoigne lay dormant for the next forty years. But it was not forgotten—over the decades, the stories were republished dozens of times in magazines, anthologies, and collections by influential publishers like Arkham House and Panther Books, keeping the tales alive in the minds of readers. Many were even translated into other languages, including German, Italian, and (of course) French. Despite this, Averoigne never quite achieved the popularity of Clark Ashton Smith's other imaginary worlds. Possibly this was because all the Averoigne stories were never published together in a single book until relatively recently—unlike Smith's more famous worlds of Hyperborea, Poseidonis, or Zothique, each of which had their story collections released by Ballantine Books in the early

1970s.

It wasn't until the 1980s that Averoigne's gradual but persistent comeback began. In 1981, TSR published *Castle Amber*, an Averoigne-based gaming module for *Dungeons & Dragons*, thus re-introducing this rich dark fantasy world to a new generation of readers. Among other adventures, the players got to visit Sylaire, Périgon Abbey, and the capital city Vyônes, interact with characters like Gaspard du Nord, Moriamis, and Séphora, acquire magical items like the Ring of Eibon and Azédarac's time-travelling potion, and battle both the Beast of Averoigne and the Colossus of Ylourgne. It even introduced a few new concepts to the universe, such as the Averoigne Inquisition.

The *Castle Amber* module also produced the first map of Averoigne, which (for better or worse) has lingered in the collective consciousness of fans. On the one hand, it introduced a few new locales to Averoigne, such as the village of Malinbois, and turning Cordeliers into a nearby city rather than a monastery within Vyônes. Later authors would use both locations as settings for new Averoigne tales. On the other hand, this map also introduced some geographical errors, such as Touraine being a village within Averoigne rather than a neighboring province. The confusion this caused is still being sorted out by fans today.

Significantly, *Castle Amber*'s bibliography section listed no less than *six* different anthologies players had to hunt down in used books stores if they wanted to read all of the original Averoigne stories the game was based upon. Despite the difficulty of such an undertaking, the first few new Averoigne stories began to be published during the 1980s, albeit in obscure and hard-to-find fanzines. In this respect, Averoigne benefited from its links to the Cthulhu Mythos of H.P. Lovecraft, which had gradually been developing a cult following over the preceding decades. Clark Ashton Smith had borrowed deities like Shub-Niggurath and Yog-Sothoth from Lovecraft's mythos for his Averoigne stories (albeit with French versions of their names, like Iog-Sotôt). Lovecraft, in turn, incorporated some of Smith's creations, such as Tsathoggua, the *Book of Eibon*, and the Château Faussesflammes into his own stories. This may explain why the first Averoigne tribute stories appeared in Mythos fanzines like *The Crypt of Cthulhu* and *The Cthulhu Codex*.

In 1984, *Crypt of Cthulhu* published an article by Glenn Rahman entitled *The History of Averoigne?* (which can be read on the Pickman's Press website) that examined the real French province of Auvergne—long considered to be the area Averoigne was loosely based upon (although that's still hotly debated by fans)—and the historical events in and around the province that may have inspired Clark Ashton Smith's stories. The next year, Rahman collaborated with Richard Tierney on *The Wedding of Sheila-Na-Gog*, a Simon of Gitta story set in Roman-occupied Averoigne. A few years later in 1989, *Cthulhu Codex* published *The Oracle of Sadoqua* by Ron Hilger, who wrote the story based off a synopsis for another Averoigne tale that Clark Ashton Smith had outlined, but never completed before he died (a practice commonly known as a "posthumous collaboration").

The 1990s saw more new Averoigne tales appear here and there. While no one can say for certain what brought about this slow-but-steady resurgence, it's fair to say the advent of the internet—and Amazon in particular—played a major role. Suddenly, it was much, much easier for fans to acquire all the various collections and anthologies needed to read all the original Averoigne stories. In 1994, *Cthulhu Codex* published another of Ron Hilger's posthumous collaborations with Clark Ashton Smith, *The Doom of Azédarac*, in which the sorcerer-bishop travels to an alternate universe and battles another version of himself. 1995 saw Brian McNaughton's World War One-era Averoigne story *The Return of the Colossus* published in the magazine *Weirdbook*, and in 1996 Ron Hilger collaborated with Henry Vester on *The Muse of Averoigne*, the story of a tapestry depicting legends from Averoigne's past, which was published in the fanzine *Fungi*. There was an Averoigne double-feature in 1998 when Michael Minnis released *The Butcher of Vyônes* and *The Circumstances of Ghostly Cats*, both tales of cruel, violent Frenchman falling afoul of something even worse.

The 2000s continued the emerging trend of new Averoigne tales being published. The Clark Ashton Smith fan website *EldritchDark.com*, begun in 1997, posted fan fiction set in Smith's fantastical worlds. One of these fan stories, Simon Whitechapel's *The Passing of Belzévuthe* about a fanatical Inquisitor obsessed with capturing a Jewish sorcerer, went on to be published in the anthology *Lost Worlds of Space and Time*, alongside James Chambers' excellent *Unhallowed Ground, Unholy Flesh* in which white wizard Luc le Chaudronnier combats a reawakened and rampaging Colossus of Ylourgne. More importantly, however, was that *EldritchDark* gradually posted the text to many of Clark Ashton Smith's short stories over the next decade. At long last, all the Averoigne tales could be found in one place—albeit not necessarily in a book—to inspire new readers and writers. Meanwhile, between 2007 and 2010, Night Shade Books released *The Collected Fantasies of Clark Ashton Smith*, a five-volume set of his weird fiction edited by Scott Connors and Ron Hilger (yes, the same Ron Hilger), which is generally considered to contain the definitive versions of Smith's stories. Now all the Averoigne tales were, if not in a single book, at least in the same *set* of books.

All this increased accessibility to the original stories may well have led to the explosion of new Averoigne tales in the 2010s—more were written in this decade than in the previous seventy years combined, and far too many to mention here. Averoigne, it seems, was more popular than ever. By the end of the decade, a total of well over two dozen Averoigne tribute tales were scattered around the literary landscape, and it seemed about time to collect them all into one volume so Averoigne fans could easily obtain and read them all.

It would be wonderful to say this anthology includes every new Averoigne story to date, but sadly there were a few that were left out for various reasons. Foremost among these is *The Door Through the Fire* by Gary Myers. Set entirely in Périgon Abbey, it involves a restless novice monk given the task of scraping the ink off the pages of an old pagan tome so that it can be reused for a Christian religious book. What happens next is . . . well, whether it's something supernatural or merely a young man slowly going insane depends on the reader's interpretation of the events. All that's certain is that it's a must-read for any true Averoigne fan. Unfortunately, it was recently reprinted in the resurrected *Crypt of Cthulhu* fanzine, and thus wasn't available for this anthology due to complicated legal reasons too boring to go into. However, Averoigne fans can still find it in Myer's collection *The Country of the Worm*.

Believe it or not, there were no less than *three* Averoigne tribute tales featuring the Colossus of Ylourgne during World War One. For the sake of maintaining a variety of stories in this anthology, however, only one could be included. Josh Reynolds' *Dead Men's Bones* from the mega-monster anthology *Kaiju Rising*, and Matt Baugh's *What Rough Beast* (a sequel to *The Gargoyles of Notre Dame*) found in *Tales of the Shadowmen Volume 7*, both deal with the Germans trying to build their own Colossus. In the end, however, Brian McNaughton's *The Return of the Colossus* was selected for inclusion instead, as it dealt with the Allies resurrecting the *original* Colossus to help break the stalemate on the Western Front.

Still other tribute tales contradicted each other. Olivier Legrand's *Lost in Averoigne* from *Tales of the Shadowmen Volume 8* features Bishop Azédarac time-travelling to the 20th century to escape capture by his enemies—only to have them follow him to the future, hunt him down, and kill him. Unfortunately, this completely contradicts how Clark Ashton Smith intended Azédarac to meet his end in *The Doom of Azédarac*. Of these two differing accounts of the sorcerer-bishop's fate, however, it was fairly obvious which story should be considered canonical, and which should be left out of the anthology.

There were also one or two stories set in Averoigne, but not really *about* Averoigne. Peter Rawlik's short story *The Ylourgne Accords*, which later became a chapter in his novel *Reanimatrix*, is a good example. It's an intriguing tale about the negotiation (and failure) of an arms-limitation treaty. However, since the "arms" being debated were reanimated corpses, Ylourgne was a perfect setting for the conference . . . but, ultimately, *only* a setting, for a story that otherwise had little to do with the world of Averoigne. This, combined with licensing complications with *Reanimatrix*'s publisher Night Shade Books, led to it not being included in this anthology.

Then there was the smattering of amateur fan fiction. For some, the writing quality was simply too poor to be publishable. Others were utterly bizarre, like a crossover story between Averoigne and the Transformers. Not all the fan fiction was low-quality, though—in fact, this anthology includes David Reid Ross's *The Cult of the Singing Flame*, which was originally found on fanfiction.net.

Not surprisingly, many of these stories' authors attempted to imitate—all with varying degrees of success—Clark Ashton Smith's personal writing style, characterized by dreamy narration, vivid descriptions, poetic language, and an enormous vocabulary. Others wrote in their own personal styles which, while being reminiscent of (and perhaps influenced by?) Smith's, are subtly different. Perhaps more interesting are the stories written in completely different styles. For example, Colin Harker's *Clotaire of the Cross* reads more like an eighteenth-century gothic horror novel, while Aaron Hollingsworth's *The Pink Flower of Saint Zénobie* can be nothing other than a fairy tale, albeit a very dark one. Rahman & Tierney's *The Wedding of Sheila-Na-Gog* is clearly a sword-and-sorcery adventure, and Matt Baugh's *The Gargoyles of Notre Dame* evokes the swashbuckling daring-do of 1920s French pulp stories.

Many readers find these Averoigne tales told in various voices to be interesting and enjoyable for much the same reason as stories set in numerous time periods: it lets the audience see Averoigne through a different lens. By examining what differs and what does not, what changes and what stays the same, one can come closer to understanding what makes the Averoignian milieu so unique and intriguing, so exotic and yet familiar. In short, why the world of Averoigne continues to appeal to readers after almost a century.

One of the purposes of this anthology was to help add to the Mythos of Averoigne, to provide an "expanded canon", so to speak. Some of the monsters in these pages were never defeated, and may still be hiding out in the Woods of Averoigne. Likewise, the heroes (those who survived) may have more adventures awaiting them. Perhaps Vyônes' ghost-cat Matois may make a cameo appearance, briefly sighted running down a dead-end alley before disappearing into thin air. Maybe the new places mentioned in this volume like the Cave of the Oracle, Château Conflans, or the Plain of Nathaire may pop up in future Averoigne tales.

For there almost certainly *will* be more stories to come. At least three other Averoigne stories were outlined by Clark Ashton Smith— some in great detail—but never written. Perhaps other authors will attempt more posthumous collaborations in the future. Moreover, large swaths of Averoigne's history are currently unknown, and fertile ground for the imagination. The pre-Roman age is a complete blank, and little or nothing is known about Averoigne in the Dark Ages. How did the province fare during the Moorish invasion of France? Or under the rule of Charlemagne? Did the Vikings sail down the River Isoile and attack Vyônes? What happened in Averoigne during the French

Revolution, or under the Nazi Occupation of World War II? Perhaps future Averoigne stories will answer these questions.

One thing is certain—if the past is prologue, there are definitely many more new tales of Averoigne yet to come. This is not the end of the story.

— Edward Stasheff, October 2019

I Sing of Averoigne

by Aaron Hollingsworth

Where once the Druids in their councils joined,
Where Gallic faces cover'd every coin,
Where fell satyrs stalk with aching loins,
I sing to thee of Averoigne.
Where Romans conquer'd what they could not tame,
With sword or spear or Holy name,
Where lamias seduce without shame,
A wand'ring lord or wayward dame,
Where vampires sleep in hidden towers,
Stolen from view by eldritch powers,
Where time is robb'd of many an hour,
Where all but the bravest shake and cower,
Into that land where Death purloins,
Poor souls from vessels once conjoin'd,
Where witches yet meet in covens rejoin'd,
I sing to thee of Averoigne!

THE ORACLE OF SADOQUA

by Ron Hilger

"Black and unshap'd, as pestilent a Clod
As dread Sodaqua, Averonia's God."
— H.P. Lovecraft

"By the beard of Jupiter! I'll not return to Rome until Galbius has been found or avenged!" thundered Horatius as he strode forth from his military pavilion into the golden morning sunlight of the recently conquered province of Averonia, leaving a much intimidated courier stammering in his wake.

"B-but my l-lord, what shall I tell the senate?" The courier had been dispatched from the Roman senate with written orders that Horatius, First Lieutenant under General Julius Caesar's forces in Gaul, return immediately to Rome under the dictum disbanding Caesar's army.

Horatius wheeled about. "The senate will have to understand the importance of teaching these pagan savages the power and justice of Imperial Rome. I suspect Galbius has been captured or killed by the heathen Druids who infest this barbarous land. If the matter is not resolved, we invite open rebellion. I shall send half my men back under the command of Romulus, but I return with Galbius or with the blood of those responsible for his disappearance upon my sword. Tell *that* to the senate!"

Horatius signed the communiqué and dismissed the courier with an air of preoccupation, more concerned with his missing comrade than with the orders from Rome. After all, with luck he would be returning long before any response from an irate senate could reach him. The disappearance of Galbius, however, concerned him greatly. Aside from tactical considerations such as where Galbius could be and how to find him, Horatius was deeply concerned about the welfare of his friend. The two had been close as brothers ever since military training, when drunken brawls had taught them each to respect the other's fighting prowess. Together they had risen through the ranks to become officers while battling their way across Gaul under the ambitious General Caesar. Now it had been nearly two days since Galbius had disappeared after leaving on a scouting foray into the woods, and Horatius could not think of a more disquieting place in which to lose a friend.

Werewolves, vampires, and lamias were reputed to haunt this unfathomable forest, as well as the savage Druids who were rumored to be tainted with a dark strain of Hyperborean ancestry. He shuddered involuntarily and wished again that Galbius would return with some tale of amorous captivity in the clutches of an insatiable Averonian maid.

Having decided at last to organize a search, Horatius ordered a detachment of his cavalry to prepare their horses and weapons to accompany him through the ancient forest to question anyone they encountered in the area of Galbius' disappearance. As they rode along a well-traveled road through sunlit meadows filled with the raucous cries of birds and the colorful pageantry of myriad woodland flowers, Horatius felt his spirits rise, as one who has been too long idle.

All too soon, the amaranthine meads gave way to higher, stonier ground, and the trees grew thicker until they crowded out all but a few filtered rays of sunlight. They wound their way beneath the cool umbrage of enormous moss- and mistletoe-encumbered oaks, and soon Horatius felt an ominous unease settling down upon him like an invisible shroud. The pagan Druids who dwelt here disgusted him, and their blasphemous sacrifices and heathen rituals filled him with horror and righteous indignation. The road soon reduced to a narrow footpath, and as a trailing vine of cobweb-covered mistletoe brushed his face, Horatius reflected that in such a primordial, god-forsaken place any number of pagan myths and monsters were likely to be found.

As the trail rounded a large outcropping of rock the soldiers unexpectedly came upon a scene which might well have been taken from some ancient myth. Two savage-looking Druids sat upon large boulders on either side of a low, dark aperture at the base of a cliff, as if guarding it. The Druids appeared barbaric to an extreme. They wore long coarse-looking robes of mottled grey. Their dark hair was long and matted, as were their beards. Gnarled hands clutched long cudgels of oak, at the ends of which long, wicked-looking pieces of obsidian were firmly strapped at right angles, in the fashion of a scythe. But that which caught and held the attention of the formidable horsemen was a pair of the largest, most ferocious-looking felines the Romans had ever beheld. The great cats sat immobile as statues, one beside each guard. The upper canine teeth of these great beasts hung several inches below the lower jaw and their hungry yellow eyes were fixed on the newcomers. Having ordered weapons drawn, Horatius dismounted and approached the larger of the two savages.

"We seek word of Galbius, second lieutenant of the Imperial Roman Army, last seen in this vicinity two days ago. Some of your people must have seen or heard of him. Tell us everything you know of this if you wish to live."

The brutes exchanged a series of low, guttural remarks, punctuated with vigorous gesticulations. Finally, they lowered their weapons and the larger Druid spoke, his poor Latin almost indecipherable beneath his heavy accent.

"The guardians of Sadoqua are at your service. We know nothing about this man you seek, but you stand at the doorway of the Fane of Sadoqua. The people of Averonia are wont to consult the oracle within for answers to questions that defy even the wisest sage . . . for a small fee," the Druid added slyly, extending a crude wooden bowl in which rattled a few small coins and nuggets of gold.

The Druid smiled malignly at the soldiers' watchful wariness of the great feline guardians.

"You have nothing to fear," the Druid said scornfully. "These are here to guard against dangers far greater than yourselves."

Horatius glared at the Druid, then suddenly knocked aside the bowl with his blade, scattering the contents.

"Tullius, Florian, come with me," ordered Horatius, "the rest of you watch these two heathens. If we return not after a count of one thousand, kill these so-called guardians and come to our assistance." He then turned and, with his sword before him, disappeared into the dark opening followed closely by his two picked men.

The three Romans shuffled forward slowly into the gloom, letting their eyes adjust to the tenebrous interior of the cave. Horatius distrusted the Druids, and suspected they might be hiding something. Perhaps Galbius, perhaps an ambush. As they made their way through the musty tunnel, the blackness slowly gave way to a dull, diffused light, and a noisome odor now began to permeate the air. Horatius perceived that the light ahead appeared to be shifting about in an eerie manner regarding which he did not feel entirely comfortable.

He now recalled stories and rumors that circulated in Rome and Greece about the barbarous northerners: that the Druids were reported to make human sacrifice to the daemon Taranit and to nurture the ancient cults of the Old Ones. The worship of the toad-like Tsathoggua and the spider-god Atlach-Nacha was confirmed by the Greek historian Hecataeus, who brought back and translated a copy of the notorious *Book of Eibon* from northern lands. In his book *Peri Hyperborean*, Hecataeus described the evil effect of Hyperborean culture on subsequent northern tribes. Horatius was compelled to mutter a short prayer to Mars, god of war and soldiers, to grant him victory over the many loathsome creatures he imagined while moving cautiously towards the wavering light.

Soon they found themselves in a grotto rifted from floor to ceiling. The light which fell through a great fissure in the roof was partially obscured by clouds of foul vapors rising from the chasm at their feet. At the very brink of the abyss, chained to an immense black altar-stone, was a hideous creature which appeared only vaguely human. The thing was almost covered with coarse black hair, except on its pale underside. Its head seemed to rest directly on its shoulders with little or no neck at all. The facial features, also, were seemingly nonexistent, save for its insanely staring eyes and toothless, slavering maw.

The Roman's heart quailed at the abominable sight before him and he grew somewhat unsteady from breathing the fetid vapors. Yet Horatius summoned his courage and addressed the fearsome oracle.

"The Druids have bidden me consult the Oracle of Sadoqua concerning the fate of my lost friend Galbius. Answer then, if you are the one of whom they speak." A cloud of roiling vapor engulfed the oracle, and as it cleared the monstrosity began to speak in half-articulate Latin.

"The fate of Galbius is before you, as is your own. As yet your friend lives, but it is decreed that he shall die before this very altar before the setting of the next full moon."

Strangely disturbed by something about the creature's voice, Horatius pressed the oracle for greater detail. Suddenly, a shaft of sunlight pierced the reeking cloud and fell briefly on the figure before him. Horatius was shocked to imagine a distorted, impossible resemblance to the lost Galbius.

"Galbius?" he whispered uncertainly. "Can it be you?"

The oracle cackled with laughter.

"Galbius is not here, and I have been the mouthpiece of Sadoqua, who reposes in eternal slumber at the bottom of this abyss, for a thousand eternities."

Horatius and his subordinates glared incomprehensibly at the squat obscenity, which now half crawled and half dragged itself into the dark recesses behind the altar-stone in apparent forgetfulness of their presence.

The Romans left the creature and soon emerged from the cavern, blinking in the strong light of noon as they mounted their steeds and prepared to depart. The great tawny cats still sat immobile. Horatius urged his mount forward and regarded them thoughtfully.

"I think perhaps these beasts permit all to pass within, yet stand ready to devour those whom you would not have escape. If I discover you have been less than completely honest with me, your heads shall be set on pikes down at the crossroads to proclaim your dishonesty and insolence before all the countryside." Without awaiting a reply, the commander wheeled his horse about and signaled for the company to ride on.

The soldiers continued their search through the forest, the trees crowded still closer together as if trying to choke the trail out of existence. As they rounded a bend, Horatius caught a fleeting glimpse of something ducking behind a tree a short distance off the trail to their left. Signaling a halt, he dismounted and plunged through the brush towards this mysterious apparition, several of his men close behind him. They soon found Horatius standing beside a huge, moss-covered oak with a young peasant girl struggling in his iron grasp. He studied his catch with undisguised delight. Shoulder-length chestnut colored hair surrounded a fair, blushing complexion, accented by her large hazel eyes. She wore a simple homespun dress that did little to conceal her youthful charms, though she had yet to achieve her fullest curves. Horatius waved away the men who had understandably begun to gather around her, and reassured the girl in the Celtic dialect of the Gauls.

"Do not be afraid—we mean you no harm. We only seek news of a missing comrade." He then described Galbius and asked if she had seen or heard of him. She shook her head slowly, glancing anxiously around her.

"I cannot say . . . Please let me go," she pleaded urgently. "The Druids must not see me talking with you!"

"My friend Galbius," he repeated firmly. "Have you seen him?"

She hesitated momentarily, then whispered close beside his ear. "I have not, but I will ask my people about him. Meet me this evening after moonrise in yonder meadow and I will tell you what I have learned." Without awaiting his reply she sprang lithely away through the trees. Two of his men leaped into pursuit, but held back at his command.

"Wait. Let her go. She may yet prove useful," he added thoughtfully.

That evening Horatius set out alone to keep his woodland tryst. He had debated with himself the wisdom of going alone. Indeed, he had thought of little else all day, but something about the way she had clung to his arm while she whispered to him, some unspoken promise in her eyes, had decided the matter for him.

He made his way silently along the path, his sword and shield strapped to his back so he could walk unencumbered through the gloom of the nocturnal forest. He had left somewhat early so as to arrive first in case of a trap or ambush. He did not expect deceit, but such preparedness had saved his life on more than one occasion. The oaks closed in around him, shutting out the stars and cutting off the breeze, making the air musty and stifling.

He began hearing slight noises—twigs snapping and night-birds calling, he even thought he heard voices rising and falling in rhythm to drumbeats in the distance.

Suddenly he noticed a soft glimmering through the trees on his left and, making his way with great stealth, he crept through the brambles until he came upon a large, moonlit meadow. The full moon was just peering over the tops of the branches, filling the glade like a silver basin with soft pearly light and illuminating the great trees of the forest like giant granite monoliths or lofty snow-covered peaks encircling the glade. The entire scene before him was bathed in soft moonlight, save only the pitch-black band of shadow under the trees, which even the noonday sun could not penetrate. Then, moving to a place of optimal surveillance, he noticed several shadows moving strangely about in the glade. Cursing, he drew his sword and crouched behind a large oak, berating his foolishness in coming alone, and envisioning a grisly death upon some blood-stained altar of these vicious and degenerate people. But the shadows moved no closer. They seemed to be moving in circles, reversing directions and shifting patterns. He watched, enthralled by what he now perceived to be dancers, although he could make out none of their features.

A small noise close by brought him instantly to a defensive position, his sword and shield raised menacingly. He discovered the peasant girl standing close beside him, and he marked the uncanny silence of her approach.

"Beautiful, aren't they?" she murmured as she knelt down next to him. Horatius regained his composure as he noticed the girl was, in fact, alone, but decided to keep his sword in hand for the present.

"What are they?" he returned, "And who are you, who managed to steal so close without my knowledge?"

She smiled, her teeth gleaming in the moonlight. "My name is Selena, and they are the folk of the forest, whom you will likely scare away with your boisterous whispering. As for my quiet passage, I have that skill in woodcraft shared by all those who live within the shadow of the forest." She contemplated the Roman a moment before continuing. "I hope you can forgive my mysterious behavior this morning, but I have good reason to fear the sorcerous Druids should they suspect me of helping you. I have heard they regularly sacrifice those they suspect of treachery in a most brutal and bloody manner."

"True—they are savage devils of the Pit," agreed Horatius. "But what of Galbius? Have you learned of his whereabouts?"

"I fear to answer that question, my lord," whispered the girl, avoiding his gaze with downcast eyes. "I will not lie and say I know nothing, for I have learned that your comrade is already beyond all mortal assistance. You cannot help him." She quickly continued, "And I fear that once you discover the whole truth, your anger will lead to your undoing." The girl glanced shyly up at the Roman before continuing. "Then I shall see you never again."

Horatius reached out his hand as if to caress her cheek, and gently tilted her face towards his searching eyes.

"And what if I promise to return to you once I have beheld the fate of Galbius with my own eyes?"

"Promise me instead a few hours of your time. Escort me about this glade tonight as befits a lordly Roman officer, and tell me tales of Rome with its paved streets and marble statues. Tell me of your people and how they socialize and their manner of dress. Tell me of your armies that rule over half the world, let me feel the glory of this Rome I hear such splendid rumor of, make me unafraid of the cruel Druids you would have me betray. Do this for me and then I will gladly tell you all I know of your friend."

Horatius decided her proposal was an attractive one and accepted, partly because of her considerable feminine charm, and chiefly because he had no alternative—the girl was his only hope thus far.

"And what of these strange folk who dance in the moonlight?" returned Horatius. "Surely they will resent our intrusion upon their festivities. Can we be sure of our safety amongst them?"

"We have nothing to fear from these shy and innocent creatures." Selena assured him. "It is more likely that they will flee if we approach them too directly. Therefore, let us stroll slowly along the edge of the glade, close to the shadow of the trees so we do not disturb them, for their dance is very beautiful to watch."

Horatius could think of no objection as she took his hand and led him along the perimeter of the moonlit meadow, plying him with questions about Rome which he answered with great pride and enthusiasm. As they picked their way through the boulders and moss-covered branches strewn along their path, the Roman's eyes constantly returned to the weird ceremony, which seemed to stir within him a strange and blasphemous curiosity—almost a desire to join the pagan celebration. The singing and chanting grew louder as their path drew nearer to the revelers, and Horatius began to notice strange abnormalities in the figures of the dancers, bizarre glimpses of horns and hooves, wings and tails, uncertain in the pale moonlight.

"Shades of Dis!" exclaimed the Roman. "I cannot tell if these beings are daemons on a dark errand from the netherworld, or only peasants in costume for some festival of Bacchantes."

"Nor can I tell you for certain, but I do not believe they are evil. One night I attempted to join in their dance, but although I approached slowly and spoke softly to them, they all fled silently into the forest."

Horatius paused and, taking the girl swiftly into his arms, he replied, "I do not know how any creature, man or beast, could be afraid of such a gentle and beautiful young maiden." He then bent his head and attempted a kiss, but she slipped away demurely and called teasingly from the protection of the woods.

"And I thought you were a gentleman! It seems I have more to fear from you than from yonder 'daemons from Dis'!" She then vanished between the trees, leaving only her silvery laughter lingering in the air.

Horatius plunged into the woods in pursuit and soon they were alone in a grassy moonlit bower, lying comfortably in each other's arms.

"I have heard that in Rome the women do not work, but stay home and invent new ways to please their lovers," Selena whispered. "Is this true?"

Horatius nodded and replied, "Perhaps you would like to return to Rome with me to await my return in the evenings?" As the conversation ceased, he could only assume that she would indeed be receptive to his proposal.

Later on, as the lovers walked about in the now empty glade, the full moon striding down from its zenith, Horatius explained his determination to find or avenge Galbius quickly, before his return to Rome.

"For I grow weary of this savage land filled with pagan horrors, and would gladly return to the quiet groves of my villa." He kissed the back of her neck, and continued softly, "There you would be clothed in silk amid the luxury of Rome. Tell me, then, what do you know of Galbius?"

"First I must know if you questioned the Druids who guard the cavern of the oracle, and their answer, if any."

"I did question the two savages," he admitted. "But they told me nothing. I even consulted their filthy oracle, but although I have a strange feeling the creature somehow knew the truth, the answer I received seemed little more than gibberish."

"But of course, you could not recognize the truth." Selena shook her head with pity. "I will explain, but you will not like what I must tell you. The Druids worship the dread god Sadoqua, who they believe sleeps eternally at the bottom of the chasm atop which the oracle is chained to his black altar. It is held to be true by local sages and sooth-sayers that Sadoqua is but a corrupt version of Tsathoggua, the god of ancient Hyperborea. The legends tell how this evil one abandoned that country after it was overwhelmed by glaciers and returned to the light-less abyss of N'kai where he still abides. Tsathoggua and others of the Old Ones first entered N'kai through a gate of foul sorcery which con-nects N'kai to a similar abyss located deep within the planet Saturn. So say the dark legends of the Druid religion, which is founded largely upon the writings of the great Hyperborean wizard Eibon. The Druids believe the vapors rising from the abyss to be the actual breath of the slumbering Sadoqua. Because of the constant exposure to these nox-ious fumes, the oracle is soon reduced to a monstrous condition in which he receives and relates the divinations of Sadoqua, who is said to know all things past, present, and future. This primal regression con-tinues until the unfortunate creature dies, or is no longer useful as a medium, being too primitive to communicate.

"Because of the inevitably short life of the oracle, the Druids must search constantly for new victims to serve Sadoqua. Usually they choose from amongst the criminals and beggars who roam the coun-tryside, but when these are scarce they will often abduct strangers who happen to be traveling through the forest. This undoubtedly was the fate of Galbius. The men from my village say that your friend must have fought well, for the remains of three Druids were found alongside the forest trail. The great wounds and cloven limbs of the slain Druids show that a heavy broad-sword, such as your own, was wielded against them by one who knew well its use. The foul oracle you spoke with was indeed Galbius, but his mind and body had already succumbed to the lethal respiration of Sadoqua." Selena attempted to pull Horatius into the comfort of her arms. "I am sorry for your friend, but can't you see there is nothing you can do to help him?"

Upon hearing these words Horatius felt a black rage rising within him. He shrugged off the girl's embrace, desiring only the comfort of slaying the murderous Druids and dispatching the hideous oracle from the torture of its existence.

"If it is too late to save Galbius, then I shall at least honor our friendship by ending the misery of that witless ruin that was once my friend. Tell me the shortest route to the cavern," he demanded, his hand tightening on the hilt of his sword. Selena pointed the way and begged him to be careful.

"For if the Druids discover I have betrayed them, they will carve my heart from my breast and devour it before my dying eyes. Such is their customary treatment of informers."

"Await me at my encampment and tomorrow we shall quit this barbarous land and return to Rome!" cried Horatius as he set forth on his errand of vengeance and mercy. He quickly found the path Selena had indicated, which showed up as a narrow, pale swath barely visible in the gloom. The Roman slowed his reckless pace and drew his sword as he realized his vulnerability. As a soldier, he had been trained to control his rage and use it effectively against his enemies. Now his tactical mind began to assert itself and he realized that by storming unprepared into a stronghold of his enemies he might achieve little more than becoming a meal for the feline guardians of Sadoqua. His wrath was too great to consider going back for reinforcements, but with caution and stealth he might still achieve his goal and possibly kill a great number of the enemy as well.

When he reached the clearing which surrounded the entrance to the cavern, the Roman peered cautiously around an outcropping of rock until he noted with grim satisfaction a lone Druid sitting in the wavering torch-light beside the mouth of the cave. The feline guardians were nowhere to be seen. The sentry had only enough time to bellow once before the Roman's sword cut off his scream and sent his head rolling across the ground, leaving a dark trail of gore in its wake. Horatius removed the torch and, thrusting it before him, entered the cavern of the oracle.

The first thing he saw in the dim torchlight was an obsidian-bladed scythe descending in an arc towards his chest. In desperation he whipped his sword beneath the falling scythe and was rewarded by a dull thud as his blade encountered the firm resistance of bone. The scythe fell harmlessly over his shoulder, the still-gripping hand and arm dragging horribly after. Horatius felt little emotion as he drove his sword through the Druid who lay writhing on the dusty floor. He uttered a mechanical grunt of satisfaction as another of his enemies died before him, leaving him yet alive to wreak further vengeance.

Hastening to the black altar, he found it engulfed by the reeking mist which soon dissipated enough to reveal only an empty, slimy shackle lying in a puddle of unmentionable filth.

The Roman cursed aloud, having been thwarted in his quest to render Galbius the final service of releasing his tortured body and soul from the noxious will of Sadoqua. Unwilling to accept defeat, Horatius held the torch aloft and searched about, hoping to find the pitiful oracle hiding in some crevice, when once again the rank, obscuring mist began to issue forth from the depths like some maleficent ethereal tide. He held his breath until the cloud subsided, then he peered cautiously over the edge into the abyss. There, not a foot below the edge of the cliff, crawled a huge slug-like creature glistening in the torchlight that could only be the transformed Galbius. Horatius thought he recognized the insanely staring eyes, although they now protruded above the body on gently waving stalk-like appendages. The thing was sliding down the sheer wall along a well-slimed trail which ended, he imagined, in the batrachian jaws of Sadoqua. In horror, he plunged his sword again and again into the quivering mass until it finally released its hold and fell silently into the yawning pit. As the Roman straightened from this grisly task, he was struck savagely on the head from behind. A hot, spreading numbness swept over him as he sank down into oblivion.

When Horatius regained consciousness, he was first aware of sharp throbbing in his head and a burning asphyxiation in his throat and chest. He could see or hear nothing and his mind seemed strangely disoriented. He struggled to his knees and became aware of the heavy chains about his waist and ankles, and noticed for the first time the abominable stench and slime in which he knelt. Dimly he recalled the events which had led to his capture, then he reached out in the darkness and felt the stone altar to confirm his fate. With dreadful irony he now recalled the prophecy of Sadoqua: "The fate of Galbius is before you, as is your own." In this pitiable state he struggled against his bonds until he thought of his friend Galbius, and with what fluid ease he must have escaped these very chains. Horatius screamed and cursed his rage and frustration into the baleful abyss until, slowly, there arose from the stygian depths a vast chuckling, such as a god might utter during an amusing dream. Horatius continued to scream his fury and horror until, wearied from his exertion, he ceased, and realized he no longer recalled why he screamed.

The following evening, having waited the long day through in the encampment of the Romans, Selena slipped away and set her face toward the Cavern of the Oracle, desperate to learn the fate of her new love. Although filled with terror, she strove to appear at ease as she told the Druid guardians of her desire to consult the oracle regarding a matter of the heart. She thought she glimpsed a knowing leer on the face of the guard who stepped aside to permit her entry, but she refused to allow herself to be frightened away when so close to learning the fate of Horatius. Shuddering at the sight of the great pools of congealed blood within the grotto's entrance, she fixed her eyes ahead and continued on. At last she came to the great black altar and its hideous oracle.

It squatted in semblance of an immense, boneless toad, tethered to the stone by massive rusted chains. Its bulging eyes stared up at her uncomprehendingly, its slavering lips muttered soundlessly to itself in the dreams of its delirium, yet still could Selena discern the familiar features of her missing Horatius. Stricken to her soul by a crushing horror, the girl yet found the strength to speak.

"Horatius, my lord!" she whispered, still fearful of the nearby Druids. "Is it truly you? Do you not remember me?" she sobbed.

The creature fixed its huge, unblinking eyes upon the girl and gave reply.

"Horatius is not here, and I have been the mouthpiece of Sadoqua, who knows all things past, present, and future, for a thousand eternities."

And then, in its madness, the oracle was seized by a fit of insane tittering laughter which grew in volume until the cavern echoed with its mindless reverberations. Selena was paralyzed by the extremity of her fear as she heard, unmistakably, the addition of another hollow, rumbling laughter which seemed to rise up out of the black abyss on the surging clouds of foulness. At last she found refuge in shrieking flight, which ended abruptly in the waiting arms of the Druids, whom she had betrayed.

THE DRUIDS' ALTAR

by DJ Tyrer

Cats with unblinking eyes
Gather in the glades of the wise
Where men's hearts easily falter
Before the gore-stained druids' altar
That is widely whispered and feared
Upon which elder demons are revered
Forgotten since Hyperborea's doom
Save here in Averoignean forest gloom
Where toads sing out a symphony
The most grotesque cacophony
In honor of gods strange and dark
The toads ritualistically bark
And druids caper and prance
In a horrific sacramental dance
And upon their backs hang capes of skin
Freshly flayed when the rituals begin
And the priests in their churches hide away
Praying till the dawn of day
To challenge such evil they balk
In glades where dead things walk
And ceremonies of the most obscene sort
To innocent maidens are taught
Who are encouraged to enjoin
The corruption of Averoigne

THE WEDDING OF SHEILA-NA-GOG

by Glenn Rahman and Richard L. Tierney

A ruddy glow lit the twisted canopy of the oak grove, casting strange shadows over the wolfish, expectant faces of the warriors squatting in a circle around the fire. All were big men with light eyes and long, fair locks that swayed as they beat their knees with horny fists in rhythm to the Gallic chant. Their garments bespoke a tribal kinship: similar tartans occasionally cut into a tunic of the Roman style, and a more prominent slashed garment with sleeves descending a little below the waist. Only a few seemed to be experienced fighters, and these bore weapons in keeping with their size: long swords hanging from their belts, tall shields, javelins, bows and slings. Several other Gauls, standing and leading the chant, wore full, red-dyed robes—red symbolizing the nature of the ceremony this night.

There was a stir as a few latecomers arrived: a half-dozen cloaked and cowled men who seemed incongruous among the Gauls. Ferchobhar, first among the Black Goat Druids, came to meet them and led them to their places without a word.

Another incongruous figure at the ritual watched their arrival suspiciously—a black-haired man in his early thirties with high, prominent cheekbones and a square, cleanly shaven chin. His expression was controlled, in no way sharing the fanatical concentration of the Gauls, but the dark eyes in his impassive expressionless face flickered with angry fires. He wore the cloak and tunic of a Samaritan, both emblazoned with symbols indicating him to be a wandering magician.

The Samaritan shifted his stare from the cowled figures to an osier cage between the roots of a spreading oak. A tough, woven mesh that might have held the men within it even had they not been bound by heavy cords, it resembled a giant oval bird-cage piled roundabout with tinder and dry faggots. The captives neither begged nor cursed—less from a fear of punishment, probably, than from a stubborn pride that would not give in to futile displays.

They were dark men, the Samaritan observed, yet unlike the elegant Semitic type that he himself represented. Rather, they appeared akin to the Aquitani—the ancient strain which, so the magician had

heard, had ruled Spain and Gaul long before the Celts had come conquering from the east. The Romans called them *Arverni*—a corruption
of *Averoni*, the tribe's own name for itself. When the Gauls had ruled,
so the story went, the Averoni were tolerated as a source of tribute; but
now that both races enjoyed a kind of equality—an equally mortifying
Roman slavery—a bitter feud raged between them in the mountains of
Regio Averonum. Every captured Averoni suffered a fate similar to
this one, or worse . . . .

"I am glad to see you have accepted my invitation, Simon of Gitta."

The Samaritan started from his trance of thought. Ferchobhar
stood close beside him, bending near—though only a few seconds before, the Druid had been within the circle of firelight. In this proximity
the old man's eyes seemed intense, intent, darkly mystical.

"Tonight you shall learn much concerning Druid-lore,"
Ferchobhar went on in his low, muttering tone, "as I have promised
you."

Simon the Samaritan grunted. "I hope your lore is more impressive
than the trick you just used to sneak up on me. I've used it on audienc-
es a hundred times, at least. Tell me—who are those cloaked men who
have just arrived?"

"Students of our Druid-knowledge, like yourself. They are but recently come to our land. I shall introduce you to them later. But now,
you must excuse me. Soon you shall see that not all magic is mere
mummery!"

So saying, Ferchobhar stood erect and strode into the circle of
men—strode tall and regal, his narrow white beard gleaming in the
firelight, a straight oaken staff clutched in his fist. The other Druids
ceased their chanting as he approached, then drew to him in a mass,
left hands clenched and staffs held upright. When all were gathered
close about him, Ferchobhar began to speak alone—to intone a low,
lilting song in a tongue unlike the Gallic Simon had been studying for
the past few months.

And while the chief Druid chanted, the Samaritan magician
thought, pondered, remembered . . . .

For three months had Simon dwelt among the Druids, more than long
enough to decide he couldn't hope to learn much from them. He had

hoped differently when he had first arrived and admitted to them his name—a name much lauded by all who hated and opposed the tyranny of Rome.

The Druids, too, Ferchobhar had assured him, used their talents to resist the Romans. He had urged Simon to stay and learn from them. And the Samaritan, who was sought by the Romans as a determined rebel, had welcomed the promise of sanctuary and study.

But as the weeks passed, Simon had grown suspicious. Ferchobhar had presented him with little more than the childish mythology of the Gallic gods and heroes, some verse of a ritual nature and a few mechanical tricks, barring him from the important conclaves and mysteries. But whenever the Samaritan had chafed, Ferchobhar had affected the role of the kindest of hosts, cajoling and flattering the younger man with promises of knowledge yet to come.

"Your studies are preparing you," he had assured Simon repeatedly. "When the summer solstice comes, you shall be ready to receive all knowledge. It is not so far away."

Simon might have concluded that Ferchobhar and his Druids were charlatans and humbugs, had he not already seen the uncanny control they wielded over mist and flame during their rituals. Furthermore, they claimed to command strange creatures that haunted the hills and valleys: cloven-hoofed monsters elsewhere considered only the fancies of ancient legend. He'd had the inhuman tracks of these beings pointed out to him, and had been told by nervous tribesmen how the monsters were created and dispatched by the Druids to harry the Averoni and even war with that tribe's own magical agents, the mystical Cats of Sadoqua.

For the Averoni, Simon had learned, worshipped the deity Sadoqua—the immortal enemy of the Druids' goddess, Sheila-na-gog, whose name meant "Lady of the Gods". The Gauls claimed that the Averoni protected Sadoqua's shrines from defilement by conjuring up hosts of demon felines, whose pelts were dark as the midnight sky and whose fangs gleamed as brightly as stars. An occasional cat's cry under the waxing moon, Simon had observed, was enough to turn a Gaul's blood to water . . . .

Suddenly his reverie was interrupted as, like a bolt of heat lightning, the heads of the staffs flamed with a brilliant blue-white light, briefly illuminating the oak grove like noonday. Simon gasped. The cowled newcomers, clearly as taken by surprise as he, lurched fearfully, one ejaculating "Jupiter!" and another letting his cowl fall back from his aquiline features when the light burst full upon him.

Romans!

Simon's mouth hardened with bitterness and apprehension; he'd half-suspected as much when he had earlier glimpsed the legionnaire-style footgear one of the men wore under the hem of his robe. No longer did he wonder where he stood with the Black Goat Druids!

He knew he was in the acutest danger—knew that his own presence had to do with this unnatural alliance. Why else would Ferchobhar entertain Romans in such a secretive manner? The emperor Tiberius had years ago outlawed the druidic religion; it was the duty of the Roman occupation troops to arrest the wonder-working priests and destroy their shrines. He would be lost if he waited until the completion of this sacrifice. Yet, how to escape, surrounded as he now was by Druids and Romans…?

A ready solution came to him. Although not a true magician himself, he had studied at the feet of Persian mages who had taught him many ruses and illusions that had served him well in the past. Not the least of these was a command of the ventriloquist's art.

Without the slightest alteration of expression, Simon threw a piercing wail out of steady lips—a frenzied wail like that of a maddened cat. The Druids stopped chanting as suddenly as if choked by a strangler's knot. Warriors sprang up, groping for their weapons; the Romans followed suit, in even greater confusion. Simon, too, feigned fear, but gave a second cat's cry and then a third, imitating the continuous yowl of a bounding feline pack. The tribesmen were all jabbering panicked appeals to the Druids at once.

"The Cats of Sadoqua!" exclaimed Ferchobhar. "They're coming to save their masters from the flames! Quickly, all of you—into the forest! We will protect you!"

The terrified Gauls needed no more urging to break into a run for the black woods beyond the spot of firelight.

Ferchobhar thrust his weirdly flaming staff into the tinder around the osier cage; the fire took quickly and threw red sparks into the darkness. Then the chief Druid whirled and followed the rout out of the grove, flanked by subordinates and bodyguards.

Simon also pretended to flee. Once out of sight in the shadows, however, he dove into the undergrowth and waited for the last Gauls to stampede past him. He hastened their retreat with several loud feline yowls, convincing the Celts that the cats were close on their heels.

Then, when the hindmost Gauls were nothing but a distant rustle in the dead leaves, the Samaritan sprang from his hiding place and ran back into the clearing. The fire Ferchobhar had kindled had grown rapidly and the trapped men were already choking on the smoke. Simon ran to the osier cage and laid to it with his Roman *gladius*, or shortsword; the springy wood clove asunder beneath his powerful blows and in half a minute he had opened a gap wide enough for a man to crawl through.

"Quickly, come out of there! You're free!"

Although surprised, the imprisoned and bound Averoni took Simon's offer eagerly and wriggled through the breach headfirst, like human worms.

"Come, now!" Simon hissed to them as they emerged. "The woods are full of Gauls and they won't go far once they've regained their wits. Hurry!"

The last of the four prisoners, a short swarthy man, finished squirming out of the cage, his kilts smoldering. Simon grasped his lean arm and helped him to his feet. "Let's be off!"

"Who are you? Why have you betrayed the Druids? They were treating you as a guest."

"The friends of Rome are no true hosts of mine! I will need a haven for several days—and provisions."

"Follow me to my village—you may have all that I possess! But, wait—cut these cords! It is a long walk and the woods are full of the Whore-Goddess's spawn!"

Simon nodded and whipped out his *sica*, or gladiator's knife—but before he could touch its blade to the Averoni's bindings someone shouted behind him:

"Simon of Gitta, I knew you were an enemy!"

The Samaritan whirled, snarling. In the shadows stood

Ferchobhar, gesturing histrionically. Beside him clustered four other men—two armed warriors and two Druids of a lower degree.

"Run!" muttered Simon to the Averoni, shoving the closest of them away. "Into the forest! I'll hold them till you get away—!"

"Take him alive!" shrieked Ferchobhar.

Immediately, like unleashed dogs, the two warriors bounded at him, screaming a war-cry: *"Gogmagog!"*

Simon crouched in a fighting-stance, then darted toward the on-rushing Gauls, his *gladius* in one hand and the keen-bladed *sica* in the other.

The foremost Gaul bellowed, his bulky frame towering half a head above the more athletic compactness of the Samaritan, and swung his sword. Steel rang and sparks flew in the darkness as Simon parried expertly. Then blow followed blow with incredible swiftness. Ferchobhar, watching from a safe distance and scarcely able to follow the strokes, remembered that Simon had claimed to have spent two years of his youth as a gladiator in Italy. The Samaritan handled himself with such skill that the chief Druid could almost mistake his darting figure in the shadows for three distinct men.

"Beware!" yelled Ferchobhar. "He's arena-trained—!"

But the two warriors, already aware of their opponent's prowess, cunningly sought to busy him while their priestly masters slipped in from the flanks to pierce his unarmored body with their long daggers. With heavy long swords they flailed away at Simon's guard, forcing him back with their greater reach—but always the Roman sword or the sharp *sica* flashed before them, turning the berserk blows, while the Samaritan's lean figure eluded thrusts by the scantest margins with nimble turns and dodges. Never did their opponent set foot wrongly or waste a motion; he was always a menace, even in defense, executing his replies so precisely that the Gauls could not coordinate their attacks properly, but seemed to fight four separate duels.

Desperately Simon leapt and whirled, snarling with rage; sweat trickled under his clothing, which was ripped from the near misses of whipping blades. Just in time he caught the edge of a long sword on his *gladius*, then stabbed in with the knife. The Gaul bellowed at the pain of his wound, then leaped vengefully at the Samaritan. His painful lurch momentarily blocked his companion, giving Simon time to pounce upon one of the circling Druids, knock his ritual-dagger out of the way, and sink the *sica* into his breast—in the deft manner the gladiators knew, so that the blade did not stick between the ribs—

A sudden lull in the fighting. Two Gauls lay moaning underfoot. Ferchobhar looked dubiously from the wounded men to Simon, who was taxed but untouched, and hesitated. He could order his remaining priest and warrior to finish the Samaritan off, but the odds had been changed considerably. If his men did not get lucky, the high priest of the Black Goat Druids knew he might find himself standing alone before a skilled, vengeful enemy . . . .

"Back, men," he called out. "Wait for the others—!"

Simon cursed aloud. "Your treachery is even more despicable than your cowardice, goat-priest! I thought you Druids were men when I sought you, but you've proven yourselves no better than the Roman masters you serve! I leave you to them!"

He spun and ran fleetly into the dark oaks—but even as he did so he heard Ferchobhar cry out after him, like an incantation:

"You have not escaped us, Samaritan. You have belonged to us from the moment you discovered our village. You will yet pay the wage of your treachery!"

Simon made his way through the night, stumbling uncertainly in the unfamiliar forest, finding no sign of the victims he had freed. As dawn broke he recognized before him a range of blue mountains distantly merging into the mists—peaks the Gauls regarded with aversion. There, he knew, was the Averoni stronghold.

The morning air was perfumed by the scent of crumbling rocks and damp gorse. The terrain sloped downward, over crystalline boulders covered by forest and sparse grass. Since the fight with the Gauls, Simon had seen no sign of human life. That was, in a measure, lucky; he knew now that he could expect little friendliness from either Celts or Romans in Regio Averonum.

He grumbled a curse, realizing that if he had to leave Gaul now, he would take little knowledge with him. Least of all had he discovered the nature of the cloven-hoofed forest creatures or the source of the Druid's alleged power over them. Druidic myth connected the beings with the goddess Sheila-na-gog, the most important and mysterious deity of the Black Goats' pantheon. Her symbol was a crone with obscenely exaggerated genitals, as if she were nearly all womb; grotesque, perhaps, but what Simon had seen of her worship was sinister enough. Belief in this monstrous goddess set the Black Goats apart from their brother druidic societies; evidently the Wild Cats, the Beavers, the Rabbits and most other Gallic cults condemned the dark magic of the priests of Sheila-na-gog . . . .

Regio Averonum stretched league upon league, a sea of hills and forests. As Simon wended his way, the woodland floor, rent with ravines and craggy remnants of rock outcroppings, extended before him toward darker groves where pigeons cooed. The sound reminded him of his hunger. A bird might be brought down with a makeshift sling; it might be eaten raw—or roasted, should he feel safe enough to kindle a fire.

Simon picked up a stone from the bottom of a gully and walked softly toward where the pigeons roosted. At his movements the birds stilled their peaceful cooing, and some of them warily changed their position in the branches . . . .

Although intent on his hunting, Simon was suddenly alert to a quick, stealthy sound behind him. He whirled just in time to see a glittering blade lifted menacingly above him, clenched in a gnarled fist— and behind the fist a devil's mask. Then the dagger plunged down.

Reacting with the reflexive swiftness of the trained fighter he caught his assailant's wrist in his left hand and drove his stone-hardened right into a muscular, hairy belly. The creature bleated painfully and staggered back.

It was a wonder that the sudden shock of seeing such a creature had not stunned Simon too much to allow him to fend off the fatal blow. Even in the dim light it could not be mistaken for a man. The face, though coarsely human, had a bestial cast in the crook of its huge nose and the muzzle-like jut of its lips and teeth; the torso, too, was superficially human, though knot-like muscles moved strangely under its sallow skin. But below the waist humanity ended; the creature was a living satyr—manlike above and a two-legged goat below.

And it was big—almost as tall as Simon, and broader. It danced strangely from hoof to hoof, as nimble as the animal whose hind limbs it seemed to possess. Protruding eyes glared into the Samaritan's face, but Simon forced himself to watch instead the curved dagger which the monster rapidly switched from hand to hand, as quick as thought and seemingly to no purpose unless to distract and confuse its foe . . . .

The creature leaped without warning, a hard, sharp hoof aimed straight at Simon's middle. Simon dodged the unorthodox attack barely in time. Landing nimbly upright, the satyr leaped again instantly, like a compressed spring, evading Simon's *gladius* and driving a hard shoulder into his chest. Both crashed into the ground, clawing at one another while rolling across a blanket of dew-wet leaves.

Simon brought up his short-sword skillfully—but the satyr, anticipating him faster than any human could have, caught his sword-arm and stopped it as suddenly as if the air had frozen thick, then began to squeeze the captured limb with the pressure of a cart wheel. The blade tumbled out of Simon's numbed fingers.

Frantically he groped for the *sica* at his belt, but in doing so left an opening through which the satyr's dagger plunged. Simon felt its cold bite in his side, heard its tip grate upon a rib, then saw it flash up into the sky for a second descent—

But instead of striking again, the monster suddenly bleated and lurched forward, blanketing the Samaritan with its hot, reeking body. Simon stabbed it and bucked furiously, throwing it off—but sensed immediately that it was not fighting back. Rolling on top of it, he saw why not: a Roman *pilum* protruded from its broad back. Simon scanned the trees; someone out there had chosen to help him at the last moment.

He spied several figures emerging from the forest. Gauls and Romans!

Urgently Simon tried to regain his feet, but a shot of pain from his wound brought him down flat. The Romans rushed him and beat the *sica* out of his fist. When he was unarmed and held hand and foot by several warriors, their leaders strode up.

"Mailaen," said a short Roman officer, "your monster was told to take him alive! Had I not given the order, the creature would have slain him!"

The Druid shrugged. "Sometimes, Commander Scaevola, the spawn obey their basic nature in spite of their orders. Ferchobhar shall be displeased that you destroyed the satyr. His type is very precious and it required a rare sacrifice to create him."

"Ferchobhar had better concern himself with *my* displeasure! My creatures must obey me *absolutely!*"

Simon had perked up his head upon hearing the Roman commander's name. The Druids were evidently not dealing with simple renegade Romans, for Scaevola—Mettius Aelius Scaevola—was proconsul of Regio Averonum. Simon knew him of old—an agent of Caligula, until that mad emperor's demise, and now, by touch-and-go maneuverings, an officer of Claudius. Whatever the Roman-Druid conspiracy, it obviously reached to the very highest circles of the province.

Scaevola turned away from Mailaen and approached Simon, pompously, as if he considered himself a conquering emperor. He was an ungainly man, plump in the belly and skinny in the limbs. His craggy face was characteristically Roman, but sagging from dissipation. Unlike most Roman officials, he sported a beard—a short, sparse fringe of hair that outlined his pallid face like a wreath of brittle moss. Without his uniform the keenest imagination would not have pictured him as a soldier—but for the last generation many worthless sorts had risen to the high ranks of Roman officialdom on the strength of personal friendship with Tiberius or Caligula.

"Your recapture is a fortunate stroke for me, Samaritan," said the proconsul, grinning at Simon's look of consternation. "Oh, yes, Simon of Gitta, I know you—by reputation. Of course the Black Goats reported your presence to me in Augustonemetum. Ferchobhar knew I needed a man like you."

"What do you want from me?" Simon demanded stiffly. "Apparently you have greater magicians than me licking your boots—and with Caligula groping in Tartarus where he belongs, there can no longer be any great reward attached to my carcass."

"You underestimate yourself, Simon. You are a remarkable man—and the Druids have use for such."

Simon fell silent. He measured up Scaevola as a man who might gloat in his own self-importance for hours without answering a simple question.

"How are his wounds?" the proconsul asked.

A centurion lifted Simon's shirt and examined the gash the satyr had made. "It's not serious if it can be dressed properly."

"Permit me," volunteered Mailaen. "We have skills even your

Greek physicians know not of."

"Get on with it," muttered Scaevola, "and spare me your boasting. The wound will not weaken his powers, will it?"

"Physical suffering," smiled Mailaen, "if short of killing, does not diminish one's soul. Indeed, some men's latent powers are enhanced by it. Occasionally—when we believe it will heighten the victim's psychic energies—we employ torture before sacrificing him to Sheila-na-gog."

Wounded, bound and closely guarded by Scaevola's bodyguards, Simon found no means to escape his cage over the next two days. His wardens—ignorant, taciturn underlings—either knew nothing about what it meant "to be given to Sheila-na-gog" or would not say.

Then, on the third morning after his capture, he happened to overhear Scaevola and Ferchobhar arguing:

"I warn you, if I don't get what I want and return safely to Augustonemetum, a legion will burn this place out! Even if you personally escape into the hills, you'll be a hunted dog, without followers to make you feel important."

"Your fear talks," Ferchobhar admonished softly.

Scaevola's eyes flashed.

"No, take no offense," the Druid went on, "for even I have my fears. Sheila-na-gog is mother of all living things, all things upon this world that ever were and ever shall be. Do not, however, imagine we would betray you. Steel yourself! If you do not attend the spawning, you cannot attain power over the beast."

"I will bring my guards!"

"Bring them."

"You agree too easily," said Scaevola, suspicion in his eyes. "What of your precious secrets?"

"Every Roman who enters that place is a traitor to his emperor and his gods. If he is not mad, he will not speak of what he has seen. And if he goes mad, his words will not be believed."

"Mad?"

"There is that danger. But the ends we pursue are great and well worth the risk. You have sworn that you will accuse the Averoni of plotting to rise as they once did under Vercingetorix, and destroy them utterly. In return, you can count upon the Gauls to march shoulder to shoulder with your own legions."

"Perhaps I would do better if the Averoni were my allies. While you Gauls were fawning at Julius Caesar's hem, the Averoni were the only ones that showed him any fight—"

"When all the Caesars have passed away," said Ferchobhar scornfully, "there will still be Sheila-na-gog. Remember, once you are emperor, the laws of the Claudians shall be abolished and a temple of the Goddess shall be raised in Rome."

Scaevola shrugged. "I'll give you your temple. There are worse gods entering Rome every day. What do I care if Sheila-na-gog becomes first among them?"

The two conspirators walked on, still speaking in low tones. Simon watched them disappear behind a hut. So that was it—a double treason, racial enemies embracing for narrow ends!

In less than an hour Simon again saw his foes, this time as part of a procession that was gathering in the heart of the village as the morning sun rose above the surrounding trees. The highest Druids, now robed in black, mingled with Gallic warriors and fully-armed Romans. A number of lowly acolytes leaned upon their staffs, bulging packs of provisions hanging from their backs. Another acolyte, near the head of the assembly, held a stake on which was impaled the severed head of a black goat with large, twisted horns.

Simon was then brought from his cage, chained by the wrists to a Roman on either side. His wound did not pain him much anymore, and he could walk with some confidence. Evidently the healing herbs and ointments of the Druids were as potent as they claimed.

Ferchobhar stepped to the side of the goat-head standard and beckoned the assembly to follow him.

He chose a path leading out of the village toward the volcanic hills. The route rose up through a forest of beech and juniper, over black basalt ledges and boulders largely clothed in a thick carpet of moss. As they ascended the growth thinned, but Simon saw little more; a strange mist had filled in around the group, almost as if summoned by the Druids to disguise the winding route they followed. Occasionally it thinned and the Samaritan could make out a ghostly peak in the distance, a peak he recognized as the dead crater of the ancient mountain

Cantal.

The trail continued to climb for most of the day, as if seeking perhaps the very roof of the world, where waited—what? What was the
thing called Sheila-na-gog . . . ?

In the gray twilight of evening, Ferchobhar at last motioned the
column to a halt on a blasted ridge near the summit of a long-extinct
volcano. Only a rare scrub clung here and there to the dark, cracked
rocks. The valley below was shrouded in a stratum of mist through
which only the evergreens on the highest bluffs managed to break. In
addition to its desolate natural appearance, Simon sensed a queer presence in this landscape that chilled him to the quick. His companions
evidently felt it too, for a subdued tension was apparent in the experienced Druids, a more open nervous agitation in the novice Romans.

"What is this place, Druid?" demanded Scaevola, a slight tremor in
his voice.

"We have arrived," said Ferchobhar simply. "Bring the Samaritan
forward."

The guards, seeming even more ill-at-ease than their captive, prodded Simon along between them.

"My warriors shall guard the entry," said the chief Druid. "Let
your own men come in with us, Commander Scaevola, if you so desire."

The proconsul nodded nervously and beckoned his bodyguards
with a wave of his hand. "Let's get on with it, Druid."

Ferchobhar deployed his warriors, then led the rest of the procession along a chasm whose walls ran with greenish slime. In places it
was gathered into blisterous shapes and, where they stepped on it, it
clung like pine gum to their boots. At the end of the rift they came upon a pit that sloped downward and gave off an acrid odor. Once it
might have been a chimney channeling black lava over the mountain's
steep side.

Ferchobhar descended by a narrow path into the pit, followed by
Mailaen and the other Druids. The Romans' faces gawked longingly at
the light they were leaving behind; then they fell in behind the priests,
who advanced more confidently—though even Ferchobhar wore a
grave expression on his face. What horror, Simon wondered, could so
affect even those who adored it the most . . . ?

The darkness was suddenly banished by the Druids, whose staffs flamed on as if by mental command. Simon, studying the enchanted torches carefully, noticed that the smooth finish at the head of the rods was neither blackened nor consumed.

"What magic is this?" Scaevola blurted. "Those staffs—?"

"A magic handed down to us by the sages of ancient Acheron, who brought our Goddess here from foundering Hyperborea," muttered Ferchobhar. "But, be silent—we approach the sacred presence."

The tunnel ended in a black, hollow space from which puffed a warm and ill-smelling draft. Blowing over the Samaritan's bare hands and face, the breeze somehow made him feel grimy and foul. The Druids, entering first, had the cavity well-lighted before the Romans and their prisoner reached it. The Samaritan, as he entered, drew up sharply in surprise and horror.

Bubbling within the vast cavern was a huge gray pool, some thirty yards across. It churned silently, constantly putting forth gigantic mouths, eyes, pseudopods and animate creatures. These last were the most incredible, swimming across the glistening surface, or flapping above it on clumsy and dripping wings. A few had escaped to the shore and grown somewhat—but even as Simon watched, tentacles or a sucking force from underneath, pulled the rest of them back down. They resembled composites of bats, toads, birds, reptiles and less describable forms of life. Thankfully, the pool dissolved them—but just as rapidly gave birth to more creatures, similar only in their hellishness.

The infant monsters on the scummy bank paid no attention to the intruding men; but the Romans gasped incoherent prayers and shrank back at the sight of those beasts that happened to wriggle inadvertently close.

"Begone!" commanded Ferchobhar, extending his staff toward a small, gelatinous lamia that was squirming toward the Romans. At once the thing dissolved and rilled back into the churning pool.

The chief Druid raised his arms. "Behold the womb of Sheila-na-gog, Mother of Life! Now, in the hour of the Lark, we bring to our Goddess a worthy mate. May his seed conceive in her a child of unsurpassed power. Receive him, O Goddess, into your sacred body!"

Ferchobhar then continued to speak, but in a tongue that Simon did not recognize. The remaining Druids struck up an undecipherable chant in support of him.

And Simon at last understood—and wished he did not! The gelatinous creatures cast off by the viscous pool had very little physical stability to them; the Greeks knew of such things and called them "*khimeras*". Although a few might escape into the outer world, they could maintain a semblance of life only by vampirizing the truly living beings who had already adapted to that world.

But such entities would not suit the needs of the Black Goat Druids, who wanted servitors of dependable physical stability. Apparently a human or animal from the outside world, cast into the pool, would provide the substance of a real monster—such as the satyr he had fought in the woods. And especially so if the victim was animated by a strong life force . . . .

Scaevola turned and grinned wolfishly at Simon. "When you fell into the Druids' power, they realized that you would provide the soul and flesh for what I demanded of them—a servant like no man has possessed before! There are men who must be destroyed and others who must know terror before I dare make my move and overthrow that limping fool who reigns in Rome. Judging from your notoriety, Simon of Gitta, you have great spirit. Surely the Druids' slime-goddess will make of you nothing less than a demon—perhaps a host of demons—and then Ferchobhar's magic shall make your spawn my absolute slave!"

"Mot take you first, madman!" snarled Simon, leaping forward furiously. The guards chained to the Samaritan responded barely in time to restrain him before his hands reached the proconsul's flabby neck.

Angrily, the Roman commander struck him across the face and thrust him back.

"Take off these chains and try that again, Roman slime!" howled Simon.

"See how he fights!" Scaevola trumpeted. "What spirit! Did I not choose rightly? What he generates in union with Sheila-na-gog will shake the throne of Mars!" He signaled his guards. "Give him his wish and remove his shackles."

One of Simon's escorts dug a key out of his pouch. As the guard opened the bracelet around his own wrist, Simon's mind raced. When his left hand was also free, he would make his move. The Romans were ill-at-ease in front of the incredible pool, partly distracted by its heavings and bubblings; he might strike one of them down with his bare hands, then seize a *gladius*, kill as many of his foes as he could before being hacked down—possibly even fight his way up the tunnel. The Gauls waiting outside—little chance to elude them, but better a fighting death than a surrender to Sheila-na-gog . . . .

Suddenly a cat's scream echoed. The Roman holding the manacle-key jerked in nervous surprise and fumbled it; it dropped into the slime underfoot. The Romans and Druids looked anxiously at one another.

"Stay where you are!" ordered Scaevola. "It's only the Samaritan! He made fools of you once!" The echo of his voice thundered between the rheumy walls of the huge cavern.

The wail of the cat was followed by the shouts of the Gallic warriors outside. Scaevola looked askance into Ferchobhar's pallid face. "We *are* being attacked!" exclaimed the proconsul. "Hurry—let's get this over with!"

He gripped Simon by the shoulder and pulled him forward. The soldier still shackled to his left hand lurched behind him, cursing in protest.

"Fool!" roared Scaevola. "Remove that chain or you'll go into the pool with him!"

"It's not my fault!" the guard protested frantically. "Rufus dropped the key into the muck!"

"Then strike off the Samaritan's hand!" barked Ferchobhar, "but in the name of the Goddess, hurry!"

Swiftly Simon shifted his weight, seized the chained guard by the wrist and upper arm, bent forward—and expertly flung the surprised Latin over his muscular shoulders. The man crashed into two more Romans, sending them sprawling also.

"Stop him!" bellowed Scaevola, retreating behind the Druids.

Ferchobhar, showing more spine, thrust his staff flame first at Simon's chest. The Samaritan sidestepped with the agility of a trained gladiator—barely in time, for the brand slid along his side, singeing his woolen chiton. Cursing, he struck out with the heavy manacle that dangled from his right wrist, bringing it down savagely on Ferchobhar's shoulder. The old Druid yelped and slacked his grasp on the staff. Instantly the Samaritan grabbed it and jerked it out of his hands—but then lost his advantage as the chained Roman gave the other shackle an angry tug and pulled him down.

Simon grappled with the man on the scummy cavern floor, while the other Romans began to push through the indignant Druids with swords drawn. The foremost legionary raised his *gladius* over the Samaritan's head.

"No!" shrieked the proconsul. "Take him alive!"

The warning spared Simon a severed neck. Instead, the Latins seized him by the legs and his free arm, controlling him despite a struggle that would have done credit to two men.

"Hold out his hand!" yelled a Roman, his white knuckles clenched upon his sword grip. Two others forced Simon down under their combined weight and wrestled his manacled arm into a position convenient for its detachment.

Suddenly a man howled in pain. The Druids and Romans glanced toward the egress as a Gallic warrior came threshing and stumbling into the grotto. A black cat clung to his bleeding back, biting and clawing his flesh.

"The Cats of Sadoqua!" blurted Mailaen.

The Gaul, seemingly blind with terror, plunged frantically through the startled men and blundered over the edge of the pit into the churning pool, the cat leaping from his back to the bank barely in time. The living muck held the Gaul for an instant, submerged to the waist, like a berry on a steaming porridge; then, as his cries intensified in recognition of his new horror, tentacles formed out of the upper surface and dragged him under.

Frenzied yowls rang down the narrow tunnel. Fear lit up every Druid face.

Ferchobhar alone had the self-control to shout: "Defend yourselves!" and retrieve his staff from under the Romans' feet. He had scarcely done so before dozens of black feline figures gushed out of the tunnel, as nimble as bats.

They rushed and sprang straight into the mass of men, claws and fangs bared, moving so swiftly that Simon, now abandoned by his captors, could make out little of them in the uncertain light and moving shadows. He glimpsed darting, shiny pelts and large eyes gleaming like moons. The Romans and Druids fought them with steel and flaming staves, but were obviously disorganized by the inhuman manner and ferocity of the attack; even those hardened veterans seemed baffled by the smallness of their foes and the supple ease with which they evaded the weapon-thrusts.

The chained guard, forgetful of the manacle in his panic, scrambled to his feet and dodged a rushing cat; the chain brought him up short and threw him off balance. Screaming out in horror, he plunged into the pool of Sheila-na-gog, feet first.

As the man was drawn under, the manacle wrenched Simon's arm with a force that rolled him over on his belly and dragged him toward the pool. Frantically he caught hold of a scum-caked stone with his free hand and arrested his slide, but the bubbling fluid was swallowing the Roman—and Simon, chained to him, was accompanying him down the gullet of Sheila-na-gog!

He strained and held on tenaciously. The edge of the iron wristlet cut through his skin, and some of his blood dribbled into the ichor. Pain shot up his forearm till he feared that his arm would tear off—a severance more painful than the quick cut the Romans had intended for him . . . .

Suddenly the tension broke and the chain sprang slack. Simon lifted the manacle.

"Baal!" he gasped.

The other wristlet hung empty, not a trace of blood on it. The Roman had been swallowed alive and dissolved.

Shaking off his astonishment, Simon scrambled to his feet—to find himself jostled and trampled by the struggling men. Except for himself, every man in the cavern had one or more cats clinging to his clothing and biting his exposed flesh. Blood reddened the black robes of the Druids and rilled down the Romans' limbs as they threshed about. Their panicked shrieks filled the grotto and mingled with the yowling of the cats—which yelling now began to shed its feline tenor and become more like screamed syllables in a forgotten tongue!

The shrill chanting seemed to drive the beleaguered men mad. They ceased to defend themselves and began to run crazily, randomly around the narrow ledge above the pool, jostling one another in their terror, striking themselves senseless against the walls or stumbling blindly into the goddess' fluid mass.

A louder voice penetrated the commotion—Ferchobhar's, invoking a protective spell against the cats' shrill voicings. Bright flashes of flame suddenly lit the cavern—searing blasts from the end of the Druid's magic staff. The fire dissolved the felines it touched in the wink of an eye, but also charred those luckless men who were mingled with them, driving them in blind agony into the clutch of Sheila-na-gog.

Then Ferchobhar made a dash for the exit, and close behind him ran Mettius Aelius Scaevola, the cats no longer barring their escape. Quick as thought, Simon grasped a Druid's fallen staff and threw it between the proconsul's legs. Even as Ferchobhar vanished up the tunnel the Roman stumbled over the staff and crashed to the rocky floor, his armor ringing. Before he could regain his feet, he felt Simon's strong hands upon him.

"Latin dog!" hissed the Samaritan, gripping his foe's throat.

"Spare me!" Scaevola gasped against the pressure. "I had nothing to do with this! I can make you an important man—!"

Disgust welled up in Simon's breast, and hate. It was corrupt Roman officials like this one who had plundered his home in Samaria, slain his parents, sold him into the arena.

"Scum who would rule the world," he snarled, "kiss the bride you would have given me to!"

Then with a surge of rage he heaved the man off his feet—and straight over the brink of the pit into the pool of Sheila-na-gog.

For a moment the Roman stuck like a fly in the surface of the seething paste; then, screaming, he sank down. Simon watched, dark eyes narrowed, feeling no pity for the dying proconsul. Scaevola howled as his mouth filled with the gray, pulsing fluid; then his voice choked off, and his frantic eyes vanished beneath the fetid surface. The depression he left behind slowly filled in with ichor . . . .

Suddenly Simon realized he stood alone in the grotto. The cats had gone and those men who were not dead or senseless underfoot had vanished into the goddess-pool. The Samaritan felt a strange heaviness begin to take possession of him . . . .

Something huffed close by. Turning, Simon beheld a creature heaving itself out of the pasty womb of Sheila-na-gog. It was a small criosphinx—a ram-headed beast with leonine hindquarters and wings still dripping with fluid. Other fetid monsters were similarly rising, most smaller and frailer—amalgamations of all manner of lowly beasts, some possessed of forms that had no known equivalent in Nature. Simon recoiled; here, he realized, were the men who had gone into the pool, now remolded into abominations not of this earth.

He backed away, and turned to retreat up the tunnel—but then he heard men's shouts and footsteps coming from around a bend. Was it the rest of the Gauls? Had Ferchobhar rallied the men outside?

Simon snatched up a Roman sword. Wounded, sickened, he would yet make a fight of it . . . .

The intruders moved cautiously into view. Simon's *gladius* wavered unsteadily. These were not the Gauls, although Ferchobhar's face was in the forefront . . . .

Aye, in the forefront—for in the fist of the first Averoni tribesman dangled the head of Ferchobhar, chief of the Black Goat Druids. Blood and horror had hideously changed the dead priest's face.

"Put down your weapon, Simon of Gitta," said their leader. "We surely have not done all this with the intent of harming you."

Simon recognized the newcomer as the last man he had released from the Druids' osier cage. He nodded, lowered his sword and slumped wearily against the wall.

"I thank you," he said, fighting to keep from passing into a swoon.

Several Averoni nudged past him and began to attack the creatures of the pool with spears, axes and knives, hewing them into lifeless pieces.

"Good," said their chief when the butchery was finished. "Now, let's get out of this foul place!"

They all hurried from the cavern; but as the last two torch-bearing Averoni helped Simon through the exit, he turned—and gasped as he observed a final creature rise from the womb of Sheila-na-gog. It had just surfaced in an obscure corner, near the spot where Mettius Aelius Scaevola had disappeared; it was small and had the shape of a rat, but its pallid, bearded face and handlike forepaws were evilly human . . . .

Then a sudden bubbling of the pool seemed to frighten the risen creature, sending it scurrying into the shadows with a loathsome, piteous titter.

THE LAND OF AVEROIGNE

by Edward Stasheff

In Averoigne country, deep within France,
The loup-garoux howl and the satyrs dance.
Where vampires drink and gargoyles soar
Sorcerers summon and lamias lure.
An ancient land of shadow and spirit,
That seeps into all creatures within it.
Of woodland and mountains, river and moor,
Of forgotten gods and forbidden lore.
Let me guide and regale you as we roam
Through the primeval land of Averoigne.

In the rotting marshes near Les Hiboux,
Handsome young boys grow increasingly few.
For a fat lusty witch dwells in the brine
Who lures in lads, and gives them drugged wine.
But should they flee from her flabby embrace,
The bog swallows them up without a trace.
While an alchemist harvests with a knife
Mandrakes from the grave of his murdered wife,
To sell potions mulled from this noxious brew
From his hut in the mires by Les Hiboux.

In the prosperous city of Ximes,
Not everyone is quite what they seem.
The saintly Bishop helps the sick and poor,
But summons demons behind a locked door
From *The Book of Eibon* he keeps nearby
Until it's stolen by a clerical spy.
His henchman pursues and doesn't give up,
Till he slips a potion into the thief's cup,
Leaving the Bishop free to plot and scheme
In the sanctified city of Ximes.

In the starry sky above Averoigne,
After a flaming red comet has flown,

A shadow beast stalks the forests and glen,
Preying on livestock, then corpses, then men.
It slaughters in silence, and then it dines,
Sucking the marrow from its victims' spines.
Travelers and peasants and nobles are snared.
Even the monks of Périgon are not spared.
For the demon is lurking within their home
Under the haunted skies of Averoigne

In the holy Abbey of Périgon
Their prayerful lives go profanely wrong
When an ancient pagan idol is found
Buried deep beneath consecrated ground.
Then many monks fail their sacred test
Between immortal soul and carnal flesh.
At night a star-beast preys upon the monks
As they lie dreaming, asleep in their bunks.
But come the morning, the monster's withdrawn
Beyond the hallowed walls of Périgon.

In remote deserted Château Faussesflammes,
Across the sylvan vale from Périgon,
Once lived a sorcerous vampire pair
Who enticed travelers into their lair.
They met their end when they suffered the wrath
Of a troubadour with a hornbeam staff.
Now curious folk who venture too near
And explore inside soon disappear
For a succubus hides far down below
The courtyard flagstones of Faussesflammes Château

In the desolate ruins of Ylourgne,
Risen, wandering corpses merely forewarn
A dwarven sorcerer's sadistic plan
To take revenge through a colossal man,
To fill the titan with his warlock's mind,
And leave his own dying body behind.

His minions butcher the horde of undead,
To stew in glowing vats of white and red.
From dead meat and bone a giant is born
In the abandoned fortress of Ylourgne.

In the great walled city of Vyônes
The ancient cathedral's gargoyles roam
Abroad in flight at night to hide until
They swoop in silence down to rape and kill.
When a vengeful Colossus comes to brawl,
It steps with ease over the city's wall,
And wrecks and kills with relentless power,
Until it's stopped by a whiff of powder.
For a loyal warlock has made his home
In the cathedral city of Vyônes.

In the ancestral land of Averoigne,
The dead leaves whisper when the cold winds moan
Deep in the forests of holly and oak
Where Druids serve and Necromancers invoke
Primordial gods from Hyperborea—
Iog-Sotôt, Azètot, and Sodoqua.
Here the Old Ways cling on to survival,
Even Christians seem like a new arrival.
And yet the Church tries to claim as its own
This old pagan land of Averoigne.

THE CULT OF THE SINGING FLAME

by David Reid Ross

Translation from Latin medieval manuscript:

I, Onfrei, have sat too long in this dank monastic cell, too long with no company save your unsmiling "attendants" outside this deadbolted oaken door. You say, O tender Inquisitors, that this is for my protection. Perhaps you are right.

You say you will provide me with quill, ink, and uncouth parchment, on condition I use these implements only for my testimony, on the recent disappearances from southern Averoigne and on the new heresy reported there. From musical notation, you forbid me, and I must write by daylight as I can no longer abide the dance of an open flame.

Your agents have doubtless learnt these facts already, from certain unenraptured citizens of afflicted Ximes, and from others in the ambit of her bishop, Azédarac: he who sent me on my mission, and he whom I divine to be your true target here. I testify that, whatever accusations be whispered against him otherwise, my lord bishop and I have opposed, and shun, this heresy as much as you do if not more so.

The Lord be witness over what I write that I, wretch that I am, be no heretic nor liar! If a flame be my fate, no pyre you can kindle should burn as painfully nor as completely as my heart has burned already.

Since your eminences require a complete record, I must start from the beginning.

I was a foundling of no parentage, so I am told, and until entering the future bishop's service I lived all my life far from the siren fires of the Martyrion, within the quiet grey-black mures of the Abbey of Périgon. I am told that Périgon, following the rule of Saint-Benoît as it does, imposes a regimen less strict than that of the Cistercian establishments; but for a youth growing to adolescence the regimen was strenuous enough. As an acolyte my lot was prayer, study, and communal meals. I am however grateful for the education I received, in Latin and Greek, although I was only passable in the former and remain barely literate in the latter. It is the custom in Périgon to shave a tonsure only upon writing correct Latin; I received my crown having the age of nine, later than most.

My true passion was in music. I learnt the eight Gregorian authentic and plagal modes, enough to compose some chants for the propers. I loved best the Office of Vespers, held in the dark grey chapel as the westering sun behind us cast golden highlights upon the sacred Table. In this Mass, you understand, the classes of singers may vary their tune, even in polyphonic harmony. Would that I could sing to the Lord only the *old* songs. . .

On the feast of Zenobia Martyr, the penultimate day of October, it was our custom to issue forth from the abbey, rustling through the falling russet leaves to the local village's church, which reveres some minor relics of that saint. Some of my compositions are perhaps still sung in that little country church, albeit not likely in Périgon Abbey itself. Not anymore. Not since word reached them I had seen and heard the Flame.

Certain of my fellow acolytes would follow a rather more independent pilgrimage to Sainte-Zénobie, especially after Vespers on the "fête du Saint-Samedi," pleading your pardon. The Benedictine Rule has forbidden such; but in Périgon some monks could be persuaded to make themselves scarce as the boys set out and returned from their nocturnal peregrinations. I suspect that the Abbot himself was not blind to their excursions; this was his means to discern the sheep, called to the Rule, from the young goats, called to serve in other ways, although the goats were not always discerned quickly. I was not the only lad there miraculously born of a Zénobienne virgin.

On mine own first ventures alongside my peers, I hesitated to join fully in their merriments, being still very young and fearing to transgress more of the Rule than I already had. They quaffed the local golden vintages; I made do with boiled and flavored water. I sat by the wall, near the flickering flames, to hear the chantaires. Many of their songs even some of your eminences will have heard. Of the unhappy count Gerard de Venteillon, lured into the ruins near Périgon by the will-o'-the-wisps there and consumed. Of the fire-haired baroness Jirel de Joiry, returned from Hadean depths with a poison kiss for her despoiler.

The minstrels employed a form of parallel and oblique organum polyphony in how they played their chords. Most of their songs were like ours, at least structurally: in our system, they would approximate the first and fourth authentic modes. Others of their songs were in musical arrangements less easily assigned. I hasten to point out the same holds true for certain of our hymns, especially the older ones. As I learnt more songcraft, in my youthful arrogance, I argued with my teachers over which hymns belonged in modal form; and which could be improved or, perhaps, restored.

And during my last spring at the abbey, I began furtively courting a buxom auburn-haired maiden of Sainte-Zénobie. Acolytes grinned; monks cast glances; at the last before it could become a scandal my bunk was overturned and my secrets revealed: an ode to *la bénie entre toutes les femmes* in that popular fourth, a version of the Magnificat in the second-plagal, and several other less-finished works on the theme. The Abbot, upon summoning me to his office, got from me the full truth, including the name of the maiden. It turned out that this name had been oft-repeated in the abbey, and I was apprised that the true object of my hymn was in character more like that of that other Maria. So I shall name her here: my heart, my damnation, my Madeleine.

After that, my aspect became, I am ashamed to confess, sullen and resentful, and my studies suffered as a result; nor was I a boon companion to my fellow acolytes. So on the last week of that October, when the then-Archdeacon Azédarac strode into our refectory, scanning us with his black-and-yellow eyes, and called out for an assistant for the great church in Ximes, one who could read and write Latin and could follow musical notation, more than one face turned in my direction, and the gloom on my face was lightened. And so I, no longer bound to Benoît's Rule but still in the Church, ended up outside the sheltering grey walls of Périgon, with my few personal effects packed, bidding farewell to my childhood home. As my brothers in the Abbey made their way to Sainte-Zénobie, I turned my face instead to the wilder musicks of the wind-tossed autumnal forest, beckoning to me like a great conflagration.

The roads of Averoigne are not always free of wolves, on four legs or two, so Archdeacon Azédarac had brought a small company of men-at-arms. As I had never ventured far from the shelter of Périgon I had much to learn about our destination, Ximes. As we rode together beneath the Averoignard oaks and pines, I plied my companions with questions. Azédarac, not being much encumbered with the virtue of humility, was more than pleased to fill a willing ear.

In the evenings, whilst the moths fluttered about our fire-lit faces, the archdeacon's men-at-arms led by vulpine Jehan spun tales of Averoigne. Some of these I knew from the Sainte-Zénobie tavern, like the sad end of Comte Gerard; others, like the tale of the satyr of La Frênaie, or of the gargoyles of the cathedral city, were then unknown to me, and their heterodox content certainly would never have been permitted in the cloister of Périgon.

The Ximes I knew from my studies was a city of many thousands of souls and the seat of a bishopric, subject to the cathedra in Vyônes. Azédarac informed me further of his master, Bishop Garaille: an elderly fellow, tolerant as bishops go, as inoffensive to the lowly Averoignian priests as he was to the Roman Curia.

At last we scented the smoke of the charcoal-burners who live outside any notable settlement; we passed some inns; and anon we crested a rise and gazed down upon the great wooden walls of Ximes. And what a sight it was: the vermilion haze of thousands of stove-fires mingling with the vapors of the River Isoile, the walls in a circle looming over the cleared fields around, and at the centre of town the great church of the bishop.

The next few days went by as if in the sepia fog from the river. Within the church grounds I was introduced to my chamber, much more splendid than the poor pallet I had as a humble acolyte, with a single bed and a desk, and shelves well-stocked with Alandalucian paper—paper! In Périgon we were still scrubbing old deerskin for palimpsests. I was also introduced to my tutors, who would be furthering my studies in Latin and Greek, and in music. The Archdeacon had even recruited for his bishopric a teacher of Arabic and Hebrew, a Jew having fled the Musselmans of Algrenade. I think that even the cathedral city Vyônes was not then endowed with such savants.

And there was the music. My patron, Azédarac, had made known that here in Ximes was a market for cosmopolitan compositions, and that coin was at hand for any novelties of quality. Here in Ximes I was *encouraged* to attend the taverns; if only I brought my pen and paper. What contrast with Périgon! Minstrels from all Europa swarmed into the streets of this once-humble city: rough bards of the Angleterre, se-ductive chantaires of the Franks, gallant poets of Alandalucy. Not all the jongleurs and chantaires were of our faith. Not all the songs I tran-scribed were in languages even known to Christendom. As the leaves turned on the trees, more trouvères arrived from even further afield: the peripatetic Rom from the Byzantine counties, and the travelers of Eire. Some told more terrific tales of a dark land in Abchazy, of blood-drinkers in Hungary. It seemed to me that Ximes had become a gaulois Baghdad, an auditory for a thousand and one songs. Some of my fel-low clerics, however, made sour comparisons with a more ancient Mesopotamian metropolis, whose king had consigned the three saints to the furnace.

As the months went by, and as my hair grew out (Azédarac, ton-sured himself, saw no purpose in baldness upon a lapsed-Benedictine assistant) I gained more of my master's trust, and was permitted to travel afield. Later I traveled as far as Lutèce des Parises, wherein I read in the libraries of Our Lady's grand cathedral (saints preserve it!) the books of polyphony assembled by its magisters.

So it went for more season-turnings, and in AD 1166 the time came when our good Bishop Garaille went home to our Lord. Azédarac led the Requiem Mass at his bier. I, still only seventeen summers old, was called to conduct the elegaic hymns. In my pride I desired to add my own voice to the chorus. I had attended funerals in Périgon, and I never liked their songs about the *Jour de la colère*, so I had some notions on the content and style befitting my theme. Without changing the content of the vocals nor the trochaic structure, which would cast disgrace on me and on my patron, I endeavored that night to adjust the music. Where the traditional music was sorrowful throughout, I introduced themes of communality (by polyphony) and of hope (by raising the tenor), gathering force at the end. In this task I struggled, not knowing the late Bishop as well as those born of Ximes knew him. I admit that in the quivering candlelight, I recalled my Mad-eleine; abandoned in Sainte-Zénobie but not forgotten, never to be forgotten.

The choir sang my song, such as it was. As it concluded, I glanced over to my master Azédarac. I will not say he was emotionally moved; he could not have been. But no sneer crossed his lips that moment, and during some of my cadences his dark eyes went unfocused and their spark more somber, which I took for compliment enough.

The late Bishop Garaille was duly interred in the catacomb with his predecessors in the cloth. It seems I had not disgraced my patron, at least: a few days later, Archbishop Clément summoned Archdeacon Azédarac to Vyônes; Clément returned him to us as our new Bishop.

Little changed in my position as Azédarac assumed the mitre. I had heard rumors that our overseer was perhaps not the holiest man in the parish; all knew then as well as you know now that he was not even ordained as a priest before ascending to the episcopacy. But all allowed that no woman nor young man of the parish would speak a word against him. He had faithfully served the Church in Ximes, albeit in a secretarial capacity, without misstep. And if Azédarac seemed a student more of matters scientific or even alchemical than spiritual, at least there was no introduction of Mahometan or Byzantine heresies in the liturgy, and—dare I say—the choir was good.

As for Azédarac as an administrator, his hand was a light one, and it only lightened with time. He left secular affairs to his hound Jehan; the conduct of the Mass, he left to his priests and to myself. Some now curse him for negligence, or worse, and they shun us his creatures as if we were devils—like Jehan "qui mau'vai en'soir", so I hear. But what did I know of the mundane duties of bishops? For my part, he left me free to bring mine own compositions to the great church.

Already we, who were charged with such duties, noticed that from Ximes and from its environs came to us fewer funerals, fewer burials of the elderly and infirm; and as I walked the town streets I observed that more than one undertaker had hung up his shingle. If I heard of someone in town who had passed away unshriven, their friends and relations would say that his or her "sun had set," an idiom foreign to me, and—I was informed, in hushed tones—foreign to Christ. Azédarac kept his own counsel, and the rest of us had not yet registered this matter as serious. But then the confirmations thinned, the baptisms were postponed, and finally even Mass attendance dropped. Such could not be ignored. The remnant Christian faithful cast aspersions upon the priests, for their sloth and gluttony; this sentiment made its way to the more daring chantaires. The priests, tightening their belts, muttered that my patron was perhaps haunted by demons of *acedia*.

But we still had weddings, amongst our remnant faithful. And one damp and sleety winter I received a letter from my Madeleine of Sainte-Zénobie: she was well, had mended her ways, was improving her handwriting, was still irritated by the local yokels, and wondered how her "favorite bard" was faring. My heart shuddered as a bird swooning over a volcano; my gut roiled like its magmal cauldron. In such a fever I wrote back to her: I was remiss for not contacting her first, I assured her I was well (and—hinting—still unattached), I threw in some wry comments about this city, and observed it was lacking in the warmth of her presence. Over the weeks more ardent missives passed between us. And then she hinted that soon enough she might be traveling in this direction herself.

Flush with this emotion with no outlet, I did what any young man in my position would do: I composed a march. I had occasion to test my composition for the nuptial of two scions of the Ximes notables. A few days later, as if on cue, as I was walking down the alley-ways in a February drizzle, I overheard my tune underlying a decidedly less sacramental lyric drifting through the sun-like glow of a tavern window. In my vanity I ducked in; by chance I saw the young newlyweds gaily singing along with the ribald chorus.

As they finished, some men and women came into the tavern. Their preternaturally lean frames were modestly cloaked in tan and yellow tunics, fastened with golden brooches each shaped like a flame. They proposed, in Rheinlander accents, to play a tune of their own. The innkeep seemed reluctant, but some of his patrons recognized them and insisted. And so the troupe assumed their positions at the minstrels' dais, and brought out their instruments. Besides that they were all wind instruments, I was unfamiliar with them all, not even of their material. One was something like a transverse flute; another was perhaps an ocarina, or some bloated Moorish shawm. Thus equipped they performed that damnable concerto, the Chaunt of the Flame.

Its melodies were not of the eight modes, nor of the old modes of the Mozarabes and Latins. These were perhaps not of any mode possible on Earth; the very chords seemed to defy Pythagorean geometry. The overall oeuvre was transporting to the degree that no-one else spoke. As they played, the flames of the hearth seemed to dance in tune with the music, like rippling Lorelei. The barmaids seemed colder to the patrons for it; even the newlyweds seemed less focused on each other than on the music. And I was swept away myself; when they ceased playing, the calls for them to continue were so raucous the bouncers started to clench their fists.

Something in me suggested that a minion of the bishop might not be welcome much longer, so I quickly settled my account and slipped out into the night. As I wandered home a part of me wondered about making use of the new alien melody, to entice the lady of my thoughts should we ever meet again. (Another part was jealous that mine own composition, which I had thought a good one, might now be forgotten.) And that night in my bed as I restlessly fidgeted I pondered if there was some threat here, at least to other chantaires and churchmen; we all serve the goodfolk in our own way, if we might not agree on much else.

Hearing in my mind a fragment of the eldritch music, I suddenly realized that—somehow—I was already dressed for a journey and packing my bags. I knew then that I must inform my patron and bishop.

The next morning in the church offices, as I approached the bishop's oaken door, I noted the hypnotic flicker of flame-like lights along its cracks that were not like the lights of a taper. I almost had to beat the door down when, at last, it opened.

The room was bathed in a weird inconstant glow from the wall-mounted mirror, whose face instead of reflecting the contents of the chamber—or so it appeared to me—was like the screen shielding a blazing kiln. This hidden flame illuminated the pages of no less than two opened codices and one partly-unrolled scroll, all of a dubious and nonlatinate script. Azédarac's dark gaze looked more jaundiced than usual and, as it lighted upon mine, angered at the introduction. His fist clenched as if to strike a blow . . . and then sagged, as if aging decades before my eyes.

"Enter," the bishop invited me. "And shut the door behind you."

I told my patron of the song at the tavern. Azédarac listened, then asked me to recite the tune. When he heard what I could repeat of it, his face locked up and the hook-shaped scar over his eyes lost its color. In his silence, I begged to be allowed to track down the font of this otherworldly melody. "The Cistercians are already suspicious of this whole province," I reminded him, "and the uncouth Franks of the north have never abandoned their ambitions for imperium over the Latins and all three parts of Gaul. If the Archbishop should cast his gaze here, we are ruined." It seemed to me as I spoke he concealed the content of his truer suspicions. But I was consumed with my obsessions; alas, I do not think that even my Madeleine, had she appeared at that moment, could have dissuaded me. In the end I wore the man down; he charged me with finding the source of the candle-song.

For a while I heard little enough of this strange music. I learnt little more except that it was somehow associated with the dark massif to our southwest, whence we quarry the bulk of our stone—the price of which was rising these days. This massif was, I knew, whither those of Ximes who were dying would travel these days; but such parties were secretive, such that I could not yet insinuate myself.

Meanwhile from the homes of those "sunsetted", paper documents were brought to me by the concerned Christian friends, and from those more reluctant whose tongues were loosened at my bishop's inquiries. You, my gaolers, have read from these codices; they contain Scripture, but arranged in a peculiar order, as florilegia. We saw an abridgement of Luke and Acts; certain sections of Paul, but not in the canonical order; the anecdote of the three saints of Babylon, but not associated with the book of Daniel. And the first chapter of John's Gospel, and its Priestly Prayer, disassociated from the Evangel.

My investigations were all very frustrating; and lonely, since I as a Church creature was now being shunned by the common man of Ximes. But at least now I had the comfort of my lovely correspondent outside Ximes. I have retained some of our letters, and sometimes I cannot help but re-read them . . .

But to return to my account, at last we were given to understand that certain of our healthier citizens, whose absence from Mass was being noticed as well as their abstention from the local inns, were making ready to depart our city. Azédarac took credit, in his priests' presence, for his "successful crackdown." We who were more directly involved knew that there had been no crackdown, but an inquest only; yet we knew enough to utter no word to contradict our master.

We also knew that this was our chance, to track the conflagration of heresy to its source. If only someone could join this caravan's train. Someone with no attachments except to Ximes and to her Church. Someone like me—or so I counseled my lord bishop. To this petition, to my ruin, my lord bishop acceded.

Thus I found my way into this group. We set out from the walls of Ximes on foot, to venture west under the pines and oaks into the shadowed hills. Along the way we passed other men and women of Ximes traveling on my way, singing the Siren song, like pilgrims. Also we passed other men traveling the other way, toward Ximes, these mostly men and women of the hills, not singing, like apostles. As I already knew the latter would look upon my person with distrust or even menace I deemed it wise to stash my rosary and other Christly accoutrements in my luggage.

Of my group, many were old and sick, such that they were carried in carts. My companions were vague about what they sought; they did not fully know, themselves. They had heard that in the hills was a way to "consolation." These pilgrims hoped to discover it, and if they found it, to be deemed worthy of consolement. To my ear it all sounded quite final.

There were some, they told me in tentative tones, whom Consolation returned to roam the world, like friars. These bore a small golden pin in the shape of a flame—like that which those minstrels in town had borne. But they numbered few: none of them accompanied us (that I knew); they had merely directed our flock to the road we traveled. I asked after those suppliants from Ximes whom we had not observed anymore in our midst, if they too yet roamed the world; this, they would not tell me, but were visibly uncomfortable, and altered the course of our conversation.

Other paths merged into ours, and other groups of pilgrims joined with ours. And at last we came to the crossroads to Périgon and Sainte-Zénobie; and thence, leading a group of about five, came my auburn-haired Madeleine. And she remembered me!

We fell in together to discuss the past few years; she was eager to learn more of Ximes, I to catch up on events in Périgon and Sainte-Zénobie. As we continued to ascend the massif and as the trees turned to pine, we spoke of matters more personal. Whilst I was away my Madeleine had wearied of the sneers and advances of the townsfolk and even of certain monks; grown heartsick of the lovers after Vespers who did not tarry for the Lauds. It was her intent to be washed clean, as Saint John had prophesied, in a medium other than water. It occurred to me that John's winnowing bonfire would not end well for the chaff, but I heeded not that still small voice. At that moment I would have followed my Madeleine to the carmine lips of Gehenna.

That evening by the camp's main fire she announced to everyone that I, Onfrei, was "the finest songwright in the county" and she begged me to entertain our companions of the road. Blushing I gathered some musicians, then led them to sing my wedding-song, altered toward that bawdy variant I'd heard in the Ximes tavern, which was now spreading like spring leaves among the jongleurs. This being a success, we moved on to other songs, to wide approval, but my Madeleine's firelit eyes radiated upon me sufficient approval.

Our swollen throng crested a rise and I witnessed the pilgrims' destination: in the midst of a treeless vale sat a dark and rectangular town, walled around. This burg looked recently and hastily constructed. It was built of pine, but many of its habitants—all very thin—were rebuilding the larger establishments by means of the local basalts. The usual city of our type, you recall, is circular; this settlement had more the character of a Roman camp.

At the centre of this dusky castra was a great building likewise rectangular, but red and tall, like a candle in the gloom; with a colossal porte barred by stout doors of a yellow wood I could not recognize. On closer look the edifice proved unpainted. Its crimson stone did not look like the surrounding Massif basalts nor like the granites of our Alps, nor yet as the marbles of the Lusitaine. The blocks did not even look like Averoignian make, nor Roman, nor of any style of which I am familiar. Later I would recall an illustrated Pausanias in Azédarac's office, depicting the lion-guarded gate of Mycènes, the walls around which—so the Greeks related—the Cyclopes had built.

As soon as we entered the town-camp's atramentous walls we were lodged in a humble, barracks-like inn with no tavern. Prominent on one wall was a strange painting, of a vast field of some alien lavender studded with immense standing stones, in the midst of which arose a red stone city, all below an orange sky with no sun. It needed no urging for us to understand that we had alighted upon a sacred site, with limited space for such revelry as we had enjoyed on the road.

On wakening, the centurions of this strange new settlement set us tasks to earn our keep. Our valuables were confiscated, to be held in common; anyone who objected was politely sent on their way out of camp. Most of us who stayed were asked to assist with construction or quarrying, replacing the wooden buildings with the local stone. Those with more specialized skills, like medicine, were assigned to the relevant stations, or reassigned if other duties needed them more. For my part I, as a literate man, but not entrusted with secretarial secrets, was assigned some basic scribal work including the copying and translation of Biblical florilegia. It worried me that I was contributing to the dissemination of possibly-heretical literature. But there was nothing in there, yet, which could attract the attention of a Cistercian.

The leaders of this castra, bearing the xanthic sigil of the flame, were Electi—those so dignified preferred Latin or Greek for the title. These, we found out, had endured the fasts and entered the scarlet building—and, the people noted, with fateful implications, they had *returned* thence. We sometimes passed Electi by this structure—they would gaze at its yellow porte, as if listening for a music the rest of us could not hear. On their faces was the haunted look of Adam and Eve outside Eden, facing the angelic guards and their incandescent swords. We learnt that only at the end of their natural lives would the Electi be permitted back through its gates. As such, it was always with heavy hearts that they ever left the compound on official business.

We others were provincially labeled Auzidors, because our lot was to pay heed and to learn. We celebrated no Mass (each night I prayed forgiveness for this, in secret); we instead attended lessons, as did the first disciples of Christ before the Paschal Supper. The Latin Church, they instructed us, was at best a waypoint like—directing this mainly to us from Ximes—the Inn of Bonne Jouissance en route to the cathedral city Vyônes. Except that the *true* seat of God was in a place not in this world and unknown to Catholics.

Between the sexes the camp was roughly divided into male and female. The Electi conducted no sacrament nor even ceremony for what we know as marriage. They did preside and mediate over pairings betwixt the sexes, or even—I beg your pardons—betwixt the same. The only rule was that no issue could flower from such passions. Several Electi, mostly male, wooed Auzidors; as I was a musician, I too attracted the notice of our superiors.

But I had eyes only for the lady of my thoughts, and all my music was composed for her ears. The camp afforded no place for marriage-songs, so I turned to more secular tropes of tragic love: of Paul and Thecla, of Olivier du Montoir and Adèle de la Frênaie, of Blaise Reynard and Nicolette Villom.

Whether Auzidor or Elect, those of us most near to death—and I was beginning to envy them—were taken into the great red building, which the Electi called the Martyrion. Such went there in pomp, in a solemn joy heralded with song, wholly unlike our funerals and more like our weddings. We Auzidors were not informed of their destination when they did not return to us. We had one, however—an Elect—who had collapsed and died before he could make this journey. His luckless corpse was borne to a crematorium outside the camp, and a service was performed there more familiar to Christians. I wondered to myself why, to the Electi, a soul was assured of Heaven in the Martyrion, but could only be prayed for outside it. I could conjure no reason that was not grossly heretical, to the point of Mahometan or worse. I could only count my rosary beads in secret and collect the information my bishop had required. At least, when not thinking of my lady.

On one evening it was announced to us that the time of Consolation was at hand. The gates to the village, or camp, were to be closed. None might enter nor leave but the brooch-bearing Electi and those in most dire need, but those once outside our camp might not return. Those of us who desired to be baptized anôthen—in the Greek—were first to be made perfect, by fasting. This would be a forty-day endurance like that of Lent. For us, volunteering to join the Perfecti was not precisely encouraged; the Electi warned us that the fast was so strenuous we might not all survive it. We had all learnt by now that the crematorium gaped ever open for those who hoped to enter the Martyrion, but proved unworthy. I was one of those who stayed apart from these perfecting ordeals. Still, many rose to the task, among whom was my flame-haired Madeleine of Sainte-Zénobie.

Those days of endurance were the hardest to bear of all the days I spent in that accursed place, as the once-buxom lady of my thoughts wasted away before me. And as we all were warned, among the fasters were those too weak to endure: some broke the fast, many just collapsed and of those who did, the doctors ruled some be taken at once to the Martyrion. One couple was caught right in the refectory pantry, surrounded with half-eaten food and clad shamefully only in oil and syrup (these two were expelled in disgrace, and I can only imagine the songs that are sung of them). For my part, over these weeks my songs grew ever more ardent and desperate for my Madeleine. Despite that I was not officially fasting I had not eaten much more than she had.

On the last night the two of us stole out under the stars, alone, and took the assais together, although I shall spare your most pious ears the amorous details, except that we passed it and that I, as a Christian bound to my bishop, still had not broken my vows of chastity. As we held each other afterward, we gazed on the spinning constellations and discussed everything except our likely parting on the morrow. This left unspoken, there was nothing left for us but to return to camp, to catch what sleep we could.

On the next morn, we assembled at the jaundiced porte of the red Martyrion, looming over us like a sanguine Punic temple. The Perfecti who had survived the endura were clad in white robes. I saw my pale Madeleine there, having survived both the fast and the assais, her bone-thin frame holding up her robes like a mast holding a fluttering sail.

One of the Electi then delivered a sermon, making reference to a Scripture at once familiar and exotic. The mind-numbing content of this sermon may have been part of its intent; I cannot recite it all. But I remember most of the end; perhaps one of your eminences might make more of this.

"As the Saviour said to James, brother of the Lord: 'Therefore, trust in me, my brethren; understand what the great light is. The Father has no need of me—for a father does not need a son, but it is the son who needs the father—though I go to him. For the Father of the Son has no need of you.' The Church imagines it holds the key to the kingdom of God; the Musselmans pretend to have the keys to the Garden. Even the Albi nation fasts and prays and seeks to work their congregants' way to Heaven. Nay! Of them, our Saviour demands to know— 'Or do you perhaps think that the Father is a lover of mankind, or that he is won over without prayers, or that he grants remission to one on another's behalf, or that he bears with one who asks?' "

The great yellow doors of the Martyrion opened, and we saw beyond it nothing but wavering red lights, like a bonfire with no visible fuel, as if from an unseen Toffète. We, starved out, or cored out from watching our loves starve, groaned and swayed before the cold and infernal blaze. And the scarlet walls of the Martyrion seemed to grow before us, to bend in our direction, or orthogonally to any direction, in defiance of all laws of Euclid or Archimedes. We hallucinated that beyond the fires beckoned to us the red stone city under that orange sky. If we knew that this was not the promised Jerusalem, we no longer cared.

The Elect went on preaching, beneath or through this abomination of space and time: "And granted unto James, brother of the Lord, as he wrote it in his book—'Therefore, become seekers for death, like the dead who seek for life; for that which they seek is revealed to them. And what is there to trouble them? As for you, when you examine death, it will teach you election. Verily, I say unto you, none of those who fear death will be saved; for the kingdom belongs to those who put themselves to death. Become better than I; make yourselves like the son of the Holy Spirit!' "

And now reaching out to us from beyond those towering yellow doors, as if to conduct that infernal shimmer, was the rumor of an eldritch vocal symphony, whose melodies the jongleurs of the Elect could only hint to us before. We yearned toward the song and the flame, swaying in tune, our jaws slack, some jaws drooling. Many of us started toward it but our guards—themselves struggling internally—held us back. It was all I could do not to push past them for a taste of immolation.

And the preacher modulated his voice with Molech's lambent piping, so each bolstered the other: "As for James, 'And when we had passed beyond that place, we sent our mind farther upwards, and saw with our eyes and heard with our ears hymns, and angelic benedictions, and angelic rejoicing. And heavenly majesties were singing praise, and we, too, rejoiced.' "

But of course only the Perfecti could join those celestial majesties. The Electi arranged them in a line; their chief rolled out a scroll and recited their names, one by one. And each one entered those gates of trilling fire, and none returned.

As the Electi called out the lady of my thoughts, she docilely took one step toward the hungry red-gold flame writhing and cantillating behind those terrific yellow doors, and faltered. She turned her eyes to me, seemed about to speak—but I did nothing. Then she smiled at me, sadly, and turned back to the porte. As she passed the Martyrion's yellow threshold toward the *flamme chantante* someone screamed out— there was a tussle in the crowd—I cannot remember—except that then I was outside the camp and the gates were being shut and locked in my face. And I was the one screaming, still screaming, my voice cracking.

I remember some of what I was shouting then: "You would have your holocaust consume us all! What kind of gods demand a world without humanity? What kind of love is this without even children?" But nothing I could argue before the pitiless wooden walls would budge them. At the end I hurled myself against them like a beast and pounded on them, also to no avail. I fell to the ground. I wept. I lay there like a stone for hours—and I think some of the people inside those walls looked down upon me, as if in judgment. And then I . . . my back and stu . . . ed down . . . to Xi –

Eds. note: *This account has been translated from a Latin manuscript hand-copied in, we think, the sixteenth century. It is mostly intact, save at the end (partially burned), although we suspect that a copyist has abridged sections he deemed irrelevant (viz. of a risqué nature) and has inlined some glosses ("penultimate day of October").*

To protect our sources we cannot divulge how we acquired a fax of this text.

Of most interest to philologers and historians, besides the record of this Kult (thus far) Unausgesprochen, will be its quotes from a pretended book by Saint James. These are strikingly close to passages from the Apocryphon unearthed at Nag Hammadi. The parallels are so close that, for the sake of this reproduction, we deferred to the Francis Williams translation at the online Gnostic Society Library.

This text would also be of use to musical theorists . . . were the MS less damaged. It appears that Onfrei disobeyed the command not to pen any musical notes, because the MS clearly once bore such; here and there on the margins, and more fully at the end. But some later hand has blotted over the marginal notes and even attempted to burn the ending; and we find occasional stains whose nature we hesitate to consider.

It is a pity that we too could not listen to the music which so bewitched our author and those around him! For ongoing attempts to reconstruct the notation, cf. Zare Gilman et al. (Miskatonic University, 2017).

SÉPHORA

by Ashley Dioses

The lovat pool produced soft ripples from her touch.
The water clung to her yet did not hide too much.
Her skin was pale and glistened like rose-petals white
And dipped in dew from charming flowers of the night.
She was as lovely as a chatelaine from great
Intriguing castles from Averoigne of late.
She was a stranger though, to this time and these lands,
For far beyond this realm, her ancient kingdom stands.

Séphora was her name, Enchantress of renown
In Sylaire, her high kingdom, where she holds the crown.
Through paths that serpentined through the dry antique wood
She saw the falling suns and rising moons and stood
At the threshold to her domain, her realm of charms.
Her magic blocked her home from those who'd stand at arms,
Yet a hermit of such fine handsome features like
Anselme, would be so hard to refuse for spikes
Arose inside her darkened heart at his sweet glance.
Perhaps this lusting lover will make her heart dance.

A wolf of deepest blacks and richest blues emerged
From lurking shadows eyeing the hermit and urged
Him, with hot eyes of gold, to stray not from her grasp.
The wolf, or maybe a true Were, began to rasp;
Its lolling tongue gave forth the savor of a root
Unknown to Anselme, some herb of ill repute.
Yet Séphora, a great enchantress, cares not for
What the hermit soon thinks or hears of Sylaire's lore.

Enchantress of aeons, fair Séphora arose
To gaze upon her catch from her window and froze.
Her ancient lover, wolf of wolves, transformed to man
In front of her new guest and spoke of some strange plan.

She knew inside, he would give the Mirror of Truth
To her hermit and would reveal then her false youth!
She waited for him to come and he soon arrived
In bloody rags so caked with fur and scars, yet thrived.
He held up the mirror and threw it in the burs
And then embraced her and she knew, he was all hers.

— After Clark Ashton Smith's "The Enchantress of Sylaire"

THE DOOM OF AZÉDARAC

by Ron Hilger

"And what of Azédarac, the Bishop of Ximes? Is he dead, too?"
inquired Ambrose, desperately.
"You mean St. Azédarac, no doubt. He outlived Clement, but nev-
ertheless he has been dead and duly canonized for thirty-two years. Some
say that he did not die, but was transported to heaven alive, and that his
body was never buried in the great mausoleum reared for him at Ximes.
But that is probably a mere legend."
— The Holiness of Azédarac, by Clark Ashton Smith

The Bishop of Ximes sat behind a massive table of ornately carven ebony, cluttered with a bizarre assortment of baleful-looking items not generally associated with one of his lofty ecclesiastic position. Oblivious of this miscellany of fulvous scrolls of serpent-skin and bubbling alembics, he gazed through the window, his somber eyes lingering over the autumnal landscape of the Averoigne countryside as seen from the topmost tower of his mansion at Ximes. The fiery points of light which had formerly flashed within the ebon depths of those eyes now smoldered with a cooler flame, for, in the Year of Our Lord 1198, Azédarac was no longer young. Indeed, the infirmities of age had begun to affect even the Archimage of Averoigne, who had been born hundreds of years before the oldest man in all of France. Only Jehan Mauvaissoir, his manservant and confidant, could likewise recall those dim years of the pre-Christian past when the Druids still held sway over much of Western Europe.

Strange magicks in the form of diabolic potions and fearsome rituals were common then, as were wizards and witches, werewolves and vampires. Among all these, the sorcerer Azédarac had reigned supreme; he had served the omnipotent entities known as the Old Ones even then, and had acquired many powerful spells and demoniac servants equal to the most horrific task or impossible quest.

For reasons into which it was not healthy to inquire, Azédarac and Jehan had deemed it prudent to remove themselves into the future by means of a time-distorting philtre, the secret of which was known to few, if any, besides Azédarac.

Now he had long been content to reside in his luxurious château, masquerading as a pious old prelate while still maintaining privately his well-established understanding with the Powers of Darkness.

After many uneventful years the ennui of his elder days smote him like some vengeful assassin from his youth, and the knowledge of his former greatness was an added bitterness in the dregs he now tasted.

"I fear I have lingered overlong among these luxurious surroundings and would venture forth to confront my doom rather than await it here as a doddering old pontiff!" he exclaimed, rising abruptly from his high-backed chair of polished oak. Crossing the circular chamber, he paused before a stone fireplace in which burned a ruddy bed of glowing coals. Grasping a certain rock with both hands, he slowly worked the stone from its socket. He then reached into the cavity behind and withdrew a small flask filled with a vermilion liquid.

Returning to the window, he held the flask aloft and swirled the contents about, peering at its peculiar color before he removed the crystal stopper and raised the phial to his lips. Gently he tested the acrid aroma, which arose from that dubious elixir, as if considering some fine old vintage of wine. He replaced the stopper, and set the flask down upon the littered table between a squat stone idol and a tattered black tome. He then summoned his manservant Jehan to the tower chamber by means of a cord connected to a bell which rang out in the main hall.

The very existence of this room was known only to these twain, being accessible by a secret stairway entered through a hidden door in the rear of the closet where Azédarac was wont to hang his many sacred robes of Episcopal service.

Jehan arrived a few moments later and approached Azédarac where he sat at his table before the window, studying a passage in the old black volume.

"Damn this Latin translation of Hecataeus! Not only is his rendering from the *Book of Eibon* done poorly, but apparently even the Druidic manuscripts that he copied were incomplete. Bitterly do I regret the day I inadvertently allowed that snooping Brother Ambrose to steal the Hyperborean original from my library. Now I am forced to recall the incantations of Iog-Sotôt and Sodaqui from the over-crowded vaults of my aged memory." Azédarac slammed the book closed, sending aloft a billowing cloud of centuries-old dust.

"Jehan, I will require your assistance in performing the rituals and incantations from which my time-distorting philtre derives much of its potency." The venerable sorcerer indicated the flask upon the table before him. "This very evening I shall attempt to retrieve the *Book of Eibon* from the past, where it was transported along with young Ambrose to prevent him from showing the book to Archbishop Clement. I have not been able to obtain another copy in the original Hyperborean script, which is absolutely necessary because most of the rituals and incantations must be recited aloud in the ancient language of the Hyperboreans to achieve the desired results. My power has been waning steadily ever since I lost it, as surely as it waxed strong while I possessed it, and I had only begun to realize the full implications of the ancient text!"

Azédarac began lighting the candles which sat in sconces mounted around the perimeter of the chamber while Jehan scattered some incense on the coals in the fireplace and filled several intricately wrought brass censers with another, more evocative fragrance.

"Shall I prepare to accompany you, your Grace?" asked Jehan. "I could assist in any subterfuge that may be required—or, should it come to a fight . . ." At this point, Jehan patted his long thin sword which he always wore in the service of Azédarac.

"Ah, Jehan," chuckled Azédarac. "I have no doubt of your swordsmanship, and your ability to outwit the pious Ambrose has already been well proven. But I am afraid I have a much more difficult task for you. I do not know how long my absence may be; it may take a good deal of time to locate Ambrose—perhaps longer to find the book. You must stay and make sure no one suspects I am gone. If necessary, tell them I am ill and do not wish to be disturbed. I shall return as quickly as possible, most likely by this time tomorrow. But now let us continue with the preparations or I shall be going nowhere! All that is lacking is the essence of mandragora. Have you been able to replenish our supply?"

Jehan rummaged around through various medicaments and soon produced a small leather pouch. "I did have some difficulty," he admitted, "but the apothecary who abides down in the marish sold me what he claimed to be the purest and most potent in the land."

The wizard opened the pouch and sniffed the contents, shrugged his shoulders, and added a large pinch to the vermilion liquid in the flask. "I believe it would be wise to test this potion on some expendable creature before I unwittingly poison myself," mused Azédarac. "Jehan, would you mind fetching one of the rats which infest the cellars?"

Jehan smiled and replied, "I'll see to it at once, my lord." He soon returned holding a large sack that writhed and heaved violently. Bits of rat could be seen protruding here and there through several weak areas of the sack.

As Jehan deposited the rat into a cage waiting upon the floor, Azédarac laced a bit of meat with the bright red potion and dropped it next to the glaring rodent. When the rat perceived the meat, it first suspiciously sniffed, and then quickly devoured the morsel. Immediately it stood upon its hind legs, twitching its nose and swaying back and forth. Finally, it pitched over to one side and vanished as it struck the bottom of the cage, as if falling magically through the floor.

Azédarac picked up the cage and shook it to make certain of the rat's departure. "Unfortunately we cannot tell where, or I should say, *when* it has arrived. However, I still regard the results as a success; indeed, the philtre seems to be quite efficacious. I shall depart as soon as the other preparations are completed."

Jehan regarded Azédarac anxiously; obviously unwilling to allow the ageing sorcerer-bishop to go unassisted into the past on such a dangerous and dubious mission. "Please, Jehan, do not worry about me," Azédarac said quickly. "In spite of my age and apparent frailty, I am still quite able to protect myself—in fact, an adventure of this sort is just what I need to cure my endless ennui."

After a brief interim, during which Azédarac consumed a large and sustaining meal, the other preparations were completed: a wineskin filled with the blood-red wine of La Frênaie, a loaf of bread, dried venison, and the emeraude-tinted philtre required for the return journey—all were packed into a leather satchel which now depended from the wizard's shoulder.

Azédarac intoned the final, thunderous phrase of the incantation, and before the sonorous reverberations had ceased, he quaffed the sanguine contents of the crystal flask, drew his sword, and crouched into a defensive position.

Jehan raised his hand in farewell and held the wizard's gaze with his own until Azédarac faded and disappeared amid the fragrant grey vapors rising from the laden censers.

When at length Azédarac regained his senses, he was immediately assailed by a lethargic feeling of heaviness that was quite beyond his experience. He was likewise baffled by the dim, purpureal sky, over which to his astonishment presided a bloated, angry-looking sun of scarlet hue. "Obviously, something must be fundamentally wrong with the time-traveling philtre," mused the Archimage of Averoigne. "I suspect the essence of mandragora was even more potent than the apothecary claimed it to be."

He soon perceived a feeble thrashing which came from the low, variegated shrubbery directly before him. Upon investigation, he discovered the hindquarters and tail of a large rat protruding from a huge, pale, writhing blossom attached to a long snake-like stem. Realizing this must be the same rodent upon which he had tested his philtre, he watched with a detached scientific curiosity as it was drawn inexorably into the carnivorous blossom that stretched and bulged to accommodate it.

Deeming it prudent to examine the foliage in his immediate vicinity, he soon observed several more of these sentient-looking flowers leaning insidiously towards him. With swiftly growing trepidation, Azédarac began shuffling slowly away from the infernal vegetation, his movements greatly impeded by the inexplicably increased gravity.

Scanning the horizon, he recognized many of the geologic features as those which surrounded the town of Ximes in Averoigne, albeit somewhat flattened and distorted. Of his château, however, he could discover no sign; although he did notice several squat edifices perched atop some of the nearby hillocks. Suddenly the leaden heaviness vanished from his limbs and he was able to move about quite freely. This strange fluctuation in gravity was in itself a most novel situation, even more perplexing because it apparently affected only him; the alien vegetation no longer swayed and crawled with malignant life. All things save himself seemed frozen in a curious timeless condition as Azédarac walked leisurely and unhindered along a sinuous path that apparently led towards the nearest edifice.

The sorcerer-bishop realized that the *Book of Eibon* was not likely to be found here in this unaccountably alien world, but perhaps he might yet discover something to justify his journey. Meanwhile, he reflected, his boredom was being alleviated most satisfactorily.

Jehan closed and bolted the heavy door, ignoring the concerned protestations from without. Leaning silently against the door, he listened patiently as the voices diminished, sighing with relief when at last they ceased altogether. "This whole affair will soon be quite out of hand," he muttered to himself. "What can be keeping Azédarac?" The sorcerer-bishop himself had expected his journey to last no longer than one day—and it was now a day and a half since his departure. To make matters worse, visitors had arrived soon after Azédarac had disappeared; Jehan dismissed these promptly enough with a tale of the prelate's ill health. Unfortunately, this seemed only to have the effect of creating more visitors who, concerned with the now rampant rumors of Azédarac's swiftly deteriorating health, were becoming not only more numerous, but alarmingly persistent. Jehan returned to his vigil inside the tower chamber, awaiting the sorcerer's return. Eventually, he knew he would have to let them in, forcing him to explain the absence of the Bishop of Ximes.

"Damn!" he muttered, sotto voce. "What can have happened to Azédarac?"

Oblivious to Jehan's dilemma, Azédarac continued to explore his extraordinary surroundings. Having spent what seemed only an hour or two at most away from Averoigne, it did not occur to him that he was overdue. As he walked he examined the bizarre forms of flora and fauna, pausing now and then to study more closely some especially fascinating specimen. On many of the carnivorous species, strange appendages protruded from the base or trunk, these apparently being organs of sensory perception. Azédarac mused that perhaps these organs might explain the uncanny rudimentary intelligence many of the plants seemed to exhibit.

He soon noticed a slight buzzing sound; as if a small insect was hovering close beside his ear, but looking about he could discern nothing to account for this strange sound. With a sudden chill, he realized the sound came from within his mind, and not from his ears. The buzzing grew louder; it rose and fell in a rhythm that the sorcerer found strangely familiar, almost recognizable.

As he reached the base of a hill upon which stood one of the strange-looking structures, he was once again seized by the paralyzing gravitational force, and at the same instant the inarticulate buzzing changed pitch and slowed into an understandable monologue.

"Welcome, Brother. Stand ready and prepare to meet your destiny! I, Caradeza, have foreseen your arrival as well as your inevitable defeat before my superior sorcery."

The Bishop of Ximes struggled against the invisible bonds which held him. Slowly, painfully, he withdrew his sword from its scabbard, and held it before him to ward off his mysterious assailant. He now perceived a figure emerge from the structure atop the hill, and descend inexorably towards him. Azédarac uttered a brief but powerful incantation of defense, but instead of projecting the desired aura of protection, he heard again the alien voice within his mind.

"Your paltry spells are ineffective against me," the voice declared sardonically. "For I am the trans-dimensional extension of yourself, your alter-ego in this dimension into which you have foolishly stumbled. I have known of your existence for many cycles, and have long desired to arrange such a meeting in order that I might assimilate your being into my own, thus giving me greatly expanded powers in both our worlds. Indeed, your visit has saved me a great deal of trouble, for which I am sincerely grateful. In fact, I shall endeavor to make your demise as quick and painless as possible, in order to show my profound appreciation."

Azédarac stared incredulously at the inhuman creature which now approached him: a short, green, pyramid-shaped torso, from which protruded three long, tentacle-like arms, and crowned by a squat, leering caricature of a human head. The method of locomotion was unclear, for there were no visible legs—the entire base of the creature seemed to undulate along the ground in a horrid slug-like manner.

He recoiled instinctively from the monstrosity, his mind reeling beneath the concept of the alternate dimension and his hideous alter-ego. He had often meditated on the possibility of such a dimension, but he had never imagined that such a world could be so fundamentally different, yet still parallel so closely his own.

His assailant now raised his arms with a rippling gesture directed at Azédarac. Simultaneously an imperative word of command droned and echoed in his mind, echoed and reverberated on and on, over and over. The Bishop of Ximes found himself completely paralyzed, unable to defend himself or even to flee, hardly able to think of anything except the word which flowed endlessly through his mind. A part of his mind resisted, but could only watch helplessly as his victorious counterpart approached and stood before him. His tortured brain screamed at his frozen body to flee, to drink the philtre and escape the abhorrent creature—the creature in whose loathsome features he now recognized a mutated semblance to his own.

The long, sinuous arms stretched to envelop him, stretched but did not grasp. With a sudden start, Azédarac realized he was free once more, the inexplicable quirk of gravity had fluctuated again, freezing the groping arms inches from his body and nullifying the endless reverberations in his mind.

Not lingering to speculate, Azédarac turned, stumbled, then fled back down the path until he reached the place where he had first entered the alter-dimension, where he paused, withdrew the crystal flask, and immediately drank the emeraude contents.

With a profound sense of relief, Jehan watched as the Bishop of Ximes materialized within the wavering candlelight of the wizard's den. Azédarac looked about, taking in the familiar surroundings with obvious satisfaction before his eyes rolled upward and he pitched forward into Jehan's arms.

"M'lord! What has happened? Are you wounded?" cried Jehan, his relief completely giving way to alarm and dismay. He half-dragged, half-carried the unconscious prelate to his bedchamber, noting the peculiar tenuousness of the form and features of Azédarac, as well as the apparent lack of any wound or injury that would explain his grievous weakness. After a few moments, however, Azédarac was recovered sufficiently to relate his incredible adventure to his concerned friend.

" . . . and even now that I have returned safely to my own time and my château here at Ximes, I feel my escape is somehow incomplete, as though a vital part of my being remains captive in the other dimension," he concluded.

"Even more inexplicable is that you relate the experience of only a few hours—yet nearly three days have passed here in Ximes since your departure," observed Jehan. He then advised Azédarac of the difficulties which had arisen during the bishop's absence, and finally disclosed that several visitors were even now firmly ensconced in the main hall, refusing to depart until they had received an audience with the ailing Bishop.

"That situation, at least, can easily be remedied," replied Azédarac wearily. "Send them in at once, but only briefly, for in truth I am not well at all."

His bedchamber was soon crowded with the concerned members of his spiritual flock, each contriving to ask him how he felt or what his ailment was or when he might again be up and around. The Bishop of Ximes, however, was apparently unaware of this barrage of questions. He was listening intently to a dull buzzing sound which seemed to originate close behind his left ear—a sound that sent an icy shiver of terror down his spine as he recognized the droning reverberations of the trans-dimensional spell!

"Please, please," implored Azédarac, waving his hand feebly. "My tale is quite simple. I have been stricken with fever and delirium these past few days, having just now returned from a nightmare world of evil dreams. The fever has consumed me, body and soul, and leaves me nigh unto death. I would now receive the Final Sacrament, for I do not believe it is God's will that I recover."

The distraught onlookers bowed their heads and murmured prayerfully amongst themselves. The eldest priest then stepped forward and quickly began to administer the Last Rites. Jehan also approached the bedside; his discreet features were contorted into a grim mask which concealed a host of struggling emotions as he clasped his Master's hand.

"Nay, Jehan. Do not grieve overmuch for me. All men must leave this world of flesh and blood; I do so now willingly. For I am assured that my being shall not end, but shall be joined with that of the greater entity. I leave to you, my trusted friend, all my worldly possessions, even as I leave to the Church all my spiritual inheritance."

The priest administering the Last Rites suddenly gasped in a most unholy manner, dropping an aspergillum clattering to the hardwood floor. The stricken bishop's body had begun to glow and pulse with an unearthly radiance, which quickly increased in brilliance as Azédarac began to shimmer and then to fade. His voice, faint and far away, seemed to echo across immense gulfs of Space and Time, ere it faded into oblivion. "He summons me, I must join him in the next world. Farewell!" The nearly transparent body vanished completely. The glowing radiance clung briefly about the bedclothes before it too faded and disappeared. The gathered clergy stared in astonishment at the impossibly empty bed which had so recently contained the Bishop of Ximes. The eldest priest dropped to his knees, the others quickly followed suit. Soon, all those present had abased themselves, utterly consumed in fervent prayer.

The legendry concerning the Ascension of Saint Azédarac (who was later to become the Patron Saint of Averoigne) is widely varied and often highly embellished by the peasants who still perpetuate it. The most widely accepted version states that while the body of the Bishop of Ximes lay helpless in the grip of a violent fever, his soul descended into Hell and there strove mightily with the Adversary. At last, the noble Bishop's strength and endurance were exhausted, but before Satan could claim victory over his weary soul, the Heavenly Powers intervened, and Azédarac was bodily assumed into Heaven. Not without telling effect was St. Azédarac's valiant struggle; indeed, many legends claim that Satan was sorely weakened by his battle with the Divine Powers, and that his ability to promote sin was greatly diminished for many generations to come. Other less substantiated rumors claim that Azédarac can still be seen at odd whiles, appearing mysteriously here and there in the vicinity of Ximes, still locked in mortal combat with an unseen assailant.

But all accounts agree that, whether because of the large number of witnesses who observed the actual miracle, or in light of their impeccable reputations, Sainthood was bestowed upon the Bishop of Ximes not only without opposition, but also with an expedience and alacrity unparalleled in all the long and illustrious history of the Church.

Night Vigil for the Necromancer

by Wade German

I have here, master, leaves from your grimoire;
And by their elder glyphs and diagrams,
The arcane, overlapping pentagrams,
Surmise you voyage now the farthest shores
Where, singing spells of great antiquity,
You search for stranger necromantic lore
And chart the death dimension and its doors,
Those barriers between realities.

In your high castle carved from crystal verse,
A spectral servant waits for your return,
And speculates on what his lord might learn
In far, occult infinities immersed,
Where alien worlds emerge from nighted streams,
The unknown gulfs in nebulae of dream.

THE PINK FLOWER OF SAINT ZÉNOBIE

by Aaron Hollingsworth

The humanity of Raquel D'Hubert came into question the day after her baptism. From her birthday day to her second month, the babe had been normal and pretty. Yet, sometime during that moonlit night, her blonde curls turned sepulchral black, her cream-white skin changed to an even shade of pink, and her firmamental eyes took on mismatched hues of green and brown. No doctor or priest could explain the transformation, but people whispered rumors throughout the town of Saint Zénobie that the blessed water had washed away a demonling's disguise or, worse, that the real infant had been stolen and replaced with a changeling fairy babe.

None dared bring these charges to Pierre D'Hubert and his wife. As the proprietors of the town's only cobbler shoppe, no one wished to anger them and be without shoes, for the soil of Saint Zénobie was laced with razor-edged shards of flint.

The tide of rumors ebbed as the child grew into maidenhood. In spite of her deformities, she became the belle of the town. She was the very feminine aspect of her father, a dashing fellow. Raquel was tall, well-formed, with skin smooth beyond blemish or pock. The men of Saint Zénobie referred to her as the Pink Flower, and one such man was bold enough to draw her affections.

François was the mayor's son and a huntsman of local renown. With his flint-tipped arrows he never failed to bring back game, even in a forest haunted by loup-garous and floating heads. Though his suit was well-received by the girl, her father, the cobbler, thought it best that the couple prolong their courtship for another year before marital vows were uttered.

D'Hubert would never fulfill the honored duty of giving his daughter away, for both she and his head went missing the night of August 14th in the year of our Lord 1196. The cobbler's wife awoke in a bed made soggy-cold by the congealed blood of her mate's corpse. The neighbors awoke in turn to the cracked wail of her horror. There was no sign of intrusion or struggle.

Brother Habile of the Benedictine Abbey of Périgon came at the mayor's behest to investigate the matter. The monk held particular repute in the knowledge of satanic lore and rural necromancies. Since time immemorial, beheadings were common about the town. Legends suggested those who lingered too long in the surrounding forest would be consumed by werewolves. The heads were then offered from bloody claws to the bony hands of some necromancer who would animate the severed members to float like aimless will-o'-the-wisps throughout the shrouded trees.

Brother Habile was unable to question the cobbler's wife, for the wretch had cried out both her heart and mind, leaving her a gibbering hysteriac until the end of her days. The cobbler, however, though now a truncated cadaver, answered many queries.

The stumped neck had been cut with a blade both heavy and sharp and swung by hands well-accustomed to making clean strokes. A werewolf's claws could never hope to sever a head so evenly. About the wound, a black pollution of the skin could be seen that was neither rot nor mold. Nothing else in the home had been disturbed or stolen. Drops of blood led from the cobbler's house to the edge of the wood.

A search party was assembled consisting of Brother Habile, François the Huntsman, and the greatest of the town guard, Jacques Brian, who bore a mighty partisan spear that, in past years, quelled many a rake and ruffian.

Before they embarked, Brother Habile interviewed several prominent townsfolk as to the myriad of rumors surrounding the Pink Flower known as Raquel D'Hubert. He also imparted a singular and queer form of blessing upon the arrows and partisan of his companions. Taking out a small earthen jar and leather pouch from his pack, he toiled in pious preparation for the terrors that lay ahead. Using a small paint brush, he coated the flint heads and steel edges with a gum housed in the jar and sprinkled powdered silver from the pouch. After a lengthy prayer, the gum dried, and the weapons glinted and sparkled with a holy scintillation that reinforced the martial resolve of those that bore them.

History tells us the trio entered the malignant forest, never to return, never to recover the missing maiden. However, their severed heads were encountered over the next month...

On the following night when the moon waxed full, the head of Jacques Brian, the partisan guard, appeared at the foot of the mayor's bed. The sight of the bloodless atrocity, with dangling shreds of neck and vertebrae, pinned the magistrate to his sheets with a fastening terror. It fixed its cloudy gaze upon the mayor, and thus it spoke:

"A league deep into that cursed forest, a swarm of human heads assailed us. Some were cloven at the neck, as if by a sword stroke. Others were disembodied as you see me now. They bit at us and shouted foul things both vulgar and blasphemous. One of these floating heads we recognized as the cobbler, Pierre D'Hubert. François' arrows had little effect on them. It took the deft swings of Brother Habile's cudgel to pulp each hovering member to inert paste.

"We continued on through coarse bushes and thorny thickets. Something large and snarling leapt upon my back. A set of hungry jaws tore half my neck away. And that is all I can recall."

Then the head of Jacques Brian floated out the mayor's window and back into the ghostly wood.

On the following night, the head of François the Huntsman appeared before his father, the mayor. This head had been cleanly severed. As the mayor wept in silence, the head continued where Jacques Brian had left off.

"We were waylaid by a pack of loup-garous. They caught Jacques off guard, but Brother Habile managed to defend himself long enough for me to fell three of them with arrows. The rest scattered. We were loath to leave Jacques Brian's remains there, but my love for Raquel and the monk's pious resolve compelled us onward.

"We eventually found her at the foot of a steep hill crowned by a ramshackle cottage of baleful aspect. A werewolf was chewing meat off Raquel's leg. Without thinking, I drew an arrow and sent it through the monster's heart. It fell dead, a man. Raquel's body had been flayed, her pink skin and raven curls stripped and stolen, but the corpse's head still housed those precious mismatched eyes of green and brown.

"Mad with rage and ignoring Brother Habile's urging to maintain our stealth, I charged up the hill with an arrow nocked. Like a spider from a hole emerged a nude hag bearing a black broadsword. She was wearing Raquel's skin, Father! That hateful, chortling woman wore the hide of my fiancé in place of her own! The witch's body was that of a bent and tottering crone, but the skin she wore was the very skin of my Pink Flower!

"I loosed my arrow, only to watch it deflect off the flat of her terrible blade. With uncanny swiftness, she charged down the hill, cackling like venomous thunder. Her emerald glare held me fixed like a statue, unthinking, unmoving. She swung her sword through my neck, and I felt my body collapse to the ground below me. Yet, my head remained as if does now, floating in mid-air like a will-o'-the-wisp.

"Oh, dear Father, forgive your son's folly! I must return now to those horrible woods. Adieu!"

When the floating head of the huntsman departed out from the window into the spectral gloom, the mayor of Saint Zénobie ignored his fatherly pangs of grief just long enough to write down all his son had told him. When the information was properly documented and sealed for his factotum to find the next morning, the old man slit his throat over his chamber pot.

Several townsfolk mourned the mayor's dismal demise, yet even more of them saw fit to vie for his now vacant seat. Life went on in the town of Saint Zénobie. Eventually, after enough people complained of sore and gashed feet, a new cobbler was brought into town to replace Pierre D'Hubert.

One month after the haunted night of the mayor's death, the floating severed head of Brother Habile found its way back to the Benedictine Abbey of Périgon and appeared before the abbot while the holy man knelt in consummate prayer. In his private chambers, the startled abbot watched and listened, rapt in pious horror as the hovering visage spoke.

"I have returned from my mission, honorable sir, though not in the way I had hoped. No doubt you have heard the accounts of those who preceded me in peculiar death. I come to report the remainder of the venture's transpirings and to seek absolution for my sin committed in that foul cottage.

"After mesmerizing and decapitating François, the hag-who-will-not-be-named turned her emerald stare of entrancement onto me. Enslaving me with succubal sorceries, she took me into her cottage and, for a month, subjected me to venereal acts so atrocious that I dare not describe them in this hallowed edifice. In that time of lusty servitude, I learned from her many secrets.

"She had enslaved Pierre D'Hubert the cobbler in this very satanic

fashion many years ago, getting a daughter from him. When the cobbler's wife bore a daughter as well at about the same time, the hag
switched the babes in their infancies. The fate of the true and legiti-
mate daughter, the real Raquel D'Hubert, was a grisly one. The witch
fed the babe to her werewolf sycophants.

"When the pink-skinned changeling became a woman grown, the
hag crept into the D'Hubert home with her black broadsword, severed
the cobbler's head as he slept, and ensorcelled the maid to follow her.
Though the girl known as the Pink Flower of Saint Zénobie was half
hag, her fate is still pitiable. Her wicked mother desired not a child to
love, but a fresh new skin to wear for the prolongation of her unnatural life. This was the Pink Flower's reason for cultivation.

"I also learned of the witch's sword, an ebon blade of necromantic
influence that animated severed heads with unliving flight. These heads
filled the forest about her cottage, acting as her familiar spies and sentinels.

"When tired of my compelled affections, she used that very sword
upon my own neck, adding yet another murder to stain her foul and
demoniac spirit. Yet, even in that state of living death—that buoyant
manifestation of earthly purgatory—my cleverness and cunning did not
escape me.

"Lethargic from gorging herself on my leftover trunk and limbs,
the hag fell into a deep slumber upon her bed of unicorn pelts. With
naught but my teeth, I drew her evil weapon from its sheath, hovered
high above her sleeping form, and dropped the sword point-first onto
her exposed throat. The blade sank deep, and the hag gurgled a bloody
death rattle before taking her place among the damned."

The abbot trembled in cold sweat and crossed himself. "You have
rid this land of a great evil, Brother Habile. I have no doubt God will
forgive your sin once we cure your earthly remains of this malefic af-
fliction. I will summon the other monks. Perhaps collective prayer and
copious amounts of holy water will free your spirit from that ghastly
shell."

The head of Brother Habile shook in grave variance. "Nay, venerable sir. We must be practical in this matter. Go and fetch a cudgel.
Pulp this head into paste and burn it."

THE WOODS OF AVEROIGNE

by Grace Stillman

Deep in the woods of Averoigne,
  Goblin and satyr, loup-garou,
Devil and vampire hold their feasts:
  Forces of wizardry imbue
Even the foliage of the oak;
  Beeches and pines in drear decay,
Uplift their bony branches wan
  Under a sky of corpse-like gray.
Evil is there in Averoigne:
  Evil I should not see at all;
Evil whose very presence seems
  Holding me in curious thrall:
Knowing it well, my feet still grope
  Nearer this force malign, withdrawn;
In dread, against my will I creep
  Deep in the woods of Averoigne.

HUGH THE DISCERNING

by Garnett Elliott

One warm spring morning, the reeve Hugh de Manchefort was out among his gardens supervising the early planting. Amidst flowering chamomile and carefully cropped bushes of amaranth, delphinium, and juniper, he stood like a stern warden; an elderly man in a woolen shirt and broad-brimmed hat, with a long willow rod tucked beneath one arm. If a servant went about his duties without sufficient zest, then— whack!—out came the willow rod across the unfortunate's back. Such was Hugh's devotion to detail that he inspected each and every seed before it was placed beneath the ground. His garden had not suffered for his attentions; a lush checkerboard of rare plants, stately trees, and polished, artfully-placed stones. Everything seemed to prosper beneath Hugh's watchful eye.

Presently, he noticed an assortment of villagers heading up the road towards his estate. A single, gray-haired figure marched purposefully at the lead. Hugh squinted his eyes in recognition and frowned. The procession drew close. The leadmost figure was none other than Matron Margeut, a woman of property nearly as old as Hugh, and no small authority in the village of Morraine. She wore a coat of green velvet and had her hair drawn up with long silver pins brought from Troyes. Hugh bluntly asked the nature of her business.

"You have not heard the news?" she asked.

Hugh scratched at the scalp just beneath the rim of his hat. "What news are you referring to?"

"Why, the ogre Chantillion of course," she said, looking surprised.

"Ogre?" Hugh said slowly.

"Yes. Even now he ravages the forests around Morraine. It is only a matter of time before he enters the village proper."

Hugh stared at Matron Margeut and the crowd behind her for several long moments. He then turned to one of his servants and began instructing him in the proper trimming of rhododendrons.

Sensing dismissal, Margeut stepped forward and rapped her knuckles against the front gate. "Hugh!" she demanded. "Hugh, I am not finished speaking to you."

Hugh looked up wearily from his flower bush. "Yes?"

"I was telling you about the ogre Chantillion, and how he threatens the common good of Morraine."

"Yes, a frightful character I'm sure." He bent to examine a clipping. "And you—along with half of the village here—have brought this to my attention because?"

"You are the reeve."

"Yes," Hugh admitted, "I am the reeve. That means I count grain. I am responsible for keeping an accurate tally for the Comte de Fleuris. I am not, however, responsible for vague supernatural threats."

Softly, Margeut said: "You are also Hugh the Discerning."

Hugh straightened. At the mention of his old sobriquet, some of the harshness drained from his face. "You have a long memory," he said, but his tone was not so dismissive now. Hugh had long ago earned a reputation for his powers of perception. When presented with several choices, it was said, Hugh could unerringly pick the best, and this had helped to build his early successful career, serving in courts as far away as Venice and Prague. Even to the present, he enjoyed the best livestock, carefully culled and bred from the farms of his neighbors; he employed the best vintner and ale-tasters in the region, so that his private stocks were always sought after; and he had procured for himself, after much haggling, the most handsome, vivacious young wife that a man of his advanced age and station could hope for.

"I am flattered," Hugh said carefully, "that you have sought my counsel in this important matter. I would advise you thusly: take your appeal to the Comte de Fleuris. He can dispatch some of his horsemen to help out, provided you can convince him of the threat posed by this creature."

Matron Margeut shook her head. "Your mind is no doubt clouded by your exertions this morning. Else you would remember that the Comte's horsemen are away raiding our neighbors in Coeur-sur-Mer, at the behest of our benevolent lordship."

"Then I would exhort you to locate the Christian hero Balthazar of Messina, a swordsman without equal, who bears the magic blade Triste. He should prove more than adequate in dispatching your ogre."

"Again," said Matron Margeut, more tersely this time, "I think the vapors of this fresh morning air have left you addled, else you would recall that Balthazar is now a prisoner of the Moors, and the sword Triste is believed to languish in some Saracen treasure-house, masterless."

Hugh reddened. "The duties of my station," he said thickly, "do not allow me time for idle gossip about far-away places. You have come here seeking my aid and I have given it. For all I know, you are having some elaborate joke at my expense, teasing me with this fairy-talk about ogres and whatnot."

"Chantillion is real," came a voice from among the villagers.

The crowd parted, allowing a shepherd to come hobbling forward, leaning heavily against his crook. His face was youthful and unlined; he had a trace of blond stubble growing at his chin. But his eyes, and his mannerisms, were those of a much older man. Hugh noticed with a start that his left leg was gone below the knee.

"I have met Chantillion myself," the shepherd said. "I can vouch for his cruelty."

"Go on," said Hugh.

Margeut leaned close and draped a comforting hand over the young shepherd. He began to talk, haltingly at first, of how Chantillion had come across his cottage in the dead of night, and Grendel-like, stole inside to devour his family while still in their beds. The shepherd had awakened and tried to escape by leaping out a window, but Chantillion caught his leg before he was all the way through and held him fast. Relishing his own cleverness, the ogre then began to explain how he had found him.

"He came across my son," the shepherd said, "while he was out grazing the flock; killed and ate him on the spot." Tears slid down his cheek and onto the fine velvet of Margeut's dress. "Then he ate every sheep, one by one, until only our old hound was left. Chantillion made as if to let him go, but then followed at a distance. The dog led him all the way back to our house.

"I feared for my life, maddened by grief as I was, but Chantillion's hunger must have been sated from his night's work. He let me escape. As I fell out the window he gave my leg one final grasp, and tore with all his strength, lest I ever forget what had happened."

The shepherd fell silent. Margeut began to help him hobble back towards the crowd, but he turned suddenly and fixed his eyes upon

Hugh. "I have glimpsed Chantillion's house in the darkest corner of the wood," he said. "Built from the bone, skin, and sinew of his victims—a Grue House, and it grows larger as the ogre ranges farther about the forest. Soon, he will come to the edge of Morraine."

Hugh gravely shook his head. "I believe you. But, as Matron Margeut has already pointed out, my counsel is lacking. I do not know what to do."

"You could take action!" Margeut said. "I have seen an old sword hanging above your mantelpiece, in the main hall."

"That sword belonged to my father, good lady. I do not have the skill to use it. Or the strength, for that matter."

Margeut looked down at her feet. The crowd shifted, trading uneasy glances and muttering, but no one raised their voice to speak. "I will pledge this," Hugh said quickly, sensing the need for authority. "Tomorrow I will have the sword taken down and brought to the square. Assemble those stalwarts among the villagers brave enough to face this threat—preferably young ones. I will choose the fittest candidate from among these, and bestow upon him the weapon."

The crowd made no response. Geese honked from wicker cages nearby; a lark circled overhead. Margeut, still sullen, nodded her head and turned away from the gate. The villagers silently trailed after her. They marched back up the road with far less enthusiasm as when they had come down it.

Hugh noticed all his servants were staring at him. "Back to work!" he sputtered, laying about with the willow-rod until they were once again kneeling and digging. He tried to concentrate on the garden, but the feeling he had shirked his obligations nagged him for the rest of the morning. At noon he found a large mound in his turnip bed swarming with ants. He watched the creatures for the better part of an hour, until he felt he had identified certain ants that were behaving in a laggardly manner, and carefully ground those beneath his heel. In this fashion he convinced himself he had helped Morraine by ridding it of inefficient elements, and was so able to free his conscience for the rest of the day.

The next morning Hugh had a servant take down the old sword and wrap it in oilcloth, which he carried himself to the village square.

Margeut was already there and waiting. She had dressed somberly for the occasion; dark blue velvet instead of her usual green, lapis earrings, and a shawl of black silk. Her entourage sat patiently around the brick perimeter of the square, now more spectators than concerned citizens. Three men, presumably the candidates, stood behind her. Hugh surveyed them quickly and frowned. He asked Margeut when the rest would arrive.

"We asked among the villagers as you prescribed," she said. "These were the only willing to come forward."

"But they're, they're all . . ." He wrung his hands in disbelief.

Margeut shrugged. "We have what we have. Begin your judging."

Hesitant, hugging the sword-bundle against his chest, Hugh walked over to the first candidate, a young man of disheveled appearance. One of his eyes stared off at a pronounced angle from the other. Hugh asked him a question and he answered with a stream of amiable babble. "I recognize this man," Hugh said at last, "as Gérard the Idiot. He is a stable-hand at the farm of Guillaume Severts."

"It is true," admitted Margeut.

"And did he volunteer for this duty of his own free will?"

"I am not completely sure. He is difficult to understand. Suffice to say that I put the question to him, and he seemed agreeable enough."

"I see." Hugh moved on to the next candidate. This was a much older man, around Hugh's own age, with great shaggy mats of silver hair. He sat cross-legged on the ground. He was clothed in old rags clotted with urine and ale, and a stench wafted up from him with the force of a stiff breeze.

"This is Antoine de Lus," Hugh said with disgust, clutching at his nostrils. "A known drunkard and layabout."

"True," confessed Matron Margeut. "But it is common knowledge that spirits can embolden a man and fire his heart to great deeds."

Hugh gave her a despairing look. "And so," he said, addressing Antoine, "how would a tosspot such as yourself hope to overcome Chantillion? I don't think you have the wits about you to find your way out of the square."

In reply, Antoine vomited up a stream of thick brown liquid. Hugh could not dash aside in time to avoid having his boots splashed. He fumed and kicked at the besotted man before turning to the final candidate. This last was more promising than the previous two, and Hugh felt his hopes soar for a brief moment. He was a young man, with intelligent features, and wore his long black hair tied back in a poet's queue. His eyes were reddened and sore; when Hugh approached, he buried his face in his hands and began to sob.

"And what is wrong with this one?" Hugh asked, suddenly weary.

"Ask him yourself. It is a sad story, and frankly makes me depressed to repeat it."

The young man composed himself and told his story. He was indeed a poet, and very much in love with a certain young Colette, whom he had courted for the better part of a year with the intention of marriage. But at the last moment, she had spurned him for an older, wealthier prospect.

"This story has a familiar ring to it," observed Hugh. "I assume you wish to win Colette back by the performance of heroic deeds?"

The poet threw up his hands. "What does it matter?" he asked, his eyes becoming wide and manic, his ink-stained fingers trembling. "Colette has already been married, and nothing I do can bring her back." He leaned close to Hugh and looked at him slyly. "In truth," he giggled, "I only wanted to obtain the sword so that I could run myself through at the first opportunity." Then he collapsed to the floor and began weeping all over again.

Hugh cursed aloud, but Matron Margeut could only profess her own frustration. "The only men willing to come forward," she concluded, "were those who already had nothing to lose."

"I find not one of them suitable," Hugh said. He turned to the crowd huddling around the edges of the square, speaking loud enough so everyone could hear. "I see no other recourse," he said. "As a group, we must arm ourselves—with torches and pitchforks, if nothing else is available—and seek out Chantillion in the surrounding woods. I doubt that even this creature could prevail against a mob. There would, of course, be casualties . . ."

His voice trailed off. Most of the spectators were rapidly leaving the square.

"What is this?" Hugh said, turning to Margeut.

"Your 'army' appears to be deserting the field."

Hugh sighed. "Yesterday, they seemed much more resolute."

"They're scared," Margeut said simply. "They've had no training as soldiers."

"And I have?"

Margeut ignored his question. A small, determined-looking group of villagers remained behind, including the one-legged shepherd, but they were not numerous enough to form a mob. Hugh shook his head in disgust. He began to stalk away from the square.

"And where do you think you're going?" Margeut demanded.

"Home. If the townsfolk are too craven to band together for their own good, then so be it. I go to arrange the defenses of my own estate."

"But your pledge—"

"I have done as I pledged."

The young shepherd's staff struck against the floor with such force that fragments of brick flew upwards, and the sound echoed through the square like a thunderclap. All eyes now turned to him. "You pledged," he said, leveling the crook at Hugh, "to choose among the candidates and pick the most suitable. None of them are suitable. By default, you are the most fit to confront Chantillion."

"That's not what I meant!" Hugh snapped. "What kind of logic is this?"

The crowd began to murmur. Margeut looked from them and back at Hugh, blinking rapidly, but just then a red-haired ploughboy stepped forward and everyone fell silent again. The ploughboy respectfully cleared his throat. "I have always heard," he said, "that ogres are stupid creatures, and easily tricked."

Hugh nodded towards the shepherd. "He found his home cleverly enough."

"Yes," said Margeut, warming to the idea, "this Chantillion may possess some base cunning, but what is this next to the brains of Hugh the Discerning? You doubt if you can use a sword: I say that your sharp tongue is a sword, and your quick wits a shield. With these weapons, you could surely overcome a simple, backwoods ogre."

"You are proposing that I somehow trick this ogre?" Hugh asked. Again, Margeut's mention of his old title had restored some pride, stoking a fire within Hugh's belly, albeit a small one.

"Yes." She looked thoughtful for a moment. "Perhaps you could lure Chantillion off a cliff."

"Or into a fast moving river," suggested somebody else.

The group was quick to paint other, similarly inane, scenarios, all involving a high degree of culpability on the part of the ogre. The one-legged shepherd did not seem as confident as the others in this matter, but he was not about to break the group's momentum. "I doubt if the creature is that stupid," Hugh said at last. "But I think the idea has merit."

Margeut brightened. "Then you'll go?"

Hugh set his finger to the edge of his chin. Pride was like strong drink to him, and now the fire in his stomach was a furnace, blazing stronger still. In the courts of Milan, in Provence, he had faced poisoners and assassins' knives; the consequences of a hundred ill-fated intrigues, and yet his agile mind had always seen him through. Was he so rusted now, after years of grain-counting and livestock-whelping, that he could not reclaim the hard-won lauds of his youth? He steeled himself by blotting out the possibility of failure. "I will try," he said softly.

The small crowd let out a cheer and rushed forward to mill about Hugh. Matron Margeut kissed him on both cheeks. He absorbed what adulation he felt appropriate, then waved the group back. The morning was still young, and if he hurried, he would have several hours of daylight to search for Chantillion in the woods nearby. He sent a message to his wife that he would be home by evening, then left the square via the main road, treading his way out of town and past the boundaries of Morraine proper. For half an hour he walked, until the tall Averoignian forest of beech and poplar loomed close. He left the road and took an old trail used by poachers leading into the thickest parts of the wood.

He was in good spirits. Grass and flowering brush reached to waist height on either side of the trail; insects droned, and in the high branches above jackdaws called challenge to one another. The sword-bundle was becoming increasingly heavy, so in annoyance he cast it into the weeds. Perhaps he would be able to find it on his way back, perhaps not. He needed something new to go over the mantelpiece anyway. By late afternoon the shadows were growing longer and the trail nearing its end, but Hugh still had not found Chantillion or his Grue House. He would need to turn back soon, before darkness overtook the woods completely. Tomorrow he could find another trail and begin the search anew; all the better, as he had failed to come up with a clever plan on how to trick the ogre once he found him. He would have to think on that during supper.

Hugh turned to leave. And stopped. Somewhere off to his left came a sound, low and rhythmic, like hammer-blows. He strained his ears. The sound was not far away.

He stepped off the trail, plunging past brush and low-lying branches. Cracks of sunlight appeared through the foliage ahead, and suddenly he was free, standing at the edge of a bright clearing. Fifty paces away he glimpsed the source of the strange noise.

A tall woodsman was carefully lining up white posts and driving them into the ground with a cudgel. Behind him, in the shadows of the treeline, he could dimly see the woodsman's modest estate. Hugh's immediate thoughts were of rest and refreshment. Perhaps he could stay the night, and with directions, resume his search for Chantillion in the morning, without having to walk all the way back to Morraine. He called out and the woodsman waved back amiably enough. He set out across the clearing.

At twenty paces Hugh began to realize something was wrong. The woodsman, in proportion to the surrounding trees and brush, seemed disconcertingly large. His hands and forearms were grossly knotted with muscle. Although he stooped at his work and his face was therefore difficult to see, when the woodsman turned to fetch a fresh post, Hugh was presented with a strange, craggy profile.

At ten paces, more details: the woodsman wore a greatcoat stitched together from bear-skins, odd pieces of cloth, and oily leathers. An enormous hat of red felt tried to encompass his head, and over his back, dropping just below the waist, draped someone's tablecloth. Beneath the brim of the hat, Hugh could see rows of shovel-like teeth set within a square jaw, and a long nose with three long hairs protruding from the tip, one golden, one black, and one green.

A sudden and uncomfortable thought occurred to Hugh. But then it was too late; the woodsman stood up to his full height, grinning fiercely, and extended a massive hand. "Good evening," he said in a low, but dulcet tone. Hugh could now see that the "posts" he had been hammering were human femurs. A thick odor, sweet and strangely familiar, wafted over from the direction of the cottage.

Hugh declined to shake his hand. "Are you the . . . woodsman in these parts?" he asked.

"I am Chantillion," the creature replied, removing any doubts.

Hugh swallowed. "I am Hugh de Manchefort, from the village of Morraine."

"Hugh de Manchefort?" Chantillion pulled at his protruding lower lip. "The name rings familiar . . . may I ask what you are doing in the middle of these woods?"

The bright morning, with its confident talk about clever tricks and stupid ogres, seemed a long time off. Hugh could not think of a properly guileful response. "I will not mince words," he said at last. "I have come in defense of my village, whose inhabitants you have been molesting. I am charged with the task of ridding you from these parts."

Chantillion nodded, half smirking as he drummed his fingers against his chin. "I admire your frankness. Sadly, I am committed to staying here for the present time."

"Then we are at an impasse."

"It would appear so."

An awkward silence ensued, then Chantillion began to laugh softly. "We could at least try to be civil," he said. He pointed with a muscular arm towards the cottage, presumably his Grue House. "The temperature will be getting nippy, soon. I suggest we retire inside and discuss the matter further."

Hugh agreed. If the ogre desired to overpower him, he could easily do so whether they were indoors or out. More importantly, Chantillion appeared to be a rational, even reasonable creature, and Hugh's skill at diplomacy might prevail where his trickery could not.

Chantillion led him up a twisting walkway, past piles of innumerable bones, to a "cottage" that was not really a solid structure at all, but a giant tent made from carefully flayed and preserved human skins. Such was Chantillion's skill that Hugh could still make out individual faces within the canvas, and personal details like moles, birthmarks, and scars seemed to have been emphasized rather than blended away. Bones wrapped tight with corded sinew provided support. The smell was nearly overpowering and thick clouds of black flies hovered above the roof.

"It's not altogether finished," Chantillion admitted, as he undid the finger-bone prongs that held the front flap shut. "Right this way."

Inside the air was warm and moist, the walls a dim pink shot through with purple veins, and Hugh was struck uncomfortably with the sensation of being inside a giant stomach. Chantillion led him through a series of chambers, all apparently kitchens by virtue of their cooking pots, racks of sharp knives and saws, and haunches of unidentifiable meats hanging from the ceiling. He at last entered a spacious, central room and was offered a seat made from some unfortunate's pelvis.

"An idea is coming to me," Chantillion said, after Hugh had been seated. "A way, perhaps, to resolve our mutual dilemma."

"Please make it known. I myself have no solid plans along this line."

Chantillion looked at him closely. "I said before that your name sounded familiar. In truth, it is your other name that I remember more clearly."

Hugh was taken aback. "But how do you know?"

"I have traveled this country extensively. Once, in the wastelands outside Pont du Planier, I at—that is, I befriended a certain Benedictine monk, who regaled me with local legends before we . . . parted ways. One of these legends was you."

"Go on."

"I mean no disrespect, but I find it hard to credit some of the wilder claims he made about your powers of perception."

Hugh smiled inwardly. Was the ogre proposing a challenge? And against his strongest suit? If so, then Chantillion was playing right into his hands—and Hugh had not even bothered to set a trap!

"I think I see where this is going," Hugh said, "and I would be happy to satisfy your curiosity. Simply name your terms."

Chantillion leaned forward in earnest. "I propose this: I will present you with three unknown objects, and ask that you discern their true natures."

"Is that it?" Hugh asked, stifling a laugh. "I have played thousands of such guessing-games, in courts all over the continent. To accept your challenge would hardly be in good sport."

"In that case, I would propose instituting a handicap—say a blindfold."

"I would insist on a blindfold at the least," Hugh said, feeling magnanimous. "And if this does not prove difficult enough, you may propose further handicaps as the challenge unfolds."

"Such confidence!" Chantillion exclaimed. "Such generosity, even before the match has begun." He looked at Hugh sideways for a moment, and then asked slowly: "You don't intend to trick Chantillion, do you? That would be a cruelty indeed! I remind you that I am a rustic, a provincial, and not given to all the worldly complications of a man who has served in court."

"You have my word that I will ply no such trickery," Hugh said. In his opinion, the ogre seemed quite adept at tricking himself.

And yet, Hugh's vaunted perception had already failed him. He had overlooked several clues pointing to the cerebral refinements of his host. On a nearby table rested a set of Plato's *Dialogues*, along with a complete copy of *The Republic*, both lovingly bound in human skin and dog-eared after much perusal. There were miniature chess sets carved from baby's teeth, a half-finished astrolabe, and a series of anatomy portfolios penned in Arabic and Italian. Chantillion was an intellectual, but Hugh's senses, distracted by the gory opulence of the Grue House, were drawn elsewhere, and he could only see the ogre as the rustic he claimed himself to be.

"We have an agreement, then," Chantillion said. "If you can discern all three objects, I will leave Morraine peaceably."

"And if I lose?"

Chantillion smiled. "There are certain sections of the house needing expansion . . . ."

Hugh silently reassured himself. Chantillion produced a blood-stained rag and carefully wound this around Hugh's eyes, making sure they were wholly covered. When he had finished, Hugh testified that he could not see a thing.

"Does the room seem a tad chill to you?" the ogre asked, as he was bringing forth the first object for discernment.

"Somewhat. I am not adverse to a fire, if that is your intention."

There was a brief moment as Chantillion stoked the requisite fire. He then placed something spherical and vaguely wet in Hugh's outstretched hands.

Hugh stroked the convoluted surface; brought it close to sniff and took a small bite. "Ha!" he exclaimed. "Cabbage. I would say it is three days past its prime—still all right for putting in soup, though." He nibbled further. "I suspect that it was stolen from a farm near here. Guillaume Severts? Yes—and from the dew still on the leaves, the cabbage was stolen in the dead of night, in great haste, so as to avoid Severts' many hounds."

Chantillion gasped. "You have described both the cabbage and the conditions of its abduction to the letter."

"As I surmised," Hugh said, quite pleased with himself. "I would suggest you impose another handicap before we go any further."

"A good idea. Let me ponder this." Hugh heard Chantillion pouring a large quantity of water. "Would you like some tea? I usually take a cup or two around this time."

Hugh politely declined. Chantillion drew close, then gently bound Hugh's hands behind his back with a length of knotted rope. "I have decided that your hands are too clever," he said when he was finished. "Let us see if you can discern the next item so quickly."

Hugh felt a small object drop onto his lap. Without the use of his hands it was indeed difficult to ascertain more, but he moved his hips in such a way that the object rolled onto his knee, and from there he was able to bend down and seize it with his teeth. Almost instantly, he knew what it was.

"This is a turnip fresh from the soil." By a combination of taste and smell, he was able to describe to the ogre the pedigree of the turnip, to the same exacting quality as he had the cabbage. Again, Chantillion was dutifully impressed.

"I must warn you," Hugh said, "that your predilection towards vegetables is making this much easier than I anticipated, despite the handicaps."

"Hmmm. I see your point. A change in environment? Perhaps if you were disoriented this time . . ." Hugh felt himself being hauled up bodily and carried a short distance. The next moment he was plunged neck-deep into tepid water. He called out, sputtering protest against the nature of this handicap.

Chantillion promptly removed the blindfold. Hugh was immersed in the waters of a giant cauldron. Cabbages, turnips, and a dozen different kinds of wild mushrooms all bobbed in the waters around him. Chantillion's mouth parted in a huge smile.

"What is this?" Hugh asked, outraged. He couldn't climb out of the cauldron as both his hands were still bound.

"Why, I would think that obvious to someone as perceptive as yourself."

Hugh's eyes went wide. "But the rules of our contest—you have yet to bring forth the third object, and therefore I have not lost!"

"Well," replied Chantillion, "I have not yet thought of a third object to present. I suspect, however, that you will be thoroughly boiled by the time I do."

"Cheater!" Hugh snarled. "Base trickster!"

"Tut-tut. Let's not make an unpleasant situation any worse." Chantillion turned his back and began preparing various implements.

The water was heating rapidly, and already Hugh's skin was turning bright pink. He pleaded with Chantillion to be spared, offering him his estate, his young wife, and sums of money he did not have.

"I am moved to a small amount of sympathy," Chantillion said at last. "Not enough to free you, of course." He produced a tray of fresh cut shallots and proffered them to Hugh. "You may exercise your gifts for a final time."

Somberly, but with an air of dignity, Hugh sorted among the shallots for those that would make the most tasty addition to the stew.

A week passed in the village of Morraine. When Hugh did not return from the woods the townsfolk suspected the worst, and dutifully went about electing a new reeve. Panic around the approach of Chantillion reached a fever pitch, then subsided when sightings of the ogre began to decline.

As hot summer swiftly overtook the spring, travelers through the woods reported a fearsome stench, almost overwhelming, emanating from a certain clearing, and great clouds of flies and carrion-birds darkened the sky. Chantillion appeared at the edge of Morraine a short time later.

He wasted no time, moving himself swiftly into Hugh's old estate. Hugh's former servants and closest neighbors fled immediately, with the notable exception of his young widow. Nothing else untoward occurred for several weeks. Matron Margeut, concerned as ever for public safety, sent an official petition for aid to the Comte de Fleuris and was promptly ignored.

Soon afterwards, Hugh's widow was seen making daily sojourns to the market and buying enormous amounts of food, mostly meat, but to the most fervent questions regarding her well-being would make only casual replies. In fact, she was often spotted in public singing idly or weaving wildflowers into her long hair. When pressed as to why she did not mourn the passing of her gentle old husband, only to have him replaced by a large and no doubt rapacious ogre, she would only smile broadly. The matter became the subject of much disreputable speculation.

Later that fall a rooster belonging to Guillaume Severts laid a reddish-hued egg from which hatched a strange worm. Severts cut the unwholesome creature into bits and threw the remains into his hay pile, but the worm soon re-formed and grew to prodigious size. The creature destroyed Severts' barn and began devouring all the sheep and cattle in the surrounding area.

The villagers were once again in disarray about what to do. Finally, Matron Margeut grew desperate and appealed to the powerfully built Chantillion for help.

The ogre pledged his support on the spot. Near Severts' farm, he uprooted a beech tree and affixed an old plowshare to one end. With this giant axe, he chopped the worm into several quivering pieces, which he swiftly collected and threw into a roaring fire. The worm was completely consumed.

From that point on, the terror surrounding Chantillion's presence in Morraine subsided into a general uneasiness, and he was hailed as a local champion, albeit from a discrete distance. Like Hugh the Discerning before him, Chantillion became known for his wise temperament. Unlike Hugh, he proved to be a man of action, and not given to the vagaries of thought that often paralyze otherwise capable people. He would on occasion break into old form and make off with neighbor's livestock, but the townsfolk agreed, Matron Margeut foremost, that this was a small price to pay for having an ogre in the village.

THE CIRCUMSTANCES OF GHOSTLY CATS

by Michael Minnis

It was a year of travail and a season of discontent for Vyônes and its people.

The battle of Poitiers had left France defeated, the flower of her chivalry cut down by English archers, her king a prisoner. Weary Vyônese knights returned from the battle to raise ransom only to be mocked by the peasants. "They ran away!" the commoners cried. "The forked beards ran away!"

The countryside now belonged to mercenaries, armed brigands released after Poitiers—English and Gascons, Burgundians and Germans. They violated the truce, looting monasteries and burning villages. None were spared their insensate cruelty. Grandfather or monk, virgin or child, they fled to Vyônes seeking shelter within its ancient walls.

Vyônes, still marked by the long-past Plague, lay half-abandoned. Wildflowers grew long in fields once tended. The First Pest had killed every third man; taxes levied to ransom the French king had left the other two nearly penniless. Now a Second Pest, lately arisen in Picardy and Flanders, threatened to carry them away as well. Faces soon became furtive and unfamiliar. People rarely went abroad. The outlands belonged to their foes.

And as for the outlands, they were closer now. Nature had been swift to reclaim its own, to subvert the work of man in the wake of war and pestilence. These days the wilderness came to the very city walls.

To Petrarch in Paris, the River Seine seemed to weep for the shame and devastation of all France. To a Carmelite prior it was as if the land had put upon itself a garment of confusion, a cloak of mourning.

Perhaps it is for these reasons that the renowned and feared sorcerer, Gasquet of Aquitaine came to Vyônes in the Year of Our Lord 1361, anno Domini.

He had left the English-occupied province of Aquitaine with little more than the robes on his back, his staff, and a single gray ass weighed down with decrepit, wormy tomes.

The Treaty of Brétigny, signed by the kingdoms of England and France the year before, had proven as grave a misfortune for the sorcerer as it was for France. Edward of Wales, the Black Prince and ruler of Aquitaine, had ordered Gasquet to leave or face imprisonment, torture, and death. The Prince would not tolerate a servant of the Adversary in his midst. Nor did Gasquet's refusal to levy tribute help plead his case.

The people of Aquitaine did not sorrow at the sorcerer's departure. Indeed, years later it was said to be the only wise decision ever made by the reckless, vainglorious Black Prince.

And so into Vyônes came Gasquet, and hardly a soul suspected he was more than a simple weary traveler, another refugee, this lone youngish man of middling height and long mouse-colored hair. Wizards and such are usually prepossessing figures. Awe precedes them and fear lingers in their wake.

This fellow excited little more than curiosity with his blandly handsome features, straggling mustache and delicate frame. Indeed, for a time the people of Vyônes were more interested in Gasquet's manner of dress than the man himself. He wore robes, an embroidered mantle of many-shaded green, and an oddly peaked black cap of the sort worn by the Wallachians. His puffed breeches and queerly buckled shoes meanwhile spoke of realms even further away—Byzantium, Tartary and beyond.

There was but one flaw, one mark upon the man and that upon his face. Gasquet's right eye was blind. Rolled half-upward within its socket, it lent a weird, fragmented serenity to his face, but whether it was the peace of sainthood or death none could decide.

The Flemish wizard Ludvig Prinn, perpetrator of the dread *De Vermis Mysteriis*, is said to have resided within a pre-Roman tomb in his later days. Gasquet, while rumored to have studied under Prinn, was not as flamboyantly morbid in his lodgings. He chose instead a lofty and drafty garret in Les Ruelles, one of the rather less savory of the city's districts.

Visitors to Gasquet's abode were very few. They acknowledged his grace and politeness, but they had little good to say of either the sorcerer or his home. True, there was never a lack of wine, nor bread, or cheese. A fire always burned in the grate. Violets were spread upon the floor. The best of the sorcerer's furnishings were at their disposal. But beneath all, there lurked something watchful and sardonic. A mute autumn gloom seemed to hang permanently over the garret, like smoke or a shroud—no amount of firelight or thoughtful conversation could dispel it. Words rang hollow and yet were without resonance, so that all speech was like that of muttering blind spirits.

And always, the sense that one was never entirely alone in that place. Things flickered and whispered at the peripheries of perception. Before long the most ordinary of objects became isolated, unfamiliar, and blackly suggestive. What was a visiting census-taker to say when an empty chair slid across the floor toward him? And what should the apothecary think when he looked upon a mirror and saw reflected there, standing behind him, a floating mass of oily iridescent spheres?

Even the most evil of men sooner or later desires a companion. The question was, who would become Gasquet's?

Perhaps he desired a mistress, the people of Vyônes said. A wife was unlikely, for an evil man can never truly give of himself in matters of love. The mistress would be pale in appearance, dark in manner, and slender as the promise of spring in midwinter. She would appear in his garden beneath a horned moon. But no mistress appeared.

Perhaps an advisor or confidante would be more to his liking, a fellow conspirator to whisper in his ear at the appropriate moment—much to the discomfort of visitors. Preferably he would be small and scuttling, with the face of a nocturnal animal. But of such men there was no sign. Gasquet did not much trust anyone's counsel besides his own.

He was a sorcerer of ability, some said. Perhaps he will fashion a companion from dead air or dead flesh—a conjured devil or a summoned skeleton. But a devil is a liar, others argued, a twister of words, ever eager to deliver its master to still greater masters—Astarte, Shub-Niggurath, or Iog-Sotôt. The summoned skeleton proves a puppetry of empty obedient bones and nothing more. Devils and the undead, they said, are best summoned in secret, far away from others.

The people of Vyônes waited, and wondered.

Eventually Gasquet's self-imposed exile came to an end. He had need of others. Sorcerers never go long unknown, and the increasing disrepute in which he was held necessitated personal protection, while the rather verminous state of his garret necessitated a companion of the four-legged variety. In Vyônes he found both.

The first, his guard, was Pierre Udon. He was a madman of the first water—lean as the Reaper himself and tattooed like a Pict with strange bluish markings. Udon wore neither tunic nor shoes. His hair was brutally cropped and of the same rusty shade as his pronounced mustache. His knotted hands spoke eloquently of savagery, whether they wrought forth music or blood.

Udon played the bagpipes. The instrument in question was of tanned goatskin, oddly decorated and its lilting chaotic tone was exquisitely strange—clearly a relic of the unknown East. The Vyônese shuddered to hear it.

Many tales surrounded Udon. He was said to be a graverobber, a Gascon mercenary turned loose from Poitiers, and an outlaw. He was the Wolf of Malinbois, who had eaten children and mated with wolves. There were those who believed he was all these things. One only had to look into his pale cold eyes, to smell the violence upon him. Ecclesiastical torturers had been unable to break him: it was said he had laughed at all the designs of pain. Exorcism could not cure him: he had merely gibbered and barked and vomited animal hair and pins, shards of pottery and squirming eels.

Udon was appalling in full rage. The mightiest of knights could scarcely stand against him. *Iog-Sotôt*, Udon would shriek, *Iog-Sotôt*, as he beat madly upon helm and shield with his great-sword, driving foes to their knees.

The second was a notable specimen of feline, as handsome as Udon was repellent. His name was Le Matois, or the Guileful One. He was large and of the shade of smoke. His eyes were of jade shot through with copper. As cats go, Matois was well into middle age—competent, comfortable, calculating but not coldly so, and as phlegmatic as Udon was mercurial.

No one truly owned Matois, though his was a familiar face at many a back door or garret window. An accomplished mouser, Matois knew every inch of Vyônes—every alley, rooftop, gangway, footpath, garden, cloister, veranda, gutter and windowsill. Vyônes was his kingdom, the hearth of the innkeeper Bertrand his court. The people of Vyônes were his subjects and he their benevolent ruler. None were so lowly or ignoble that their king Matois did not visit them at least once in their lives, even then if only by circumstance, chance, or in the case of the newly-arrived Gasquet, curiosity.

Had times been better, perhaps this tale would not end so strangely. Had times been better, sorcerer and swordsman would have been turned forth, banished to the unknown.

But they were not.

There were none to challenge the two who were not preoccupied, or afraid, or sick at heart. With the agony of existence multiplied three-fold, was there any reason to seek further trouble? God had sent the Pest, and then he had sent the English. Who wished to know the third scourge? Let him come forth then and ask of the sorcerer's designs. Let him come forth and ask why Gasquet should ascend the tallest of hills to speak with the dread demon Iog-Sotôt, or why should his foul servant mock the people of Vyônes and speak of the unfathomable Old Ones and a terrible reckoning long overdue?

And so if someone should suddenly disappear and the circle draw smaller yet again, the people of Vyônes nervously named it an act of God and pleaded His mercy.

Matois, however, knew as little of God as he did sorcery.

It was a mystery to many why he had chosen to live among the doubtful goings-on within that strange, high, blackened garret, where sulphurous lights flickered and odd sounds emanated in the dead hours of night. Normally he was the most staid and conservative of creatures, disliking any disruption in routine and all things unusual. So why this taste for the fantastic?

Matois will leave soon, the people of Vyônes said. He is like the wind. He visits much but seldom stays.

But the Guileful One remained with Gasquet and Udon. He was often seen sitting in the garret windows, a smaller shadow among shadows. Or atop the steep roof, like a diminutive gargoyle, his paws tucked beneath him. He visited no one. Such portents greatly upset the people of Vyônes. Had their Matois abandoned them? What deviltry bound him to that shunned place? The innkeeper Bertrand, Matois' greatest friend, offered his finest meats and richest creams to the disinterested feline in an attempt to lure him away. Matois did not heed him and Bertrand came to believe that Matois was bewitched.

The half-blind old woman Dulot, who kept toads and mice as pets in her tiny home, did not think so.

Gasquet, on occasion, consulted with her upon matters she felt unwise to discuss. She had been to the lofty garret perched high above its crooked cobblestone alley. She said it was thick with spirits and the comings and goings of doubtful things. A mere man should not enter such a place—but one wise in certain arts, as she, was relatively safe.

As for Matois, he did not appear to be in any danger. She had heard the delicate jingling of a bell-toy in an adjoining room, and Gasquet told her he thought it odd that Matois preferred to play alone and out of sight. Nor did Dulot believe the cat to be ensorcelled. Rather, he seemed more to await something—what, however, no one could guess.

Udon grew to hate Matois.

Perhaps man and beast were too akin for the liking of either; Udon almost like an animal, Matois very nearly human. The former did not care for the way in which the latter looked upon him. The cryptic jade eyes were full of secrets a tattooed savage born of snow and wilderness could not hope to understand. Why did his master tolerate this imp, this insolent little bastard?

Udon's hatred was a terrible thing, like him a wild beast. He cursed the cat. He kicked at it. He chased it.

Matois was not unduly disturbed by Udon's antagonism. Driven to a rooftop, he attended to the cleaning of his paws while below the Wolf of Malinbois raved and promised black revenge. Offered a present of fresh meat tainted with hemlock, the cat disdainfully left dead field mice upon Udon's rude bed. Through Udon's fevered dreams the smoke-shape capered, tantalizingly out of reach. In time the people of Vyônes came to laugh at Udon. The fiercest of outlaws was sorely lacking in wit. He was no match for Le Matois.

Gasquet, too, was rather amused by the affair and did not intervene. He once told Dulot that he wished to see who was stronger, cleverer, who would prevail: man or beast.

A sorcerer after all, he said, should never have too many companions.

In the end Udon prevailed. With rabbit skins bound about his feet to muffle his footfalls, Udon cornered Matois one wet spring day, and strangled him.

Matois fought furiously, tearing so with his teeth and claws that the latter's hands and wrists appeared to have been flayed. Udon, his breath hissing through his teeth, squeezed the cat's throat ever tighter. Matois' struggles weakened. He cried out helplessly. Soon he was dead, though Udon in his blind fury continued to throttle him.

When Udon finally realized that he had killed his hated foe, he howled his triumph and threw the body at the wall. He raged at invisible foes. He kicked and trampled the pathetic corpse. He laughed madly and danced in circles, crooned to himself as he touched his blood to his chest and face drawing strange designs. He was the Wolf of Malinbois. The Terror of Averoigne. No man could stand against him, let alone the worthless little rat-chasing bastard Matois!

Outside the garret a fearful mob had gathered, drawn by the agonized shrieks of the cat. Udon threw the corpse at them.

Bertrand was first to approach the body, and he wept when he saw that it was Matois, the lithe body limp, the handsome face bruised, the lovely eyes puffed shut. Udon laughed at Bertrand, who cursed him and started forward. He was held back by his friends. They knew that the portly innkeeper was no match for the Wolf of Malinbois. Udon spit at the people of Vyônes and called them dogs fit only for beating. There could be only one Beast, he said, and that was Pierre Udon. Now take your silly little King and go. Feed him to the worms.

In tears the people of Vyônes wound a shroud about Matois and brought him to the gentle hills that lie beyond the city walls. There beneath the lime trees they laid him to rest within an isolated tomb among giants long dead: knights and princelings, monks and crusaders.

The people of Vyônes sealed the tomb shut. Rain began to fall, pattering among the leaves. Of the mourners, Bertrand lingered longest.

Cats do not readily leave this world. Le Matois was no exception.

Like Bertrand, they linger at the door between existence and spirit, in life and in death. They are hardly discomfited by their new circumstances. Their kingdom is as it has been before; only they have changed—silent as fog, twisting like smoke. Of barriers there are none. They pass through air and earth and stone with equal impunity. Among the wind and leaves and pebbled streams they move, high into the sky, deep into the secret places under the earth. But ultimately, they are creatures of habit, and follow the dictates of the physical world—especially if they have unfinished business there.

Matois visited first his old friend. Bertrand was certain he heard the cat's plaintive homely cry from his cellar one shadowed April day. Astonished, he went downstairs to investigate. He found nothing but swore to his puzzled patrons that he felt Matois brush up against his ankle, and heard the swift patter of cat-feet up the stairs.

Soon others spoke of similar sights and sounds. Matois was seen sunning himself upon the stone sundial in the nunnery garden. He leaped from rooftop to rooftop in the dead of night. From another room might be heard the soft tattoo of paws, the scratch and scurry of claws, the jingle of his favored bell-toy.

A few were dismayed by Matois' apparent return and expected some form of hideous retribution for his death.

Others found a certain poignant comfort in his presence. He was here to bid farewell to those he knew and loved best. Perhaps God was not entirely displeased with them, and the world not entirely indifferent to their suffering.

In the end, both theories proved true.

It was neither philosopher nor demonologist who later learned the truth of the matter, but Arnaud, a humble woodcutter.

Admittedly, Arnaud was slightly simple and prone to fantastic sights and stories. He was a lonely man given to wandering the hills and forests of Averoigne, often amidst lowering storms. While it is true he had been to places seldom visited by others, no one entirely believed his wild tales—talk of faerie rings and wyverns and rivers that flowed uphill. The good people of Vyônes knew better.

Arnaud claimed to have been approached by Gasquet and Udon one evening, as the sun sank into the west. He had liked neither the unctuously polite sorcerer nor his oddly marked grinning servant, but they offered Arnaud a goodly sum to lead them far into the hills beyond Vyônes. The coins in question, to some astonishment, were later found to be gold and of Roman make.

And so Arnaud had brought them to the tallest and most wind-swept of hills. It was well into sunset by then, and stars innumerable had begun to fill the darkening sky. With stick and chalk Gasquet had begun to scratch into the earth signs the woodcutter did not like, and then a circle. Then even the simple woodcutter was alarmed. He tried to slip away but Udon seized him by the wrist and asked Arnaud where he might be going. The countryside is full of dangerous men and . . . wolves. Perhaps it is better you remained with us, *bon ami.*

Yes, Gasquet had said, please remain with us. There is one other we must yet meet.

Gasquet and Udon stepped within the circle. Confused, the wood-cutter thought he should join them, but was roughly pushed away by Udon.

Damn you, the Wolf of Malinbois said. Do you realize what you're doing?

The woodcutter replied that no, he did not.

Then watch where you step, Udon replied, grinning. Because you nearly ruined my master's circle, and bad things happen to people who do that. You don't like bad things, do you?

The woodcutter replied that no, he did not.

Then stay back.

The wind lashed at the long grass and though night was close a cu-rious luminosity filled the air, so that Arnaud saw far away the green ridges beneath the blue-black sky. Something flickered silently there, like lightning, revealing the bones of the land.

It was toward this that Gasquet turned, his staff above his head. He began a sonorous chant in a language that Arnaud thought to be Latin, though he was not certain. For a seemingly endless time came the outpouring of mysterious words, while Udon, clearly restless, swayed from foot to foot, and on occasion turned to offer Arnaud a gaunt knowing grin.

Gasquet's voice grew louder. The lights on the horizon blazed in muted violence, seemingly in time and measure with the sorcerer's words. Arnaud contemplated running, but he was certain the limber agile swordsman would have no trouble catching him. A fear had fallen upon him, greater than that of the visions that plagued his waking or the nightmares that snaked through his sleep. Something was coming—he knew it.

Slowly he inched away from the surreal scene. Gasquet and Udon were preoccupied with events, with the glowering horizon. Then there was a particularly brilliant flash, Arnaud said, so that the entire sky went white. At that moment Udon began to play his pipes and an eerie ululation filled the air, the notes swirling like smoke.

Arnaud saw at first what he thought to be the sickish, shifting spots that accompany such phenomena, but realized with cold dread that this was hardly the case.

No, it was no corneal illusion taking shape before him, drifting slowly up the wind-whipped hillside. It was in fact something, a being, an inhabitant of the outer void. Over the hissing grass they came: a universe of oily iridescent spheres of all dimensions, some no larger than a man's fist, several large as horses and one tall as a tower. They orbited one another to bizarre music, flowed into one another, broke and coalesced in a hypnotic saraband of muted color: dull orange and russet, muddy green and blue, ochre and mauve. Some were swift, sparks in the gloom. Others proceeded with far less alacrity. But all converged to became a restless, shapeless congeries of protoplasm that massed overhead, touched with fire, burning brilliantly in the last light of the day.

Higher and higher rose the utterly silent, unknown being, revolving ponderously in its courses. The smaller spheres clustered about and between the larger in strands, like amphibian eggs, slick and fluid.

Arnaud was sick with dread. He crouched down into the grass. The poisonous colors shimmered and wavered. A purposeful, almost palpable malevolence filled the air and he knew it was alive, and aware after some awful fashion. Then a voice rose above the shrill whine of wind and pipes, uttering words of malignant and terrible potency: *Iog-Sotôt!*

Arnaud turned to run. Something was coming toward him, however, through the grass. It was too small to see. Up the slope it came, darting first one way, and then the other, swiftly, stopping only for the briefest of moments before its pell-mell progress resumed. As the grass grew shorter near the hilltop, Arnaud saw that it was a cat—a big fellow, gray and handsome, with something in his mouth. At first he thought it might be a mole, or a mouse, but it was a small toy, and it jingled merrily.

The cat darted between his legs, intent on some private game. How could it not notice the horror before it? It paid no mind. Instead it dropped the toy and began playing like a kitten, knocking the thing about, leaping and pouncing. Closer and closer it drew to the circle. Udon, disturbed by the delicate bell, was first to see the cat. His wild music ceased and astonishment clouded his features. It became terror when the capering animal chased his toy through the carefully drawn magic circle, breaking utterly its spell of protection.

Bastard! Udon cried.

With a thunderous crack the conglomeration of spheres swiftly broke apart, and descended upon the two men. The smaller globes swarmed like wasps about them, and Arnaud shuddered to describe their effect upon bare flesh, which was like that of *aqua regia*, or flames touched to parchment. Like will-o'-wisps the spheres went in pursuit of the fleeing cat. Yet even as Arnaud watched, the animal faded from view.

Soon it was gone and it was only then that Arnaud saw that the demon Iog-Sotôt intended to take him as well . . .

Arnaud's flight from that dreadful place became legend—undoubtedly the most fantastic of all his tales. It chased me, he insisted later. And it would have had me, had I not ran so swiftly, and had it not already taken the sorcerer and his accomplice!

The people of Vyônes simply smiled and shook their heads. Poor old Arnaud. Perhaps if his wife were still alive, and his children not far away, he would not be quite so mad. But it was a story worthy of Le Matois.

Bertrand remained curious, however, and months later he visited the hill. That he should find its crown scorched as if by a great fire was alone disturbing, but to find among the cinders yellowed bones and two skulls frankly unnerved him. Little else was left besides a rusting great-sword, a ruined set of bagpipes, and the charred remains of what might have been a staff. Silently he blessed the place, so that no evil creature would return here.

The skulls he crushed underfoot.

Then he said to the empty air: Matois . . . though you are no longer within this world, I ask you to return. The city will continue without its king, but I am lonely for your company. Please return to me, if only for a day, or an hour. You know that in my house, you are always welcome.

With the wind at his back, and his thoughts far away, Bertrand left the hill.

Perhaps something heard him that day. The innkeeper is certain of it. Should one chance upon his inn talk is sure to turn to Matois, the Guileful One, when the ale is flowing and the fire burns low. Matois, clever as an old peasant, even in death. Not even the demon Iog-Sotôt could catch him. Le Matois, who still walks among his beloved, the people of Vyônes.

To this day, visitors to the inn are said to occasionally hear the homely cry of a cat from the cellar at odd hours. Sometimes it is scampering and scurrying. And sometimes it is no more than the jingling of a toy bell.

SONG OF THE UPROOTED MANDRAKES

by Dan Clore

The last love of the homicide
Bespewed the slime that gave us birth,
'Neath the gibbet, sprouting inside,
The miry matric of the earth.

Mandrake wine may fulfill the wizard's cup
But a curse on the cur who digs us up!

Beneath the shade of gallows-gloom
We saw no sun, but did not die,
We grew without a woman's womb,
Stunted, deformed homunculi.

Mandrake wine may fulfill the wizard's cup
But a curse on the cur who digs us up!

The virtue in our blood anon
Shall quicken or de-drowse the breath;
Mingled with dwale and hebenon
To make the drug of love—or death.

Mandrake wine may fulfill the wizard's cup
But a curse on the cur who digs us up!

At witching-hour and plenilune,
Culled for a mage's venefice,
We shriek and groan this baneful rune
To end our days with malefice:

Mandrake wine may fulfill the wizard's cup
But a curse on the cur who digs us up!

UNHALLOWED GROUND, UNHOLY FLESH

by James Chambers

In those fear-blasted days of winter, Isobel's parting words haunted him more than the dread monstrosity that rose up to threaten the land of Averoigne. Many a night he passed dozing bathed in the carmine glow of a dying fire as the mists of his memory swirled about and chilled him like a tempest of dreams. Some nights ill visions of the deepest corruptions visited him, and the shadows of his modest chamber writhed like serpents coiling to strike, agitated by the unconscious stirrings of his great power. In these black hours he would start to wakefulness at the sensation of some nearing entity, some form devoid of all warmth of life, some mindless demiurge entreated with his apprehension. And though his countless sorcererous attempts to divine the nature of the thing had failed to unveil it, knowledge of its cause dwelled deep within his heart, waiting for the moment when he would allow himself to recognize it.

On one of these specter-branded nights a heavy pounding dispelled the gathering storms of his consciousness and drew him awkwardly from troubled slumber. Shivering and sleep-addled the solitary mage passed through darkened chambers, threw back the bar, and swung wide the stout door of his home.

"The hour is quite late, and the winter air is savage and sharp," he said. "Who comes through such unpleasantness to disturb my reverie?"

Two men shuffled into the meager warmth of the entryway, one a broad-shouldered figure of taut muscle and sinew with a crossbow slung across his shoulders and the other a young man of slight build but possessed of a steely posture. The flickering of the wizard's taper brought their visages into gentle focus—the scarred and hardened face of a warrior beside the soft, querulous aspect of a monk.

"I am Brother Albert," said the cleric. "With me is Henri Giroux, the Marshal of Vyônes. We seek Luc le Chaudronnier with word from the Archbishop of Vyônes."

"And what does his holiness wish of me?" said le Chaudronnier.

"Though our interruption may be unseemly, sir, we have traveled the better part of the day to arrive here. We are frozen to the marrow,"

Brother Albert said.

"Enter, enter," said the wizard, with obvious exasperation.

Le Chaudronnier shut the door firmly and then led his guests to his study. He threw fresh wood on the fire, and poured the men portions of a potent brandy to restore the color to their flesh. As the remnants of sleep fell away, he grew more even-tempered and welcoming of the diversion that had rescued him from his nightly torment. What could bring to his door men such as these, who under most circumstances would shun him? Ten years had passed since his brief and secret discourse with the Abbot of Périgon, when in return for a service only he could provide, he had received dispensation from the Archbishop of Vyônes to carry on his arcane studies and occult explorations with impunity from the region's religious authority. Since then the Church's periodic inquisitions against those of le Chaudronnier's calling had steered wide and far of the mage.

As if reading his host's thoughts Brother Albert resumed his purpose. "His holiness wishes me first to remind you of the great service you provided some ten years hence in dispelling the comet-spawned beast that ravaged Averoigne."

The sorcerer nodded. "Of course."

"He noted in particular your discretion in attending to the reputation of Abbot Théophile whose life was forfeit in that misadventure, and to this day is remembered for his good works rather than his ignominious demise."

"Yes, yes," said le Chaudronnier. "Whatever your god may give you cause to think of me and my work, Averoigne is my home. I want the best for it, and I am willing always to aid in its protection. Without one of my knowledge and power, the dark forces that haunt this land would surely overrun your congregation."

Henri Giroux chose then to break his silence. His coarse, gravelly tone boomed in the close surroundings. "No wizard have I ever met with such noble intentions. You would do well to realize that there are those who wonder if your affection for Averoigne is not fostered by a wish to guard some secret purpose. Many feel that seeking the aid of your kind is akin to consorting with the devil."

"I am aware, Marshal Giroux, of all that is said of me. Rumor and jealousy must surround all those who follow my path, deserved or not.

What is it your archbishop would have of me?"

Evading the direct question, Albert continued, "His holiness also asked me to offer his continued assurance of immunity for your studies and work."

"Is it blackmail, then?" said le Chaudronnier. "Consent to his request or face trial by torture?"

"No! Please don't misunderstand," said Albert. "His holiness is an honorable man and wishes only to reconfirm your status. In exchange for your cooperation in this current matter, he is prepared to grant reburial on hallowed ground of the Scotswoman Isobel Aickman, dead by her own hand these past eight months."

Le Chaudronnier toppled into the high-backed chair he kept by the hearth. An icy sensation seized his weary figure, and he found no words with which to respond. With numb fingers he clutched the nearby brandy decanter and poured himself a full measure. The amber liquid revived his senses and brought tears brimming to his eyes.

"The archbishop is aware of your dispute in this cause with the Bishop of Ximes and has made arrangements to assure that his colleague will not interfere."

The wizard leaned forward, his narrow gaze searching the monk's features for signs of guile but finding none. "What is it he would have of me?" he whispered.

"You are familiar, I assume, with Nathaire's Plain?" Albert said. "It's a patch of land along the banks of the Isoile, a wasteland not far from Vyônes, said to be the final resting place of the dwarfish necromancer Nathaire and his ten devil-given pupils. Its soil is poisoned and fit nurture for only the vilest of plants and fungi. The water that passes there beneath the hollow remains of its once-strident pines often becomes polluted. For nearly a century the land has been left undisturbed by men. But in recent weeks travelers on the high-wooded road have glimpsed the flames of bonfires on the river's bank in the night. They have heard the faint discordant echoes of voices carrying through the lifeless woods. The archbishop sent two monks from my abbey to investigate. Three days later their bodies washed ashore downriver. Their bones had been crushed near to powder. Since then several head of livestock have been found in similar condition among the farms outlying Vyônes and a number of barns and other structures have been demolished. Whatever wreaks this destruction draws closer to the city with each new slaughter. His holiness fears the worst for Vyônes and implores your kindness in directing your expertise to solving this mystery and mayhap saving many lives."

Le Chaudronnier tested the monk's tale against what he knew of Nathaire's Plain and the history of the dread necromancer. He was more familiar with the story than Albert suspected, having visited the plain on more than one occasion to secure certain rare alchemical ingredients that grew exclusively in such forsaken places. The land there did indeed suffer the miasma of impenetrable evil. It suffused the soil and girded the air, and le Chaudronnier conducted his business there in haste so as not to fall prey to its unhealthy influence. He had often concluded that one who set foot upon such benighted ground in the wrong frame of mind would be easy victim for its lingering malice.

"If you agree, we are to provide you with what supplies and men you might require and escort you to the River Isoile," said Brother Albert.

"With or without you we must return to the road at dawn," Giroux said. "And I would take some measure of rest while night is still upon us. What say you, sir?"

The mage rose from his seat and showed his visitors his back. He peered into the hungry flames beyond the hearth. Amber, iridescent embers swirled and floated into nothingness. Isobel, for all her exploration of things occult and mysterious, had never fully relinquished the faith of her birthright. With her body interred on holy ground, might her tortured soul finally know peace? If a chance existed, le Chaudronnier must take it.

"I am at your service. You may rest here, while I prepare," he said, "I will need little, but I must consult my archives and resources. Do not leave this room. Ignore whatever sounds or voices you may hear. We three are the only men present regardless of what your senses might tell you. You will be safe under my protection. Follow my instructions and we shall leave at first light. Any interruption will perhaps prove unhealthy for us all and delay us. Agreed?"

Albert and Giroux traded questioning glances then nodded in consent.

"We shall remain here and await your summons," Albert said.

With that the monk knelt directly before the fire. The heat drew beads of perspiration from his bald pate as he clasped his hands about a rosary and settled into quiet prayer. The marshal poured himself a fresh dram of brandy and eased into his chair to count the long, slow hours. But neither man passed the time in restful repose. The horrific cries and unearthly howls emanating from the deepest recesses of the dwelling fueled their wakefulness and unease until daybreak.

An hour before sunrise a gentle snow began to fall. The wind settled into a steady blow that kept up without quarter and stole the riders' warmth. The trio encountered few signs of life along their journey. Le Chaudronnier viewed this absence as a bad omen, and the gathering blackness on the western horizon only reinforced the sense of hopelessness gnawing at the back of his mind. His nocturnal investigations, which he had hoped would arm him with useful knowledge, had served only to deepen his puzzlement and consternation.

Giroux rode ahead, a stain against the deepening intensity of the snow-clad forestland as he marked the trail and set the pace. Brother Albert drew aside le Chaudronnier and attempted to enjoin him in conversation. The mage had little to say, but the monk expounded at length of his monastery and his Cistercian brothers, of their long history and tradition in the region, and of the ruined remains of the castle of Ylourgne, which stood above their cloisters in the deepening woods. The young cleric possessed a worldliness uncharacteristic of his years, and the few times he succeeded in engaging his companion, he demonstrated a knowledge and facility that extended well beyond the traditional realms of his religion.

"You've a surprisingly open mind," le Chaudronnier said.

"This is Averoigne, my friend, where a closed mind can lead to a sure death," Albert said. "Besides, the abbot's library is among the finest in the land. I believe you have underestimated me and my brethren."

By noon they came upon a small camp at a fork in the road, where three men-at-arms huddled around a sputtering fire that demanded their constant attention amidst the swift wind and downy precipitation. At the riders' approach the men rose and readied their weapons, but at a sign from Giroux, they gladly sheathed them again. What orders the marshal gave his men were lost on the intervening wind, but when le Chaudronnier and the monk reached the campsite, the fire had been doused and the soldiers had mounted their steeds.

"You say you have all you need for your investigation, Messire Chaudronnier," Giroux called to the mage, "but with these three men at my side, I would brave the gates of Lucifer's domain. They travel with us whether it suits you or not."

Le Chaudronnier assessed the fighting men, their coarse bearing and bodies toughened by rough lives. Love of honor burned in their deep-set eyes. They would do all within their power to secure their good standing with their leader and with their god.

"Their presence is of no weight to me," he said after a moment. "They will not interfere. Let them attend and test their souls against Nathaire's Plain."

The afternoon passed without measure. The sky grew uniform and coal-dark. Clouds swirled like silt stirred from a river bottom by mad currents, and though light sometimes slipped through, none among the riders could determine the location of the sun or mark its passage. The snow continued to descend and coated the woods with inch upon inch of accumulation. It was only Giroux's masterful scouting that enabled them to find their way. Even with good fortune they would not achieve Nathaire's Plain before nightfall, which meant passing hours camped on the edge of the most polluted land le Chaudronnier had ever known. The idea brought him no comfort, but they would have little choice—to enter the plain by dark would be the sheerest stupidity.

The riders knew they had begun their descent into the Valley of the Isoile when the road embarked along a circuitous decline. What scant speech they had shared ceased as they neared the river. A thick mist drifted up to them, spawned by the dank, unseen waters below. It floated in patches and mingled with the snow to form a tattered veil that obscured their surroundings. The steady thumping of their horses' hooves grew muted and dull in the shroud of weather. The quietude embraced them like a sleeping lover.

Through the stillness came a horrible and unexpected cry, penetrating the thick atmosphere with the power of a hot needle. It rose from the trees, wild but human, pregnant with mourning and anger, and announced the presence of others approaching around the bend in the road ahead of them.

Giroux drew his stallion to a halt and waved for the riders to fall in close to the side of the road. They complied, their bodies weary from travel and their lungs seared by the relentlessly cold air. They shivered with the wetness that had finally suffused even the deepest layers of their clothing to mingle with the cold perspiration of their bodies. And they watched. From past the edge of the hilly outcropping appeared a trio of ragged peasants, two of them dragging the remains of what once had been a wide, sturdy cart. Le Chaudronnier identified them as two men, both with streaks and splotches of blood smeared on their faces and clothing, and a somewhat less blood-stained woman. The males tugged the fractured wagon along on its two front wheels while the woman straggled beside them, wailing her grief to the uncaring wilderness.

"Stay where you are!" bellowed the marshal.

He raised his crossbow and drew it taught.

The frightened peasants obeyed. Giroux marched forward and identified himself. Fatigue and discomfort had worn away his temper until his impatience crackled in his voice. Le Chaudronnier could tell the marshal would not long brook the silence the peasants returned to his questioning demands. The mage coaxed his mount forward just as the marshal's anger reached its breaking point.

"Can't you see their wits have deserted them?" he said. "How can they be expected to answer to your dogging when they've barely got hold of their senses?"

Le Chaudronnier produced a flask and handed it to the eldest male with a warm invitation to drink. The liquid recalled the old man's wits in moments. Crimson patches burned flush in his face, and he swallowed another gulp before returning the container. Steadied by the draught, he attempted to explain the predicament of his family, but though his words came forth in coherent speech, what he spoke of only deepened the sheathe of mystery that enveloped them all.

The family had set forth three days ago with a cartload of charcoal, hoping to reach the gates of La Frênaie while the weather held, but the snow had come quicker than anticipated and forced them to tarry along the stretch of road that paralleled Nathaire's Plain. For a time they became lost when the road vanished into the mists. Some hours later they rediscovered their proper route, but barely had they set foot upon it when disaster assailed them. The sky above gathered into the form of a pale, titanic arm, raised a mighty fist, and plummeted through the hazy air to slam thunderously onto their wagon, killing their young daughter who slept there. What coal escaped being turned to dust by the blow erupted through the air, striking the old man and his son and scattering out of sight among the snowdrifts. The gargantuan hand then seized their workhorses and crushed them in its palm, spewing blood and pulped horseflesh in all directions. A cascade of demonic laughter shook the earth. Then the thing vanished. Stillness returned but for the woman's tears, and the men had seized up their damaged cart and fled.

The man spoke in the tones of an automaton, his mind able to produce a record of what he had experienced, but at the same time incapable of comprehending it. At hearing the tale recounted the woman fell to her knees, her body wracked with fresh waves of sorrow. Brother Albert, who had drawn near for the telling, dismounted and helped her to her feet, whispering prayers in her ear. He pressed a small crucifix into her open palm and bid her put her faith in the Lord who watched over them all, and who surely now watched over her daughter. Some small composure restored her, the woman took her place beside her husband and son, and the family carried on along the fast disappearing road. Before the peasants left, the riders gave them a share of their provisions to carry them through the night. It was meager succor for such broken souls, and most likely a futile kindness. Le Chaudronnier had seen dull madness gleaming in their eyes.

The peasant's story bolstered some of the mage's worst expectations, but he elected not to give them voice until he found certainty. He read concern in Brother Albert's eyes and knew the monk gave far more credence to the old man's account than their martial escort. The men-at-arms had already shrugged off the tale as madness and made ample folly of it once the shattered family went on their way. Giroux carried on, his expression equivocal, his attitude dismissive. It was an improvident mixture with which to face unknown evils, but le Chaudronnier had known far darker moments in his time.

Further along the road the riders encountered a meager hillside cove that offered reasonable shelter and so they chose to camp there for the night. Crepuscular gloom gave way to full darkness, and the men scrambled to clear the ground and gather suitable fuel for their fire. Le Chaudronnier was grateful to go no further for even here he could feel the black energy of Nathaire's Plain probing at his soul. Its power had grown since he had last traveled here, and its influence had spread outward. The night to come would be a difficult one, and their simple stores, which only satisfied their growling stomachs, did nothing to fortify them for the ordeal.

They set watches at intervals with two men to share each duty. In the morning they planned to descend to the plain, though the thickening snow threatened to trap them should it continue without pause. Le Chaudronnier and Brother Albert took the first watch while the men-at-arms went quickly to sleep within the small shelter they had constructed. Giroux sat upon a high boulder protected from the wind, enraveled in his thoughts, and intent upon staying awake until morning.

Brother Albert passed the time seeking conversation. Le Chaudronnier resisted, but even his stony silence and cold stares failed to dissuade the earnest monk. Thus Albert spoke at length of his monastery where he found all the needs of his existence fulfilled by a simple life of austerity and contemplation. Trouble, he explained to the disinterested mage, did not avoid the monastery. Conflict came to their community just as any other, but all things were resolved after a fashion. Tragedy did not leave them unattended as their long history in Averoigne attested, or even events as recent as Brother Garamond's vanishing a month before while carrying communications between the archbishop and the monastery.

"No doubt fallen prey to the vampires and specters of Averoigne," Albert said. "But tell me, Messire le Chaudronnier, what is the tale of Isobel Aickman? Was she your wife? Your lover? Why might one so young take her own life?"

"Fool," le Chaudronnier spat. "What would you know of it? You live protected by your god, shielded by your meaningless optimism. A monk lost in the woods is your concept of tragedy. How dare you question the life of one beautiful beyond words in both form and spirit?"

Brother Albert mumbled an entreaty for forgiveness then fell silent.

Le Chaudronnier saw genuine embarrassment in the monk's eyes, his words born only of the thoughtless inquisitiveness of youth, and he looked somewhat more kindly upon his companion. "Isobel was my student, then my friend, and finally my lover. She came here because those in her homeland—even her closest family—hounded her for her beliefs and her chosen life. Her father disowned her and cut Isobel off from her sisters. In the end it proved a blow too powerful to sustain. For all we accomplished, for all we had together, she knew it would never win back her place among her own kind, and in an oblique way, her entire life had been lived toward that unattainable goal. When she ended it, she left me a final letter that simply said, 'What would the weight of the world turned against me matter had I won over the lone voice whose hatred cuts the deepest? I cannot live without that which has been obliterated. Farewell.' "

"Do you believe burial on holy ground will soothe Isobel's dissatisfied soul?" asked Albert.

Le Chaudronnier nodded. "Perhaps. She never lost hold of her upbringing. But perhaps it is no more than foolish superstition."

"I called Brother Garamond's disappearance a tragedy because his situation was not unlike that of your beloved," said Albert. "What little Garamond spoke of his family made it clear he had joined our order as a last resort. His father demanded a son better attuned to the sword and more likely to provide suitable heirs for the family name, one like his two brothers before him, and when this proved not to be, he turned his last son away as a stranger. Deeply troubled, Garamond lost himself among the libertines of the Vyônes' underworld, but eventually his soul revolted. He craved redemption. He wished no more than to heal the wound that daily assailed him. Had he lived, perhaps he might have. I shall pray for Isobel. And for you, as I have prayed for Garamond."

"Do as you will," said the mage. "Our watch is over, and I wish to rest."

How long le Chaudronnier lay lapsed in fitful unconsciousness, he could not estimate. He awoke to Brother Albert's hand upon his shoulder and the dying echo of an awful scream lingering in his ears.

Fear coursed through him like poison. His lungs heaved for air.

"Luc, you are safe! We are camped on the high road along the Isoile," Albert stated. "You were beset by night terrors. You have trembled all night like a man whose conscience suffers. What is it that bedevils you?"

"I screamed . . . ?" asked le Chaudronnier.

Albert nodded.

"Then the better question to ask is what bedevils us both? For if I called aloud, why hasn't our brave escort attended us?"

Albert and le Chaudronnier peered through the slight opening of the shelter. The darkness rendered no secrets. Only the barest pale glow of their fire remained. The snow had ceased and all around them stretched a crystalline void.

"Giroux?" the mage called out.

Silence reigned for a scant few moments before response came in a tremendous pounding from the west. The ground shook with unnatural tremors. A ghastly peal of laughter thundered across the sky, turning the two men's stomachs to knots. They leapt to their feet, shocked to action by the realization that they stood alone and defenseless against an unseen power. The dreadful thumping of the massive, unknown thing grew closer.

Le Chaudronnier fled the shelter with Albert behind him, but both men succumbed to a fresh wave of dread at the sight that awaited them beyond the campfire. There lay two of the men-at-arms, their bodies smashed and crumpled like discarded parchment, their figures mangled and embedded into the snow and earth, blood and organic matter splashed around them within the perimeter of the shallow crater in which they rested. Realizing that the position of the shelter at the back of the cove had kept it hidden in shadow, le Chaudronnier surmised that the hulking abomination whose approach pounded through the night like a landslide had been recalled by his cry in the stillness. He scooped armfuls of snow and dirt onto the fire, smothering it until the sputtering flames sizzled and died, sending forth a diaphanous column of grey smoke. Without waiting for the final coal to fade, the mage dragged Brother Albert toward the road, hoping to hide amidst the snowdrifts and tangled dead wood on the far slope.

A burst of terrible cackling reverberated through the night, laughter like a thousand mad voices choking in convulsions of absurdity, shrieks like the demon-tainted spirits of a host of slaughtered innocents. The sound burrowed into their minds with fetid tendrils of fear that devoured rational thought and left only panic in its place. Blind, all-encompassing horror overwhelmed their beings and threatened to consume them. Le Chaudronnier struggled against the invasion, demanding the full extent of his arcane prowess to erect a fragile shield against the raw, undiluted insanity that imperiled him. Brother Albert had no such resources. He crumpled to the ground, whimpering and terrified, curled into a ball, and clamped his hands over his ears in a futile gesture. The mage grabbed hold and dragged the incoherent monk from the road, but his strength was fading and the dead weight proved too great until abruptly the burden lightened and both men tumbled off the edge of the road into the deep culvert.

Before le Chaudronnier could orient himself, Marshal Giroux clamped a hand around his mouth and revealed his presence. With him was the third man-at-arms. It was they who had helped carry Brother Albert to safety.

The explosive footsteps crashed all around and the land quivered with their weight. A heavy, unclean stench permeated the air, and though the abyssal darkness left him quite blind, le Chaudronnier sensed an immense presence towering above them, lingering, sniffing the air, hunting. He caught an unwelcome glimpse of its dead, glazed eyes reflecting a stray beam of moonlight high above, farther up than the tallest spire of the cathedral of Vyônes. The beast hesitated, waiting, seeking some sign of the noise that had recalled it to the campsite. Finding none, it soon shifted and resumed its retreat, marching through the heavy woodland toward the heart of Nathaire's Plain. When its bombastic footsteps faded, the marshal released le Chaudronnier's mouth.

Giroux grabbed the wizard by the arms. "No earthly thing so massive could be so stealthy," he blurted. "It came upon us without warning. Truly we face some pit-spewed demon. Jean and I were standing by the road when it came, but the others, by the fire—they had no chance. It smashed them with but a blow." Giroux clasped his head and turned away as if to hide the unfettered emotion dancing across his face. "My God, le Chaudronnier, what is it?"

The mage slid a small brass container from his pocket and un-clasped the lid. A faint glimmer emerged as he opened it, and he held the light up to Brother Albert's mud-caked face. The monk remained enraptured with terror, his mind lost to the world, driven from reason by fear. At that moment the demonic beast unleashed a last inhuman shriek that reached them across the expanse of bare treetops and shook their convictions.

"Will he recover?" Giroux asked.

"Somewhat, but he'll never be the man he was. For one so young to be so enfeebled is truly a loss," answered le Chaudronnier. "But I know of none who succumb to the mad cries and laughter of *le revenant* and later regain their faculties. Yet, three of us weathered the assault with our minds intact. I possess defenses against such dangers, but why you and Jean were spared, I do not know."

"Jean is deaf," said Giroux. "As for me, who can say? But you call this thing a revenant—you tell me it is a ghost?"

"Not a ghost. It's a necromantic monstrosity, vengeance given form through the most black-hearted of spells. It is the rotten flesh of the dead infused with vicious new life. Such is the creation of thrice-great Nathaire who sought to revenge himself against the people of Vyônes in 1281. Derided for his hideousness and small stature, Nathaire knit a patchwork giant from the bodies of the dead with which to terrorize Averoigne. Only his former pupil, Gaspard du Nord, stopped him. But once raised a revenant cannot be destroyed for a hundred years. The beast has lain fallow beneath Nathaire's Plain, waiting some new soul with a fresh thirst for vengeance to revive it."

"Then Nathaire has returned?" asked Giroux.

"Nathaire's festering soul and flesh remain forever a part of the revenant, but it is not his will that guides it. A new call for evil has arisen," said le Chaudronnier.

"How can you be certain? Nathaire was a powerful necromancer."

"I am certain because before we left my home last morning I summoned Nathaire's soul from the hell in which it abides and asked it," le Chaudronnier said.

Giroux recoiled at his memory of the otherworldly voices he had heard in the mage's dwelling. His stony face trembled with disgust. "In the morning we must find the revenant, and put it to its final end."

"Have you not listened to me?" argued le Chaudronnier. "The year is 1379. Nathaire's abomination is but ninety-seven-years old. It cannot be destroyed for another three years, and even then the task presses the impossible."

"But it has been stopped before?"

"Yes, after a fashion. Put to sleep by du Nord," le Chaudronnier confirmed. "That option, however, is no longer open to us. The powder du Nord used was of Nathaire's own devising and knowledge of its manufacture died with him. Nathaire's spirit refused to grant me the knowledge. Our best chance will be to slay the one whose wish for vengeance awoke the thing and drives it."

"Then we shall go to Nathaire's Plain and carry out an execution."

Le Chaudronnier said nothing. What would be by daylight would be. He comforted himself with thoughts of Isobel and the prospect of her happiness wherever she had gone after leaving him. If his deeds on the morrow could secure peace for his beloved then he would willingly let slip his mortal frame to accomplish it.

The next day began in dispute. Sunlight pried through the cloud cover. Narrow patches of blue sky lay exposed, but the horizon's persistent darkness signaled that the respite would be short-lived. Le Chaudronnier woke to Giroux and Jean arguing while they buried their fallen comrades. The lack of ceremony or rites to accompany the interment upset Jean, and Giroux criticized him for his sentiment. Tempers flared again when the marshal demanded that they leave Brother Albert behind so that they might face Nathaire's revenant unencumbered. But Le Chaudronnier, who had developed an unexpected affection for the monk, refused. In the end they strapped the mindless cleric into his saddle and let le Chaudronnier lead his horse by rope.

Thus they entered the wild desolation of Nathaire's Plain.

The putrescent energy of the place sickened them and sapped their willpower. All around stood nothing but long-dead vegetation speckled by fresh growth and fetid matter too abhorrent to consider. Like rotten wood beneath its bark, the snow-encrusted earth gave softly under the weight of the horses' hooves. The air came laden with the moist slickness of oil and fat, and with each step the grotesque setting worked its vile notions into the cracks of their minds, drowning their moods in a tide of futility.

Le Chaudronnier tried to guide the others to protect their thoughts and block out the deathly illness that intruded upon them. It was all that stood between them and utter despair, and in a subtle manner, Giroux fell back so that the mage became their leader—they were now beyond any territory the marshal felt competent to chart.

By the river's edge the stench reached unimaginable intensity. Brother Albert, who seemed slightly more aware of his existence than he had that morning, vomited upon himself several times when confronted with the noxious fumes. The others gagged back the bile that rose within them. They traversed the majority of the plain without incident. The sky darkened once more with the renewed threat of snow. Wary of the stillness, le Chaudronnier gathered them in a circle.

"Something is amiss," he said. "We should have encountered the revenant by now."

"Could it have fled?" asked Giroux.

"From us? Don't be ridiculous," answered the mage. "Perhaps it is hunting along the road."

Le Chaudronnier, with his back to the river thirty feet away, reacted not to the sudden torrent of water that fountained upward, but to Jean, whose face paled with shock as he drew his blade. Giroux immediately followed, urging the mage to order his horse around to face the river. Their quarry had approached beneath the oily surface and erupted forth casting toxic sludge in all directions and forcing the scum-coated water crashing over the bank. The creature surpassed nightmares. A towering, decomposed homunculus lashed together from the flesh and bone of hundreds of dead men, a gigantic receptacle for hatred and rage so fiery that even the worm-riddled clay of the giant threatened to rupture from containing it. Its face burned with an eldritch aura, a death mask caricature of the long dead necromancer who had crafted it. Ropy tangles of obsidian hair flailed about its skull like eels. Clinging to the abomination's back were the remnants of a massive basket strapped between its shoulders. Dangling there with limbs and bones embedded in the revenant's gelatinous skin were the squirming forms of Nathaire's ten pupils. Among them an eleventh figure, one still human and living, clung to his footing at the base of the undead Titan's neck.

The revenant arched its back, dropped wide its crooked jawbone and screeched to drown out the wind. Like the foul, feral grunts of pleasure uttered by the Satyr's consort, like the howling of witches burned alive for their ungodly ways, like the whisper of skin flayed from living muscle magnified a million times, the voice crushed the riders' souls. Even Jean, who could not hear the dreadful wail, reacted as the raw waves of sound rippled through him. He fell from his mount in unfettered panic. The assault threatened to splinter le Chaudronnier's defenses. He looked to others. Giroux contorted in agony but somehow clung to his wits. Brother Albert, unfazed in his madness, giggled like a child, gazed upward, and waved to the dark figure atop the revenant. Albert's mouth moved, but his words died in the discordant echo of the revenant's undead song.

Le Chaudronnier dropped from his horse. Familiar black shapes swam around him, indigo silhouettes that circled like wanton sharks, and an oft-tasted dread welled inside him—the black thoughts of his subconscious drawn forth by the revenant's summons. Already the riders were incapacitated. The mage saw no chance of survival, but Brother Albert's actions resounded with his intuition. In the monk's senseless gesticulation and yelling lay some piece of the puzzle, and though oblivion loomed mere seconds away, he refused to let go of any small hope.

Le Chaudronnier grabbed Albert's cloak and yanked him downward to his ear. The howl of the revenant dipped in a lull, and the mage picked out Brother Albert's words. "Brother . . . Garamond . . . hello, Brother . . . down here . . . Garamond . . ."

The mage whirled about and peered through the gloom at the commanding shape clutching foul strands of the revenant's hair like reigns. The man wore the clothing required by Brother Albert's order, the soiled and torn garb now barely recognizable. His hair was trimmed in the accompanying manner. The missing Brother Garamond had come to Nathaire's Plain and found himself a monster. The lunatic monk flailed like a mad puppet and cried inaudible obscenities into the cold air. His sight fell upon Albert and le Chaudronnier. The revenant raised its arm of withered flesh and mineralized bone. A deepening shadow engulfed the two men upon the river bank.

Seconds passed, but the crushing weight did not fall.

Le Chaudronnier, who had turned away from his imminent doom, coiled around in time to see the limp figure of Brother Garamond drop like a stone into the ebon waters of the Isoile. A long shaft protruded from his torso. The revenant stood frozen in place, the tatters of its being fluttering in the wind, a hateful grimace locked on its face. Its eyes simmered with cold anger.

Still atop his mount Giroux seized a fresh bolt from the quiver at his side and reloaded his crossbow. His chest heaved with exertion.

"It is done!" he cried.

But le Chaudronnier could see that the revenant yet seethed, awaiting a new command. Brother Garamond had only been wounded. He gathered Albert and fled from the prone giant, helping Jean to his feet as well, and leading them to rejoin the marshal.

The deaf man refused to take his place by Giroux's side. He unbuckled his sword belt and threw it to the ground at the feet of his leader's mount. He spat and barked words malformed by his passion, his meaning beyond le Chaudronnier's grasp. Giroux turned his cold eyes toward the man and shrugged.

"Then so be it, idiot," the marshal said. "I trusted you with my life, yet you cast off my loyalty."

Giroux turned his crossbow toward Jean's chest. The tortured man-at-arms punched himself and screamed more words that only Giroux understood.

Le Chaudronnier thrust himself between the two men. "Enough!" he bellowed. "Settle your petty bickering later. Your bolt has bought us but a brief reprieve, Giroux. Brother Garamond yet lives, and so the revenant. We must stand together."

"That is the matter at hand, Messire le Chaudronnier," Giroux said. "Jean has renounced my leadership for he does not approve of how I have treated my son."

The troubled le Chaudronnier searched Jean's tear-streaked face. Rage, heated and righteous, burned there. The deaf man pointed to the place in the river where Brother Garamond had slipped beneath the surface then gestured to Giroux, croaking again in speech only the marshal could decipher for his years of friendship with his soldier.

"Garamond . . . your son?" breathed le Chaudronnier.

"Jean thinks I drove him beyond reason with abuse and torture.

He says I brought this renewed evil upon all of Averoigne," Giroux said. "He calls me inhuman because I did not pause to mourn those sons I lost in the night, Garamond's brothers. And for this insolence, he must die. Now, stand aside, devil-worshiper!"

Le Chaudronnier enjoyed no time in which to make his choice. The crumbling roots of a long-dead, uprooted pine crashed among them, hurling him to his back. Jean disappeared amidst the tangle of old wood and Albert fell into the mud. The heavy base of the trunk collided with Giroux and projected him from his saddle with brutal force. His mount toppled sideways onto him.

The revenant screamed, and the whole of the dark plain quaked with the awful cacophony. Brother Garamond dragged himself free of the river muck and stalked along the bank. Nathaire's necrotic giant followed him. Twisting its powerful, unnatural muscles, it hurled the tree into the distance and then crouched behind Garamond, who had knelt beside his father. The lunatic monk chortled and gasped, probing his father's broken body, touching and prodding, caressing, testing the extent of his progenitor's wounds. He leapt to his feet and danced in circles, hopping from one foot to the next, unleashing discordant guffaws of pleasure, gyrating and bouncing with sinister glee unleashed. With a sudden move, he dropped to all fours and spat in his father's face.

Giroux struggled to breath. Blood soaked through his tunic, but the terrible hardness in his eyes had not faded. He stared at his son like a cat might survey a plump insect. When Garamond next crouched beside his mortally-wounded patriarch, Giroux seized the boy by the neck and thrust the broken shaft of a crossbow bolt through his throat. Vermillion poured forth and Garamond's noxious joy turned to choking gasps. The marshal snapped his wrist, wrenching the arrowhead deeper, and then Garamond fell lifeless across his father's figure, his last breath gushing out of him.

The revenant remained, alert, the horrible glow still alight in its eyes. Fresh laughter cut through the afternoon. The towering, charnel golem crouched until its hideous, leering face hung inches from le Chaudronnier.

Giroux struggled to raise himself on his elbows. "You . . . sorcerers . . . brought this to us . . . you . . . claimed my last son . . . ," uttered the marshal. "Now . . . you pay . . . ."

The revenant swayed and thrust to its full height. It lingered for a moment, gazing downward before it raised its horrendously thick leg and poised its foot above the head of the weary mage. But once more, something stayed its blow. In a heartbeat all life fled from the dread creation and it crumpled backward plummeting into the thick waters of the Isoile, roiling foulness in every direction, until the black waters flowed back to embrace it and claim it as their own. Le Chaudronnier looked to Giroux. The marshal lay dead with Jean's dagger embedded in his heart, his lust for vengeance extinguished. Jean and le Chaudronnier gathered the two surviving mounts, placed Albert in the saddle of one and then fled Nathaire's Plain for the cold comfort of the empty road and the heavy, slate sky.

Some weeks later le Chaudronnier stood beside the freshly filled grave of Isobel Aickman, now interred on the grounds of the cathedral of Vyônes. Sunlight came down in welcome pillars through the hazy morning. A single priest presided over the burial. The archbishop had refused le Chaudronnier an audience, but the mage had delivered his report through intermediaries who had also brought word of its acceptance.

Brother Albert was returned to his monastery and the care of his order. Henri Giroux's remains were left to rot beside those of his son on the lifeless riverbank where both had fallen. It had been Giroux's own secret wishes for vengeance that had shielded him from the madness of the revenant, and so the plain made a fitting grave, thought le Chaudronnier. Of Jean, nothing was known. He left Vyônes within a day of their arrival and said nothing of his destination.

Le Chaudronnier passed the bright morning alone by the new grave of his beloved before undertaking the long journey home to his solitude. Whether Isobel would now know peace, le Chaudronnier could never discover. But that night his dread visions tormented him still, and he felt certain in his bones that the blackness would haunt him for many nights to come, a revenant of sorts that was all his own.

THE RING OF EIBON

by Ron Shiflet

The Ring of Eibon, forged with reddish stone
And set with a gemstone of purple hue,
Contained a demon of whom it was known,
Would reveal the answers long hid from view.
When desiring esoteric answer,
Over burning amber the ring was held,
Much less ghoulish than the necromancer,
With his rotting corpses and truth to meld.

The greatest sorcerer of any age,
Was Eibon, so the histories reveal,
Even demons were wary of this mage,
And the truth from him could not conceal.
Eibon's Ring compelled those summoned to speak,
Revealing all knowledge that he might seek.

THE LITTLE AND THE BIG

by Michael Minnis

It was widely known throughout Averoigne that Mère Antoinette was a witch and mother of toads. It was also widely known that she was a rather amorous creature who'd had many lovers, most of them unwittingly duped by her spells or potions.

What was not known was that Mère Antoinette had a mate and husband of sorts—a hulking, jealous, ill-tempered thing named Gros Vert.

He, like her children, was a toad but enormous in size, big as an ox. His warty skin was as thick and tough as triple-boiled leather. He was, unlike most toads, a muted shade of green, like verdigris. His head was the size of a wine cask, while his great lipless mouth was as wide as a trapdoor. All toads are fat, of course, but Gros Vert was exceptionally so. In fact, he could hardly hop, and preferred instead to waddle awkwardly about on his spindly, misshapen legs like a spider.

Unlike Mère Antoinette, Gros Vert could neither assume a fair form nor cast spells. Magic was a matter of profound indifference to him. Nor could he disguise the faint earthy mustiness of his odor. He understood speech but could not speak himself, and in fact made very little sound whatsoever for a creature of his size. The most warning a victim ever had of his presence might be a snort or clotted snuffle before he ungainly lumbered forth to snap them up.

He was a spiteful thing, was Gros Vert, and only the innumerable little toads of the marshes near Les Hiboux loved him. They thronged about him, sang to him, eagerly awaited his silent bidding. In the long dry days of late summer they covered his gross body with their own, to protect him from the sun. Come snow, they dug deep into the mud to prepare his winter bed. Should man or animal stumble into their shadowed, creaking kingdom, the smaller toads did their best to herd them toward their master. In lean months they became his food. But the marshes of Les Hiboux throng with innumerable little toads; never once did Gros Vert's appetite diminish them, and never once did they disobey his wishes.

Few men had ever seen Gros Vert, for he lived deep within the marshes and rarely came out. Occasionally a herdsman might run back to his village with a breathless tale of the monster that had suddenly lumbered forth to spread ruin among his flock, and occasionally a child disappeared in the marshes, but few paid these stories any mind. A great toad, indeed—a toad whose head, like that of all toads, was said to hold a buried jewel of unsurpassed beauty, a jewel said to pierce the minds of animals and make their thoughts known. A toad that ate sheep and men like flies. Preposterous. The peaceable kingdom of animals did not allow for such hideous permutations on God's grand design.

But it was thus, and so it came one day that Mère Antoinette took one lover too many, and Gros Vert decided he had endured this state of affairs long enough. When the huge toad came across his mate's latest unlucky conquest, he snapped the poor lad up and swallowed him whole. Gros Vert had done this before, so while Mère Antoinette was annoyed, she was not unduly upset. There were always other lovers to be had.

Gros Vert was far angrier than usual, however, and the little toads that crowded about him sensed it. They, too, became agitated, and hopped and thronged and spilled over one another in their eagerness to punish and hurt. And so finally one clear, rushing spring day the toads cornered Gros Vert's duplicitous mate—a swarming mass of flopping, flabby, cold little bodies that for once Mère Antoinette could neither command nor dispel. Gros Vert then confronted her, and though he could not speak the jewel allowed her to dimly sense the furious pall about his crude but powerful mind.

Because many of Mère Antoinette's lovers had come from the village of Les Hiboux, she was loath to name that place for fear of its destruction, so instead she said, "The world outside your land is full of men who seek the wives of others. Far and wide these men wander, even into such distant and dismal realms as your own, my noble lord. They come from the great and wicked city of Vyônes."

And so for three days Gros Vert remained sunk deep within thought. His lesser brethren were baffled and milled about uselessly in the absence of his authority, falling back upon their old, instinctive habits. But by the third day the great toad had arrived at a decision. The smaller toads were summoned in unheard of numbers. That night

Gros Vert lumbered forth from his kingdom into the undisturbed countryside, in his wake an immense living, hopping carpet of little toads.

Gros Vert was not alone in matters of fidelity and the heart, for on a humble farmstead near the city of Vyônes there lived Robert, a farmer of indifferent skill, and Brigitte, his long-suffering wife.

Robert was not a good husband. He was not a good farmer. In fact, he was not much good at anything apart from drinking, fighting and avoiding work. The latter he left largely to his young wife, so that after a long day in the fields she often returned to their cottage to find the spinning wheel or the little ones awaiting her, and her husband in blissful bibulous sleep.

Usually such chronic male indolence breaks many a female back. But in Brigitte it cultivated a great cleverness and unshakable will, and she did what was necessary to provide for herself and the three children. She played at love with the ugly but wealthy seigneur of their tiny village so that he might not seize Robert's land for failure to pay rent. She feigned tearful, pleading piety so that the tithe collector as well left her family alone. She sometimes took to the road for weeks at a time in search of paying work—hauling wood and water, tending to livestock, spinning wool, cleaning ovens, loading manure, separating wheat from chaff. And if work was not to be had, or if the families she helped sought to cheat her, she stole, filching eggs from chicken coops and milk from cows. It was a situation to excite neither pride nor happiness in the young woman, but it had made her strong and far more clever than most.

The same, however, cannot be said of Robert. Unlike his wife, he had decided long ago that the contest was lost. The little people, the *petites gens*, could not hope to best the rich and powerful, *les gros*, the Big People who dangled succor tantalizingly before their lessers and then pulled it away should they clutch for it. The efforts of his wife alternately amused and exasperated him. It was all entirely in the hands of fate whether the harvest succeeded or failed, or if the children should thrive or die. Besides, what was Fate anyway but one of *les gros* itself, like the King and the Church, the seigneurs and the tax collectors and the merchants? And which of the *petites gens* had ever triumphed against that lot? Better that his young wife should simply accept the dismal state of things, grudgingly do the minimum expected of her, and seek solace in drink and sleep and dreams.

Brigitte endured such cynical musings as she did her life, for there was really no escape from either. Should she protest or complain, Robert would threaten to turn her and their three children out of their home for good and let the wilderness receive them.

"A woman alone in the great wide world, with three little ones tugging on her skirts, hungry and afraid," Robert once said, grinning while his wife went about her countless chores. "How could you hope to survive? It is best to remain here with your good husband. It is best to accept the rule of *les gros*, of Fate, and accept your situation." When drunk he liked to fancy himself a dispassionate philosopher amused by the futility of others.

"I do not believe in Fate," Brigitte replied. "And I do not accept my situation."

"Then by all means, take your brats and go forth," Robert said. "Seek something else. I don't care. Find company in wolves and bandits, if you wish. But remember—you will leave here without so much as a *sou* to your name. And, if by chance I should I come upon you again, I will kill you."

Robert laughed at his wife as if this was some grand jest, but Brigitte knew he was not joking. So instead she returned to her bitter, endless labor, wondering all the while if her worthless husband knew that she considered him no better than one of *les gros* herself.

It was at this time that curious calamity and frightening phenomena struck the countryside, with little in the way of warning or omen.

It all began subtly enough, so that the peasantry noticed little beyond the sudden disinclination of their livestock to roam and feed where they usually did. Sheep avoided the lowlands in favor of the hills. Cattle kept close to their pens. Even the pigs forsook the woods and the acorns they love so dearly.

This puzzled the peasants greatly, for there was nothing to explain such unaccountable behavior. There had been neither comet nor eclipse. There had been neither blasphemy nor monstrous birth. In fact, nothing whatsoever had happened, but for the increasing number of toads one found underfoot, in the grass and on the doorstep.

At first, there were only a handful of them here and there—fat brown complaining things with pebbled skins, which gave ground only if prodded. Perhaps the recent rains had flooded the swamps where they lived, allowing them to go abroad. But more and more of them appeared as the weather cleared and the day wore on. Before long the landscape was studded with their ugly little forms, and they grew increasingly bold. They filled the ditches and the culverts. They burst into dwellings and nothing could be done to keep them out of the wells or the food stores. They launched themselves at those who came too close or kicked them or tried to sweep them away.

Then, as if from nowhere, came the mass of them, burying the golden fields beneath their countless bodies, the hopping vanguard of some vast unknown migration, some flapping, flabby, flat-footed horde. It was a wave of toads as high as a man's waist and broad as a castle wall, hopping and crawling and squirming, a tide that knew no obstacles. Crossed by a stone fence, they simply piled upon each other and then over it. Confronted by a barred door, they merely heaped against the house's walls and spilled through the windows. They drove all other animal life before them—deer, rabbits, stoats, foxes, field mice, and any number of birds. All fled the foul, thronging bodies as well as the great hideous green shape among them, the shape that fell upon any man who dared stand his ground.

Hideous tales soon reached the people of Vyônes, as did any number of frightened refugees, their carts and wagons piled high with whatever belongings they could take with them.

Les gros, of course, were initially disinclined to heed the wild talk of their inferiors, feeling it the sort of collective hysteria to which simple folk are prone. A plague of toads led by a monster of their breed, indeed! What did the commoners think this was, the Egypt of antiquity?

It was a season of war with the hated English after all, so nerves were running high. That, and the *petites gens* had always been, well, *imaginative*. But when villagers began pounding on the city gates and a royal hunting party reported no game in the countryside but for numerous toads, the Big People gathered to take stock of the situation.

As the number of toads increased, *les gros* grew proportionally more concerned. There was much learned discussion among them. The Big People stroked their beards and assured themselves that this was no more than a curiosity, a passing madness among the lower life forms, some inexplicable impulsive drive that would dissipate as suddenly as it appeared.

The toads waxed ever more numerous, however. The land was alive, crawling with them. Something should be done, but what?

A general mustering of arms was out of the question. Most of the city's soldiery was committed to campaigns further north and besides, whom would they take the field against? Toads? And just how should such a battle be fought, if it could be fought at all? It was ultimately decided that the outcome of the contest lay with the fate of the *gros crapaud*, the great toad that bound his lesser kin to his will. But who was willing to challenge such a creature?

In the end a knight came forward—Louis-Charles de Morineau, who had fought at Nicopolis and Rachowa during the last great crusade against the Turks. He had narrowly escaped execution as their prisoner, and been ransomed for a handsome sum.

His bravery and skill in combat was unquestioned. He feared nothing, so that the flopping horde was beneath his contempt—so far beneath, in fact, that he initially would not take the field against the toads. It was an insult, a task for the peasants! But the city burghers pressed de Morineau, speaking of a great monstrous toad that must be slain if this plague was to end. Still, the knight did not heed the townspeoples' pleas. It was only when many extravagant promises and offers of gold and silver were made to de Morineau that he finally took action.

It was a grand spectacle, this knight come forth to do battle, mounted and in full armor. But if his bravery and splendor were exceeded by anything, it was his vanity and love of luxury. Saddle blankets of satin, servants in silk livery, and trumpeters with silver instruments were requested of the stunned citizenry, as were silver platters and gold vessels, the richest of delicacies and the finest of wines, footpillows and cooks and man-servants and hunting falcons.

Soon the entourage numbered one hundred in all, of which only one could fight. Among their number was a monk to serve de Morineau in matters of piety, as well as a winsome and nubile maidservant to serve him in matters otherwise.

And so the entourage went forth to slay Gros Vert, and de Morineau boasted of what he would do to the great toad when he found him. He would lay open his head with his sword, spit him on his lance! He would cut the great jewel from his head! Why, his *horse* would trample the pitiful toad army beneath their hooves, should the little creatures dare show themselves! And so de Morineau ate and drank and made love to the maidservant, and never once displayed the least bit of concern or caution, so that his expedition came to resemble a carnival, a festival of indulgences.

And like all festivals, it drew attention from afar. De Morineau awoke late one morning to find many toads within his camp—fat little things, hopping about as if they owned the place. The maidens were beside themselves with disgust. The man-servants kicked them aside, knocked them off the chests and stools and tables. Away the toads hopped, back into the long grass. It was not discovered until later that they had gone to great lengths to foul the food and wine and silk with their own wastes, so that the whole camp soon smelled abominably.

The entourage was still in some disorder when the toads later returned, in numbers that struck fear in the hearts of all—a great flopping wall of them and *him*, the great beast, Gros Vert, upon whose massive back his smaller kin clustered like Carthaginians upon a war elephant.

De Morineau, though amazed, was not dismayed. The trumpeters blew a challenge and de Morineau's lover tied a silken scarf to his arm as a blessing. None of this appeared to impress Gros Vert, who merely squatted on his flabby haunches and waited.

Again the trumpeters blew. The knight leveled his lance, spurred his huge horse, and charged. Thundering across the plain de Morineau came, and his entourage watched with great confidence and anticipation. And as if at some invisible signal, the horde of little toads went forward to meet him like a tide of mud.

What happened next left all incredulous, struck them speechless. As de Morineau had expected, the little toads were utterly helpless against the full might of his chivalry. They were crushed, extinguished, trampled into jelly beneath his horses' pounding hooves. But such were their numbers that his mount soon lost its footing in the slick mire of slime and blood. Screaming the horse fell, sending its master crashing to the ground.

Even so, there was still little the pattering toads could do, for the knight was clad in the thickest and heaviest of plate armor—so heavy in fact, that he had extraordinary difficulty in righting himself. Even when he did, he soon fell again, and so up and down he went like a broken toy.

Gros Vert finally lumbered toward de Morineau, and a clumsy battle of sorts began. Neither toad nor man could best the other, and instead each awkwardly fumbled and strained and pushed against his foe so that the gathered entourage began to smile, then chuckle, and finally guffaw at this ludicrous spectacle. The monk lost his ethereal reserve and laughed until he choked. Even de Morineau's lover could not suppress a smile.

It was true that even Gros Vert could not bite through such armor, but that was not his intent. Instead he finally bore de Morineau down, seized the knight by his feet with his huge mouth, and dragged him to a nearby, sodden cattle wade. The humor of the crowd rapidly faded. It evaporated entirely when the great toad remorselessly pressed the screaming man facedown into the liquid mud with its great webbed feet until he drowned, and then pissed long on the lifeless body as if to demonstrate its opinion of knighthood and chivalry in general.

Gros Vert then charged the late knight's entourage, but it was no more than a feint, a gesture, an idle amusement. Nevertheless ninety-nine souls fled in abject terror, abandoning trumpets and foot pillows, wine casks and satin blankets, silver platters and gold cups. The little toads swarmed over the aftermath of the scene. Immensely pleased with the havoc their master had wreaked, they crowded about him and sang his praises.

With the demise of Louis-Charles de Morineau went the city's single opportunity to stop the monster. In the days that followed, more and more peasants spilled into Vyônes from the surrounding country. Among them were Brigitte, her husband Robert, and their three children.

The family rode in a two-wheeled cart piled with their belongings. The little ones did not understand what was happening, and were inclined to think it all some grand game. As for Robert, he was blissfully drunk and could not have cared less—he sat in the back of the cart bouncing the littlest child on his knee. Brigitte, as usual, was alone with her fears.

She knew salvation lay not in chivalry—the humiliating demise of de Morineau was ample proof of that, as was the fact that the seigneur of her village was among the first to flee the onslaught. Nor was piety of proof against this latest menace—the village priest had barricaded himself within his church and answered to no callers. No, sanctuary lay only behind thick stone walls. And it seemed the intent of the city guards to allow no one else behind them.

"The city is full, we can take no more!" they cried. "Go back!"

"We can't!" the peasants replied. "There is nowhere else to go! Let us in!"

Rising fear led to ugliness. The peasantry and city guards pushed against each other, shouting and cursing. There were threats and offers and wild accusations, any number of shaken fists. There was talk of rushing the gate—the guards were outnumbered. They could be overpowered. Scuffles broke out within the crowd and between the two sides, and while no real injury was done Brigitte sensed real bloodshed was not far off.

Robert, on the other hand, watched the apish gesticulations of his worthless fellowmen with good-humored contempt. Then he had an idea. He hopped down from the cart, searched about for a stone— there was a *les gros* among the guards whose looks he didn't like, a warden of some sort. Some self-important bastard giving orders. Best to teach him a lesson in humility. Robert let fly with his stone. It struck the warden just above the eye and opened a great cut, driving the man to his knees. At this, a great shout erupted from the city guard, and they tried to push through the peasants toward Robert and his family. The two sides came to hard, bloody blows then, and Robert found himself in his natural element, swinging drunkenly even as his children cried in terror and his wife screamed at him to stop.

The melee may have gone on for some time had not Brigitte seen them, crawling through the long grass toward the city gates. A multitude of toads, not hopping but creeping, as if they expected to take the stymied caravan by ambush. Among them, the great lumbering monster, the beast that had crushed de Morineau underfoot like an insect.

"It is here!" Brigitte cried. "The monster is here!"

Then the peasants saw him as well, and in a great, shrieking, panic-stricken crush all pressed toward the city gate, abandoning weapons and wagons and livestock. Some escaped before the gates were shut. Others were trampled to death by their fellowmen in the press to flee, or snapped up like insects by the great toad. The smaller toads swarmed triumphantly over the bodies of the dead—among them Robert, slain by a city guardsman in the confusion.

Gros Vert, meanwhile, pressed hard and with appalling strength against the city gate but found he could not break it. City guards high above threw spears at him, and the huge toad was forced to retire. Three times in all Gros Vert tried to break the city gates, and three times he was driven back.

The Big People, recovering from their shock, celebrated their victory. Gros Vert, indeed! A stupid puffed-up beast that had finally encountered something greater than himself, walls neither he nor his brethren could surmount! And so *les gros* mocked the drab host gathered at their gates, and even the *petites gens* joined them in their fun—a rare camaraderie, indeed.

Brigitte was not among them. Not only was Robert dead, she knew the field belonged to Gros Vert and his vast army, and that the great brute was unlikely to relinquish it. A siege was in the making. When she told the others this, they dismissed her.

"What can they possibly do, little woman?" asked a jovial, ruddy-faced man-at-arms. "They have no guns. They have no ladders. They have neither siege towers nor battering rams. What can they possibly do, this army of toads, but sing to us?"

"If you are so sure of yourselves, then take the field against them," Brigitte replied.

The city guards merely laughed.

As for Gros Vert, he was not about to uselessly throw his kin against such mighty walls, where they would be slaughtered by stones and arrows and molten lead. No, instead they must probe this fortress, seek out its weaknesses, the chinks in its armor, overcome its defenses, as he had overcome the vainglorious knight.

So he contented himself by swallowing a goat, and prepared for a siege.

For two weeks little of import happened. The army outside Vyônes' walls made no attempt to enter the city, and the garrison within made no attempt to break out. Autumn had begun to burn in the country-side, and there was a general consensus among the besieged that once the weather turned cold, the little toads would either be forced to re-tire, or die. Few took the siege seriously, in fact. They treated it as a biblical scourge turned comedy. *Les gros* laughed at the toads. So did the *petites gens*.

That is, until the little toads found their way into the city. No one was quite sure how they managed it. Perhaps they had squirmed their way up through the extensive, half-flooded catacombs beneath the city—no one knew precisely how far or where they went, after all. Or perhaps they had hidden themselves among the belongings of the flee-ing peasantry. There were many theories, of course. Some claimed to have seen toads falling from the sky during a particularly violent storm. More learned sorts spoke of the mysteries of *spontaneous generation*, and that the toads had simply sprung up from the earth like ambulatory fungus.

All that was certain was that there were now toads where there weren't toads before. A man might leave his house and notice one squatting upon a nearby barrel, watching him. Still another might find two or three under his bed, or be presented one of the ugly things by his child. A stable-boy might chase a small phalanx of them out of a stall with a broom, only to have them return later and in greater num-bers. Then a monk found the nave of the cathedral thronging with them—an ugly and contentious mob of tiny parishioners who blanket-ed the pews and made sport of the holy water.

People began killing them. They drowned them, burned them, crushed them underfoot, threw them into sacks and struck them against walls, smashed them with whatever was handy. The little toads suffered dreadfully and fled to secret places, and the people congratu-lated themselves upon their victory. But they had hardly gone to their beds that night when the little toads began to sing. From the gutters and sewers, from the middens and cellars, from under the floors and between the walls came their song—a monotonous cacophony of chirps, creaks, squeaks, peeps, scrapes, cries, trills and lilts, a choir that could not quite find the right key. It was a dreadful, ancient sound; disturbing yet hypnotic, eerie but lulling, precluding all sleep. The commonplace stopped their ears, grumbled, put their pillows over their heads. More sensitive folk listened instead, and to them the little toads' music spoke of something. It spoke of mud and deep still water and the endless cycle of the seasons, of burrowing and hiding, of a time long before Man, before Eden, before even the reign of serpents and dragons when all was wet, all was lush and steaming. All had belonged to them, the young sun and rain—this world but newly formed out of chaos, out of dust and gas. From this chaos they had crawled and squirmed and hopped, breathing fitfully, between worlds, and into this chaos all would someday return.

Night after night after night the little toads sang their song of time, and the people of Vyônes began to go quite mad with frustration and weariness. Only the stone-deaf were able to sleep. By day the besieged populace stumbled witlessly through their duties, but more often than not they slept at their stations—the man-at-arms leaning upon his spear, the smith with his head upon his workbench, the baker beside his oven and the monk in his garden. Even the beggars slept, clustered like winter birds in the alleys and gangways, their heads tucked together. The cathedral bells were silent. Scarcely a child shouted or a dog barked. Only the nocturnal cats were unaffected, but even they were amazed by this supreme upset of their familiar world. And over all things, toads—hopping and crawling or simply sunning themselves upon the bodies of the sleeping.

Not all were under their spell, however. Brigitte, used to little sleep, had known enough to stop her ears and those of her children with wax each night, but knew this state of affairs could not continue. The city stores of food and water would soon run short—the little toads had already fouled much of it—and the harvest could not be brought in. No help could be expected from the outside. By the time the cold weather that all hoped for arrived, things could be very bad indeed. Lastly, the men would not fight the monster, so the work fell to a woman. As usual.

Brigitte proposed a bold plan. She would go forth and confront the monster, this great toad, and attempt a ruse, or parley, or at least convince it of the hopelessness of its siege. She knew, too, that the great jewel within his head might lay his clouded thoughts bare to a perceptive, keen mind like her own. Trickery was better than force, but in her defense she took a long dagger of Damascus steel, though she knew it would be of little real use against the monster.

With great reluctance the city fathers opened the gates just enough to permit her outside. Everywhere toads, numerous as autumn leaves, comported themselves with the air of little seigneurs. In places they were so thick it was difficult to tell where the dead lay. Robert was among them. It was a pity, yes, but a breaking of bonds as well.

The little toads reluctantly parted to let her pass, but gathered and closed in from behind, channeling her, guiding her. Brigitte knew what they were doing, so she did not resist. Before long she possessed a great insistent escort of the hopping little things, and they took her to their master.

The monster, Gros Vert, lay in the cool mud of a cattle wade. Upon his back was gathered his court—a cluster of very large, ill-tempered toads. Brigitte was taken aback by Gros Vert's size, by the cold disdainful gold-black glitter of his eyes. She did indeed sense his murky brutish thoughts, uncolored as they were by higher sentiments or refined emotions. It was as if she gazed into the black, writhing, tormented soul of the mire itself, the collective blind rage of all lesser things, the hatred for all who went upon two legs. Rebellion and tumult would one day overthrow Man the master. Slime and wilderness would swallow whatever remained.

Yet there was simple jealousy here, as well, the pride of a lover deeply wounded, and Brigitte sensed her opportunity. Hardly had she spoken, however, before Gros Vert lunged at her. He snapped up her arm to the shoulder.

Brigitte cried out, but she forced herself not to panic. To do so would mean her doom. Instead, she said, "Do not devour me, great beast! I am hardly a mouthful under the best of circumstances. And besides, I know what troubles you!"

Gros Vert reluctantly released her. Shuddering with disgust, she daubed at her arm, knowing that she must speak swiftly and convincingly. "You are angry, are you not?" she asked.

The great toad pressed close, snorted foulness in her face, the mouth set in a wide scowl. Tentatively Brigitte took the huge snout between her hands, sensed some confusion on the part of the monster, but curiosity as well. The great yellow pouch of his throat pulsed rhythmically. As for Gros Vert, a patience of sorts had settled over him. He would hear the little thing out, but not for long.

"You are," Brigitte said. "You are angry because you have been wronged. You have been betrayed by a useless mate. Am I not right?"

The great toad's enigmatic eyes and expressionless face did not hide the swirling, chaotic thoughts within. Brigitte felt as if she were staring into a dark pool alive with deep, deadly currents. But one who knew them might be able to contain them, to channel them, to use them.

"Yes. Yes, you *have* been betrayed, once too often. It is Mère Antoinette, is it not? The Mother of Toads and a most unfaithful wife, yes? And because of her faithlessness, you have come forth to punish all Men, to pull down their cities and fill their fields with your kin.

"I ask, great beast, what do you possibly hope to accomplish?"

Gros Vert twitched at this, as if mildly affronted. The great gold-black eyes darkened. A few of the little toads, angered by her presumptuousness, snapped at Brigitte's dress and feet. She ignored them, and continued to speak:

"I mean no insult, O master of swamp and mire. I only point out that which is true, and that is though you may bring about the deaths of many and even destroy the city of Vyônes, you cannot hope to usurp Man entirely. All is against you. Stone and steel. Weapons of war. The seasons themselves. Your army will win the day, but not the war. And the sacrifice will all be for naught—all for the foolish dalliances of a faithless mate. All because the little shall never triumph over the big."

Gros Vert shifted his weight, as if he were growing tired of her voice, but Brigitte would not release him. Instead, she cradled his head, pressed her face to the knobs and carbuncles and goose-egg warts of his own, his leathery palpitating skin. The little toads watched her with displeasure and suspicion, but there was little they could do.

"I know what it is to hurt so," she whispered. "Pain is the constant companion of all thinking things, of Man—pain at what is, and what should be.

"Look upon your little ones. They know nothing of jealousy, or faithlessness, or lies. They do not remember the past, and do not care for the future. They do not weary themselves with such things. How simple and free are their lives! And yet, here you are—burdened with the rudiments of thought, enough to know rage and pain and the desire for vengeance, and little else."

She stepped away from him, caressed the great blunt snout.

"Yes . . . it all burns within you, this thing, beneath skin and skull. What some might think a gift is actually a curse. A deep, mortal curse—that of thought. Of emotion. Of awareness. All of which drive you and your little ones toward doom, because the little shall never triumph over the big."

A great sigh escaped the enormous toad and he slumped ever so slightly, as if beneath the burden of this truth, of his own consciousness.

"But! But there is hope yet, O great beast, however slight. I am but one of the little, yet wise and with clever hands. That is why I have survived where others have perished. It is why I am alive today. I am full of tricks. I know many things. And I believe, great beast, that there is a solution to your dilemma, if you will allow me to act upon it."

Brigitte gazed steadily into the monster's eyes. "Allow me to remove the jewel from your head," she whispered. "Allow me to end this curse, and peace will be yours forever. You will know nothing of anger or jealousy or the struggle between great and small. You will know nothing of faithlessness. You will know nothing more."

For what seemed an interminable time, Gros Vert debated this course of action, but it was really only moments. And the burden of thought, of deliberation and self-awareness, however dim, did seem immense. So he lowered his huge head to allow this squeaking, whispering, soft little creature to administer to his woes. Out from under a hidden fold came the dagger of Damascus steel, and through Gros Vert's skull and brain it swiftly plunged.

The great toad died almost immediately. He jerked, stiffened, the watchful malice faded from his eyes, and he slumped, still.

The little toads went berserk. They flew at Brigitte from all sides like shot from catapults. She screamed, covered her face, was certain she would be overwhelmed beneath the crush of their flabby bodies, that the little *would* triumph over the big in the end.

Then the attack began to falter by degrees. First a few toads drifted away, and then more, and then many more, hopping aimlessly back into the grass and brambles. No more did their master's will blindly drive them. Simple instinct had reasserted itself, and try as they might they could no longer do harm. Instead they chased insects, sought shelter from the sun, began to seek out their old haunts. They hopped away from Brigitte, suddenly afraid of her feet, of this towering thing among them. A great retreat began back to the swamps, to mud and deep water. Behind them they left their dead master, whom they no longer knew.

So ended the siege, as well. The exhausted Vyônese awoke toward dusk that day to find the night blessedly silent and the little toads gone. They were not to be found in the cathedral. They were not to be found in the castle. The streets and gutters and alleys were entirely empty of them, as were the fields beyond. It was as if the besieging army had never existed. They were entirely gone, and they never returned.

As was the same with Brigitte and her three children. She had taken the great jewel with her, cut from the skull of Gros Vert. It was the shade of dark wine and burned with a dim, inner light. She knew she must hide it, must leave Vyônes or other *les gros* would claim the jewel for themselves in the name of faith or fealty. No, this was a prize for her and her children. This was a prize for the *petites gens.*

No one is entirely certain what became of Brigitte or her children afterward. Some say she and her family fell prey to wolves or robbers while in the wilderness, as her late husband had once predicted. But there are others who point to the rise, some years later, of a formerly unknown but immensely clever noblewoman in the region of Picardy. Marrying into wealth, she was said to have built a great castle upon the Somme River, while she numbered among her distinguished sons a knight, a scholar, and a moneylender.

The big people, of course, huffed at this absurd notion and said that this woman and the farm-wife Brigitte could not possibly be one and the same. One must never forget, they told their lessers: the little will never triumph over the big!

And when told this, the *petites gens*—who often know better than their masters but nonetheless indulge their follies—simply smiled and thought quite otherwise.

The Passing of Belzévuthe

by Simon Whitechapel

"Vous avez pour père le diable, et vous voulez accomplir les désirs de votre père."
— *L'Évangile de Jean.*

"Ye are of your father the devil, and the lusts of your father ye will do."
— *The Gospel of John* (8:44)

It was in such things that the hand of Providence was seen clearly at work, Thomas de Tourcrémée, the Dominican Prior of the Monastery of Sante Pierre at Vyônes and Grand Inquisitor of Averoigne, had stated at the beginning of the letter he wrote to his uncle Jean de Tourcrémée, Bishop of Ximes. The Jew Moïse ben Belzévuthe, a notorious sorcerer and fomenter of heresies, had three months before vanished, on the eve of his long-planned arrest by agents of the Holy Inquisition, from his cramped but richly furnished house in the Jewish quarter of Vyônes.

For those three months, despite the immediate circulation of his description for many leagues in all directions, there had been no word of the fugitive, not even the most fragmentary, and no sighting, not even the most uncertain, and it had been judged that he had fled with præternatural and indeed unwholesome despatch far beyond the borders of the province, or else had sought the shelter of the great forest of Averoigne, a perpetual nest of heresy and sedition and the scene, in hidden ceremonials conducted by woodcutters and swineherds, of certain survivals of pre-Christian days against which the clergy of Averoigne had long thundered their anathemas in vain.

But these guesses as to Belzévuthe's flight were entirely wrong: the Jew, with all the native cunning and perfidy of his race, had concealed himself far closer at hand than any had guessed, as was discovered when the watch upon his house was finally called off and officers of the Holy Inquisition conducted a final search preparatory to its demolition and the levelling of the site as a perpetual *in memoriam* of

Belzévuthe's crimes. The floorboards had been wrenched up in the days following Belzévuthe's disappearance and the friable earth beneath probed with rods of iron, but nothing had been detected at the time. The house had then been sealed and a watch placed upon it, that all who knocked on its portals in coming days might be arrested and taken away for interrogation. Three unfortunate peddlers and a great-aunt of Belzévuthe's from Ximes now languished in the dungeons of the Inquisition, but even the Dominican Prior Thomas de Tourcrémée, a fanatic whose drawn and haggard features spoke of chronic self-mortification and whose eye glimmered perpetually with the light of the *auto-da-fé*, was half-convinced that none of those arrested, not even the great-aunt, knew anything of Belzévuthe's whereabouts.

Now, with the passage of three months, it had been decided to call off the watch and conduct the demolition and levelling of the house. Accordingly Prior Thomas went thither through the mists and snow of an early winter morning with a notary bearing parchment and quill, with which to take record of any discoveries, and eight brawny friars bearing hammers and crows, with which to begin the work of demolition. When the wax seals on the Jew's front door were broken and Thomas stepped within, his narrow nose, super-sensitized by prolonged fasting, caught at once a faint but unmistakable odor of *cooking*, as of meagre meals fried or stewed over exiguous flames, nor, as he advanced further into the house, did he discover the air lacking in other, less savory odors, as of certain other, less nominable activities connected with the consumption of food.

The rufous spark of the Prior's eyes glowed more fiercely still and his voice, hoarse with the same fasting that had sensitized his nose, trembled with ill-suppressed excitement as he ordered the friars to make a renewed search of the house, reporting any suspicious signs, however small, of recent change or disturbance. The friars scattered and almost at once his attendance was shouted for from a rear room. Balancing nimbly on the beams that criss-crossed the naked earthen floor of the house, he hurried to the spot with the notary, noting a suddenly waxing odor of cloying sweetness underlain noxiously with decomposition; and when he entered the rear room he discovered the friar who had called pointing to a singular herb, source of the troubling odor, that had burst through the earth of the floor in the glaucous light filtering through a window of cracked horn.

The leaves alone of the herb would have excited Thomas's sincere reprobation, for they were fleshy and black, mottled with purple blotches and spots suggestive of crawling flies or beetles, but they, with the scent, were the lesser of the herb's distasteful features, for it bore atop a repulsively veined and swollen stem eight or nine sanguineous flowers whose swollen and lewdly gaping petals counterfeited, in some unwholesome and surely diabolic correspondence, the vertical lips of lamiæ or succubi. Indeed, a thick and glistening nectar was trickling slowly like spittle or drool between these lips and even as Thomas paused before the thing, crossing himself with well-justified distaste and disbelief, a large bead of the nectar sank slowly floorward on an extended thread that did not snap until the bead touched the earth of the floor, whereupon the thread was slowly and obscenely sucked back to the floral lips that had released it.

Had Moïse ben Belzévuthe been a prelate of high standing in the Church Herself, with a character untouched by the slightest breath of scandal from his earliest days and bearing letters of accreditation from the Pope and all the College of Cardinals, the presence of such a growth in his former dwelling would have served to damn him irrevocably as a trafficker with the Devil. Thomas spoke two words and the friar who had discovered the nefandous herb stepped forward and aimed his crow with righteous vigor in a blow intended to sever the stem half-way up its length. What happened next was never fully settled: the friar himself, a devout but obtuse youth of some twenty-one summers, insisted that his sandal slipped as he aimed the blow; another witness, the notary, maintained less vehemently that the herb itself evaded the blow by an uncanny spasm of its stem; Thomas himself would not speak of what he had seen, saying only that it provided unneeded confirmation of what he had already decided of the herb on first setting eye to it, *viz.*, that the parent whereof it was seeded had grown on the banks of the Acheron or Styx, nourished daily with the waters thereof.

What is certain is that the blow aimed by the young friar went sadly astray, leaving the friar sprawling on the earthen floor, his crow flying from his hand to crash through the window of horn, and the unharmed herb quivering sinisterly as though with righteous indignation at the violence offered to it. Thomas ordered the friar to his feet and the blow re-administered once the crow had been retrieved. The friar hastened to retrieve the crow, then stepped back to re-administer the blow, which Thomas accompanied this time with a murmured verse of the *Gloria Patri*. Whether the young friar took more care with his balance or the sacred syllables paralyzed the malefic will of the herb, the second blow went home, and with a repulsively moist crunch the stem was broken in two. A vile and blood-like ichor instantly began to ooze from the severed ends and the half-sweet, half-sickening odor redoubled, forcing the three spectators involuntarily back. Thomas indeed was heard to retch as he ordered first the notary to make careful note of what had occurred and second the friar to uproot the thing and delve beneath it in the earth, to see whereof it had sprung.

At this juncture a friar elsewhere in the house called for the Prior's attendance, and he gladly left to see what else had been discovered. When he returned with two more friars, the very flames of an *auto-da-fé* were flickering in his eyes, for a fall of fresh soot had been discovered in the fireplace of the main room and the Prior's suspicions had hardened into certainty: Moïse ben Belzévuthe had not fled Vyônes on hearing that the Inquisition intended to arrest him, but instead had concealed himself with a supply of food and fuel in his own house, no doubt hoping to find some opportunity to slip therefrom after some weeks had passed and the vigilance of the Inquisitors, as might naturally be expected, had relaxed from its initial high pitch. However, the watch placed on his house and street had apparently proved too tight for him to perfect his scheme, and he had been forced to remain in hiding until now, like a rat in a wood-pile.

"Alas, *Seigneur Juif*," Thomas murmured to himself as he gazed with satisfaction at what had been discovered in the rear room while he had been away, "the wood-pile is about to be set afire, and *nolens volens* thou must come out into the Godly light of day. This, I believe, will prove a most satisfactory tinder."

What he referred to was a small chest of dark wood that had been unearthed beneath the roots of the herb, which had itself sprouted through a hole driven in the lid of the chest. It appeared that one of the rods with which the earth beneath the Jew's floorboards had been probed had broken into the chest without meeting sufficient resistance or making sufficient noise to alert him who wielded the rod to the presence of some buried object. Thomas decided to seek out and punish the slack-witted friar who had been responsible for searching this room, but when, on his brief order, the chest was hoisted from its hole, it was apparent that it had been constructed with just such a search in mind, for the wood was of the very lightest and flimsiest kind, and the chest broke apart even as two friars lifted it forth, spilling the manuscripts and small clothen bags with which it had been cunningly half-filled.

"See there, *fratres mei*," Thomas pronounced, pointing at the chest with a fasting-sharpened index, "note the perfidious cunning of the Jew. He hath made his chest of light wood, nor hath he filled it to the brim, lest the enclosing wood yield to the probing rod and the tight-packed contents yield not. Nay, *Frère* Jerôme, read not the blasphemies of that paper thou holdest, lest they work the ruin of thy soul. Gather everything, and bring it with me to the fireplace for purification."

Blushing for shame, the friar who had paused to examine the papers spilling from the chest obeyed his superior's order with the other friars. The chest and its manuscripts and clothen bags, which proved full of strangely and sternutatorily scented herbs and seeds, were lifted and carried after Prior Thomas to the fireplace of the main room, where the chest and its contents were piled atop the fresh soot already reported to the Prior. Thomas gazed upon the pile with satisfaction, but as the most skilful of the friars busied himself with flint and steel to kindle a flame, he clicked his fingers sharply for a pause.

"A moment, *Frère* Lucien. *Frère* Renault, bring the remnants of that blasphemous Jew-wort too: we shall send the Jew's papers and Hell-flower up together in flame."

Brother Renault, the clumsy youth who had required two blows to break the herb, hastened to obey, but in seconds his moon-face was gaping back through the door of the rear room to report that the herb had deliquesced with unwholesome speed, leaving only a patch of foully dampened earth that was already attracting unseasonably belated flies through the broken window. Indeed, even as he spoke a fat black fly buzzed over his shoulder, made a circuit of the main room, then returned whence it had come, disappointed of more enticing nourishment than the deliquesced Jew-wort. Prior Thomas scowled at the young friar.

"Cover the patch with fresh earth at once, thou great lummock! Those unnatural creatures must be the Jew's familiars and may yet contrive his escape if they gather in sufficient number. Quickly! And thou, Lucien, light the fire. Aye, you heard aright: I said the Jew's escape. Are you all so dull of wit that you have not read the significance of the soot already present in the fireplace? Mayhap he is in hiding up this very chimney, as a few moments' work with flint and steel will serve to test. Unless, *Seigneur Juif*," he went on, raising his voice and turning to address the walls and ceiling, "thou care to honor us with thy presence at once and save us the labor of bringing thee forth?"

Whether the hidden Jew cared or no, the honor of his presence, after a fashion, was quickly vouchsafed, for the first smoke had scarcely gone curling up the chimney than a coughing and choking was heard from above, followed by objurgations in a voice of superhuman resonance and depth proceeding from the chimney itself and speaking in a guttural language with which none of the Christians present was familiar. Brother Lucien blanched and stepped back from the fireplace, the flint and steel falling from his nerveless fingers. "*Prieur* Thomas!" he cried, trying to cross himself. "It is the Devil Himself, come to rescue Belzévuthe! Let us flee for our lives!"

But the Prior laughed, shaking his head so that gorged lice in his beard flew left and right like grains of ruby. "Nay, *Frère* Lucien: it is not the Devil, it is but his servant, our long-awaited guest, the Jewish sorcerer Moïse ben Belzévuthe. As I told thee, he is concealed in the chimney and must come forth presently or roast. Do thou liven the fire for a moment, that he may feel it kiss his skin more lingeringly still. Nay, do not let his words affright thee: it is only the chimney that deepens his voice so. I know the coistrel's habitual tones, and his chords are tuned to a higher pitch by far."

A little uncertain still, Lucien stepped back to the fire and encouraged it to burn higher, exciting a further round of objurgation from the Jew hidden above. Prior Thomas watched with satisfaction, then ordered the fire banked before stepping forward to the chimney himself and stooping to shout up it: "Moïse ben Belzévuthe! Hearken to me! Thou canst not escape, but thou canst, for the nonce at least, save thyself further blistering. Come down now or I will order the fire piled high with fuel and let thee roast for a time before offering thee the choice again."

He paused, waiting for an answer. None came, but as the Prior opened his mouth for a final taunt, there was a sound of scrabbling high above and lumps of soot began to descend into the hearth, shattering there to create a black and thickly billowing cloud that drove the Prior back coughing and spluttering, his face converted on an sudden from famished pallidity to startling negritude. Having wiped his lips with a hand that shook with rage, he spat for several moments, then said, almost as to himself: "The deicide will pay dearly for that." He then turned to the friars: "*Frères* Abraham and Bertrand: meseemeth that our guest seek to decline our humble hospitality by climbing up the chimney and out onto the roof. Go you two outside and watch how he fare. *Frère* Lucien, thou hast made a poor job yet of this fire. I wish to see it burning high as our heads, if thou please, and we will give the Jew a foretaste of what certainly awaits him in his master's infernal domain. If the foretaste translate into the reality, that will be sad, no doubt, but the Jew is already destined for death and we will have done no more than anticipate it by a month or two. Ah, *Frère* Renault: hast thou done in there? Yea? Hast covered the patch with earth? Good: then go with *Frère* Germain and gather fuel for thy brother Lucien."

All this, and not neglecting the undignified episode of the soot, Prior Thomas described in the letter to his uncle the Bishop of Ximes, before, his quill beginning to shake with the memory of it, he went on to describe the hilarious *sequela*, when the Jew Belzévuthe, despite the extreme thinness consequent on three months of exiguous aliment, had become wedged in the chimney-pot of his own house as he sought final egress to the roof. There, with only his grey-bearded head visible, he had stayed for some time, throwing down curses of increasing virulence and blasphemy in his harshly accented French on the Gentile crowd that gathered below to jeer at him and rejoice in his discomfiture. *He looked a veritable imp from the Pit*, Prior Thomas wrote, *with smoke still billowing up around him, though doubtless the lungs of the imps of the Pit are better adapted to a diet of smoke; and it was not until the Godly folk of Vyônes began to supplement with stones the dung and refuse with which they were responding to his blasphemous maledictions that I ordered them dispersed and the Jew brought down. He now awaits my tender attentions in the deepest cell of our dun-*

geons, but I have decided to let him lie for a week or t

Here the letter broke off with a blot, before resuming in a swifter, less legible hand, for the Prior had been brought most disturbing news: the Jew Moïse ben Belzévuthe had escaped from those very dungeons. Once the Prior had added this startling intelligence to his letter, signed and sealed it, and handed it to an underling for despatch with the week's mail to Ximes, he hastened to examine the Jew's cell for himself, promising to arrest on the spot any guard on whose breath he detected the faintest trace of wine. Belzévuthe should have been under the closest possible guard in the deepest cell of the Inquisitorial dungeons, and his escape bespoke either a wholly reprehensible incompetence or diabolic intervention, or both.

When he came to the dungeons, Thomas therefore sniffed carefully first for wine, on the breath of the guards he had paraded before him, and second for sulfur, in the cell in which Belzévuthe had but an hour before lain chained; but he detected in the former case only stale garlic, and in the latter only the stench of the Jew's close confinement, for he had, on Thomas's explicit orders, been suffered to sit up and move only when he was fed and watered at midday. The chains with which he had been bound, rusted with his sweat and excrements, were lying on the floor of packed earth, and Thomas gagged with nausea as he stooped to peer at them in the flickering light of a torch held by the guard who had accompanied him into the cell.

" 'Tis the Jew-stink, your beatitude," said the guard; "from the first day I remarked it. A Christian would not smell sweet from the first day, I grant you, but he would not truly stink till day three or four, but a Jew, like this Belsebouthe, he—"

"Silence, thou fool," said the Prior. "I am still inclined to think that if thou and thy addle-pated fellows had kept closer watch on the deicide this could never have happened. These chains: do thou examine them and tell me what thou thinkst of the manner in which they lie."

The guard stooped too and peered at the chains.

"Well, your beatitude, it seems to me that the chains lie as though he whom once they bound had melted into air. They are not broken in any link and the lock—"

"Aye, aye, enough. I think the same. There has been devilry at work here: the stink of it is as metaphorically plain as the veritable stink of that damnable Jew."

"So I said as soon as I was brought news of his vanishment, your beatitude: the Devil has had a hand in this, I said, else the Jew could never have—"

"Aye, aye, that is enough. The walls are thick, the stair steep, the cell was locked, and the Jew himself chained upon the floor. He could not have escaped but by some devilry, and that is why, much against my initial inclination, I will take no measures against thee and thy fellows. Nay, do not thank me: escort me out of this place. I have matters to arrange, as I told thee before."

What matters Prior Thomas had to arrange were known to the guard himself by midday and bruited throughout Vyônes by nightfall: six elders among the Jews of the town had been arrested, chained, and thrown into the cell from which Belzévuthe had escaped, and would remain there until Belzévuthe had surrendered himself to justice or been re-captured by information received from his own people.

By the end of the month one of the elders was dead and the rest seriously ailing, but Thomas merely ordered a fresh hostage taken to replace him who had died, with orders to renew the procedure after any subsequent fatality among the occupants of the cell. If the supply of Jewish elders gave out, he was prepared to arrest merchants or maids—indeed, to sacrifice the entire Jewish quarter of Vyônes, from the most venerable patriarch to the youngest infant, to his lust for vengeance on the Jewish sorcerer who had already twice cheated the righteous justice of the Church.

Having issued the order for this fresh arrest, Thomas climbed to his cell for meditation and prayer. It was now the depth of winter and his breath steamed freely on the stairs, yet redoubled in inspissation when he entered his cell, for he had chosen it specifically for its narrow southward-facing window, through which the sun never fell whether by morning or evening. The resultant bone-deep cold was another of the mortifications he willingly imposed upon himself, believing he gained much merit by them and shed many centuries in Purgatory.

He knelt on the floor before the open window and began to pray, but even as he did so he heard a low, thick bombilation and looking up saw a great black fly lift from the pages of his Bible where it sat open on a lectern by his narrow pallet. The fly circled the room once, buzzing more obscenely still, and then vanished through the window before the astonished Prior thought even to move. Now he did so, his knees cracking sharply as he rose to his feet and hastened to the window himself. For a moment he thought he caught a glimpse of a black speck moving against the snow-smothered landscape outside and heard a final mocking bombilation, and then both were gone. Muttering with superstitious dread, he turned away to examine the Bible, which he knew he had left firmly closed and clasped.

But it was open now, to the Book of Exodus, and a cry of horror burst from the Prior's lips as he saw that the fly had blasphemously obelized its presence there: a streak of excrement lay in one margin, angled like an obscene rubric to a verse of the scripture. Even as he tried to scrape the foulness away with a trembling finger, his eyes were moving involuntarily over the rubrick'd verse and his lips pronouncing the following words: *QVOD SI NON DIMISERIS EVM ECCE EGO INMITTAM IN TE ET IN SERVOS TVOS ET IN POPVLVM TVVM ET IN DOMOS TVAS OMNE GENVS MVSCARVM ET IMPLEBVNTVR DOMVS AEGYPT-IORVM MVSCIS DIVERSI GENERIS ET IN VNIVERSA TERRA IN QVA FVERINT.* For-tunately the excrement was still fresh and came away easily enough, and Thomas hastened out of the cell to wash his soiled finger, carrying the Bible under his other arm lest the fly return in his absence and de-file the book again.

He spoke of the incident to no-one, though he wrote of it to his uncle the Bishop of Ximes, who confirmed his decision to keep si-lence, and he ordered his window covered with sackcloth; nor did he ever again, in the two months remaining to him, leave his Bible unat-tended in his cell. By the vernal thaw three further Jews had died in the dungeon cell from which Belzévuthe had so mysteriously escaped, and Thomas had twice dismissed petitions from the guards that they be al-lowed to swill the cell of its accumulated filth, lest it bred a pest in the

---

* *Exodus* 8:21 Else, if thou wilt not let my people go, behold, I will send swarms of flies upon thee, and upon thy servants, and upon thy people, and into thy houses: and the houses of the Egyptians shall be full of swarms of flies, and also the ground whereon they are.

days of heat that would succeed the thaw. He told them that he would sacrifice every Jew in Vyônes to re-capture the criminal and count it cheap at the price, reminding them that it was all upon the Jews' own heads in any case. It was more than likely that one, at the very least, among that sly and perfidious race had some clue to Belzévuthe's whereabouts, and by his refusal to come forward that one rendered himself, not the Prior of the Monastery of Saint Pierre, culpable in the deaths of the elderly Jews.

However, it was but minutes after a friar announced a third petitionary delegation from the guards and Thomas was, in customary fashion, letting them await his pleasure, that the news for which he had long prayed at last arrived: a messenger burst into his cell to inform him that Belzévuthe was re-taken, though not in such fashion as he had wished. Following the departure of the third petitionary delegation of guards from the Inquisitorial dungeons, waters of the vernal thaw had flooded the lowest cell, drowning two of the Jews before the cries of the remainder, who had managed to wriggle in their chains to the highest-lying section of floor, had alerted the guards on duty to their predicament.

The survivors had been dragged forth still in chains, but when guards re-entered the cell to retrieve the two corpses, they discovered to their astonishment that there were now in fact three: the water had collapsed the roof of an oval cavity in the floor from which the corpse of Moïse ben Belzévuthe, bound in curious leathery integuments, had floated free. In this way the mystery of his escape was solved for the second time as it had been for the first: Belzévuthe had never actually left the site whence he had been supposed to have fled, though how, in this second instance, he had managed, chained as he was, to delve a cavity in the floor without attracting the attention of the guards, let alone discard his chains and conceal himself in the cavity leaving the floor apparently undisturbed, none could yet conjecture.

Thomas hastened to view the corpse of his enemy at once: it had accompanied the messenger who brought the news, dragged behind the messenger's horse on an ashen hurdle. When he saw it laid out on the hurdle in the shadow of the walls of the Priory, the joy he had felt as soon as he heard the news was tempered with unease, for the curious leathery integuments of which the messenger had spoken were more curious than he had imagined. Indeed, so tightly did they convolve the corpse, and so closely did they seem to merge with its skin, that the dead Belzévuthe seemed more like a huge pupa or chrysalis than a human being, and Thomas could not rid himself of the notion that the dead Jew's lips were curled in a cryptic and mocking smile.

He said nothing of this to the messenger or the friars who crowded to the spot to see the recaptured sorcerer, however, and his voice had all its wonted authority as he ordered an *auto-da-fé* prepared for the following day, at which Belzévuthe would pay in death the penalty he should by rights have paid in life. As he turned away, having delivered the order, his path was blocked by one of the delegation of guards who had come to petition him, and he was asked if it was permitted now, seeing as the Jew Belzévuthe was found, to release the hostages held against that eventuality in the Inquisitorial dungeons. He stared at the questioner for a moment, fixing his features for later enquiries into his name and antecedents, then nodded curtly.

"Aye, let it be so. They can attend the *auto-da-fé* with the rest of the perfidious crew. Dost thou hear that, *Frère* Anselme? Send criers into the Jewish quarter and order attendance at the *auto* on pain of the customary fines. Nay, on pain of a *doubling* of the customary fines. We want a goodly attendance of his brethren to see how the Church repays those who assail Her."

That night he began a letter to his uncle the Bishop of Ximes, telling him the long-awaited news of Belzévuthe's re-capture. He laid the letter aside to be concluded with a description of the *auto* held the following day, and it was thus it was discovered on the afternoon of the following day by an official of the town council, who added a hurried *postscriptum* informing the Bishop of the death of his nephew, into which the severest investigations were already proceeding. No coherent tale ever emerged, however, despite the urgency with which the few surviving witnesses were pressed in the torture chambers of the Inquisition of Vyônes, which had been hastily re-staffed from Ximes and Périgon.

Most of the crowd, Jew and Gentile alike, had scattered in panic when Belzévuthe's corpse, propped up amid the freshly lit faggots of the *auto-da-fé*, had first shown signs of commencing its alleged transformation, and only Thomas and his friars had voluntarily remained, the drone of their exorcisms contending, in the ears of the fleeing crowd, with the shrill cries of the elderly Jews whose emergence the day before from imprisonment had been too recent to allow them chance to recover use of their limbs.

It was these elderly Jews, indeed, who were the only surviving witnesses of the final act of the *auto-da-fé*, and it was upon them, in consequence, that the Inquisition centered its investigations into the curious exsanguination discovered in the corpses of Prior Thomas and his friars. The stories wrung from the Jews by torture contradicted most grievously, however, and contained details too fantastic for even the credulous Inquisitors brought in from Ximes and Périgon to readily accept. That the corpse of Belzévuthe should have *burst* as it burnt was quite within the bounds of credibility: had not such things been observed many times before when sentence of *ignis crematio,* death by fire, had been inflicted *post mortem*? That the corpse should have swollen to oliphauntine proportions and greater *before* it burst, however, quite smothering the fire atop which it had formerly stood, could not be accepted with equanimity, and as for the tales of what had *emerged* from the corpse as it burst—no, such things could not be, or at least could certainly not be admitted to be, lest the populace come to doubt the power of the Church over all such manifestations of the Satanic Host.

Nevertheless, there was more than one nervous friar of Ximes or Périgon in attendance at the first of the *autos-de-fé* held at Vyônes later in the year, in which the elderly Jews were burnt *seriatim* for their part in the assassination of the widely respected and loved Prior Thomas de Tourcrémée and his friars; but when the first elderly Jew burnt in customary fashion, without supernatural manifestations of any kind, these lingering fears were laid finally to rest. It is true that the condemned man, like several of those who succeeded him, called upon *"Moïse! Moïse!"* as he died, but this was almost certainly a misplaced invocation of the Patriarch, not of the accursed sorcerer Moïse ben Belzévuthe of Vyônes. Indeed, Belzévuthe's memory was already beginning to fade, though his corrupted name remained attached for some decades to come to a large black species of fly popularly known as the *moche de Belfoute*, which was unusually numerous in the summer and autumn of the year in which he died and which possessed at that time a painful and occasionally veneniferous bite.

THE INQUISITOR'S SIN

by DJ Tyrer

The Inquisitor aroused the fury of the crowd
Against the witch who dwelt deep within the wood
Promising them her evil would be overcome by their good
If only they were not by curses cowed

The Inquisitor led them by blazing torchlight
To the cottage of the witch they strode.
He flung the door open but saw nothing but a toad
He sighed, in spite of himself, that it was no fearful sight.

But then the toad spoke, called him by name
The Inquisitor recoiled with a cry of shock;
He looked about but saw only cats and no sight of his flock.
The toad chuckled then transformed: a maid naked without shame

Who smiled and to the Inquisitor said:
"I am here, the one that you seek."
The Inquisitor was silent, he could not speak
Nor resist as she led him to her bed

Where maiden-witch and man-of-the-cloth
Proceeded to enjoy the passion of physical love
And the former-celibate found he could not get enough:
"Once more, once more," he begged, lips rimed with froth.

Then came morning and he woke not alone
Woke with an awful, fearful scream
To no nightmare nor putrid dream
For the maiden now was a toad-faced, flaccid crone

Who laughed to see the Inquisitor distraught
Disgusted and despairing to see his mate
And realize his lust had sealed his fate:
In the witch's lustful embrace he was caught.

From the cabin, through the woods, the Inquisitor fled;
In Averoigne he could no longer stay
So boarded a ship to far-off lands to carry him away
But could never forget his night in the toad-witch's bed.

THE BUTCHER OF VYÔNES

by Michael Minnis

It had long been a joke in Vyônes that the ribald butcher Maurice Daumard was little better than the animals he slaughtered. Few dared repeat it in his presence, though, and those foolish enough to make this mistake invariably made the acquaintance of his raw, knotted knuckles. It hardly mattered if they were nobleman or pauper, knight or knave. The butcher's fondness for jest did not extend to himself.

Outwardly, at least, Daumard was a good-humored brute with a booming laugh, quick with a bawdy song. His body was hardly less rude than his speech: thick-armed and bandy-legged he went about in great thumping knee-high cockers, weather-stained gamash, and leather apron. His blunt nails were tiny sickle moons of dried black blood. His hands and forearms were tempered as old blades with nicks and faded scars. That he was still physically robust at his age was without question. But a youth of drink, debauchery and fighting had battered Daumard's face, left it florid and ugly and vaguely truculent, with broken nose and the suggestive dim glint of violence still deep within his pale eyes.

It was widely rumored that as a younger man Daumard had killed his first wife in a drunken rage and then disposed of her body in the river Isoile. It was said that only the intervention and influence of his own guild had spared him the headsman's axe.

Ever since this no woman of Vyônes, or Averoigne, would have him. He seemed destined to live his remaining years out in loneliness, and there was no reason to believe he would not die in the same manner.

And so it was with great astonishment and some consternation that the people of Vyônes received news one summer day that Daumard was to be married again, to a woman less than half his age.

Her name was Catherine Demoulin and no one was entirely certain of her origins. Some said that she was the daughter of an impoverished peasant, a peat-digger or charcoal-burner desperate to be rid of another mouth to feed. Others said No, that was not possible. The girl, though small, was entirely too sleek and well fed to be a child of "Jacques Bonhomme", of the peasantry. She must be the secret progeny of an official, a *seigneur* perhaps, or a crusading knight long since perished in battle against the infidel Turk.

A few thought she was the bastard child of the mad King Charles' scandalous wife, Isabeau of Bavaria. And some believed her even worse, the offspring of sorcerer and succubus.

But all could agree on one thing: that the girl was fey and wise beyond her years, that something strange was deeply imprinted upon her, in her eyes and expression. But like the unknown depths of a still pool it was not readily apparent—her emerging loveliness obscured it, was like the bright glint of sunlight on water. While those of a sensitive nature might dimly glimpse it, in the exotic curve and impassive green eyes of her faun-like face, in the petulant set of her lips—full lips with the slightest hint of coiled hell—Daumard was a man of no such thoughts. In her reddish ringlets he twined his thick fingers, in the growing curves of her hips and breasts he simply saw a young lover and mother of many children.

That they should be together was of hardly less puzzlement than the nature of Catherine herself. Daumard was so crude, so ill mannered, so loud! And when he was in his cups . . . why, such a man would only make her thick and coarse as himself someday, a sway-backed harridan, broken by grief and labor.

If he didn't kill her as he had his first wife, of course.

November came to Vyônes and summer disappeared into the loam with the leaves and the yew-berries, into the dark earth. The empty fields were given over to that timeless triumvirate, the rulers three of all passing things: wind, rain, bleak autumnal sun. Men found their words suddenly short and few; the silences hung between them, watchful and as long as the empty horizon beyond, awaiting winter.

November came with the end of All Hallow's Eve and doubtful moonlit shapes returned to their uneasy slumber. Goblins and imps no longer pressed their hideous faces to keyholes and Judas-slots. They ceased their mockery of the devout and righteous and fled unseen into the night. No longer did wan lights flicker about the ancient ruins of Faussesflammes or Ylourgne. Auguries were at an end and omens were laid to rest.

November was the time of the Feast of St. Michelmas. November in Vyônes, as always, was the time of slaughter.

From far and wide they came to that unfavored part of Vyônes known as Les Ruelles, where live and work a diminishing enclave of butchers and tanners—peasants and shopkeepers, nobles and commoners, all with animals for the knife.

Daumard set to his task. From sunrise to sunset he cut flesh, sliced throats, split skin until his arms were ensanguined to the elbows, until he stank of sweat and blood. He laid bare bellies, dug into the steaming entrails and membranes with his fingers, stripped meat from bone. He laughed at the upside-down piglet's frantic struggles, at the fowl's indignant flurry of flapping. He reflected jokingly upon mortality, and called himself kissing cousin to the Dead One, Death himself. The only difference in their work being that he salted his when he was done.

Haw, haw, HAW!

And so one day came a visitor, a *langueyeur*, an inspector of tongues, to see the results of Daumard's butchery, and judge it fit or not for the people of Vyônes. He was also here to see that the butcher was a man of his word and did not take more than his allotted portion of flesh, as some rumored he did.

Gilles le Roye was the *langueyeur's* name—young, foppish, and uncertain of his authority. In the time it took Daumard to slit a throat of a piglet and catch its blood in a cup, he had Gilles le Roye amiably bullied and quite bewildered.

Bewildered enough, in fact, that Gilles at first failed to note the presence of the butcher's young wife. She touched Gilles' arm and he startled, excused himself, and then remembered the proper pleasantries.

Daumard thundered, "Here is my little one!" and set aside his cup. He wiped his hands on his apron, took her by the waist and held her aloft in triumph, spun in a slow circle, set her down again. Catherine did not smile. Daumard laughed. Gilles simpered and nodded uncomfortably; the two had been married hardly four months and already the young woman had grown silent and sullen.

"So this is the young lady I've heard so much about," Gilles said, taken by the girl's demure beauty, despite her reticence. Suddenly he remembered himself. "Oh, please forgive me." Gilles removed his shapeless feathered cap, and bowed.

"Gilles le Roye, *langueyeur*, at your service."

The gallant moment hung in the air like a carcass.

"Catherine . . ." Daumard prodded gently.

Catherine curtsied. "Catherine Daumard at yours."

Daumard split the air like an axe with his laugh. He took the young woman by her slender pale wrists, held her soft hands up to Gilles as if a pearl might be found within each palm.

"An inspector of tongues, you call yourself," Daumard joked. "Perhaps you should consider a new line of work. Look at these hands! *Look at them!*" He rubbed them covetously with his own, and Gilles blushed, embarrassed for Catherine.

"Soft as a baby birds, I tell you!" Daumard said. "Nothing like the claws of my first wife. Here, see for yourself—"

The butcher clumsily thrust Catherine's hands under the *langueyeur's* narrow, patrician face, but the girl pulled away. Like storm clouds passing before the sun, Daumard's expression darkened for a moment. The old violence flickered in his eyes, was quickly gone. His hearty laugh again filled the room and he released his captive.

He returned to the tin cup of blood and raised it. "A toast," he declared. "To one whose spirit is as strong as her flesh is delicate."

He drained half the cup at a swallow. Gilles' face pinched in mild momentary disgust. Catherine, however, watched her husband with what Gilles thought was more than common interest.

It was not over yet, as Gilles had feared. Daumard was not through making fun. With an impish grin, he dipped a finger into the cup. Slowly he walked toward his wife, the finger extended.

"And now, a baptism for a butcher's wife."

Catherine closed her eyes, and Gilles marveled again at her exquisite beauty, the pallor of skin, the hair shimmering like beaten copper, the eyelashes soft as dusk. The lips, voluptuous, set and yet full of promise. That such a cherub should be married to a brute like Daumard was godless. The toad had taken the nightingale for his own. The unfairness of things!

With great care Daumard dabbed blood upon Catherine's flawless lips, painting them red. When he was done, Catherine opened her eyes again. Gilles glanced away in embarrassment. Daumard laughed at him.

"I wouldn't have figured you inspectors to be such delicate sorts," he said, and to Catherine, "and now you are almost a proper butcher's wife. But first!"

He held the tin cup to Catherine's lips. She glared at Daumard.

"Go on, love. Drink."

With both hands he gently pressed the rim of the cup to Catherine's mouth.

Finally, clasping her own pale fingers over his, she drank, slowly. Smooth muscles worked beneath the milky skin of her throat, like ripples through a subterranean pool. Before long the cup was empty, and it was lowered. An enigmatic smile played about Catherine's lips.

"Is that all, love?" she asked.

And the butcher smiled then, with a wisdom Gilles would not have expected in a commoner, and cupped his young wife's chin.

"We all receive no more than we are due, little one," he said.

Late that winter Daumard made a sudden and most peculiar visit to a noted surgeon of Vyônes.

The surgeon, François Hemery, awoke to a pounding downstairs at his door. Finding at last a candle stub, he went to the window and opened it. It was night and the roofs and gables of Vyônes lay under fresh snow, while flakes danced through the bitter air. The sky above was a frozen vault of glittering stars. In the courtyard below he spied the unsteady orange glow of a torch, and what appeared to be two men, close together.

Summoning his courage—for he was an elderly man, and frail—he said, "Who is this who disturbs me at this hour?"

"It is I, Jean Guisay," replied a voice, "and Maurice Daumard. He is wounded, and needs help!"

François gave pause. Jean Guisay was known throughout Vyônes as being something of a ruffian, sometime rat-catcher, drinker and brawler—a fine example of the people Daumard chose as company. The man would steal your very breath, given the chance . . . and the surgeon had many fine things in his home.

"Can't you go to the nunnery?" the old man asked.

"It is too far!" Jean replied. "And the snow is up to our knees! For the love of God, monsieur, let us in!"

François shook a gnarled fist in frustration. His breath pluming in the winter air, he said, "Very well. I will be down. But I warn you! No trickery, or I'll raise a hue and cry, yes?"

"You have my word," Jean replied.

Grumbling, rubbing the sleep from his eyes, shuddering at the drafts and eddies in his high shadowy old house, François hastily clothed himself in the purple gown of his station and shuffled down the narrow steps to the door.

Hardly was the door half open before Jean Guisay pushed his way into the room. Tall, with lank black hair that hung in his eyes, drooping mustache, Spaniard's skin and a cloak of crudely stitched rabbit and squirrel fur about his shoulders, Jean Guisay seemed more ogre than man. For a moment François quailed—but it was Daumard at the Jean's side, leaning heavily upon him. Both were dusted with snow, but whereas Jean was flushed and ruddy, Daumard seemed oddly pale.

"Where is he wounded?" the surgeon asked.

"In the thigh," Jean replied.

A table was cleared of books, and an old blanket laid upon it. Daumard they helped atop the table. The surgeon, now in his element, cut away at Daumard's blood soaked legging with deft, precise motions. Jean he ordered to stir the smoldering coals in the stingy hearth back into life. Soon the guttering light grew, and the fire cracked and snapped. Daumard, reeking of ale, watched the operation with the singular interest and incomprehension of the dismally intoxicated.

Now François was a competent surgeon, well versed in astrology and human physiology. He was an expert in bleeding, the extraction of ill humors, and the influence of the planets and constellations upon the body. In secret and against the will of the Church, he had dissected corpses to further his knowledge of anatomy. He was familiar with the methods of necromancy, though he did not practice it, and saw in many strange events and things the designs of Satan and other foul demons—Astorath, Belial, Iog- Sotôt.

When François had washed the blood away, he saw that the wound, though ugly, was not as serious as previously thought. It was on the inner thigh, close to the groin, bruised purple and yellow, and bleeding. It was not, as François first thought, a slip of the blade that would have easily been fatal. Half-moon indentations rather suggested the work of teeth, of chewing and tearing. Here and there the teeth had broken through skin, and the edges of these tiny gashes were ragged and mangled.

He asked Daumard just what in the name of all saints had happened to him.

Daumard, made utterly indifferent by drink, shrugged. "Dogs," he replied. "Dogs did this."

"Dogs did this?" the surgeon repeated uncertainly.

"Well, *a* dog," Daumard said, correcting himself. "You see . . . good Doctor . . . on occasion, when I am working . . . I like to tease the dogs with a bone or a scrap of hide. They get to fighting and . . . I have a good laugh. No harm done. But . . . well . . . perhaps I teased one of them a bit too long and, well, as you can plainly see . . . ."

His eyes narrowed and his shoulders shook with sodden mirth. "Yes, as you can plainly see . . . a finger-length or two higher . . . and my little wife would be looking for a new husband!"

Daumard thundered with laughter then. "Am I not right, Jean?"

Jean Guisay, who stood beside the fire rubbing his reddened and raw hands, muttered something in reply.

"Speak up, you filthy catcher of rats!"

"Yes, you are right, Maurice," Jean replied.

"Ha! See, good Doctor? I am right."

Daumard chuckled and mumbled to himself, and soon lapsed into a semi-conscious stupor, in which he did little but stare somnolently at the patient ministrations of the surgeon. Twice Daumard fell asleep, head upon his chest, only to jerk awake and stare groggily about. In the grate the fire burned yellow and blue. Guisay remained close to the flames. About them the ancient house settled into sleep. Outside snowflakes chased each other, whirling madly against the high window.

On Daumard's cuts François placed lint and cobwebs, plugging the gashes—so much like bloody little mouths, he thought. He then wrapped a length of white linen bandage about the man's thigh, with the help of Jean the rat-catcher. He was grateful that Daumard's injury was not more serious, but still puzzled by its incongruous nature. Did butchers not wear thick leather aprons to avoid just such calamities? And what sort of dog could chew through leather?

But Daumard was asleep, and the angular pockmarked face of the rat-catcher did not invite questions.

As winter lengthened, and the days grew longer, a slow, subtle change came over Daumard that soon became evident to the people of Vyônes.

He had always been a vital, hardy fellow, inured to hardship, able to drink any other man under the table. As François Hemery had hoped, Daumard recovered swiftly from his wounds. Doubtlessly the planets had favored him, as had the Blessed Virgin, which François had ordered Daumard and Jean to offer prayer to that bitter night—but Daumard walked with a limp now, and was not quite the same man. He seemed troubled now. Oppressed.

Not that he was alone. The winter of 1410 was proving unusually long, cold and harsh in Averoigne. Food was running short. Ancient stores of flour and grain were found despoiled by mold, half-eaten by rats.

And meat—for many a luxury in the best of times—was not to be had, though the increasing absence of cats and dogs among the peasantry was duly noted. It was said to be even worse elsewhere. In Ximes it was said that the peasants had resorted to stealing corpses from the gibbet. In Les Hiboux, graves were found empty of their occupants. Wolves stalked the forests of Averoigne, and their moonlit howling intruded upon the uneasy sleep of the people of Vyônes. Small wonder that even the indomitable Daumard should become taciturn and brooding.

But stranger still was the gradual transformation of his young wife.

For Catherine the prospect of famine held little fear. So far its effects upon her seemed negligible. If anything, she seemed oddly blessed—*increased*—rather than diminished by events, in mind and spirit as well as form. No longer was she silent. No longer did she trail after Daumard like an unwilling shadow. No, she was first to receive visitors now, with wry ethereal smile and lustrous eyes, taking their hands into her own. She spoke, laughed, made affectionate mockery of the habits and doings of the people of Vyônes, and her knowledge of them was astounding in its depth and breadth. It was as if she sat with them at their tables, slept with them in their beds.

And was she not larger than before, more full? Jean Guisay thought as much. One could see it in her face, in the ample swell of her bosom and hips; Catherine was growing plump. Or heavy with child. There was some disagreement as to just what, exactly, was happening. Jean the rat-catcher had called upon husband and wife once, and thought the latter not only rather nervous, but flushed and somehow subtly *swollen* in body. As for Daumard, he was nowhere to be seen.

At any rate, this much was true: the butcher and his wife were privy to some secret. Daumard was providing handsomely for his little one. That she should eat so well in such times was obscene.

And so the common folk gnawed on their bread crusts, grumbled to themselves, cursed both wife and butcher, and plotted against them.

With spring the snows finally receded, though the weather that followed was hardly less foul. Rain came with vengeance, lashing the stubbled fields into soup, falling in violent torrents from gutters and the twisted mouths of leering stone gargoyles. The cobblestone streets of Vyônes became rushing streams choked with flotsam and debris. Cellars and crypts became dank dripping pools.

From a gray lightless sky rain fell, sometimes a sullen blurred curtain, at others like the crashing waves of the sea. With it came hail that clattered upon rooftops and gathered in white drifts. No more than tiny pebbles of ice at first, soon missiles the size of a man's fist fell through the air to smash against stone and wood and the flesh of the unwise.

But the rain could not accomplish all disasters, and so the wind gave wild voice to the torments besetting Vyônes. It shrieked about the battlements like a tattered ghost, tearing at the cloaks and faces of the men-at-arms so that each drew into himself and saw nothing. It gibbered in the ears of blind beggars and half-mad lepers, who drooled and chuckled in toothless delight, certain they had been favored with unfathomable secrets. It rattled at shutters and doors at all hours. Against the wan and cold sun it sent massed storm clouds to shut out all light but for the jagged skeleton-thin flicker and flash of lightning.

Beleaguered, beset, the people of Vyônes were in a quandary. While some might gather in the battered cathedral to seek absolution, most merely shut themselves away from a world dissolving into a Biblical nightmare of wind and storm.

There they lit candles and contemplated the nature of their sins, of punishment and the unknowable designs of God. The pious accepted their fate. Others, however, gnawed at their predicament. Snow, hunger, storms—had they not suffered enough? And the wind and rain—was this not an omen, the sign of other hands at work, of sorcery and the Black Arts? For what other reason did the wind mock them or the lightning stab the earth? For what other reason did the heavens weep, day after bleak day?

More and more suspicion turned to the butcher and his wife. Soon there was wild talk everywhere—in the taverns, in the shops, in the hovels of the poor and the manses of the rich.

A mendicant friar claimed to have seen Catherine atop a steep roof near lauds. She had leaped from building to building with the grace of a cat.

A wife of a lowly charcoal-burner, Marie Fauche, had seen Catherine riding through the night upon a headless black horse, whose hooves struck sparks on empty air. The beggars and cutthroats of Les Ruelles worshiped her as a goddess and called her Queen of Rats.

Not to be outdone, a renowned huntsman and falconer, Pierre Maillart, told his fellows that he had spied Catherine deep within the woods of Averoigne seven days ago, in the company of a great man-like goat.

Gaston the Miller argued that this was not possible, for that very day, she had slipped like smoke through the keyhole of his door. Confronted by the miller before she had fully taken shape, she stole up the chimney. Gaston, undaunted and armed with a poker, had prodded about the darkness, only to be confronted by a pair of lambent eyes staring down from the black flue.

That had been quite enough for the miller.

Seemingly no one was without a tale, and no one lacked for listeners. Apathy gave way to fear, fear to indignation. A monster existed in their midst. Ghost or ghoul, vampire or revenant, the arguments made little difference, for they all lead to even blacker conclusions concerning the fate of Catherine Demoulin. She must be burned, beheaded, a stake of ash driven through her heart. She must be broken upon the wheel, whipped, her fingernails torn loose and her eyes gouged out.

Evil was afoot. Something must be done.

In even favored times, Les Ruelles was not a well-regarded or liked place in Vyônes. There was always a stink in the air—sometimes the bite of urine, sometimes the copper heaviness of blood—the rough work of tanning and butchery. It was an odor that varied in sharpness with the season, yet invariably clung to one's clothes like filth, and to the tongue like bile. Fires, lit on order of the guilds, did little more than bring a smoky redolence to the stench, sending ash into the air like wayward bats.

Here everything seemed wrong, but in a manner not evident until some time was wasted among its cracked walls and crooked alleys.

First were the people who, like dead leaves descending into a still black tarn, had settled into the old stones of the fortress wall and fortifications Vyônes had outgrown and abandoned centuries before. These people had done little to cheer or improve the place, and were not well favored. Scattered fragments of their misery clustered in secret places—stump-limbed beggars, forgotten soldiers sodden with drink, perhaps a pair of pickpockets or a blind prophet familiar with the dead. From a high narrow garret might lean a pock-faced harlot made frightful by powder, a leering midday ghost. Below, lumpish patchwork shapes that met no other face roamed the buckled streets. Up crumbling stone steps they limped, down odd gangways they shuffled, only to disappear behind mossy rotting doorways.

Second was Les Ruelles itself, which some called The Shambles. Once it had been a meeting place of sorcerers and vivisectionists. True, they were long dead and gone, put to sword or torch by papal inquisitions, but the mercurial atmosphere of their weird work—fluid, indestructible, poisonous—remained.

Few outsiders were at ease between the blind vaulting stone walls, with their sparse, tiny, high windows like misplaced eyes, their soot-stained chimneys and gables like broken rotting teeth. The walls seemed too tall. They rose like giants to close off forever what perilous little light and sky remained. Movement and sound tugged at the peripheries of the senses like half-forgotten dreams—scuffling heard within a heretofore-undisclosed alley, the flicker and fade of a pale face within a dark window.

But there is security in numbers, and the milling mob that had come for Daumard and Catherine was not so easily deterred. They filled the narrow streets like a river in flood, crested by a bristling foam of makeshift weapons—scythes, pitchforks, glaives, bill hooks, axes and hammers. Men and women, peasants and tradesmen, city guard, merchants, students, laborers—at their head a nervous and thoroughly bewildered monk with cross, aspergillum and flask of holy water. Dogs wheeled and yammered in their vanguard, children trailed in their wake.

A break in the rain allowed them torches and an additional degree of ferocity. Flames to stave off the bereaved gloom of the day! Flames to scatter before them the astonished bundled shapes lurking in the shadows, to burn monsters! Oily and orange they twisted in the wind like hellish banners. A young boy with an angelic face beat inexpertly upon a drum.

Their rage was not for the butcher and his little one alone. No, there were others who must be punished—accomplices, familiars, spies and servants of the Devil, driven out of their holes like rats!

They smashed windows and battered doors. They threw stones at fleeing figures. With cudgels and maces they set upon any ragbag beggar or urchin too slow to escape. Cats and lepers were set aflame.

A tinker's cart was upended. The tinker's hands and feet were bound with his own colored ribbon, and he was thrown from a bridge into the foul water below.

Another man of displeasing—and therefore evil—appearance was drowned in a rain barrel.

A terrified gravedigger they beheaded; his companion they disemboweled.

Jean Guisay they pursued to the very rooftops. "There he goes," came the cry. "There goes the rat-catcher!" Here several of the mob met their deaths when they slipped, stumbled and fell—including Guisay, who chose to throw himself to his own doom rather than allowing his pursuers the honor.

But the closer they drew upon the butcher's abode, the less vociferous the mob's fury became. They were deep in Les Ruelles now, and far from the familiar. Bloodshed and retribution had scattered them widely. The wind was in their faces. The clouds had returned. The children had departed. They shouted to one another for courage, aware all the while that doubtful shapes had begun to gather along the rooftops and chimney pots.

At last they arrived at Daumard's home—a weathered corner of ancient fortification and crumbling buttresses within a courtyard. Its crest was overshadowed by an angular bartizan speckled with small empty windows and murder-holes and archer-slits looking inward upon blackness. From corners and cornices grinned fractured gargoyles made nearly featureless by years of rain, freeze and thaw. To the side was a short flight of wide worn steps that ended before a great arched door.

They shouted for Daumard. When there was no reply, they mounted the steps to hammer on the door with clubs and fists.

A small window, very high up, finally opened. Inside was naught but darkness and a suggestion of watchful movement.

"Who is this at my door?"

It was Daumard. A cacophony of shouts, curses and threats rose in reply.

"Is it the people of Vyônes," the monk announced. "We are here—"

But Gaston the miller interrupted him. "We are here to put an end to the mischief of the devil-spawn you claim as your wife, Daumard!"

This was greeted with cheers and the shaking of weapons. With a singular look at the miller, the monk continued: "We are here to see whether or not all is well in the house of Daumard, Maurice. There is reason to suspect the company you keep."

A pause, and a reply: "The company I keep is my own business. Stay away."

"Let us in!" Maillart thundered, and made as if to break the door down with his sword. But the monk intervened, and held the cross before Maillart to bar his way.

A strange laugh came from the black window.

"So," Daumard said, "I see you are quite anxious to learn if all is well within these walls. So anxious, in fact, that you come as a mob, armed and bearing torches. Insistent guests, I should say . . . .

"Very well. Good people of Vyônes, I bid you enter."

The small window closed.

Silence reigned outside Daumard's door, but not for long. A murmur of nervous conversation, whispers and muttering rippled through the crowd, until the monk raised his hand.

"What in Hell's name is he doing in there?" Maillart grumbled.

Claude Rebec, a gangly blond scarecrow youth of twenty years, glanced uneasily about at the roofs and walls. "They're closing in all around us. Look."

Claude's observation provoked even louder muttering and a wave of consternation. Tiny shapes clustered high above, like rooks. Faint manic laughter, more a shriek, drifted down upon them. Yet another distant voice roared and slobbered moronic repetitive nonsense.

"We're safe as long as we stay together," the miller said bluffly.

Finally, the door swung soundlessly open to shadows so deep and textured the people of Vyônes might have well gazed upon a void. Nor was all still within. In obscure spaces unimagined things—great spiders? Crawling bats? Fragments of shadow?—struggled and fumbled to escape this unwelcome intrusion of light and air.

As one the mob shuddered and recoiled. The monk quite forgot his Latin exorcism. "Bastards!" Maillart cursed them, and stepped through the threshold. "Who will follow me?"

Behind Maillart, reluctantly, between terror and wonder, came the monk, the scarecrow youth, the miller, and a pair of stout men-at-arms bearing spears.

The others preferred to remain behind.

A faint but cloying stink entered the nostrils of the six men—blood, and something worse. Torchlight was not sufficient to reveal all to Maillart and his companions, and they cast about warily for other sources of illumination. But none was to be had. The oddly shaped windows were elaborately barred and locked, or set out of reach in the remote angles of the vaulted ceiling above, while the archer slits offered only slivers of tempestuous gray.

Through a hall they passed silently, like shades returning to the grave. Up a narrow steep flight of stairs they ascended, the way occasionally marked by a wan arrow-slit angle of light. Otherwise the darkness scarcely gave way at their approach.

Little but growing dread hindered them, though there seemed any amount of cold curiosity in their progress. Rats, as if seeded by the shadows, clustered in twos and threes on this step or that step. They were ever ahead—watching, waiting, fleeing when the men drew close, claws scratching on stone. The gloom was eloquent with their tiny, hateful voices. Each man expected to feel the sting of little teeth with his every step.

Again the stairs ascended, in an opposite direction. The air was closer here, still and stagnant, heavy with the odor of rotten growth. Water dripped hollowly from the ruined ceiling. Its trickling had stained the walls in the shades of corruption. Every crack and flaw was filled with rank black-green moss. It permeated the wet stone like a strange wasting disease.

The stairs ended beneath a carved arch. Through a heavy oak door they passed into a dim stone chamber. Maillart noted the angular walls—they were in the many-windowed bartizan.

Within was little. Scattered furniture, hard and bare. Rotting straw scattered upon the stone floor. A hearth cold, a black tongue of accumulated ash extending out from it. Bolted windows. A circular flight of stone stairs leading even further upward. Dust and filaments of depending cobweb that trailed with the exhalation of some unknown current. And indeed, it did seem like breath—the breath of something dying yet vaguely aware, foul, spoiled, passing into nothingness bit by awful bit.

The monk sprinkled holy water upon the floor, and resumed his exorcism. His tremulous tones reverberated, rippled through the chamber—empty words, stripped of their potency by fear. In the vault above the echoes gathered, and grew in strength, and returned misshapen, hollow and mocking. Or were the fragmented intonations all the trickery of empty space? Were there other voices that whispered and hissed and muttered and mumbled, in Latin, in nonsense, in tongues unknown? The blasphemy swelled, became manic gibbering and babbling, blackly bubbling lunacy, songs insectile and inhuman.

"Stop!" the monk cried, and the cacophony did, suddenly. He resumed his sonorous chant. Without warning the great door swung shut, plunging them into even deeper blackness. Claude ran to the door, threw his shoulder against it.

"I can't open it!" he cried.

"Be still!" the miller hissed.

All tensed to hear slow footsteps in descent. Maillart gripped tighter his sword, the men-at-arms their spears.

It was Daumard—slow and dragging, with a limp, come down the circular stairway. In one hand he bore a short sword. A hood lay heavy upon his head, hiding his eyes, and thick furs hung upon his shoulders, for it was cold in that chamber. But it seemed that his body bulked oddly, like that of a hunchback.

He regarded the men before him in silence.

"What do you want with me?" he asked at last.

"Where is she?" Maillart demanded. "The witch. Is she here?"

"She's closer than you think."

"Then show us to her," the miller said. "Or we'll kill you."

Daumard laughed. "I doubt that will be necessary, Gaston. She is already here."

With one hand he undid the bronze clasp of his cloak and hood, and pulled them away from himself. The assembled men gasped at what they saw, and the monk called upon the saints to protect them.

Catherine was there. She clung bat-like to her husband's back, her legs about his waist, pale hands clasped to the black curls of his chest. No one saw her face. It was buried in Daumard's throat. Reddish hair spilled down his navel. From the white figure came occasional soft sounds—sucking, they coldly realized—and the occasional dream-like movements of fingers and legs steadying their grasp.

Daumard gently stroked the mass of Catherine's hair, whispered something to her. She twitched, stirred as if in a dream, but continued to feed.

Maillart swallowed his fear and said, "You'll burn in Hell for this, Daumard. The both of you."

"Better to burn in Hell than beg forgiveness of rot such as you, Maillart. Come at me, if you dare."

A swift imperceptible communication passed between Maillart and the men-at-arms, knowledge of what was necessary seen in each other's eyes. With a fierce cry Maillart swung at Daumard, who easily turned the huntsman's blade aside. The shorter of the men-at-arms thrust with his broad-headed spear, and this, too, Daumard parried, but only just. Almost simultaneously the second man-at-arms made his attack. The spearhead struck deeply into the smooth flesh of Catherine's hip.

Catherine gasped. Lips parted from flesh in a bright arc of blood. Her body went taut. Daumard turned upon this new threat. Swinging wildly, he forced the second man-at-arms back until the man stumbled over a table and fell. Claude, bearing little more than a stout oak staff, went to the man's defense. Maillart again pressed the attack, but Daumard proved his match, and sent him reeling with a shallow gash to his cheek.

The combatants parted, panting, unnerved, Catherine staring in black animal fury, a single drop of red upon her chin. Nor was any more blood to be seen from the wound inflicted by the man-at-arms— only a thin line of crimson rounding the curve of her hip.

Sudden resolve steeled the monk, and he strode forward, cross held high. In tones of unexpected force and conviction, he damned Catherine Demoulin to Hell. He named her Beast, Servant of Satan, and Queen of Rats! She would go forth from Vyônes, broken in Mind and empty of Form!

The rage left Catherine, and her eyes dimmed. Uncertainty seemed to fall upon her, and her enemies were heartened.

Then a luxurious slow smile spread across her marble face, and it tilted forward, like that of a lover anxious to be caressed. Her expression was one of gentle rapture—almost kindly. The monk's words began to falter. Like some dark-dwelling species of vine or serpent she leaned, ever so slightly, further and further over the shoulder of her bleeding, horribly patient husband. The voluptuous lips parted.

There was a horrid, clotted gurgle. A jet of smoking blood erupted from Catherine's mouth with the all force and violence of a dragon's flames. The monk was blinded. He fell to the ground, clawing madly at his face and skull. The blood burned like Greek fire. Flesh slid from bone, and he lay there in hideous hissing dissolution, groaning and bubbling.

Claude, too, was wounded—smoldering blood droplets had landed upon his arm, eating through the wool tunic, setting to the skin beneath like hot needles. In agony he curled into a dark corner, clutching his injured limb.

"So," Catherine asked. "Who else denounces me?"

"We'll kill you yet!" the Maillart cried. With him came the men-at-arms.

Daumard fought with wild abandon. Slowly he was forced back up the stairs, fighting at every step. He clove the face of one of the men-at-arms nearly in two—the blade of his sword smashing through teeth and jawbone. He dove under the miller's cudgel like a striking serpent and threw the man off the stairs.

It was then that Maillart saw his chance, and thrust his sword through Daumard's chest and into Catherine Demoulin.

A shrill cry of agony rose from them both, twined and become one—so terrible a sound that Claude and Gaston stopped their ears. Only then did Daumard and his little one part, the former dying, eyes already clouded, the latter with a mortal wound, a horrid gash in her flawless flesh where the blade had thrust between her breasts.

She clutched her hands to this unexpected stigma. She swayed, her mouth trembled like a petal on the verge of autumn. Below her lay Daumard, dead. Her trapped gaze passed between him and Maillart.

"You bastard," she snarled, and stumbled up the stairs, back into darkness. Maillart cut at her ghostly fleeing form, but slipped and nearly fell in the blood that ran in rivulets down the stairs.

"Come on!" he cried in frustration to Claude and the sorely injured miller. "We have her now!"

Claude struggled to his feet, but his arm was seemingly in flames. Gaston, ghastly pale, muttered, "My leg . . ."

Maillart glared in contempt at them. "Christ!" he said. To the man-at-arms he said, "Quickly! Before she escapes!"

Up the stairs they bounded, and out of sight.

The miller limped painfully to Claude, who leaned against the wall, lost in pain. A tight, hurt, forced smile crossed the miller's lips.

"Let's go, lad," he said. "There's nothing more we can do here."

Claude protested, but the miller only repeated his explanation. Reluctant, afraid, Claude finally agreed.

They pushed against the door. To their astonishment, it opened without resistance. Gaston laughed in mad delight. "See? See, lad? She's finished! Over and done with! Now let's be on our way! Quick, now! Don't linger! Here, give me your arm!"

They began their awkward descent in near-darkness, the miller leaning upon Claude for support. "Steady," the miller said. "Steady . . . we'll be heroes when we return, lad. Yes, we will . . . for putting an end to this. Perhaps now we'll be rid of this abominable weather . . . that would be reward enough for me . . . ."

They rested at the bottom of the flight. Claude collapsed against the wall. The world had become gray and lifeless to him, dull with pain. To speak was an effort.

Gaston, however, was neither still nor quiet. He muttered to himself, to his leg: "Christ, if it isn't broken, I'm blessed." He rose, hobbled about. Over the landing was an archer-slit, angled so as to protect some long-gone archer from return fire. The miller leaned within its recess. Outside, it had grown darker, the gray afternoon shot through with the black and blue of storm and twilight. Lightning flashed stark and white. The miller grumbled and confessed amazement at the weather, at the sounds outside—shouts and screams. The smell of smoke. Christ, now what was happening?

Claude ignored him. The pain of his wound had subsided, though it still ached. Looking up at the dark door above, Claude wondered aloud where Maillart and his man-at-arms companion might be. His question was lost in a sudden crash of thunder so loud it resounded within his skull—that, and the throttled choking of the miller.

A hand held Gaston by his throat—held him suspended, in fact, so that his eyes bulged and his feet thrashed at the air. It was a slight pale hand, attached to a slim graceful arm that emerged from the narrow opening of the archer-slit.

The fingers dug into the flesh of the miller's throat with unreasoning strength. With a yell Claude struck the arm again and again with his staff. He might as well have tried to break marble. The hand's grip eased not in the slightest.

When the miller's struggles had finally become spasms, the hand released him and swiftly withdrew. Gaston fell in a lifeless heap to the floor.

And before Claude could run, or so much as think, Catherine Demoulin pulled herself through the six-inch wide aperture.

She came in a tangle of limbs, like a spider. Fingers, heels, toes— all dug into the stone, all strained and grasped to pull her forward. Into the gap she pushed, distorted, misshapen, taking shape, her body a pale puppet envelope of bones unconnected, a kaleidoscope of flesh, flowing siren hair and lolling loose head. Swiftly the frightful, attenuated face was made right again. The limbs no longer moved in ways unpleasant to see. Bone fused, the body swelled and took form. Catherine stood before Claude, unmarked, and lovely as ever.

"Maillart—" Claude stuttered.

"Dead," Catherine replied quietly. "The both of them."

"My God," the youth muttered. "I—I saw Maillart's sword go into you."

"It did," she replied. There was no sign of the wound.

"They're right. You are from Hell."

"Perhaps" she replied. "And perhaps you are as well."

She regarded the youth with gentle derision.

"Do you even know what I am?" she asked.

Catherine walked slowly toward Claude, who backed away until cold stone would allow him no further. He slumped, shrank away from her, but still she pressed closer. Closer, until her face nuzzled the bare flesh of his neck, her breath warm.

"Answer me. What am I? Ghost? Vampire? Demon?"

"I," Claude stammered, trembling, "I don't know."

He heard the slight slick churn of tongue against teeth, the maddeningly delicate pressure of lips on the sensitive skin of his terribly vulnerable throat.

"Nor do I," Catherine replied. "But I do know this: I grew to love Daumard. As I now love all of you. Your flesh. The blood that beats beneath it, full of so many dark things. Passion. Hatred. Lust. Violence."

Her teeth pressed hard against his throat, nearly breaking the skin. Claude gasped, in terror of the explosion of blood sure to follow. But it did not happen. The tension eased, and Catherine whispered:

"I knew you were coming to kill me. You lied to one another, as you always do. Each story more fantastic, more terrible than the last. And then madness descended upon you, as it has before and forever will.

"Into this place you entered, like wild beasts, and like wild beasts you tore out the throats of those unable to escape, and thought in your fury what you did was right and good."

Catherine's lips left Claude's throat, and pressed close to his ear.

"I saw what you did. All of you. None were innocent, and I was joyous. For I knew then that my husband was wrong. I knew then that I was to receive much, *much* more than is my due."

"You—you can be killed," Claude said. "You *will* be killed."

She laughed darkly, gently in his ear. "You can no more kill me than your own shadow, Claude Rebec."

Her hand cupped his face, and turned it gently, irresistibly toward her own. Her impassive luminous eyes were close to Claude's—green and still as deep water. Lightning flickered in their depths.

"However," she said. "There has been enough play today. I release you for now, though I will come for you sometime. In a form perhaps familiar or a form unexpected. Perhaps in the next moment . . . the next day . . . or many years from now, when you are old and alone and afraid. It hardly matters in the end.

"Now go. Swiftly."

He emerged sometime later—haggard, pale, alone, clutching his wounded arm close. The sky was weighted with clouds. He blinked in the growing gloom, stunned at the chaos before him. They had lit fires. Many fires. Flames licked several buildings. Spatters of rain had begun to fall.

Figures darted through the littered streets. From the rooftops came unintelligible shouts, stone, jagged pieces of slate that smashed into the courtyard below. The deadly missiles had already claimed several victims, dashed out their brains. Discarded weapons lay on the ground.

A man staggered toward Claude, obviously drunk, and clutched the youth's tunic. "All is lost!" he bellowed. "Save yourself!"

Claude tore away from the man. He must tell them! She was not dead! He must tell someone!

But there was no one to tell in that welter of blood and smoke. His shouts were lost in the din. Those he approached fled, not matter how loudly he cried, "She still lives! Catherine Demoulin still lives!"

Wait! Through the smoldering haze Claude spied the glint and flash of steel, like lights beckoning from a distant shore, the heavy thunder of hooves on cobblestone. Mounted knights in full armor and foot soldiers in mail began to fill the courtyard. Relief akin to joy filled Claude. The full might and flower of chivalry was at hand. God's ene-

mies would be driven before them like dust. All was not lost to madness and chaos and dissolution!

Claude Rebec went to them. Christ's own would hear him. They
would triumph where he and the others had failed.

The knight in the lead, captain of war, brought his horse to a halt,
and raised high his sword. At this signal, fierce cries went up and his
men surged past him like water about a stone. Men-at-arms grasped at
the cloaks and arms of fleeing peasants. With crossbows they shot at
the rooftop figures that dared show themselves. Any the soldiers could
not catch were pursued by the knights, to be cut down or trampled.
Shrieks and screams filled the air, rose above the shouting and the roar
of flames.

As if unseen or saint, Claude Rebec passed untouched through the
swirling carnage. He stumbled toward the captain of war, astride his
towering stallion, chillingly faceless beneath his flanged sallet.

"Sir!" Claude cried. "Hear me, good knight!"

The knight took no notice of him. The thickly muscled horse
shifted from hoof to hoof, wide nostrils fluttering and flaring, anxious
to join the milling slaughter.

The youth came closer, and called again.

At last the knight saw him. The anonymous helmet swiveled, and
an inexplicable chill passed though Claude. The sallet with its narrow
dark visor and tiny ventilation holes . . . they were too much like archer-slits and murder-holes and tiny windows forever barred against the
light. But the youth mustered his courage and pressed on.

"Please, good sir," he said, "we have need of your succor. You,
who stand as one with Christ against His foes, be they Wizard, Turk,
or Devil! So please heed me, and know that Catherine Demoulin still
lives! Know that—"

Raindrops pattering upon his armor, the knight urged his horse
forward. Closer, steadily faster he came, a dripping juggernaut. The
blade of his sword gleamed dully.

The words of the youth died in his throat, and what hope remained in him fled on terrified wings.

He turned and ran. But the knight was mounted, and swifter.
Hardly five or six strides Claude Rebec had taken before the knight
overtook him. He struck the youth a slashing blow to the throat that

nearly severed his head—the throat against which Catherine Demoulin had so lately pressed, whispering of bloodshed, of lust and madness, of the darkness of souls and unnamable things.

BLACK ART IN VYÔNES

by Keith Chapman

Alain's mother, the Widow Villon, pulled him to her and hugged him in her frail arms. It was as much as he could do to choke back tears. He tried to straighten his back and hold his head high, but his country-strong shoulders were bowed by the sorrow of parting.

Looking into his mother's careworn face reaffirmed the wretchedness of their circumstances. Her complexion had assumed the ominous finality of coffin grayness; grief and hardship had produced worry lines deep as the cracks that scarred the mudflats bordering the sluggish River Isoile during a summer's drought.

But Alain saw affection and pride, too. A piteous courage was in the black-gowned, prematurely aged woman's forced smile.

"Go forth to the city bravely, my son," she said. "You've done well to win a place in the studio of so famed a painter as Joost van Veen. But tread warily in Vyônes. Never forget your good father's maxim: 'People are not always as they seem.' The city may have a great cathedral at its heart, but its crooked lanes and alleys are steeped in the evil histories of our demon-pestered land. How can it be otherwise when a great forest—the haunt of thieves and outlaws, phantoms and loups-garoux—presses on two sides to its very walls?"

Alain strived to put some manly strength into a voice inclined at times of emotion to betray him still with the breakings of adolescence. "I mustn't let such somber things daunt me, Mother."

He was the son of a deceased tenant farmer. He and his mother had been living frugally in a small village on a well-cultivated plain which was one of the most wholesome habitats in all Averoigne.

But Alain was not content with this lot, and now he was leaving to make real his dreams in the province's principal city.

By virtue of the good offices of the village schoolmaster, who was related to Bartelomie, the Archbishop of Vyônes, Alain had secured an apprenticeship with Joost van Veen, the immigrant Flemish painter.

Van Veen's work for the Church had been much applauded by Bartelomie who, as a Christian prelate, was liberal to the point of civic scandal in his appreciation of fine art. Consequently, the painter now enjoyed the patronage of the noble classes—a wealthy clientele surprisingly willing to follow others' personal tastes.

Alain had gathered that the Fleming felt, as an accepted outlander, that he owed a debt of gratitude to the good Archbishop, and was conveniently willing to oblige such of the ecclesiastic's relatives as Alain's old pedagogue.

"No, Mother, we must be neither gloomy nor tearful in our farewells," Alain said, but not without a certain gruffness that evidenced his true feelings. "Joy shall mingle with my sadness. Van Veen is reputed to be a stern master, I know, but his fame is spreading wide and his genius will be my inspiration. He has brought to Averoigne the art of painting with oils, which has swept away the older traditions. Oil will allow me to take more time over a painting, since it dries far less quickly than tempera. They say it makes painting more accurate; more easy to shade off one color into another."

Alain paused. He had started to muse, distracted from the emotion of the occasion by the tug of his ambitions—his youthful desire for fresh knowledge, no matter the dangers.

"And there are whispers of other, far greater secrets to which I would fain be privy," he went on. "They say van Veen has colors in his palette with occult ingredients that bestow his work with incredible power. It's averred the Archbishop himself has been entranced by the beauty that issues through the channel of van Veen's brush."

So it was, with his mother's misgivings overshadowed by seductive opportunity, that Alain Villon took leave of the humble village where he had resided all of sixteen years and traveled the main highway across Averoigne, through its ill-legended forest to the walled city of Vyônes.

Now in that late summer of 1469, as yet unbeknown to the people in remote rural reaches of the province, a new horror had laid its cold hand on the metropolis. Sanctified though Vyônes was by the presence of a cathedral, a monastery, and two nunneries, it had been no stranger in medieval centuries to the infamous workings of the Archfoe and his hench-things of the Pit.

On the very night of Alain's arrival, a chilling outrage took place in a cobbled city square flanked by tall merchant houses of red brick and black timber that proclaimed the prosperity of their proprietors.

The vintner Louis Lagrange was hastening in the late hours to a backstreet tavern where he had a secret tryst in a private upstairs room with the comely wife of an associate who was journeying out of town on business.

Suddenly, a weird shape interrupted the light of the full moon. A menacing shadow was cast over the amorous M. Lagrange. Scant seconds afterward, a foul-smelling creature swooped hawk-like upon him with clasping talons and a ripping beak. It was human-sized and ferocious in its attack.

M. Lagrange stumbled backward across the empty square. He bleated in abject terror. With just his bare hands, he was helpless to beat off a winged attacker endowed with appendages that were weapons of lethal sharpness. He collided with a stone water trough beneath a cherry tree and cowered beside it as the salty blood ran from multiple wounds on his hands, arms and scalp, blinding him.

The dreadful screams of the distressed vintner roused the neighboring citizenry from beds or night pleasures. But there was nothing they could do to thwart the act of carnage they witnessed in train before them. The small mercy was that the avian aggressor, disturbed by their horrified outcry, screeched in anger and took off with a short ungainly run and a feathery flaps of its wings before it had enjoyed due time to gorge on the flesh of its prey. (Though later, town gossip alleged it had managed to tear open M. Lagrange's breeches and peck off a most delicate morsel.)

The dying vintner gasped his last breaths. "Methought it spoke with—with a woman's—voice. But it was the Killer Beast and has done for me!"

"Summon the guards! Call the surgeon!" said an affronted burgher.

But another pointed out that the cry was futile. "No surgeon can stanch such venous blood." And the monster was already flying away like an interrupted vulture into the night, silhouetted momentarily against the bright silver disk of the moon.

On the morrow, Alain Villon paid cursory attention to the wild gibbers that drifted up to him through an open, dusty-paned attic window. The latest attack by the Killer Beast occupied the chatter of the populace to the exclusion of all else.

Alain was newly lodged in his eyrie at the top of Joost van Veen's three-story mansion. These quarters were furnished as sparsely as a monk's cell. The garret afforded Alain a narrow plank bed with a single blanket and a thin straw pallet on which he could recline comfortlessly in silent dismissal of trivia and in contemplation of more important matters.

"Beasts, flying monsters . . . what incredible tales whereby these foolish city dwellers frighten themselves!" Alain wrote to his mother. "There must be a truer explanation of the unfortunate M. Lagrange's gory death. And yet how equally inexplicable are my new master's ways: I came to paint, but he has forbidden his pupil candle, chair, or table lest I practice outside his presence."

Happily, Alain soon found an ally.

Joost van Veen was an ageing, gray-bearded man dressed seemingly always in a smock both grubby and paint-daubed. His habitual expression beneath a once-scarlet velvet cap was of unyielding strictness. But his daughter, Elisa, was a delight for Alain to behold.

About the same age as himself, she was a pert, pretty girl with a mass of curly gold hair she held off her face with a silken band that matched the color of her sparkling blue eyes. In all the feminine charms, Elisa seemed to Alain equally blessed: the neatness of her eyebrows, her dainty nose, the softness of her rosy little mouth, the alabaster stretch of her neck, the slender waist . . . the promise in the swell of bosom and hips of a voluptuousness that would be fully attained when her virgin years were passed.

A blood-tingling heat mounted within Alain whenever he was in the presence of her girlish beauty. This was frequently since Elisa's prime duty was to assist her father in the studio. Van Veen entrusted her alone to help him produce and mix the colors that gave his paintings their unique qualities. She would sit in a short-sleeved linen frock, its very plainness underscoring her natural attractions, grinding mysterious ingredients to powder in a mortar with a pestle, while Alain cleaned the master's brushes. And, hallelujah, she would exchange fleeting glances and secretive little smiles with him!

"You are like a breath of fresh air in this stuffy studio," Alain said. He paid the compliment after a few weeks' acquaintance had abated their mutual embarrassment and, perhaps as importantly, when her father was out of the room.

"Ah, poor Alain!" the sweet girl said. "I fear Papa's strict rules vex you, but I shall contrive to do all I decently can to soothe the irritations of his tutelage."

Footfalls on the stairs outside curtailed their promising exchange.

Van Veen had returned with a most important visitor—no less than the Archbishop Bartelomie.

"Make way, children!" van Veen said. "His Grace has arrived to survey *The Cross Upon Calvary*."

Alain knew that the purpose of the cleric's visit was not to bear religious witness to some re-enactment of the central event of Christianity, though low hills possibly suitable for such sanctification were visible across the city's crowded roofs and gables from the south-facing second-story windows. Instead, he had come to appraise Joost van Veen's latest work, which had just been completed and was ready for framing.

The painting *The Cross Upon Calvary* had been commissioned by the Church, at the behest of its art-loving Archbishop, as a model for the panels of a huge altar-piece which his grace envisioned for the added beautification of the Vyônes cathedral. The Archbishop expected many realistic scenes of worshipping saints and pilgrims, and possibly several angels or sentimental cherubs.

Alain helped put up the canvas for display on an easel, and Bartelomie clapped his podgy hands.

"Truly, it is a delight!" he told van Veen. "Your passionate figures are so much to be preferred to the hitherto stiff and rigid figures of the Gothic style. Why, I would have said you must have gone to a ghetto and studied Jewish types from life. These characters are so real. And such vibrant color! The verdant green, the blood-red vermilion. It surpasses the magnificence of the illuminated miniatures kept at the Benedictine Abbey of Périgon, which are acclaimed for their brightness and love of detail."

Van Veen laughed. But it was not clear to Alain if he did so to make a joke of his embarrassment at such high praise, or for some other reason.

""Ha! Ha! It is the *paint* I use, your Grace. Mixed in the correct proportions, my colors give a painting the power to depict the true nature of the subject, reflecting in the fullness of time benevolence or malevolence as the case may be. Say it is the paint!"

"Well, then, sir painter," Bartelomie said, "you must bring your wonderful paints to our great cathedral and commence the masterwork expeditiously. The presence of an uplifting diversion for our congregations at this moment is most required. The townsfolk talk of nothing but the Killer Beast, and even the loyalest servants of our Lord are urging me to approach that ancient heretic Luc le Chaudronnier about options for eradicating this foulness that threatens the integrity of the archdiocese."

Alain was familiar with the name of le Chaudronnier. The astrologer and sorcerer had lived, it seemed, as long as an Old Testament patriarch in his house at Ximes, and was Averoigne's foremost practitioner of arcanic arts. He was reputed to know all the spells to summon and dismiss devils, and his talents would appear pertinent to the baleful circumstances.

"But of course," sighed Bartelomie, "it would be unseemly for an Archbishop to call upon wizardry for the city's deliverance from evil, no matter how abominable."

Van Veen nodded. "Indeed, indeed. The whispers have been of the pagan Greek deities of discredited myth. This filthy, hungry creature is a harpy, it's rumored; a latter-day sister to Aello, Podarge, and Ocypete, the impure daughters of Electra, who were taken into loathsome service by the vengeful god Zeus."

Discomfited, Bartelomie lifted a rebuking hand to command the artist's silence. "Speak not of these heathen beliefs in my presence. It is dangerously close to apostasy. Give no credence to the chatter of the erring under-classes. Think upon the good work you will do tomorrow for the glory of the Lord's house."

"Well, not quite tomorrow."

Van Veen essayed an apologetic cough.

"There is first the small matter of a picture I must paint of Isabelle, the wife of Henri, Comte de la Melicourt. Messire Le Comte has determined that her charms should be disclosed while they are yet in full bloom and captured on canvas for his private gallery. Tomorrow, she comes to this very studio to pose for me."

Alain wondered if the Archbishop was at bottom just a common man with all the weaknesses to which flesh is heir, because he certainly betrayed an irreligious thrill at this tidbit of news.

"Madame la Comtesse is acclaimed by the gallants as the most beautiful woman in the province," he said. "It will, I'm sure, be a most—ahem—memorable occasion which I should not presume to obstruct."

Then Bartelomie made a brisk exit. For all the world it struck Alain that, stimulated by his imaginings of the sitting, he was rushing to seek the solitude of his private quarters where he might meditate upon the enrapturing scene and ease his torment.

While Alain conjectured about the Archbishop's lonely ecstasies, *The Cross Upon Calvary* was stacked away amongst a pile of other canvasses and the van Veen household took an early supper before retiring. Van Veen was anxious that he should be rested and restored for the challenges of the morning.

Alain, however, had other plans. The evening hours were the only hours he and Elisa had to themselves and tonight they would seize the chance to use them.

"Goodnight, Papa," Elisa said. "May you sleep well."

Before the clocks of Vyônes chimed another hour, Elisa's wish was granted. She ascended the stairs to the dark landing outside Alain's garret, a flickering taper in hand.

"Come, Alain," she whispered. "Papa is snoring and I have unlocked the studio."

The conspirators, their lusty young hearts thumping, pressed beeswax candles onto the prickets of brazen holders in the studio and Elisa lit them from the taper.

Alain, close behind her, slipped his arms around her slender waist, but Elisa was nervous at the intimacy and averted her blushing face.

"Now, what would you paint, oh great artist?" she asked, possibly to deflect the kiss he intended.

"I shall steal a march upon your father by starting the finest portrait in Averoigne *tonight* . . . and you shall be my subject."

Smothering giggles, they prepared the materials.

"Papa is always very fussy that I should mix this rare ochre with the oil in exactly the right proportions," Elisa said. "He told me once it was ground out of chippings from the mummies of the priests of a lost religion in the Orient."

"I wonder if that's true. Your father has a strange sense of humor."

"You're right, but he does assert most gravely that a living person's portrait wherein 'tis used becomes a mirror, entirely true to life as it might be conducted on occasion by that person."

Their preparations hurriedly completed, Elisa reclined on the divan where the celebrated Comtesse de la Melicourt was appointed to display her sumptuous attractions after the sun was next arisen.

Alain would have liked to dally over the arrangement of his subject's lissome limbs in the soft glow of candlelight, but he forced himself to attend to the task of applying paint to canvas, and the work commenced to take shape.

"Verily I have never worked with such fine colors as your father's, Elisa. These flesh tints are remarkable."

"They're the secret of Papa's success, I trow. Observe how the well-to-do and the highest-placed clamor for him to paint the likenesses of their loved ones."

The stolen hours passed all too swiftly for Alain and Elisa. The cathedral clock began tolling midnight and Alain stepped back from the easel, his face drawn and tired.

Elisa put a hand to her mouth and yawned.

"I weary you with this sitting," Alain said. "We must finish another night."

Elisa eased her cramped muscles into movement. "Let us hide your work behind some old canvases where Papa never thinks to look."

Vyônes' clocks pealed twelve times apiece, hastening the furtive pair to their rooms.

In another quarter the midnight chimes heralded a sinister stirring.

In a château in a broad glade of the gloomy great forest of Averoigne, light spilled from a single window, though the impressive edifice was a place of many rooms and turrets and balconies.

The lighted window, which gave onto one of the ornately railed balconies, was thrown open and heavy drapes fluttered out in the wind.

A hideous creature with a woman's head and body, but the wings, claws and beak of a vulture, came out onto the balcony and flexed its pinions before taking to rustling flight.

Later, in the gray light shortly before cock-crow, a horse drawing a cart laden with turnips on a road approaching Vyônes whinnied and shied as a monstrous winged shadow passed over it. The animal's eyes bulged and rolled with fear. The boy on the cart bench cracked his whip and struggled to control it.

"Whoa!" he cried. "Easy, I say!"

But the panicking horse crashed into a ditch at the side of the road, breaking both its forelegs. The cart was overturned, spilling its load. Then the Killer Beast swooped down and plucked the sprawling boy from his bench with gleaming talons.

One load of turnips never reached the city's market that morning, but a boy's bloodied and broken corpse was dropped onto the cathedral steps. Two early-rising priests recoiled in horror as it crashed down headfirst to the cold hard marble with a stomach-turning squelch. The head broke open like a melon, its contents made into a sanguine pulp that spattered the priests' robes.

They looked up to the sky, crossed themselves and prayed to the Holy Mother that the Lord deliver the city and its environs from Satan's she-demon.

The city trembled to talk of the new slaying. The talk was brought to the grand château of the Comte de la Melicourt by a woodcutter returning to the forest.

"Aye, the harpy was abroad in the night. It was seen over the cathedral almost at daybreak," he told the groom attending a carriage drawn up before the château's porticoed entrance.

The groom growled: "The Killer Beast grows bolder. Some say its lair must lie within the city itself."

Isabelle, Comtesse de la Melicourt, was already seated in the carriage and she leaned out. "Enough of this abhorrent gossip! To Joost van Veen's at the gallop, or I shall be late for my sitting."

Alain had been banished to a shadowy corner of the studio to complete an exercise in figure drawing. The exasperatingly poor light was scarcely conducive to accuracy in his sketching, but his station kept him out of the way while the sure strokes of van Veen's brush reproduced Isabelle's glowing beauty on canvas.

After three days' work, the picture that Alain could see showed a woman reclining in the sunlight, aged thirty-one with fine complexion, pool-dark eyes, and full tresses of lustrous black hair. An adoring small brown lap-dog reached up to her on hind legs to receive a pat on his head.

Isabelle was pleased with the results. "Such faithful work is a wonder to behold! You and your pretty daughter must attend my ball tonight, Messire van Veen."

The Flemish artist was flattered. "We will be most honored to accept your invitation, Madame la Comtesse."

Elisa put the knuckles of a clenched hand to her mouth to stifle her excitement.

"Alain," she hissed. "Did you hear? Papa and I shall dance with the nobility!"

"I'm happy for you, Elisa. And for myself, too . . . . With the house empty, I can put the finishing touches to my picture of you without fear of discovery."

That night, Alain cautiously descended the dark stairway to the deserted studio. Elisa had promised to leave candles and had hidden the key under a loose floorboard.

When Alain unlocked the forbidden studio, he was faced with a sight that chilled him to the marrow of his bones. He staggered back, white as death, eyes and mouth wide open with horror.

A shaft of moonlight through a high window sliced a sharp-edged silver swathe through the crypt-dark room and fell upon Joost van Veen's easel and the canvas thereon.

"Merciful heaven! The picture of the Comtesse . . . it's loathsome! Obscene!"

Alain's sensations were those of one who has cut into a choice sweetmeat and found it crawling with maggots. Revulsion swelled within him until he tasted foul bile in his throat.

Since he had last seen it, the picture had changed dramatically.

Isabelle, the Comtesse, was depicted as a harpy; a rapacious monster with a vulture's vans and claws. Her nose was deformed into a cruelly curved beak, but her other features and torso were as they had ever been, and as a whole she was vaguely recognisable. The wings were like great hunched shoulders. The talons were clutching the blood-spurting body of the squealing, struggling lap-dog.

Alain was suddenly struck by a thought more grotesque, more alarming than the fiendish tableau before him. If the true likeness painted by Joost van Veen could be thus supernaturally changed by the moonlight, what had become of the Comtesse herself?

All the bizarre legends he had ever heard of the shape-changing were-things commonly supposed to stalk the forest of Averoigne tumbled through his spinning brain.

"Oh my God! Elisa, her papa . . . they're at her château: this harpy's lair!"

Alain set forth from the house of van Veen at a run. He was too consumed by his feverish visions of the significance of the distorted picture to be daunted by a journey that must take him through the somber forest where the road was but intermittently lit by the rising moon.

The city gate was soon behind him. Stray felines and small, innocent woodland creatures forsook their nocturnal wanderings and fled from his path as he stormed like a madman to the Château de la Melicourt.

He had to speak with Elisa. He had to warn her. But first, he had to see that she was safe.

A full half-hour elapsed before he reached the château, disheveled and scratched by the clutching twigs and branches into which he had occasionally veered. Panting, he flung himself at the oaken door of the porticoed entrance and hammered his fists on it for admittance.

The bored attendants to the ranked carriages of visiting high society were roused from their somnolence and watched with curiosity. An indignant footman attempted to turn him away.

"What means this rude pounding at Messire le Comte's door? Be gone, wretch!"

Alain blurted his business. "Good sir, let me speak with Elisa van Veen, the painter's daughter! 'Tis a matter of life and death, I swear by all that is sacred!"

Though grim-visaged, the footman relented and Alain was conducted to an antechamber to which Elisa was summoned. She was a welcome sight to Alain, but he found himself awkward, discomposed as she came before him in her stunning ball-gown of purple silk. The puzzled girl's greeting was cool and though moved by his agitation, she was clearly displeased that her pleasure had been interrupted.

Through an archway behind her, Alain could glimpse the crowded party in progress: musicians, dancers, drinking and laughter against the brilliant ostentation of the château. Men wore velvet cloaks and proud airs; women daring dresses and bold glances. Alain's eyes passed over the lofty salon's intricately woven tapestries, the dazzling rugs from distant realms, highly wrought vases in gold and silver, and many gilt-framed pictures the study whereof would normally have enthralled him.

Even to his own ears, the garbled story he had to tell sounded ludicrous. "And so I do beseech you, dear Elisa . . . take leave from this place before 'tis too late."

"Your tale's preposterous, Alain," Elisa said when he was finished. "What you imply is enormously insulting, both to the Comtesse and to my father who has painted her likeness so diligently and well. Were there no fumes on your breath, I'd say you'd partaken of too much wine. You fancy these things. Return to our house forthwith and rest yourself."

Alain repeated his pleadings for her to accompany him but he was unable to sway her. Moreover, she remained utterly skeptical of the macabre transmogrification of the picture, refusing to put its veracity to the immediate test of her own eyes.

"Go, Alain! As for Papa and I . . . no, no! Depart we cannot. The Comtesse would be deeply offended."

His heart heavy with foreboding, Alain withdrew. His steps were reluctant and, being distracted by the fathomless terrors crowding in on him, he brushed clumsily against a drape of rich damask that flanked the open doorway. He was startled to see that it concealed the chatelaine, Isabelle, the Comtesse de la Melicourt.

Had she merely been about to enter, or had she been standing there all the time? If the latter, he wondered how much she had overheard of his talk with Elisa.

Mumbling an apology, he made his departure, followed by her darkly inscrutable gaze.

After a brief rest in the cool night air, Alain trudged back to the city and the house of van Veen, dogged by a sense of unreality all the way.

He lit the candles in the studio and, though he feared its uncertain omens mightily, he sat head in hands before the malevolent moonlit picture of the harpy Comtesse, to contemplate its hideousness and its meaning, and to await the return of the van Veens. For sure, they were going to be deeply shocked by its foulness. That the picture as a piece of artistry was as perfect from every technical aspect as it had been originally when portraying a beautiful woman by sunlight only added to the hellish malignity of its metamorphosis.

Lost in horrible conjectures, and with fears for Elisa—whom he realized he loved deeply—still very much alive, Alain did not hear the eerie, forewarning beat of wings across the neighboring rooftops, nor the scrabble of claws as they found purchase on the window ledge of the studio.

It took the shattering of glass to jerk him from his dark reverie. The shards cascaded into the room, tinkling around him. Gleams of fantastical light danced on the sharp new edges like corposants.

Alain jumped to his feet and tried to back away as the harpy hurled itself with apparent impunity through the jagged opening where the window had been. Evil intent was written large on those parts of its form in which it took after an eater of dying and dead flesh.

The student painter ducked and dodged the flapping wings, the claws and the hooked beak. He had no weapon with which he could counter the unclean creature's vengeful fury, but as he was finally borne to the floor, he saw beside him a stack of paintings, leaned against the wall.

He snatched up the picture that was outermost, one returned that day from the framer's, thinking to use it as a shield.

And fortune in that moment chose to smile on Alain Villon, for he unknowingly took up a weapon as deadly as any he desired. The painting he had seized with both hands was *The Cross Upon Calvary*.

Alain swung the heavy, framed artwork between his vulnerable body and his demonic assailant who collided with it, shedding feathers. The picture was wrenched from Alain's grasp, its canvas ripped. He feared renewed attack . . . .

But the harpy's screeches of wrath suddenly intensified and became spine-chilling shrieks of agony.

The sprinkling of holy water could have provided no more potent an exorcism. The body and members of the harpy were unnaturally convulsed, dissolving into a misshapen, plasmic mass. Then, stage by stage, the formless matter reconstituted itself, taking on the symmetry of a beautiful woman, much as Alain supposed a werewolf would metamorphose as it returned from beasthood to its human form.

Yet when the slender, shapely body began to assume a cover of purple that took on the shimmering texture of silk, Alain's nightmare did not end but plunged him into the blackest of its depths. He was devastated, horror-struck.

"No!" he cried aloud. "Not you . . . ! I vow 'tis trickery. My eyes deceive me!"

Poor Alain! What he saw was no illusion. Of that, the studio, disarranged by his struggle with the harpy, provided bitter confirmation.

Disturbed from its hiding place, tossed amongst the litter of pictures across the floor, and illuminated by moonlight was a canvas he had painted himself with the wonderful paints of Joost van Veen. It was his novice picture of Elisa and, like the painting of the Comtesse de la Melicourt, it was now also a true likeness.

Of a harpy.

THE COCKATRICE OF CORDELIERS

by Michael Minnis

It is said that in the town of Cordeliers, near the heart of Averoigne, that nothing stayed the course of business and commercial life; not holidays, not proclamations or edicts, not war or plague, not Death or God, not even Sunday. But there was one event that always brought everything to a standstill—a public execution.

Public executions were a great source of entertainment for the people of Cordeliers, perhaps the greatest of them all. From far and wide they all came to witness the event: shining knights and stinking fishmongers, pilgrims and rag-pickers. The desire to witness, to participate vicariously in the awful event, was so powerful that all traditional boundaries, jealousies, observations, and decorum were discarded no matter how old, respected, or entrenched. Magistrates in gold thread stood next to beggars in sack cloths. Occasionally the mob surged and pushed. Tempers then flared and noses were broken and teeth knocked out. But mostly it remained oddly, frighteningly docile, an excited, anxious press of cheek and jowl and elbow and belly and bosom and ass—a sweaty composite of glee, keen interest, morbid curiosity, and potential violence.

The crowd that particular day was unusually large, even by the usual dismal standards of those dismal days. That the scheduled executed was to be a rooster only heightened its interest.

The rooster—the cock in question—was nine years old, decrepit, half-blind, balding, and in many ways quite pitiful. His red and green finery was faded as old brocade, his comb like a ragged banner, and he walked with a limp. He had no name, had lived an unexceptional life and would have died an equally unnoticed death but for one detail: he was accused of having birthed during the days of the star Sirius that most fearsome of monsters, a cockatrice.

When the headsman appeared at last, bearing the rooster under his arm to the scaffold, the crowd exploded into uproar. The headsman, unmoved, stroked the rooster's frail head and muttered, "There, old fellow, soon it will be over. Pay no mind to them. Pay no mind to these fools."

The headsman was not a favored man. When the bloody-minded cheering subsided somewhat the crowd was quick to remind him of this fact. "Hoi, Heap!" a heckler shouted.

Heap was the headsman's nickname because that is what he most resembled: a shambling, hairy, thick-limbed, roughly conical hillock of flesh, slow, but solid as a mountain, with strength to match. Supposedly no one had ever seen his face; it was said to be too terrifying to look upon.

"Heap! Have a mind to the middens when you're done here!"

This prompted laughter; the headsman dealt in the removal of refuse as well as criminals, political undesirables, minions of Satan, thralls of Azètot and Iog-Sotôt, and upstart sorcerers.

The headsman bore the jibe without reaction.

A stout woman asked: "What's that you've got there, a finger-chopper?"

This was in reference to the headsman's tool of trade; normally, he bore a great, nicked, stained axe whose head was in the shape of a crescent moon, and whose heft required the full use of both his hands. But such a weapon was too much for the slender neck of an elderly cock. So the headsman had sharpened his much smaller wood-hatchet for the grim occasion. Besides, he would need the other hand free to hold down his prisoner.

The headsman sighed. Always, they wanted a performance, this lot. He should have been an actor.

"A finger-chopper, you ask?" he replied. "Well, yes. And, if you should like, dear lady, I will loan it to you after I am done here, and you can use it on that philandering husband of yours."

There was chuckling and some laughter, but the stout woman was confused. "Chop off his fingers, then?" she asked. "All ten?"

"No. Chop off only the one that is not on either hand and yet is most troublesome to you—the eleventh."

The rougher sorts burst into raucous laughter, which quickly spread to the better elements—such as they were in that mob. The stout woman, bested, merely scowled and folded her impressive, reddish forearms together.

"You're a shit-pile, you are, Heap!" a rag-picker cried. "Lowest of the low!"

"And you, sir, pick rags! So, come, then, and polish my arse!"

A good deal of this was sport; but Heap had to be careful. There was a reason there was a line of men in armor below him, armed with staves and halberds. The crowd might storm the scaffold, like Ottoman Turks storming the fortress of Rhodes. More than once Heap had had to set the matter straight himself with the butt end of his axe and his boot soles. But today he was safe—the old rooster was unable to excite the sympathy of the crowd. No family or friends to incite a riot or attempt a desperate, last-moment rescue, no final soliloquies, pleas, or curses to sway hearts and inflame minds. The old cock was mute and entirely doomed.

"Show him! Show us the prisoner!" someone shouted.

"Yes, show him!"

"Then behold the prisoner, you rabble!" Heap shouted, "and be grateful that his fate is not yours!"

He held high the rooster, which fluttered weakly. The crowd dissolved into cacophony and insults. Fiend! Bastard! Servant of Satan! You poisoned my crops! You slew my cattle! It is because of you that I'm plagued with boils!

Drums put an end to the tumult, beating out a slow, solemn, steady dirge one felt in the guts and in the bones; the sound of final minutes under leaden skies. The moment had arrived, and the crowd waited.

Heap gently pressed the bird's neck to the blood-stained block upon which so many had been unceremoniously dispatched. The rooster did not resist. It was a pity, really.

"There, old fellow," Heap said. "Only a moment, and then sweet dreamless sleep, forever."

Taking careful aim, he raised the wood-hatchet. The drums rolled. The crowd fell silent. A single blow was all that was needed; the block made a hollow, final sound as the hatchet blade bit through meat and gristle and into hard wood. Out the blood spurted and the gathered throng stamped and cheered. They roared when Heap held aloft the decapitated, fluttering corpse. Death to the begetter of monsters! Death to the spawn of Satan!

"Bastards," Heap muttered under his breath.

It was not the only beheading to take place that day. The elderly cock, after all, had had accomplices. They were the old, half-mad woman who owned him and the creature who reputedly had sat for nine years upon the leathery egg that bore the cockatrice—a toad of contemptible character.

Forward Guy Broche stumbled along the cobblestone streets of Cordeliers.

"Idiot!" one of the wedding party shouted at him—a woman with bobbed locks like a man's, who sported huge silver Tatar spurs. "Watch where you're going!"

"Sorry, sorry," Guy muttered. Sweat had run into his eyes and momentarily blinded him. He shifted his burden best as he was able. His shoulders ached and his feet were smoldering coals. Peasants and tradesmen stopped in their labors to stare at him. They leaned out of their windows to watch.

"Pardon, pardon," Guy said.

"Step back, you rotters!" the woman shouted. "The wedding train of Odette de Berry and Jean le Roye approaches! Make way!"

And so they came, a crest of cold scaled gray and silver and winter blue and wine red, thrusting aside brown and black, the women dressed as men and the men, in turn, as women, so that no one might be as fair as Odette. Guy and his burden brought up the rear.

"Men with plucked brows and pattens on their feet," said an innkeeper in disgust as they passed his door. He cupped his hands around his mouth. "Scandalous!"

"Fuck off," replied the woman.

The men tittered and threw flowers. The women answered any challenges with the hilts of their swords. A nose or two was bloodied before the crowd learned to keep its indignation to itself.

"Pick up the pace," the woman said to Guy. "This isn't a funeral march."

"Yes, sorry, I know."

"Move!"

Guy trotted forward under his burden, which was also the wonder of its age. It was the prized possession of Odette de Berry of Vyônes: a slightly convex circular mirror of glass clear as a raindrop, and nearly three feet across. Adding to its already considerable weight was an

elaborate frame of tortoiseshell and ivory depicting the seven deadly
sins in unsparing, satiric detail; from its inlaid, starry center a sun and
moon of veneered walnut, larch, and Cedar of Lebanon went through
their courses. It was priceless and beautiful to all but Guy, who wore it
strapped to his back like a turtle to its shell, continuously and without
cease, for Odette to gaze worshipfully into from the moment she rose
in the morning to the time she finally went to sleep. Lady de Berry
quite literally believed herself to be "singularis atque incomparabilis"—
that is, peer without peer. No other woman was as desirable, as arche-
typical of courtly love, as she. Nor would they be allowed, when she
made men as women—and the women as men, deprived of all powder
and scent and comely things, and encouraged in the arts of swearing
and fisticuffs. Only Guy in his lowliness was left unaltered, Guy with
his cropped black bowl of hair, his reddened weather-beaten face,
smudge of mustache and perpetual squint; mud-stained, rain-drenched,
sweat-soaked, dust-choked, always suffering some form of extremity.

He comforted himself with the knowledge that others had suffered
worse in the employ of Lady de Berry: a poet from the city of Vyônes,
in fact, was once "commissioned" to compose verses in honor of her
shapely white bosom. The epic, titled *A une Poitrine* (To a Bosom), was
1,427 lines in length and still incomplete at the time of his mysterious
demise. None ever quite deduced his death; perhaps day after endless
day spent comparing his patron's defining feature to everything from
billowing sails and white hills to nesting doves and cantering palfreys
eventually sickened even him, and thus merited a headlong leap from
Vyônes' tallest tower. Guy had contemplated suicide on occasion as
well, but only half-seriously. Besides, heights made him dizzy.

Not that it mattered. He was sure he would die today, here, in the
streets of Cordeliers, he was so tired. And if not today, then soon. Lady
de Berry was to be married to the maimed Jean le Roye, who was as
cruel as she was vain, with a predilection for violence. The future, for
Guy, held very little promise and of luck, none.

Inevitably, he fell behind again, then further. His foot caught upon
a loose cobblestone, and he stumbled and fell. There was a crack. The
mirror!

A strong hand lifted Guy up. "Ho, there! You'd best be careful of
that."

His eyes smarted with sweat so that Guy had difficulty discerning who spoke to him. There was a great deal of black. A hood. Guy wiped at his eyes. A headsman, with a hatchet in his belt and a huge axe slung over one shoulder.

"Are you all right?" the headsman asked. "You look all right. Damned street! Every week I write to the Guild of Roads and Lesser Pathways complaining about this, and is anything ever done about it? Of course not!"

"The mirror!" Guy said. "What of the mirror!"

The headsman made a cursory examination. "What? Oh, that. Hmm. Seems all right. Well, wait . . . here, this."

The headsman handed Guy a small wood fragment. "Must have come from one of the lower corners, I would think."

Guy swallowed thickly. His mouth tasted of dust. The world collapsed into ruin. "Then it is over," he said. "I'm dead. Please, cut off my head, if you would."

"Excuse me?" the headsman asked.

"My head. Cut it off. I'm doomed."

"Why? It's just a mirror."

"No, you don't understand. Nothing must ever happen to my Lady's mirror!"

"Well, why not just have it repaired?"

Guy shook his head.

The headsman removed a pouch upon his broad belt. "In that case, I'm willing to pay for damages. Here, take it."

"No!" Guy cried.

"Idiot!" The spur-wearing woman approached. "You're supposed to keep up with us! You know that!"

"Yes, yes, I know, sorry," Guy replied.

"So why then are you dithering with him?"

"I . . ." Guy stammered. Panic set in, swarmed about his brain like stinging insects. He lost all capability for thought. He displayed the wood fragment. "Look! Do you see! It's *his* fault! He did this! He knocked me down for a joke and *this* happened! This!"

Guy held the fragment high for all to see.

"That's a lie!" the headsman exclaimed. "I did no such thing! If anything, I tried to help him. You all saw me, didn't you?"

But every peasant seemed equally blind, and apparently saw nothing.

"Quiet," the woman said. To Guy she said, "You, move along. I'll deal with this fellow."

Guy did as he was told.

"So," the woman said. "What say you?"

"Here," the headsman said, and tossed the small leather bag of coins at the woman's feet. "It's all I have. It should be sufficient. It's just a little piece, after all."

The woman kicked the bag aside. Her hard expression hardened further. "You dunghill," she said. "There's isn't enough coin in this entire wretched town to pay for that mirror!"

"Dunghill, is it?" the headsman replied. "I should prefer *Heap*, if you don't mind, for I shall fall upon you like one if you continue to insult me."

"Do you know who you're talking to?"

"Who? No. Or *what*, for that matter," the headsman replied. "Perhaps *you* should be the one wearing the hood here, and not I."

Several peasants chuckled. The woman flushed. The laughter stopped when she pressed the point of her sword against the headsman's neck.

"Drop your axe," she said.

The headsman did as told. The huge axe clanged hard against stone; the peasants flinched at the sound. The woman appeared to deliberate for a moment.

"The hood," she said.

"And why?"

"Because I'll need something to carry your head in, that's why."

The headsman made no move.

"The hood. Now."

The headsman sighed and began to remove his hood. Then, as quickly as a man blinks he palmed the woman's sword aside, seized her by her mailed wrist with his other hand, and pulled her off balance, past him, swinging her in an arc so that she flew wide-eyed through the air and face-first into a foul, squealing, muddy clutch of nearby pigs.

Befouled with offal and furious, the woman went for her dropped sword. The headsman brought his foot down upon the blade.

"Tut-tut," he said, as if to a misbehaving child.

An unseen peasant was his undoing. The headsman sustained a blow to the temple with a sturdy hunk of firewood. He did as his name, which was to collapse to the ground in a heap. Considering the impressive, reddish forearms of the stout matron wielding the makeshift weapon, it was a wonder his head wasn't entirely knocked off.

Wiping smut from her face, the spur-wearing woman said, "He's coming with me. You, you, and you, help me with him."

The stout matron slipped easily away, and went in eager search of the bag of coins, but street urchins and ragged beggars had already found it and were dividing the coins among themselves. She chased them, yelling, and they scattered in all directions like crows.

And as for the cockatrice, the monster, it was abroad and about its business, along the lengthy, lonely stretch of dark fir which shadows the road between Vyônes and Périgon—darting between the trees, alert, missing nothing. It was hunting. It snapped up a dragonfly. The cockatrice chased a terrified badger all the way back to its burrow and then lay outside, waiting—the badger within snarling mightily—until thirst compelled it to drink from a nearby spring-fed stream.

Territoriality preceded thirst. Briefly mistaking its iridescent reflection in the water for an interloper, it struck—and the foe wavered and disappeared in widening circles. Satisfied that its dominance was asserted, the cockatrice drank.

The cockatrice moved on. To paraphrase the Roman naturalist Pliny, it did not impel its body along like other serpents, by a multiplied flexion, but advanced lofty and upright—and, with what Pliny would have discovered, unnerving speed and agility.

The cockatrice as described by Lucan and Avicenna is something of a paradox, in that it is perhaps the deadliest of monsters, able to split rocks, shrivel plants, poison life with its breath, and able to kill with its mere gaze. Yet it is little more than a foot long, a disheveled compilation of watery-eyed, ragged cock and flicking serpent tail, a patchwork of tarnished red-gold feathers and gray-green scales. It would likely elicit pity, or ridicule, were it not for its reputed powers. *This* particular cockatrice, however, was different.

It was gaudily shaded, like a cock. Its feathers, which were iridescent-black along the length of its sleek body, flared into the blazing autumnal yellow-orange along its spine, tail, and limbs. Its throat and underbelly, by contrast, were of purest dove-white, the head dark, shimmering, metallic green. The reptilian eyes, set deep in their white orbits, were coolly opalescent, shifting by slight, entrancing degrees in color, gorgeous but for their inhuman coldness. This particular cockatrice could no more kill with them than it could with its breath, but this was not necessary. It had sharp teeth and claws for that task, but its chief weapons were the long, cruel, sickle-shaped spurs it sported on each foot, like a cock. But its most striking feature was a small, bright white blaze of a marking set high on its head. This mark, shaped like a diadem, was the mark of royalty according to the Egyptian Horapollo in his work *Hieroglyphica*. To Pliny, it meant that the cockatrice was king of all serpents.

But it was a king without subjects. At one time there had been others like it; scattered, bonding temporarily to hunt and for mutual safety, but they had never been numerous. In *The Book of Vule* an unknown Cistercian monk writes of the similar *basilicok*. At the battle of Châlons-Sur-Marne in AD 451 a score were seen routing among the dead Huns and Romans. One was even discovered within the vault of a chapel dedicated to Saint Lucea during the reign of Pope Leo the Fourth; its poisoned breath caused much death in Rome. From there royal hunts and goodly Christian knights took their toll; slayers such as St. George had entered the picture. By the time of the Black Death no more were seen, and the monk was left to conclude that the eradication Man had begun, the Pestilence had finished. But one, the cockatrice of Averoigne, still remained, a survivor.

A relative newcomer, the cockatrice at first behaved more like bandit than lord. It ate carrion and mice and insects. Its boldness growing with familiarity, it ventured into the environs of Man. A peasant might awaken one dewy morn to find it nosing among his turnips. It found livestock easier prey, and began killing pigs, goats, sheep, cows, and finally, the occasional peasant. Travelers, too, it took when it chanced upon them—for unlike the creature of Pliny and Lucan, the cockatrice of Averoigne was much larger and stronger. And because it had had much practice removing gauntlets, sabatons, and helmets from dead men while scavenging battlefields, armor was no proof against it.

Someone was poking Heap. A voice whispered:

"Ho, there! Are you all right?"

Whoever it was sounded familiar. Heap stirred, shifted. Something soft and dry under his palms—straw, it smelled like, a musty, smelly bed of it.

Straw? Where in blazes was he?

He rose and hit his aching head against something else.

"Ow!"

"Careful!" the voice said. "Not much room in there, eh?"

"No," Heap replied. All about him he saw crude wooden bars. "It's—"

"A cage. I know." The regretful voice belonged to Guy, who stood outside. Without the mirror upon his back, he stood straight. "Normally they keep the trained bear in it, but it seems like you've . . . taken his place. I'm sorry. Really, I'm sorry for everything."

"Oh?" Heap said. "I see. Well, then. Here. Come close. Closer. I have something important to tell you."

Guy, as usual, did as he was told. Heap seized him by the throat.

"So help me, God," Heap said softly, the hood but inches from Guy's face, "I am going to squeeze your neck until your head falls off. No! Better yet, I'm going to break every bone in your body pulling you through these bars . . ."

"Wait!" Guy gasped. "Wait! I can help! I want to help you!"

Heap's grip relaxed slightly. "How?"

"I know—will you stop choking me?—I know where to find the key! I can get you the key!"

"The key, you say?"

Guy nodded. Heap released him.

"So, who holds it?"

"Either the Lady de Berry, or her betrothed, the knight Jean le Roye."

"You'd best not be lying again . . ."

"I'm not!"

Heap eyed the heavy padlock upon the cage door.

"So, you'll get the key and help me escape?" he asked.

"Yes."

Suspicion was second nature to Heap. "And the catch would be?"

"I'm coming with you," Guy replied, grinning.

Guy stood before Sir Jean's tent. He cleared his throat. "Sire?"

"Enter."

Guy stepped into lavishly appointed half-darkness. The speckled skins and spotted hides of rare beasts were spread upon the ground, and upon them, silk cushions. A carved teak table in the middle of the tent was heavy with silver and gold dishes. Sturgeon, pickled eel, and crisped peacock in lemon sauce were the order of the day; *hippocras* and honey mead to drink. A large velvet-collared hawk eyed Guy from its gilded perch with scarcely less coldness than Jean himself.

"Oh," Jean said. "It's you."

"Sire," Guy said, and bowed, trying not to stare. It wasn't easy, and this was not because Odette sat rather indelicately upon Jean's lap as she trimmed his mustache. Nor was it because Odette was especially striking this day, attired in a laced bodice of azure and fawn trimmed with white Muscovy miniver, her long reddish coiffure bound by ribbons and tiny rosettes, her forehead by a delicate, filigree ferronière. It was because Jean was *sans* armor. And, when not in his armor, it became plain just how much Jean was missing. Having warred for years against the Poles, Lithuanians, Teutonic Knights, English, Navarrese, and Ottomans, he retained in his possession no more than a full leg, a half-leg, and his sword arm. The Hungarians, not to be outdone, had accounted for his left ear. The Frisians, meanwhile, were still out for his head.

"You even manage to bow badly," Jean said. "Tell me again, why do we keep this one?"

"My mirror, love, remember?" Odette replied.

"Oh, yes. *That*, the mirror, of course. That's the fellow, then? Strange, I could have sworn he was that blasted poet."

"Poet?"

"Yes, you remember, that addlepate you commissioned to write verses about you, your . . . well, until he—" and with the fingers of his remaining hand Jean pantomimed a little man leaping to his death from the arm of his chair.

"Oh, yes, him. I remember. Tragic, really."

"The coin I misspent on him was the *real* tragedy," Jean said. "Gold doesn't come cheaply, you know."

"I know, love," Odette replied.

"Now, as for you, what do you want? Speak up."

Guy muttered, stumbling over words. "You see—well . . . it . . . sire—"

"Are you sure he isn't the fool?" Jean asked Odette.

"Yes, he's my mirror-bearer.."

"See here, you," Jean said. "That was quite a good crack you gave my beloved's mirror—quite a good crack. You're lucky it didn't break entirely. Had that happened, it would have been your head. So, count yourself fortunate that I am a magnanimous man."

Guy nodded. One always nodded when Jean spoke, whatever he said. Swallowing a lump of fear, Guy continued: "About—about the hooded one, sire. I—I think you should release him."

"And why?"

"Because," Guy said, "because I am the one at fault. I—I tripped. He didn't push me. I lied. It's my fault."

"I see," Jean replied coolly. "Well, I—blast it, woman, if you keep trimming it there won't be anything left!—as I was *saying*, I am a magnanimous man. I am a man of God. Your . . . honesty . . . impresses me. If, say, my late master of kennels were of the same make as you, I would not have had to turn the hounds loose on him. So, then, what do you propose? Clemency? Forgiveness? Absolution?"

"Um, the key, if you would," Guy said. "The key to the cage. I should like to set him free myself."

"Yes, I see. Admirable." An idea seemed to be forming within Jean. "Yes, so admirable, in fact, that I shall put you in there with him. Guards!"

"What?" Guy said. "But—"

Two men in mail entered the tent. "Sire?"

"Put this one in the bear cage, too."

Strong hands grasped Guy by his arms. "But you're making a mistake!"

"The only mistake made here was your own," Jean replied.

When Guy was removed, Odette resumed her work. "So, what do you plan to do with them?" she asked.

"Haven't decided yet," Jean said. "I thought a little fun might be in order, what with the bear already having been, well, used for archery practice. And the hounds are getting restless. They need to run. So a hunt on the morrow, at dawn. How does that sound?"

"Rather barbaric," Odette said.

"The Ottomans are barbaric, love; I am merely cruel."

Odette resumed trimming her betrothed's mustache. "And our wedding?"

"Soon enough, soon enough," Jean said. "By God, the courtship's hardly over and already you're becoming a shrew. *Ow!*"

"So, if I understand you correctly," Heap said, "you went and *asked* for the key. Right?"

"Yes," Guy replied.

"Thinking that if you asked for it, you'd receive it."

"Yes."

Heap chuckled helplessly. "And here I thought maybe—just maybe—that you might prove me wrong. That you might prove to be some . . . hell, some accomplished thief or robber-king, who would call upon all his wits and guile to steal that key right from under the very eyes of the guards themselves and deliver me from my fate! Yes, you! Guy of the Shadows! Bandit Extraordinaire! Dauntless, daring! Faugh! What was I thinking? You're like all the other fools, the idiots that come to see me lop off a head or two. There's absolutely nothing more to you than what's to be seen, and *that* isn't much."

A change came over Guy's expression, one Heap had not seen before. "Oh? And what about you? What have *you* done exactly besides mope? You with your *terrible* big axe and your *horrible* black hood—oh, behold the Terror of Cordeliers, oh, hide your children, mothers! Bolt your shutters, good citizens! Pfft. One tap on the pate and you're done for."

"Careful," Heap said. "One look under this hood is all it would take."

"One look, eh? Then show me."

But Heap did not lift his hood.

Guy leaned against the bars, sighed, and closed his eyes.

"So, what happens next?" Heap asked at length.

"You really don't want to know."

"No, tell me."

"A hunt."

"What? Us?"

"Yes. Us."

"You can't be serious. We're to be hunted?"

Guy nodded. "Just like the master of the kennels."

Thunder rumbled in the distance.

"All over a mirror," Guy said at length. "All over vanity."

Evening settled over the camp. A few torches and camp fires were lit. The wedding was not until tomorrow, but many had already decided to get an early start on the festivities: the wedding party was a rather undisciplined lot. By nightfall, many were drunk. Song and ribaldry gave way to sleep. Fires burned low and torches guttered out. When the cockatrice emerged as silent as a phantom from the deep woods, briefly illuminated by lightning, not a soul noticed.

Normally, it avoided such large concentrations of men; in numbers and armed, they were dangerous. But the sounds and smells of the camp were so intoxicating—the bitter peaty stink of small beer, the tang of smoke and ash, hide, leather, oil, gilded meat, spun sugar, horseflesh, sleeping dog, sleeping man—that it was compelled to investigate. But it was the faint must of bear that particularly intrigued the monster. And so from beneath the whispering pines it crept, crouched, stepping carefully toward the camp. Not a soul noticed it.

Guy was awakened late that night by a small, suspicious sound. The wind had risen, but there was still no rain, only restlessness and dark. The storm was circling but had not broken yet. Guy listened: the rush of grass, the snap and flutter of tent flaps and banners, the pop of dying embers, the snore of a drunken guard—nothing exceptional. Nerves and night. He rubbed his eyes. The stink of bear was all about him. Heap muttered in his sleep. Guy wished suddenly that he *was* a master thief, an escape artist, a creature of shadows. Why, if so, he would have had the lock to their cage picked by now, and both Heap and he would be free—

But where would they go? Cordeliers was out of the question; so was Périgon to the south. They would be outlaws, forced to live off the land. And while the settled parts of Averoigne might be safe, its forests and wastelands and marshes were not, home as they were to wolves and snakes and less mentionable terrors: werewolves and phantoms and stalking things. Demons and cockatrices. Monstrosities. But then it had been Lady de Berry's idea to have this woodland wedding; it was the current rage among the upper classes, followers as they were of Dionysus and Pan. The Lady de Berry had sent invitations as far as England and the Papal States. Too bad that such illuminated guests as Chaucer, Petrarch, and Boccaccio had already died many, many years before—

Damn, there it was again—that faint scraping sound.

"Go—"

Words failed him. He did not make a sound, but simply stared in amazement at the sleek, pebbled, iridescent snout that protruded between the bars. Inhuman eyes devoid of expression blinked at Guy. The thing snorted. Then, with utmost unconcern and white teeth as long as a man's finger, it resumed gnawing upon the bars of the cage, working its fangs deep into the wood, worrying it like a dog.

Guy crossed himself. The monster outside . . . it was—of course, a cockatrice! But, it was huge! Why, it stood as tall a man. And with that powerful tail it must be twice as long.

With utmost effort to maintain his nerve, Guy crept toward the armored death's head of the creature. It displayed neither fear nor even much interest in him.

He kicked it, hard, upon the snout. The cockatrice snapped back; the jaws barely missed his foot. The remote eyes were now very much interested in him, and Guy was alarmed to see just how much of its head it could force between the bars. Terrified, Guy waited for the poisonous breath that would slay both him and Heap. Yet from the cockatrice's throat came nothing but a livid, powerful, continuous growl.

"Heap," Guy squeaked.

"It's a franc per head," Heap muttered.

"Heap."

"What? What?"

Heap saw the cockatrice.

"Don't move," Guy said.

Still growling, the cockatrice resumed its work, but with greater effort than before, tugging and pulling with such strength that the entire cage shook.

"Help!" Heap cried.

"Quiet!" Guy said.

A torch bobbed toward them through the darkness.

"What in blazes is going on over here?"

It was the woman with the bobbed locks; she appeared half-asleep, unaware of danger.

"This had better be good, you—"

The cockatrice hissed at the woman. The curved white spur upon each foot cocked, tensed, and it leaped at her.

The sound of a scream in camp was really not out of the ordinary to Jean le Roye; the men, as said, were rough, and the female company they kept indelicate. Jean was inclined to turn in early and was generally not disturbed by drunken revelry, singing, and even the occasional fight, as long as it didn't get out of hand.

He rolled over, grumbling. The wedding was tomorrow; so was the hunt, which he looked forward to rather more. Then, there was Odette's mirror. He'd have to find some other dolt to carry it, and no doubt *that* dolt would damage it too. Why couldn't she just hang the damned thing up on the wall like anyone else?

Now there was shouting and a general stir. Damn. Blast. Obviously, there would be no sleep tonight. Jean kicked off the blankets. It was time to knock some sense into some heads. Where was his squire?

Odette stirred in her sleep. "Love?"

"It's nothing."

Jean found his crutch and hobbled toward the entrance of the tent. In the distance dogs barked. Placing two fingers in his mouth, he gave a piercing whistle that always brought his squire on a breathless run.

"Jean!" Odette groaned, irritated.

Footsteps, swiftly approaching, the sound of grass trampled underfoot—*thump thump thump thump thump!* Odd. Had his squire always been so swift to reply?

The cockatrice's sudden appearance—peering as it did from under the heavy tent flap—left Jean dumbfounded, convinced he was in the grip of an unusually disturbing dream. He realized that this wasn't the case when the cockatrice bared its red teeth at him.

With dawn came gray spotty rain. The light was muted, the periphery of the green country flashing white.

The camp was deserted, tents collapsed, fires guttered out, swords and banners scattered about like leaves in autumn. As far as Heap could tell, only he and Guy remained. Everyone else had fled the cockatrice or been killed by it. And so the camp belonged to the cockatrice, and his victory feast some poor, maimed fellow it had dragged out of a tent, from which it now tore and swallowed chunks of flesh with bird-like movements. The opalescent eyes were alert, however, and Heap knew himself to be under watch.

Guy stirred awake.

"Look at him," Heap said. "Gaudy bastard, isn't he? Who's he nibbling on, anyway? Do you know?"

"Sire Jean," Guy replied.

"You mean the fellow who was going to hunt us and all?"

"Yes."

"Ha! Guess that's off, then. But we're still in a bind with *him* around."

"He'll go away," Guy said.

"Oh, and you're sure of that, right?" Heap asked. "And when, I ask?"

"Soon, I suppose," Guy said, rather doubtfully.

"You seem to have a way of being *wrong* about things, I've noticed." Heap turned his attention back to the cockatrice. "By God, but he's much bigger than I expected. Twice the height of a man in length, I'm thinking. And swift, like a greyhound! And those terrible spurs on his feet, why he—ach, I don't like talking about it. Mayhap his breath isn't a poisonous fume, and mayhap the grass doesn't wither under his feet like it should, but this fellow—he's the spawn of Satan. We don't stand a chance against that."

Guy stroked his chin. "Perhaps—perhaps it isn't a cockatrice at all," he said.

"No, he's a cockatrice, all right. He's just a little different, like we're a little different from each other."

"What?"

"Listen, we're both men, right? We've both got two arms and two legs and heads, right? But we don't look exactly alike, do we?"

"No."

"Of course not! I'm big, you're small! I'm sturdy, you're relatively frail—"

"You always go about with that hood on your head, whereas I never wear a hood except in poor weather, and then only a cowl."

"Right! Exactly! But, if you were to, say, run either of us through the heart with a sword, we'd both die. Do you see what I'm saying?"

"That we should consider running ourselves through and dying?"

Heap sighed. "No. No, no, no. What I am *saying* is *that* monster out there is a cockatrice as surely as *I* am a headsman and *you* are a buffoon. And what kills a cockatrice? No, on second thought, don't answer that, I will."

"What, then?" Guy asked.

"A *mirror.* If it looks into a mirror it will die, it is so appalled by its own hideousness."

Guy glanced at the feeding cockatrice, which cocked its colorful head warily at him before resuming its meal.

"He's really not that ugly, though. *Striking* is a better word for him."

Heap slugged Guy in the arm.

"Ow!" Guy cried.

"*That's* striking!" Heap said.

Thunder and rain eventually gave way to rushing, ceaseless wind; somehow, it was worse. The sopping banners and tent flaps flicking and snapping in the wet, the grass undulating like water, the whip and whine—it grated on Guy's nerves, ground them down.

"Do you see it?" Heap asked.

"No," Guy replied. He had not seen the cockatrice since mid-day. Having eaten its fill, the creature had retired somewhere; with any luck, that would be back into the dark woods beyond. This didn't seem likely, however. And so, they had waited to see if it would return. But of the cockatrice, there was no sign.

"Good," Heap said. He kicked again at the wooden bar the cockatrice had chewed halfway through; he had been at it for an hour. The bar was slowly growing loose—or Guy was imagining things.

Heap grunted with each kick. No, the bar wasn't loose, it was as stout as ever. Hell, the cage was meant to hold a bear; it could surely contain two tired and frightened men.

"It's no use," Guy said. "Give it up."

"Not yet," Heap replied. He smelled of sweat and prodigious exertion. He continued to kick the bar.

"Come on, you bastard," he muttered. "Come on."

"You know, we might be better off in here," Guy said.

Heap was incredulous.

"What? You aren't serious, are you? We'll die."

"And we'll die out there, too! At least in here we won't be torn to pieces."

Heap kept kicking the bar. "Do you know where that stupid mirror is, by the way? Because we're going to need it."

"One of the smiths would have had it, I think—"

Crack! The bar was suddenly loose.

"God, you did it!" Guy said.

"Shh! I know," Heap replied. With swift, careful motions he removed the bar from its socket and set it aside. "Now, wait. Listen."

All Guy heard were wind and dripping and the eerie, somehow dispiriting sound of cloth flapping in the wind.

"I think it's gone," Heap said. "But keep an eye out."

With some effort he squeezed his bulk between the bars and out of the cage. Guy followed. Heap, stiff and sore, rubbed his elbows and bottom and the back of his neck. From the ground Guy retrieved a spear for himself and a short sword for Heap. They were finely made weapons; the two men felt more secure with them in hand. Searching among the debris for additional gear, Guy retrieved a heavy sallet, which he put upon his head. The effect was semi-comic rather than formidable.

"What I wouldn't give for my old axe," Heap said of the short sword. "A toothpick is what this thing is, a rat-sticker."

Upon seeing Guy he asked, "And what in hell are you supposed to be?"

"Guy of Averoigne, Frenchman of Peril!"

He leveled the spear at Heap's chest.

"Of course," Heap replied. "Come on, let's find the mirror and see what can be done with it, Guy of Averoigne, Preposterous Frenchman."

In little time Heap was even more annoyed with Guy than usual; the latter had led the former to believe that he knew where the mirror was, and that finding it would be mere trifle. This wasn't the case. Sire Jean was known for the military exactitude of his encampments; he did not tolerate amateurism in any form. Tents were laid out in straight lines in the manner of a well-kept town, complete with "streets" and "quarters" where those of similar profession worked, slept, and ate. But the cockatrice, the storm, and now the wind had all dramatically altered that; the encampment was now a wilderness. Wreckage and scattered miscellany only added to the confusion. Here and there lay a half-eaten body. The air smelled heavily of ash and blood.

Heap kicked a collapsed tent aside; nothing underneath but for rain-soaked hides. "Are you sure they didn't take the mirror with them?" he asked.

That possibility had not occurred to Guy. "It was likely too heavy."

Prodding with his spear under a tent had an unpleasant result: a severed head rolled out from under it. Guy cried out and kicked it away.

"Quiet!" Heap said. When he saw what had startled Guy, he chuckled.

"Frenchman of Peril," he said.

"Look! Here!" Guy exclaimed.

There it was—the mirror, beneath the shelter-half. Apart from being wet, it appeared undamaged. The scale of it still impressed Heap. As for its beauty, well, he was never one to pay overmuch attention to the surface of things, no matter how fine they might appear.

"So, this is how we'll kill the cockatrice," Guy said.

"Right," Heap said. "Put it on, then."

"What? You can't be serious," Guy replied.

"Yes, I am. Put it on before the cockatrice comes back."

"But it's heavy."

"It'll only be for a little while."

"No. I won't."

"Then how do you expect to slay the damned thing?"

"And how do you know it's a cockatrice? What if, what if it's something else altogether and this mirror does nothing to it? Then what? I can't run away with it on my back . . . or is that how you planned it all along?"

"What? Are you mad?" Heap asked, astonished.

"Yes, I see how this works. If it all goes wrong, Guy gets eaten, Heap gets away. I should have seen it before. Base treachery."

Heap bristled. "Well, I certainly can't wear it, because it isn't fitted for me. So are you going to put it on, or do I have to *make* you put it on?"

Guy's answer to this question was to suddenly bolt away like a rabbit.

"Hey!" Heap shouted. He chased Guy for a short distance, but he had no real hope of catching the more nimble man. Guy disappeared into the woods.

Frustrated, Heap returned to the mirror, which reflected the dull leaden fishy-gray skies above and his own lumpish, forlorn silhouette.

Heap cursed the wind. It hissed through the leaves and fern brakes, the eglantine and cedar. The skies remained oppressively overcast. Upon the horizon stood a heavy bank of rumpled gray clouds with the war drums of thunder. But rain was the least of Heap's worries: it was a long march back to Cordeliers, even if he pushed hard.

The mirror he wore like a shield upon his left, adjusting the straps so that they were bound tightly to his left forearm. It was an unsatisfactory arrangement. Heap was a strong man, stronger than most, but the mirror was no proper shield: it was unbalanced and heavy and pulled him to one side. Still, if he could trick the cockatrice into gazing at it, that was all need be done; but he could see why Guy detested the damned thing—

Guy! That little rodent! When everything depended upon their mutual cooperation and a clear chain of command (meaning Guy obeying

Heap's orders), Guy went and ran away. Why, why in God's name did he not simply leave the little fool lying in the street?

Dark woods rose upon slopes to either side of the road, vast stretches of oak, of beech and wild cherry and towering pine—ill-favored country and on a day like this, thoroughly gloomy. It was the sort of dreary place where every sound one makes is somehow louder and more ominous, so that Heap thumped along the muddy, stone-littered road like a cart horse. *Thump, thump, thump . . .*

thump thump thump thump thump

Wait. What was that? An echo? Heap strained to listen. Wind whipped through the bracken. Somewhere a distant bird of prey uttered a piercing cry, but otherwise all was silent.

"Imagination," he told himself, but he gripped tighter his sword and the mirror. This was just as well, for at that moment there was a blur of movement off to his left, a brief glimpse of black and white and flaring yellow-orange, of claws. He brought the mirror up just in time—the impact threw him to the ground in a spray of mud and knocked the sword from his hand. The cockatrice tumbled over him, sprawling, but was on its feet again with astonishing speed—it hissed and shook its feathers, advancing, a growl rumbling from within its vitals. Heap thrust the mirror into the face of the beast so that it might behold itself and be struck dead.

"Ha!" Heap cried.

Nothing happened.

The cockatrice shook its feathers and snapped at its reflection. Its head bobbed in a sort of curious, rhythmic dance; it fell back, as if uncertain, and hissed. Heap backed away. He cast about for his sword. Yes, there it was . . . slowly . . . steadily . . . damned thing was supposed to *die* . . . slowly . . . almost there . . . just stay where you are . . . don't come any closer . . . don't do that, don't—

"NO!" Heap cried.

The cockatrice charged at him—or more precisely, the mirror, biting and snapping. Teeth and claws gripping the frame, the cockatrice lashed out with its spurs, narrowly missing Heap's legs and groin. It was all Heap could do to keep the mirror between him and his assailant—until with a wild yell Guy pierced the creature's side with his spear.

The strike was not well-aimed or even particularly serious; Guy was no warrior and his clumsy charge was proof. But it forced the cockatrice to release Heap and confront this new threat.

Heap dropped the mirror into the mud. Useless thing—

"No, don't!" Guy shouted. "The mirror has it confused! Don't take it off!"

"It doesn't WORK!" Heap roared.

Sensing an opening, the cockatrice lunged at Guy, but he struck it a smart blow to the temple with the flat of his spear head. The cockatrice stumbled, and Guy stepped forward and thrust—too soon. The jaws of the creature seized the spear shaft. It wrenched the weapon— and Guy—this way and that, until it disarmed the man. Guy went sprawling. The cockatrice broke spear the between its jaws and advanced upon the terrified man.

"Hoi!" Heap shouted, now armed. "Bring your teeth this way, king of serpents! You won't find much meat on that one!"

The cockatrice bore down upon Heap, striking like a snake, biting and clawing. Only with great effort was Heap able to fend off its attacks with his short sword. The cockatrice grew fiercer with each attack, and it did not tire. It was only a matter of time before Heap would be killed, slaughtered like a pig. Cruel, terrible fate! He *really* should have been an actor—

A blow to its head robbed the cockatrice of its impending victory. Using his broken spear like a club, Guy struck the cockatrice on the nose. Enraged, the monster lashed out at Guy. Glass shattered into silver fragments as its head collided with the mirror Guy held; pieces of all sizes—some as large as a thumb, others as small as a fingernail— were embedded in the face and head of the King of Serpents, a net of white jewels that brought pain and blood. With a shriek the cockatrice leaped away, clawing helplessly at the shards bristling from its maimed head. Half blind, it staggered toward the woods, still screeching. *Thump thump thump thump thump* went its feet, receding. And then it was gone.

Heap stood there, gasping. Guy was nearby, streaming sweat. Summoning what little strength he had left, Heap went to Guy and helped him remove the shattered mirror from his arm.

"And I still say it was a cockatrice," Heap said.

"I'm not so sure," Guy replied, gnawing upon a hunk of hard cheese, his mouth half-full. The sky was clearing and the sun peered at them from behind retreating clouds. The open road lay before them. They had already walked far.

Heap sighed. "All right, then. Have it your way. I'm just glad we won't be seeing him again."

"Perhaps it was a dragon," Guy said.

"A dragon? Don't be ridiculous. If it was a dragon, it would be picking us out of its teeth right about now . . ."

Guy shrugged, took a swig from a wine flask, and asked, "How far is it to Cordeliers, anyway?"

"Not much further," Heap replied. "But we're not stopping there for long, mind you; only for the night. Then we push on."

"Really? Why?"

"Because I'm done with that place and those people. Done with severing heads and shoveling shit. Done, done, and done. So, the next *fool* who comes stumbling along is on his own, for Heap shall not be there to rescue him."

"Well, I rescued you, too, from the cocka—from—from the monster."

"I had the situation well in hand," Heap said, only half-seriously. "You merely expedited the impending victory of the ex-headsman."

"Well," Guy said, "if you are no longer a headsman, I doubt you'll need *this!*"

With that Guy snatched the black hood from Heap's head. The huge man cried out in surprise and chased Guy for several paces, and then stopped. He was no terror; he was homely—broad and wide of face, incarnadined about the bulbous nose, porous upper cheeks and underdeveloped ears, heavy about the spotted brows and jowls. The hair and beard were cropped short as wheat stubble in winter; the eyes were deep-set and dark, weary, intelligent, nestled in crevices and crows' feet of aging skin. Where Heap was not red, he was flecked with white and gray, and this was what astonished Guy most; that Heap was not horrible but Old, and growing Older.

"Give that back!" Heap retrieved his hood.

"But you're an old man!" Guy said.

"And you're a rude young fool," Heap replied, pulling the hood over his head again, "who should have more respect for his elders, particularly when they have appearances to keep."

Heap hurried on ahead with a perspicacity that was anything but that of an old man. Guy hesitated, uncertain as to what he should do.

When he was some distance ahead, Heap stopped. "Well? Come along, then, Frenchman of Peril. Help this poor old man on his way. Or have you entirely forgotten your manners?"

Guy, smiling, hurried to catch up.

The cockatrice did not long survive his injuries. Years later, an enterprising necromancer chanced upon the scattered, bleached remains of the creature, washed down from the hills by spring floods. The skull—and only the skull—was of especial interest to him; he thought it a marvelous and fearsome addition to his bookshelf. And such was the fate of the *Coatleraptor*, last surviving member of the Dromaeosaurids.

CLOTAIRE OF THE CROSS

by Colin Harker

Part One

Sir Jean-Claire de Vair has grown very old and his memory is not as it once was. Often his mind will wander and he will speak of years gone by as though they are not of the past but the present. Customarily when he is in these moods, I myself am abroad hunting and, as I do not return until dusk is nearing, I hear of his rambles from my wife Elaine who spends the day tending to both him and our young son.

It was typical of my sort of ill-starred luck that upon the thirteenth day of October, Elaine chose to visit her aunt in Vyônes and left me to look after the old man. Fortunately, he was silent for the most part, dining upon his meager portions of porridge with no attempt at conversation. But as the long shadows of evening drew nigh, his tongue began to wax suddenly voluble. I could barely catch any of what he said for he spoke in a low tone as though conversing with himself. However, I did discern one name that he reiterated more than once. I began to wonder whether he was not speaking of a past leman of his youth or something of that nature. At last I asked, "Sir Jean-Claire, who is this Clotaire that you speak of?"

He blinked at me as though he had not realized that he was speaking aloud, and I was surprised at the look of sudden intelligence in the old man's eyes. Then, in a sorrowful voice: "My daughter has not spoken to you of him?"

"No."

"She would not—no, she would not." He smiled and I thought I caught a hint of sorrow beneath his bearded lips. "François, you have been very good to both me and my daughter. What is your opinion of this old man before you? Do you believe him thoroughly spent and useless—a sick, dying fool of no use to the world any longer?"

I spoke gently. "Sir, you were a great knight in your time, and your knowledge of how best to combat the forces of darkness never failed you. They say that there was never daemon nor spirit that ever successfully resisted—"

"Then they lie!"

I stared, shaken, at the quivering old man as he gazed back up at me with eyes that were shadowed with shame. "There was one such spirit who defied me—yes, and defeated me. And may God forgive me, but I am half glad of it; and in the end I still wonder if I truly did all that could be done against him or if I, like so many others, was ultimately seduced by his wiles."

"But who was this daemon, sir?"

He looked at me with eyes full of a terrible, guilty fear. Then, in the faintest of whispers, he replied, "*Clotaire . . .*"

Few in Averoigne, even a cloistered huntsman such as you, François, can have avoided hearing of the reign of the Marquis de Conflans who dwelt within his stronghold close by Ximes so many decades ago. His citadel was much like a small city unto itself, for his serfs would till the land close about the castle and merchants would dwell within the walls of his castle, selling their wares to both courtiers and lord alike. For he had made a great profit off of his part in the Crusades and thus had risen from a lowly soldier to a great lord in little less than a few years of military glory.

There was one who dwelt within those walls and who had served within the Crusades alongside the Marquis de Conflans. This man, however, had suffered as grievously as the Marquis had prospered, having both lost his fortune and fallen prey to a lingering, malignant illness which, though not apparently contagious, had left him shunned by all. The Marquis, out of a sense of obligation more than anything else, allowed the unfortunate man to remain within the walls of his Château Conflans, but only within the lower regions of the castle where none but the dungeon-confined dwelt. In spite of all of this, those who met him invariably accounted him a mild-eyed, kindly soul bearing little more than a melancholic resignation against his harsh fate. He was called Clotaire de la Croix—Clotaire of the Cross.

It was said that the dubious mercy which the Marquis had granted him was only due to the fact that during one the many battles they had fought together, Clotaire had saved the Marquis' life from certain death at the hands of the enemy. For the Marquis was a harsh lord and given over to all manner of cruelties against those who disobeyed his edicts—certainly not one usually inclined towards mercy. He defended his severity with the simple reminder that justice may only be kept when it is enforced with as little reserve as possible. His torture chamber and dungeons were often as crowded as his castle market and, ironically, he appointed the gentle Clotaire as the torture chamber's primary overseer—against the unfortunate man's will, of course. This was fortunate to his prisoners however, I expect; I also imagine that there was quite a bit of pig's blood spilt upon those racks during the evening, save when additional guards were appointed to overlook a particularly egregious convict's execution.

The passage of time began to wreak unpleasant changes in the Marquis. His sense of justice steadily diminished and yet his peculiar appetite for vengeful punishment did not desist in the least. Both his wife Jocette and Clotaire attempted to curb his cruelty, but to no avail—and, indeed, so frequent were the Marquis' outrages perpetrated against those who defied him, that it was not considered wise to protest too loudly against even the most callous of his policies.

Now it came to pass that one of Jocette's chambermaids, a young woman named Katriane, caught the eye of the Marquis. When she resisted his advances, he inevitably fell into a rage and sentenced her to torture and death, thus delivering her into the hands of Clotaire de la Croix. As the sentencing and execution were to be fulfilled in secret so that no word might escape of the matter to the Marquis' wife, there were no guards present. Clotaire alone was to administer to the girl.

She was brought down and bound to one of the iron tables frequently used within such chambers and left to await her punishment. Clotaire arrived, perhaps with a dagger hidden within his cloak—hoping to slay her swiftly, as was his custom, and then carefully mutilate her features so as to allay any of the Marquis' suspicions. Yet the story goes that upon beholding her exceeding loveliness, the recluse was moved to more than pity and she in turn also fell as deeply in love with him, for in spite of the leprous paleness which suffering had cast upon him, he was by all accounts not an uncomely gentleman. He concealed her in a remote cell within the dungeon and the two lovers planned to secretly depart together from the castle as soon as possible.

To conceal anything for long within a castle—even such a large citadel as the Château Conflans was—is a vain hope, however. Their plan was soon found out and the Marquis grew still more incensed, declaring himself as having been betrayed by a foul ingrate to whom he had shown a great measure of leniency and mercy. Katriane was cast into the deepest of the dungeon's oubliettes and Clotaire was condemned to the rack as payment for his treachery. The very guards, indeed, who had observed his merciful dealings with the Marquis' prisoners were those who presided over his torture—and they, of course, were not prepared to show him the same sort of lenience.

Yet though he observed the pallid anguish of his former friend, the Marquis' sense of justice was still not satisfied. Even as the screws turned every minute or so in order to stretch still more the ravaged tendons, the castle's bishop was summoned. The priest looked down upon the prisoner and marveled at how strangely silent he was in the midst of his torments. Then, at the Marquis' prompting, he asked the prisoner if he had repented of the crime. The Marquis drew closer to hear the inevitable words of agonized regret and supplication.

Clotaire's voice was as broken and distant as though it issued already from the lips of a spirit rather than a living man, but his reply was audible to all—one of soft yet eternal defiance against his tormentor. Then, again at the Marquis' prompting, the bishop spoke and his tongue was not soft in the least but heavy and cruel, pronouncing a harsh and terrible curse in the sight of God upon the unrepentant prisoner. He declared that his soul in death would not escape torment but would die the second and far more fearful death of which the Scriptures spoke so dreadfully. In an unholy, incorruptible form would the dead man's soul rise forth and—against even his own will—bring to damnation those whom he loved.

It is said that the sufferer's face grew grey at these words of spiritual condemnation and that tears of despair lightly bedewed those cheeks that had paled so often at the torment of others. Then he was taken from the rack and the Marquis, at last satisfied, had him dispatched swiftly with the sword. Several weeks later Katriane, still imprisoned within the oubliette, fell victim to a sudden, wasting illness and died a short while after. The two of them were buried in unmarked, unconsecrated ground and there the tale ends.

I myself was a child when these events—which seemed to my mind more to be taken as legendry—took place, living many miles away from the Château Conflans in the cathedral city of Vyônes. I had heard, as all others had, of the splendors of the Château but had never guessed to venture there. Even as I grew to manhood and achieved a certain renown as a vanquisher of evil in its many guises, both natural and supernatural, I still had not the slightest expectation that I would ever behold that citadel, magnificent though it undoubtedly was.

It was in my forty-fourth year that I opened the door of my home to find a man with a pinched, narrow face garbed in violet robes, identifying himself as Jacques, and bearing a scroll. It was a summons from the Marquis de Conflans himself demanding my urgent presence due to a matter of the gravest importance. I pressed Jacques for details, but he was either reluctant or ignorant and refused to divulge anything further. Yet I saw within the man's quick temper and hatred of delay that there was a fear which drove him as harshly as I guessed his master the Marquis did. Though, unsurprisingly, I felt no great wish to aid this tyrant, I had sworn an oath to remain embattled to all forms of evil and to help in particular those who called upon my assistance. Thus, albeit with an unwilling heart, I accompanied Jacques and, as I did not know how long I would be gone, I brought my daughter Elaine, who was then in her twenty-first year, with me.

It was a long journey from Vyônes to the Marquis' château close by Ximes, and by the time we wended our way through the shadowed forests of Averoigne, my heart would have been gladdened at the sight of even a hovel. In spite of my fatigue, however, I could hardly prevent myself from gazing in well-nigh astonishment at our journey's destination.

For the Château Conflans, that citadel of shining prowess that had stood stalwart for so many decades, stood before me like the face of a stranger—like a mocking refutation of the portrait which had forever been in my mind's eye. The walls were still richly clad with ivy, but they were overgrown as well with a dank, clinging moss. The waters of the lapping moat that surrounded the Château were thick and black like those of a marsh, and seemed to breed a foul mold that crept up the stones of the castle like the black, streaking prints of some taloned beast. A drifting white mist also issued from the sodden, rain-damp ground upon which we trod, cladding us in a thick wetness that rose wraith-like about us. There seemed to have fallen upon the land an encroaching, rotting sickness that caused the very trees that we passed to take on the shapes of immense, hulking skeletons.

At last, we came to the edge of that dank tarn of a moat and the drawbridge slowly lowered for us. After we had passed into the castle's courtyard and dismounted, Jacques informed us that he would take our palfreys to the stables and then conduct us into the Marquis de Conflans' presence.

I had hoped that the inhabitants of the castle at the very least would prove to be slightly more congenial than its exterior. The people who passed us by within the courtyard, however, were not the friendly merchants and farmers who usually dwell within the walls of an Averoigne castle. Rather, they gazed upon Elaine and me with expressions as blank as an unwritten parchment, their hair clinging to their skull-like foreheads as though drenched with the dew of that swirling mist that hung all about. Indeed, when I passed a hand across my own brow, I found that my fingers were wet as though with a feverish perspiration.

At last Jacques returned and led us beneath a stone archway and through a door into the castle's interior. After ascending several flights of a steep, spiral stairway lit only with a few torches, we at last reached an oaken door at the very top which, when opened, revealed a dim bedchamber. There, upon an immense canopy bed bloated with cushions and framed by four tall candles at each bedpost, I beheld a thin, shrunken figure lying there.

"Monseigneur," Jacques said in a low voice. "Sir Jean-Claire de Vair has come from Vyônes as you have requested."

A yellow hand hanging limply by the side of the bed gestured feebly for us to draw nearer. Jacques stepped back while I came closer to the lord of the château.

"Sir de Vair." The voice rattled forth from between those dry lips with the sound of a worm creeping through withered autumn leaves. "I have heard much of you."

"And I of you," I replied.

A low chuckle escaped his shriveled lips as they drew back to form a skull's grin. "And does my château exceed your expectations?"

"Marquis, it would do me good to first know why you brought me here."

A look of satisfaction spread across the old man's appalling visage. With a jolt I was reminded of the tales of the Marquis' various outrages perpetrated against his enemies, and shuddered in spite of myself. Unheeding, the Marquis spoke: "It is as I feared. Though I have not been out of this room for twenty years, monsieur, I have long suspected that a change has been worked upon this château—yes, and upon the men who dwell within it. Before I sickened, de Vair, I knew the ignorant rustics and merchants who crowded my courtyards and held fairs within my grounds. They were not the pockmarked, lisping gnomes that enter my room and tell me that I do not have many more days to live." The Marquis, seeing my discomfort, added, "Do not feel any embarrassment on account of that man," his yellowed eyes flickered towards Jacques. "He knows what I think of him."

"Monsieur, I believe that you have misunderstood where my talents lie," I told him. "I cannot make for you a new court."

"I do not wish for you to give me a court—I wish for you to give me health!" His excited state caused his breathing to grow all the more labored and dreadful to listen to. "Save me from the tortures which I must endure every night—from this sickness. You *must*. If you do, limitless wealth and lands shall be yours, I promise you."

I stood amazed for a full minute. When I finally found voice to speak, my tone was one of abject astonishment. "Marquis de Conflans, I am truly flattered by your faith in my abilities, but I am no physic! I fear I can do nothing for you."

"Fool!" the Marquis snarled, almost rising from his bed, his face a working, wrinkled mask of fury. "Do you think that it is mere old age and fever that keeps me in this state? Stay a night in this room and you shall see—you shall see!"

Jacques led us out and silently showed us the quarters in which we were to stay, one floor lower than that of the Marquis' bedchamber. "Do you believe it wise for me to stay a night with the Marquis to see how he fares?" I asked him.

"If you believe that you can stand such close proximity with the damned swine, then by all means," the messenger said, adding a few choice words in reference to the Marquis—surely the longest sentence I had ever heard the man utter during our acquaintance.

Part Two

"Are you comfortable enough, Sir de Vair?"

"Yes, Marquis." The truth was that the straight-backed, armless oaken chair that I had been given was easily one of the most unpleasant examples of its type, but I comforted myself with the knowledge that I would certainly not fall asleep during my vigil. A single storm lantern burned upon a low table by the bed, illuminating the face of my "patient".

I had inspected the Marquis previously that evening and found that physically he was indeed a hopeless case: the joints at his wrists and ankles were swollen in a manner that I had not beheld even within the joints of the extremely aged. It was clear that any sort of movement was extremely painful to him, thus accounting for his current helpless and bedridden condition. I had to allow myself utterly baffled, though, as to what could be the cause behind it and once again felt in my heart of hearts that the Marquis would be better off in the hands of a physic than a knight.

I heard the shutters of the window bang as though they were loose and I rose to fasten them shut. As I did, I noticed how thickly the fog outside pressed against the glass panes, like a grey, suffocating wall of darkness. Turning away, I settled myself down again in my chair, watching my charge with the belief that I was to have a dull, though somewhat wearying evening.

I was awakened by the sound of a cry from somewhere downstairs. My eyes flew open and I caught up the lantern which now burned low with a blue flame as though without air. With shaky steps, I made my way down the narrow staircase to my daughter's room. To my relief, I found that although frightened, she was perfectly safe. She apologized, saying that she had only dreamt that someone had entered her room. As soon as I saw that she had recovered from her fright, I returned to the bedchamber of my charge.

To my horror, I found that he was lying rigid beneath his bed-clothes, his face contorted and his teeth clenched tightly as though he were in terrible agony. Upon hearing my shouts for help, Jacques rushed in. Seeing the cause of my concern, however, his appearance was one of nervous unsurprise.

"*Oui*, Monsieur, the Marquis experiences such difficulties every night," he said in a low voice. "No physician has yet been able to discern the cause." As he spoke, his eyes—as well as mine—were drawn upwards towards the ceiling: from somewhere above, there resounded a distant creaking. It was an odd sort of sound, and I would have thought it but the wind battering against the foundations of the château had it not held such a solid, mechanical quality to it. Its steady rhythm put me in mind of a churchbell's toll, even though the sound that it produced was altogether different: rather like the clicking of a stick caught within the spokes of a wheel or something of that nature. I certainly caught the solid feeling of wood behind it at any rate.

"Is there anyone living above us, Jacques?" I asked.

"No, Monsieur," he replied. "Ours is the uppermost floor."

Our attentions were abruptly transferred to the Marquis, who let out a piercing shriek as though some sudden, unspeakable pain had transfixed him. Then, like a child's plaything rudely cast down, he sagged limply upon the bed, his mouth and eyes still hanging loosely open.

I hastened to his side, fearing the worst; he had all the appearance of a dead man. As Jacques chafed at the Marquis' wrists with little enthusiasm, I took up a mirror that lay upon a nearby mantelpiece and held it up to his yellow lips. At first I saw nothing, but at last to my relief the faintest of mists began to appear upon its surface over his mouth.

"He still lives?" Jacques enquired.

I nodded. "You may go about your business, Jacques. All appears to be well for the moment."

He bowed and exited, leaving me to ponder the strange manifestations of the Marquis' illness. I decided to take advantage of the deep, exhausted slumber into which he had fallen and began examining him for any sign of physical deterioration. As I had half-feared, the swollen quality of his tendons had become still more noticeable. Wonderingly,

I replaced the coverlets and fell into silent thought.

As I stood within that dimly-lit chamber, I noticed how heatedly oppressive the air seemed to be, as though it had not stirred in decades. I moved towards the window, lantern in hand, with the intention of opening it. As I stood there, however, I happened to turn my eyes down towards the landscape below the window. The mist had dissipated somewhat, and I observed that not only was the wall below us too steep and high for climbing, but that directly below us lapped the moat itself. Then, glancing upward, I noticed the faintest trace of an oval-shaped patch of mist upon the glass pane, much like the mist of the Marquis' breath that had appeared upon the mantle's mirror. But as I continued to gaze, my heart quickening with sudden recognition and disbelief, the mist disappeared and I could see naught but the pressing darkness without.

The next morning, I found the Marquis in the same poisonous humor as the one with which he had first welcomed me.

"Think you that your holy water will save me from death, Sir de Vair?" he enquired with a light laugh.

I did not bother to reply to his question, but continued to silently sprinkle the windowsill and the perimeter of the bed with what little blessed water I had in reserve within my glass vial. Turning to my daughter Elaine who was nailing a crucifix above the bed as I had instructed her, I asked, "Have we any more of the holy wafers?"

She shook her head. "No, father. But surely the château's bishop would be willing to aid us in such a matter?"

I nodded. "We shall seek him out at once."

As the two of us started for the door, the Marquis called after us, "Then you are convinced that my malady is not of a natural origin?"

"I am indeed convinced."

"Do you know what it is then?"

"I may."

"Would you like me to tell you?"

The Marquis' voice, needling and self-pitying to the point of loathsomeness, at last caused me to forsake every ounce of civility and self-restraint. "Marquis," I returned, my voice rising. "I do not wish to know. You have called upon me that I might rid you of your torments.

Very well; I shall. Take care, however, that I do not discover the cause of them or I may find myself siding with your tormentor rather than with you—by God, even if he be the Devil himself!"

And with that I departed, my daughter hiding a slight smile as she followed me and I busily cursed myself for my foul temper.

"Father, you seem to be more versed in the Marquis' ailment than you have told me," she said, her voice one of mock reproof as we emerged into the mist-laden air of the courtyard.

"I am well versed in the Marquis' cruelties," I replied with a heavy sigh that still held a good deal of the resentment that I felt. "And now that I believe that I know what the cause of his mysterious ailment may be . . ."

My voice trailed off, but Elaine was not to be so easily deterred. "What is your theory?" she demanded.

"Of little value until it has been verified," I replied. "Which we shall hopefully manage to do very shortly."

The chapel of the Château de Conflans was a tall, stone edifice built into the side of the castle wall and across the courtyard from the château proper. The clinging mist was as thick and impenetrable as it had been the day before and I sensed once again that stifling, sickly quality that it held. As before, my brow and body began to take on the clammy feel of a fevered man's frame, and as I breathed in the fog I actually began to feel myself grow ill as though a lingering, smothering hand had been laid over my face, hindering my breath.

I was relieved when Elaine and I finally managed to escape that poisonous air and enter the comparatively wholesome atmosphere of the cloister. I found that I preferred the dust of the pews to the open air of that unhealthy courtyard. Above us were the ribbed arches of the chapel's sanctuary and around us there hung about the whole of the place an echoing quiet. The chapel seemed to be entirely empty, save for a crimson-robed figure who stood a few yards ahead of us before the altar. As is the custom within such places of worship, an ornamental cross hung suspended by several ropes over his head; however, the ropes seemed to have sagged and loosened over time, causing the cross to sway crookedly above his head, with a creaking akin to that of a loose shingle.

"Sir, might I have a word with you?" I called as my daughter and I approached him.

He turned his head very slowly, the muscles at his wan neck rippling like those of some reptile's. His eyes moved like a reptile's as well: slitted, cold, quick, and glistening. Only the fear in them endowed them with some form of human emotion. He was very old, easily as old as the Marquis, with graying hair that clung to the sides of his skull but a comparatively smooth face.

"Who are you?" he asked, his voice little more than a hoarse whisper.

I introduced Elaine and myself and told him the purpose of our visit. He nodded silently and beckoned for us to follow him. As we followed him, I was startled to hear the Marquis' previous question issue from his lips, though with a telling variation: "Well, my son—do you believe that you can save the Marquis de Conflans from his tormentor?"

"I shall do all that I can, Father," I replied.

"Shall you?" His eyes were hard upon me; then his gaze turned away and his hands shook as he opened a tabernacle built into the side of the stone wall close by, withdrawing the sacramental bread.

"Yes," I replied. After a pause: "And who *is* his tormentor, Holy Father?"

"I would think that it would be obvious, Monsieur." His eyes shone as though tears stood within them, though there was an iron quality in them that told me that they were not tears of sorrow. "The Marquis and I had him within our power decades ago, and have had to pay a terrible price for our mercilessness—a price that is still being exacted. We tortured a man's body and then consigned his soul to the Pit—and with him our own souls as well." He smiled at me, his quivering lips compressing still further. "You have been within this château long enough to feel the fevered mist that surrounds it like a tangible malady—a slow, lingering sickness—*his* sickness. Know you now who it is that has racked the Marquis with torments until his joints have withered and grown useless? Know you now who it is who has made himself the new lord of the Château de Conflans?"

All that he said coincided with what I had half-guessed, but I still felt a pang of wondrous disbelief at the utter fantastic nature of what he was hinting at. "It cannot be . . ." I murmured.

"Yes," the bishop replied and then, his voice cracking as though revolting against uttering the very name: "Clotaire de la Croix."

I would have spoken, but at that moment my glance shifted towards my daughter who, upon hearing the name, had turned as pale as a winding sheet and would have fallen had I not steadied her. Wondering at her sudden terror, I heard the bishop say, "Do you still think to expel our tormentor, Sir de Vair? Know, then, that I attempted to do so once and failed. He has made this land his own, Monsieur, and it is of no use to drive him away for he is manifest within every element of it. You would just as well attempt to exorcise Satan from Hell as purge the Château de Conflans of its daemon."

"Anything is possible, Holy Father, so long as God is on our side," I replied.

He returned my gaze unwaveringly. "God is not on our side." He pressed the holy wafers into my hand and, as Elaine and I turned to depart, I heard him murmur to himself, "Would that the Marquis had not dealt so mercifully with the wretch but had left him upon the rack, alive to suffer rather than dead to punish! Else we would not have been damned so swiftly . . ."

Part Three

My daughter retired to her chamber early and as the evening drew on, I resumed my station within the Marquis' own chamber, hoping that my ministrations might prove successful in warding off his torments. After what I had seen the night before upon the windowpane, I half-dreaded to see some new token of a spectral presence, yet all I saw was the moon's reflection against the glass.

I must have been wearier than I had imagined, for I lapsed into a light sleep almost as soon as I sat down. My dreams were of a dark, shifting nature and I sensed myself being drawn slowly into a shifting, sinking whirlpool of a thick, yielding material resembling quicksand. As occurs often enough within such dreams, I felt myself lose all sense of balance and was about to jolt awake when something within my dream caught my hand and pulled me upon solid land. The landscape about me was still shadowy and ephemeral, but I felt a sudden lucidity and awareness come over me as I had not experienced before within the dream.

Looking about for some sign of my rescuer, I beheld a man standing close by. He was tall and slight of frame, attired in a dark garment
that contrasted with the pallor of his skin. I was struck by the kindly
compassion and gentle sorrow within his gaze as he silently regarded
me, as well as the subtle, contemplative lineaments that bespoke an
otherworldly comeliness within his visage and also a certain implacable
command. With the usual irrationality of dreams, I felt a great calm descend upon my soul as though all the evils that lay ahead were as nothing compared to the presence of this being who I had become convinced must be some sort of holy, succoring spirit. With a sort of desperation, I spoke, asking how I might save the Château de Conflans
from the evil that had descended upon it, as though this spirit alone
might have the answer.

He parted his lips as though to reply; then his eyes darkened with a
look of both shame and suffering. With a pitying wonder, I realized
that the man before me was half-dying with hunger and I grieved that I
had nothing to give him with which to ease his agony. Then, with that
strange understanding that one often has within dreams, I realized
what must be done, and I acted as I never would have acted had I not
been under the influence of the dream and of a power far greater than
my own. Drawing the dagger that hung sheathed at my side, I drew the
edge of it across my palm just deeply enough for the blood to leap
forth.

He came towards me then and grasped my wrist with fingers as
cold and inexorable as steel; yet the look in his eyes before he brought
his lips down to my hand was one of such wrenching remorse that
tears of pity sprang to my eyes and I did not resist when he began to
drink the drops that seeped from my palm. At length he ceased and I
saw him avert his face for a moment to dab at his lips with the edge of
his sleeve; the streaks he left thereon were dark and crimson and I felt
a sickness come over me as I watched. Then he turned back towards
me, his eyes shining with more than their former languid luster and his
cheeks having taken on a slight hint of color other than their previous
deathlike pallor. His smile as well held the faintest hint of watchful irony.

His gaze lowered from my stricken eyes to my throat and my hand instinctively sought to shield it. However, as I did so, I touched something cold and hard and my fingers fastened around the tiny shape of the crucifix amulet that I wore about my neck. And of an instant, the glamour that had darkened my perception disappeared to be replaced with a loathly knowledge of what I had done and who it was who stood before me. I slowly unfastened the crucifix and, as he watched with a wary absorption, held it out to the man before me.

"Take this," I said. "As a token of my estimation—for is the crucifix not your namesake, Clotaire of the Cross?"

He did not blanch or shrink back as I advanced, but seemed rather to be transfixed with a fascinated despair at the approach of the holy symbol. Then he outstretched his hand and with a trembling finger touched the shining surface of the crucifix. He then drew it back with lightning swiftness as though he had touched a hot coal and met my gaze, his eyes shining with a hopeless grief. The whole world about us rippled and billowed about and I felt a great darkness descend over the landscape.

"Father!"

I came awake with a start to find my daughter kneeling before my chair, her face bedewed with tears. Horrified, forgetting the circumstances of my strange dream, I asked her what had happened. She was too distraught to reply immediately and I, being fearful that the Marquis might awaken, led her back to her chamber. To my surprise, I found the bedclothes to be in utter disarray and the casement unlatched and open. After crossing the room and closing the window, I took my crucifix and with trembling fingers pressed it against her brow. When there was no effect, I almost wept with joy, knowing that her soul had not been harmed in any way by whatever evil it had been that had frightened her.

"Father," she murmured. "You remember the night before when I told you that I believed that someone had entered my chamber?" When I nodded, she continued, "I thought it but a dream, as I told you, and returned to my bed. But hardly had I drifted to sleep, when I was awakened once again by the sound of my chamber window's shutters flung open and rattling in the wind. I was about to arise and refasten them when a shadow rose by my bedside and a hand, cold as the moonlight itself, pressed me back against the coverlets. I then heard someone shut the window and the candle by my bedside was lit, albeit with a dimly wavering flame of blue as though the air of my chamber had grown stifling and unhealthy.

"Within its dim light, I beheld the figures of two persons standing at the foot of my bed—a man and a woman. The woman wore a gown dyed a deep, sea-like blue that matched perfectly the ethereal blue of her eyes, and her hair was as thick and golden as a lion's mane and hung flowingly down below her waist. Her full lips held a lovely, ambiguous smile that one could easily interpret as either infinitely cruel or infinitely tender. In contrast to the vibrant glow upon her cheek, the man beside her was pale as though at the point of death, and his lips were as livid as though he were overcome by some terrible agony. I saw then that above his right breast, his cloak was drenched with blood as though he had been savagely pierced through the heart by some blade. Like the woman, his eyes harbored that same tender-eyed malice; but there was also a kindly sympathy and sadness within his watchful gaze as he regarded me that served to soften his unearthly intensity and to sharpen the unvoiced appeal within those eyes."

I shuddered to hear her speak thus but, recalling my own visitation and seeing the long, fresh gash that ran like a thread across the palm of my hand, I knew that I had not proven altogether invulnerable to this appeal myself. Elaine continued in that same shaken, faraway voice:

"I lay there, silenced by both my utter fear and amazement, and somehow far too afraid even to call for help. No, Father, that is wrong. It was not fear alone that stilled my voice—it was something far more deadly. I had both a knowledge that I was in the presence and power of a thing far greater than I and, though I do not know why, I also gained a strange comfort from this knowledge. Ever since we arrived at this château, Father, I have felt no peace—only a vague feeling of unease and a wish that we might leave as soon as possible. Somehow, though, as if this man and woman were two holy seraphs, I felt myself to be safe so long as they remained. I knew that it was useless to resist them but I did not wish to resist.

"Then, in a voice as soft as though it was but a thought within my mind rather than a spoken phrase, I heard the man ask that I read aloud a passage from the Scriptures. I did as he bade, though I do not remember the particular text that I read—it may have been one of the psalms. All the while, I could feel their eyes upon me, drinking in the words with a silent avidity. When I finally ceased and looked up, I saw that the woman had departed but that the man remained. Seeing that I was finished, he thanked me with great gentleness and humility as though I had performed some indebting service towards him, and then he crossed the room towards the window as though to depart through there. At once, gaining my voice at last, I asked him falteringly who he was. He gave me the name that the bishop within the château's chapel gave us: Clotaire. At that moment, I heard from above a piercing scream—then, I must have fallen asleep, for I remember no more."

I recalled the agonies of the Marquis during the previous night but said nothing as my daughter continued:

"Do not think me weak, Father, because I did not tell you of all this earlier. You see, with the coming of the morning, my memories were so dim that I felt convinced that I must have dreamt the whole thing. Would that the memories of *this* night had faded as well." She turned her face away from me, her voice growing lower as though she half-wished that I not hear. "I felt very tired this evening as I told you and so I was soon asleep. It was a very deep slumber that I fell into and I do not believe that I would have naturally awoken at all during the night if it had not been for my shutters banging in the wind, once again having been unfastened. I rose to shut them but even as I did so, I caught a glimpse in the moonlight of a man standing within my chamber, half-hidden in the shadows. It was without a doubt Clotaire de la Croix. His smile chilled me as much as it had comforted me the evening before, and though he held his pallid hand out to me, I shrank back from it as though from a hissing adder. But, as if the shadows themselves were allied against me, I felt slender, waiting fingers grasp my wrists from behind, effectively pinioning them in their icy grip. More frightened than ever, I struggled in vain as Clotaire silently looked on. Though I guessed that my captor was the lady whom I had seen the night before, I could not overcome her strength and at last ceased trying.

"Seeing that my own strength was altogether spent, Clotaire's haggard visage went alight for one brief moment with a half-smile that bespoke both pleasure and pity. He softly informed me that no harm would come to me so long as I did not cry out for help but did whatever he asked of me. Then, his gaze moving over my shoulder to meet the woman's eyes, he gave a slight nod as though in acknowledgement of some delayed order. The woman released my wrists and led me towards my bed, forcing me to sit upon its edge as she sat by my side. She no longer held me fast with her cold fingers, seeming to trust that fear rather than brute force would keep me from fleeing. For one long terrible interval, the two regarded me with silent, avid gazes: the woman, with her shining, pitiless eyes and the man Clotaire with that kindly glance of his which pierced my heart through with its searing despair as mercilessly as a knife.

" 'Clotaire,' the woman spoke. 'You must begin first, for hunger hast made you the frailer of us two.'

"He regarded me with wistful consideration for a moment. There was such a gentleness mixed with such a resolute implacability within his countenance, that my heart was unresolved whether to give itself over to terror or to trust in his mercy. As though reading these thoughts within my face, he said, 'No, my love, you shall have her alone. It would be an unforgivable cruelty to disappoint the trust of so blameless a soul.' Then he knelt before me, taking my clasped hands in his own fingers. To my surprise, I found that his hands, though as bloodless as death, were as feverish to the touch as though fire ran through those grey, parched veins or as though he had bathed his fingers in some flaming lake. 'Elaine,' he said in a voice as subtle, as gentle, and as caressing as the cool of some autumnal brook. 'You rendered me a kind service last night in allowing me to hear the Scriptures once again and from your own innocent lips—words that I have not heard since before your own birth. Now I must ask a greater service of you. My wife is suffering deeply and yet she cannot die. Only you, my dear, may put an end to her sufferings. Do you understand?'

"I felt myself go rigid with fear once again and, sensing this, his grasp upon my hand tightened. Raising me up until I stood before him, he said, 'I see that we are become loathsome in your eyes, dear one, and with good reason. Will you but show mercy this once to my wife—as you would wish a stranger to do to one whom you love dearly?' I met the sorrowful appeal within those eyes and though I said nothing, I felt my will weaken and collapse under his subtle pressure. I do not know how it happened, but somehow, I found myself forgetting entirely what it was that he asked and thinking only of he who asked. As though sensing my faltering irresolution, he drew me close to himself; to the woman, he said, 'It is time, Katriane.'

"I saw a brief glint of silver as he passed her a thin-bladed dagger. Then, as he continued to hold me breathlessly close, I felt her grasp my wrist and a moment later I shuddered as a sudden pain seared against my arm. Then I felt a moving wetness along my wrist and knew with an unutterable pang that it was the woman Katriane's tongue and that she was drinking of the blood from my fresh wound. I do not know whether my tears were provoked by the helplessness of my terrible circumstance or by sheer horror, but I wept silently as I felt a great faintness overcome me and as I felt Clotaire's fingers against my back. Presently, I ceased to feel her lips pressed against my wrist and Clotaire's grasp upon me relaxed. In the moonlight, his face appeared to have grown still more drawn and haggard and when I met his eyes, I saw that they were fixed upon my face with a look of piteous suffering and hunger. His fingers twined the hair at the back of my throat, drawing my head back so that my throat was bared before him. I did not struggle but remained transfixed as he leaned closer, his lips barely an inch above my throat. I felt his breath brush against my throat and my own cheeks flamed with a terrible anticipation. Then, of a sudden, he wrenched me away from him, so that I stumbled back. The spell upon me was broken and, weakened by the blood that I had lost, I fell into a swoon and only awoke a few minutes ago." Elaine's eyes were shining with tears as she held out her poor wrist, upon which I saw the unmistakable mark of a knife's edge—identical to the one upon my own hand. "Father, forgive me for my weakness."

As I held her and whispered what words of comfort I could summon, I heard from somewhere upstairs the rising, agonized groans of the Marquis and over them, like the ticking of some hellish horologe, the steady, rhythmic creaking that I heard the night before—so very much like the creaking of some monstrous rack.

Part Four

The following evening, I made as comfortable a bed as I could for my daughter out of blankets and pillows in a corner of the Marquis' room and settled myself once again in my chair to now guard my two charges. I fell to thinking over the stratagems that I had laid out the whole of the day as I tried to shut out the din of the wind as it howled outside the single window of the chamber. It was evident what sort of blasphemous phantoms I had—for the Marquis de Conflans' dubious sake—pitted myself against. These creatures were the Un-Dead and they maintained their deathless state through thirsting and feeding off of the blood of the living. The only way that such a one might be vanquished was if a sharpened stake is driven through his heart and the rites of the dead are spoken over him. It had been difficult to convince the reticent villagers to aid me in procuring such a stake and, taxed for time, I simply bought a bundle of wood from one of them and set about sharpening their ends myself.

The element that made my plan somewhat difficult to carry out was due in a large part to the cruelty of the Marquis. Because he had buried his unfortunate victims in unmarked, unconsecrated ground and because such a great length of time had passed since their deaths, it was impossible to find anyone who remembered where precisely they were buried. Thus, though it was the generally accepted custom to slay these re-animated spirits during the daylight hours when they were asleep, I realized that a new plan of attack would have to be drawn. The creatures, inhumanly strong though they were, had to be confronted at night for that was the only time in which they were even abroad. Fortunately, in spite the added dangers involved, I had something of a plan in mind.

Elaine was restless that night and rose out of bed frequently to stand at the window and gaze out upon the storm as it raged across the courtyard and the farmlands beyond. Then, complaining at the stuffiness of the room, she unlatched the shutters and opened the window, leaning her head out into the maelstrom of lightning and whipping rain.

It flashed within my mind that perhaps I ought to tell her to close the window—to tell her of what I had seen two nights before upon its glass panes. But even then I was older and feeble-minded and did not think to speak until it was too late. Two white arms like albino serpents came down from somewhere above the window and seized Elaine by the arms, lifting her as easily as though she were but a child and bearing her upwards before I had even time to spring to my feet and dash to the sill. Peering desperately through the wind, I could see nothing through the darkness but the tossing of branches and the clouds as they went livid with lightning.

Throwing on my cloak, I raced out of the Marquis' room—down the spiral staircase, past the bewildered Jacques who uttered a startled "Monsieur!"—and finally out into the empty courtyard. I shouted Elaine's name several times but received no answer and, sickened with fear, I ran across the lowered drawbridge into the fields beyond. Catching sight of a white figure lying some distance ahead at the edge of the forest, I ran forward until I reached its side. It was indeed Elaine and although she was wholly unconscious, she seemed to be unharmed. I lifted her in my arms and proceeded to return back towards the Château de Conflans; when we reached the gate, she suddenly awoke, clutching my arm as though affected by a sudden, agonized terror.

"Father, there is a tomb close to the edge of the forest—I saw it as she bore me up above the battlements. It is not *their* tomb but someone else's . . . ."

I stared at her breathlessly, beginning to realize that for all of my preparations, a sinister trick had been played upon me and that I had catered to it in precisely the fashion that *he* had expected. Taking Elaine roughly by the shoulders, I said, "You say that *she* took you. Do you mean to tell me that Clotaire was not there?"

She shook her head, her visage one of deathly fear. Seizing her hand, the two of us hastened back into the château and reemerged in the Marquis' chamber. The single candle within had been extinguished, but a brief flash of lightning from outside revealed precisely what I had feared and expected. The Marquis was gone.

I caught up the holy instruments of defense that I had collected and gathered them into a satchel. I could not remember where I had put my stakes, but had no time to organize a search for them, deciding that I would have to make do with what I had. The main thing was to find the Marquis and return him to his château alive. Motioning for Elaine to follow, the two of us once again departed from that cramped little chamber, closing the door behind us. Though we did not realize it, it was the last time that we would ever enter that room again.

We passed out of the courtyard and once again into the farmland

and forest outside of the château's walls. The rain had died down and in its place a white, warm mist had blanched the landscape, impairing my sight considerably. I asked Elaine, however, if she remembered in which direction the tomb in the forest lay—the tomb which she had sighted when Katriane snatched her into the air in order to lure the two of us away from the Marquis. Elaine pointed towards the western edge of the forest and thither we went—I with my hand firmly clasped about my crucifix and prayer book. We soon entered into the deeper darkness of the forest, the rain dripping down upon us from the overhanging branches above. Then, ahead, rising before us like the brooding, uplifted bulk of some dark, shrubless mound, we saw the grey granite walls of a small chapel-like sepulcher. It was nearly as large as a goodly-sized stable and its iron-hinged door hung open. I saw by the inscriptions above the door that it was the mausoleum of the Conflans family—and I also saw by the flickering shadows that danced from within that there was a light that burned somewhere within.

Pressing the holy wafers into Elaine's hand, I told her of what I had in mind and what I wished her to do if the worst occurred. Then, crossing myself and uttering a whispered prayer that no harm might come to Elaine if I myself proved too weak, the two of us entered the Conflans crypt.

I expected the smell of ancient decay and corruption to meet us; instead, I smelled the bittersweet scent of incense, mingled with a sharper, more metallic scent that seemed familiar but which I could not quite place. Stepping forward past the flickering torches upon the walls and the rows of coffins that lay upon stone shelves, we at last reached the stone altar that stood at the far end of the mausoleum. Here, I supposed, the funeral services were held; and here, with two tall candles at his feet and at his head, lay the body of the Marquis, still and silent. And rising out of his chest like some monstrous growth and dabbled horribly with blood, I saw one of my stolen stakes driven deeply into his heart. Elaine turned away and I gazed on with a sickened amazement, the reality of my failed mission not yet having fully come over me yet. Then, as I raised my dazed eyes, I saw a cloaked figure standing within the shadows behind the altar, and I knew when I met those dark, languishing eyes and saw that fatal wound upon his breast who indeed it was. I heard a sharp intake of breath from Elaine, but I kept my voice steady as I spoke: "It seems as though you have glutted yourself with vengeance, spirit. Why, I wonder, did you not glut yourself upon his blood as well, since you have such a taste for it?"

"Were I starving and all other mortal throats denied me," Clotaire replied, his low, resonant voice reverberating within the sepulcher like the echoing voice of a stone lost within the depths of a cistern, "were I enduring already the agonies of the damned and my very salvation depended upon it, I yet would not thirst for *his* blood. Think you that I, who suffered so greatly at his hands—I, who was cursed by his priest to this blasphemous existence—I, who was forced to draw upon the blood of my own Katriane and thus damn her to my side—think you that I would wish such a one as the Marquis to continue within this world as a marauding spirit thirsting for blood as well? Nay—far better, Sir de Vair, that I godspeed his way to Hell now rather than delay the inevitable and ruin other souls during the interim!"

"Why did you not draw upon my daughter's blood when she was in your power the evening before?" I could not keep a slight tremor from my voice as I spoke, for I could not understand the motivations behind this mercifulness.

"Because you are a stranger here, Monsieur," he replied with a certain warmth. "And a stranger whose occupation I respect greatly. I was once a knight as well—before I sickened and was forced to become a torturing instrument of the Marquis. I would no more force your daughter to become one of our kind than would I dishonor the daughter of a dear friend of mine. My spiritual contagion may only be caught if I draw upon the pulsing blood at my victim's throat." His watchful eyes wavering between Elaine and me, he continued, "Shall you depart from this place now?"

"Yes," I replied. "Once I have released your soul from its dreadful state so that you may at last be at peace."

"At peace," he murmured in a hollow voice, his eyes lowering to the dead form upon the altar. "And are you so tender-hearted that you believe that once you have exorcised me, that I shall wend my way to the Fountain of Life where every tear is wiped away and night becomes a thing of naught?" The redolent irony within his voice deepened as he continued, "Or rather, do you not believe that I shall follow the soul of the Marquis de Conflans into the Outer Darkness where there is weeping and gnashing of teeth? For I have sinned knowingly—I have shown myself merciless rather than merciful towards those who have treated me shamefully, renouncing our Savior's example and thus renouncing all hope of Heaven. It is because my vengeance has not yet been sated that my soul is condemned to this state—it is not wholly the fault of the bishop of Conflans. I pray, Monsieur, that you show pity and not consign my soul to the Lake of Fire so soon."

I met his gentle, pleading gaze with one of stern resistance. "That is impossible, as you know. I cannot in good conscience allow you and your consort to remain, preying upon the living and swelling the ranks of your cursed kind."

His gaze moved somewhere behind me and he murmured, "I do not see how you intend on preventing me, Monsieur."

I turned and beheld a woman standing only a few feet away from me, her eyes two steady blue flames fixed upon my face and her loose, golden hair gleaming in the torchlight like a coronet of flames.

"You have been clever, Clotaire, but your desire for vengeance has caused you to blunder," I said. "Elaine, catch hold of Katriane's arm. Do not be afraid—you have the holy wafers. She can do you no harm."

As Elaine did as I bade, I saw Clotaire start forward, his face full of an agonized fear. Swiftly, I moved forward to stand betwixt him and Elaine. In my hand, I held my crucifix aloft so that he might clearly see it. He stopped short instantly with a visage of such frozen dread that one would have thought that he was faced with the severed head of the Medusa.

"It is checkmate, then," he murmured, his lips pale. "Sir de Vair! Of your kindness, I pray that you do not torture Katriane with these holy objects. I am yours entirely—what is it that you would have of me?"

"I believe that you know." I gestured towards the altar. "I shall remove the Marquis—and once I have, I wish you to lie there in his place."

Clotaire watched silently as I hauled the lich off of the stone altar and wrenched the stake out of his heart. Then, crucifix still in hand, I gestured for him to do as I had commanded. He complied with the same wordless resignation, though as he lay upon the altar before me, I heard Katriane utter a shaken, grief-stricken sigh that wrenched my very heart. "I beg you, Monsieur—" she began, but with trembling fingers, I opened my prayer book and sought to drown her out with the beginning words of the last rites. As I prayed aloud, I fumbled in my pouch for my vial of blessed water and, wetting my fingers with it, I bathed Clotaire's forehead and throat with it. His skin felt burningly hot to the touch and I noticed that his breathing had slowed and become less regular as well. After I had finished the prayer, I raised the stake and placed it above his breast. I felt him shudder beneath its weight and, unwillingly, I met his gaze. It was one of such transfixing despair that there was almost an element of serenity about it and, as before, I felt a foolish pity rise within me. As I drew out my hammer from my satchel and raised it above the stake he spoke, and his voice held such a gentle humility and concern that I could not help but know it to be unfeigned: "Sir de Vair, once you have done what you must here, depart from the environs of Conflans as soon as you are able— for it is not safe for you to remain."

"I shall," I replied and, moved more than I should have liked to admit, I pressed his white, fevered hand. "Do not be afraid. A repentant heart with a love for God need have nothing to fear at the judgement seat."

"I have proven myself disobedient to the edicts of the God whom I have professed to love," he replied steadily. "Vengeance is the Lord's, and yet I took it upon myself to carry it out—and both Heaven and Hell know that I would do so again had I the chance. You are kind, Sir de Vair, but let us make no mistake about which realm it is to which you send me."

I wrenched my eyes from that cursed gaze and raised my hammer to strike it home, intending to finish him with one swift, powerful stroke. At least, though I could not promise him salvation, I could ensure him a swift departure from this world...

Part Five

"Madman—stop!"

I froze at the sound of an intruder's voice and glanced up to see Jacques, torch in hand. Several other men stood behind him with naked swords in their hands.

Jacques spoke again: "Monsieur, drop your stake and crucifix or I shall be forced to run you through."

I did as he bade and saw another man seize the holy wafers from my daughter and force her to release her hold upon Katriane. Watching with dread and disbelief as Clotaire rose from the altar, I said, "Jacques, you are making a terrible mistake. These persons whom you believe to be saving are two damned spirits who prolong their existence through drinking upon the blood of the living." Jacques stared at me as though I were out of my mind. "Here, you fool," I continued, swiftly losing my temper. "Perhaps this will convince you." Stepping forward and seizing him by the collar, I dragged him before the blood-spattered body of the Marquis de Conflans. "Look at what they have done to your lord!"

Jacques gazed upon the fallen figure for a long moment. Then, turning to his men and raising his voice, he cried, "The Marquis is dead!"

They took up the shout: "The Marquis is dead!"

Outside the crypt, for the first time I heard the swell of voices cry: "The Marquis is dead!"

Advancing towards Clotaire, Jacques knelt upon one knee before the shrouded figure, taking the pallid hand and pressing it to his lips rapturously. "The Château de Conflans is now yours, Monseigneur. As for this, your intended murderer—we saw him depart and pursued him, suspecting him of foul intent. Yet haply he shall dog your steps no longer." Rising, he unsheathed his sword and stepped towards me. My hand went to my hip out of instinct, but I found that I had neglected to take my sword with me.

In one swift, inexorable motion, Clotaire seized the man's arm, effectively staying his murderous progress. "Perhaps you should have been secularly armed as well," he remarked to me. Then, to Jacques: "None of you shall lay a hand upon either Sir de Vair or his daughter." After a pause: "Any who do so shall be answerable to me." His eyes then lowered to the fallen Marquis. "Pray give him a proper burial and join us within the château when you are finished with your task."

Jacques bowed and this time I thought I caught the glimpse of two red marks like rashes upon his throat, though I could not be sure in the dim, flickering torchlight. Then Clotaire, taking my daughter and me by the hand with a gallant smile as though we were dear comrades rather than mortal opponents, led us out of the crypt with his lady Katriane following. We found a great gathering of men bearing torches and farming implements; at sight of me, their pale eyes filled with a great fear and loathing such as I had never beheld and I believe that, had Clotaire not seemed so at ease in our presence, that they would have verily torn Elaine and me to pieces. As it was, a shout of rejoicing rose up within their ranks at sight of Clotaire and Katriane and with a shuddering amazement, I heard every tongue declare the two as the lord and chatelaine of the Château de Conflans.

"Are these the ones whom I thought to save from death?" I murmured. "It seems that *I* have become the ghoul, the object of fearful hatred amongst them."

"Better to be regarded as a monster amongst the damned and yet be blessed by Heaven than to be loved by the whole of the world and yet be barred from Paradise for all eternity," Clotaire replied. For the first time I glimpsed a certain bitterness within his gaze as he glanced at me before averting his eyes. Like a cloud which, veiling the face of the moon, endows the midnight with a sudden, deeper darkness, his habitually aloof, melancholy visage darkened still more with a silent, concentrated hatred that shadowed his haggard eyes and endowed his smile with a livid, pitiless quality. I felt as though I were looking less upon a man and more upon some awful, concentrated embodiment of hate: hatred of man, hatred of self, and hatred of the peace that he had lost. For a moment, I felt as though a different man, a man with a grasp as tight and deadly as the jaws of a lion, strode beside me. Then, with a slight shudder as of a sigh, he glanced at me again and I saw that it was the old Clotaire once more: the eyes held all of their former kindness and sufferance with only that touch of bitter irony to hint at the diabolic alteration that he had undergone only a moment ago. Yet I knew that this aspect of his nature still remained and the knowledge did nothing to lessen my fear of him.

We soon reached the Château de Conflans and as we passed over the drawbridge and into the courtyard, we were met by still more of its inhabitants. Men with the same blanched, wan look that Jacques and his henchman had sported advanced, hailing Clotaire and his lady

Katriane as the Château de Conflans' new master and mistress. Fair maidens, their streaming hair adorned with white petals and their hands bearing fragrant bouquets of flowers to strew upon the path, knelt in reverence before the sweeping hem of Katriane's gown and caught Clotaire's hand to lay lingering, lascivious kisses thereon. It was as though every man and woman among them had been but awaiting this night and, as a city awaits the return of its conquering lord, were now lavishing upon the pair all the adoration that for long months had lain repressed within their hearts. And upon nearly every throat, be it the wrinkled throat of a doddering old man or the white neck of a young woman, I beheld the two red welts of the vampire's kiss.

Of a sudden, I saw that a certain group of men were pushing through the crowd, dragging someone along with them. As they drew nearer to the light of the torches, I saw to my surprise that their captive was none other than the bishop of Conflans. Halting before Clotaire, one of the men spoke: "Monseigneur, we found this man, rather than rejoicing at your return, hiding within the church with the intention of hanging himself."

Clotaire remained silent for a long while. When he spoke, it was in a voice so soft that even I, who stood beside him, could barely hear: "Pray come nearer."

Though his captors released their hold upon him, the bishop stood his ground, his gaze fixed glassily upon his former victim. His eyes would roam at turns from the wound at Clotaire's breast, to the limbs which he had seen ravaged upon the rack, and finally to the pale, drawn face itself. Hatred, fear, and remorse warred within the bishop's visage as he gazed at the phantom before him.

"You," he murmured. "So you have finally come for me."

Clotaire nodded silently.

The bishop's face went slack with abject terror as though transformed into a tragic mask of Grecian antiquity. At the same time his reptilian eyes flashed with a grotesque fury like two embers scattered from a hell-pyre. "Too merciful by far was the Marquis upon you, and these last few years have witnessed the encroachment of your evil upon the people of this citadel. You have brought Hell itself to this realm—are you well-pleased with what you have done?"

Almost inaudibly, Clotaire replied, "Yes."

The bishop's voice grew tremulous. "Poor fool—do you wreak your terrible revenge simply because of a few hours spent upon the rack?" Seeing that Clotaire grew pale and silent, he persisted, "Speak, daemon!"

"Had you suffered your wrath to be spent only upon me, you should have lived to a hale and sotted age," Clotaire replied. "But there was one other. Perhaps this shall remind you."

And, releasing his grasp upon Elaine, Clotaire took Katriane's hand and drew her forward. A look of terrified recognition blanched the bishop's face for one terrible moment. Then his eyes of a sudden dimmed and he fell forward, the blade of one of Clotaire's stealthy guards plunging deep within his back.

Even as the guards dragged the body away, I felt the crowd around us of a sudden begin to surge and press forward towards some particular destination, bearing me along in their midst. I lost my grasp on Clotaire's hand and ceased attempting to resist the human tide on which I was borne, struggling instead to find Elaine within that mob. Searching that sea of grey faces and sickened, feverish eyes, I at last caught sight of her pale, frightened face as she was hustled forward as well. Pushing past the villagers, I managed to catch hold of her hand tightly and the two of us were borne along with the throng. So dense was the mob that I could not see too clearly in which direction we were heading, but soon I saw ahead the tall spire of the château's chapel built into the wall of the citadel.

As we passed under the church's doorway, I saw that to the right of the entrance leading into the main chapel there was a wooden staircase leading to a higher story. Farther ahead upon the staircase, I beheld Clotaire pause in his ascent for a moment, his dark cloak trailing at his feet like the skirting shadow of an attendant familiar, and the lady Katriane standing at his side, her slender-fingered hand resting upon his shoulder. I gazed upon those two tall figures—the clear grey eyes and piquant features of the woman and the dark, haggard eyes of the man, filled with such a proud, tortured implacability. I believed then and still do believe, damned though they are, that in that moment I looked upon the fairest sight that I have ever been worthy enough to behold.

Clotaire took a torch from one of the men standing by: in his hand, the golden light mounted to a tall, eerily blue flame that stood steady and motionless in spite of the draughty staircase. His eyes wandered consideringly over the silent throng before him, finally resting upon Elaine and me. With a peculiar smile, he said, "We have here among us an honored stranger and guest—Sir Jean-Claire de Vair, a renowned scourge of evil." His irony softening somewhat, he added, "Would that both he and his daughter might become a friend of our company."

"Perhaps," said Katriane. "Perhaps they will join us all within the chapel's upper chamber before they depart."

As the two departed, I felt something catch hold of my shoulder. Turning, I saw that it was Elaine, her face white with distress. "Father, you are not unwell are you?"

I shook my head, asking her why she should think thusly.

"Your face seemed very odd when you looked upon the two of them."

Part Six

We were jostled up the stairs by the mob and soon found ourselves with them in a vast, bare room. From the altar at the end of the room, I gathered that this must once have been some private sanctuary; yet all of the holy objects had been removed, and even the walls were covered with tapestries as though to shield from view the stained glass windows.

The throng gathered within that room and stood by, watchful and expectant. I saw Clotaire standing by one of the tapestries; the hanging was translucent enough to allow the moonlight to filter somewhat through, framing him with the vague outline of seraph wings.

Then I saw Katriane point one long, slender finger at one of the men standing close by. Instantly, he drew nearer until he stood close enough for her to take his hand, to catch the hair at the back of his neck, and to lay her beautiful white teeth upon his throat. Horrified, I stepped forward but was instantly stayed by the hands of those closest to me. As I watched helplessly, I saw that though the man was clearly growing weaker: he did not resist the woman, but remained as passive under her lovely, avid lips as though senseless of the bitter prick of her teeth. When she had sated her thirst, he sunk to his knees before her, bowed low, and then rose again to rejoin the rest of the throng.

Clotaire then lifted his eyes and glanced speculatively about the room; not a one of those who stood there flinched beneath that wandering gaze, but rather returned it with a look of long devotion. At last, with the crook of a finger, he beckoned a young woman with dark, russet hair, barely older than Elaine. Her naked white feet hardly made a sound as she crossed the wooden floor and timidly came forward. She then went easily into his arms, letting her head rest upon his shoulder and baring her throat to him. When his lips at last reluctantly left her throat, she seemed about to kneel in reverence and depart; however, he restrained her from doing so and instead gave her a light kiss upon the brow in lieu of spoken thanks. A trace of blood was left upon her forehead in the wake of this kiss and, with a melancholy little smile, he wiped her brow with the hem of his shroud's sleeve and restored her face to its original purity before returning her to the rest of the devotees.

Men presently entered bearing platters and goblets upon silver trays, but though the wan men and women about me began to partake of the viands, I chose not to, preferring to keep a close eye upon Clotaire and Katriane in the hopes that Elaine's and my release from the château would be imminent. The two seemed deep in earnest conversation: often I would catch the overtone of Katriane's soft, languorous voice and see a thoughtful smile appear upon Clotaire's visage as he listened. Often as well I would see their eyes wander towards me and I wondered with a nervous restlessness as to what they could be discussing.

"Father," Elaine whispered. "May we not depart now?"

"Yes, as soon as—" I stopped abruptly, for once again the gazes of the two spirits were fixed upon me, and Clotaire was now beckoning for me to come forward. Elaine may have said something in order to prevent me, but I did not hear it above the voices of those about us. I pressed forward until I had reached the two of them.

"Sir Jean de Vair, you have been an honorable enemy and a clever opponent." Clotaire hesitated. "I do not doubt that had my men failed to notice your departure from the château, both my lady and I would assuredly now be safely ensconced within the infernal regions."

"And yet," Katriane continued, her brilliant eyes flickering towards me. "Though you overcame us, methinks that your sympathies still lay with us even then."

I denied this, feeling myself grow a little heady under their gazes. Clotaire then took my hand and turned it over so that my palm faced upwards, tracing the long, crimson wound there with the tips of his pale, gaunt fingers. "Was this not pity?" he enquired, his smile a mixture of kindly amusement and sorrow.

All about us, I felt that a hush had descended over the rest of those in that room; or perhaps I had grown deaf to them.

"What do you want of me?" I returned, my voice hoarsening to the faintest of whispers.

"Stay with us." Katriane's eyes gleamed within the torchlight.

"Yes, stay with us." The warmth of Clotaire's voice belied the subtle implacability that had entered his gaze. "I have imposed already upon your pity—I do so again. No harm shall come to either you or your daughter—you shall not become as we are unless you *wish* to. Only do not bereave us of your company so soon. It has been long since I have had the pleasure of meeting another knight so worthy."

"You are no longer a knight," I said, loathing myself for speaking thus but feeling that I must.

The sorrow within his eyes deepened, but his voice lost none of its warmth. "Perhaps that is why I crave your companionship still more."

An uncomfortable silence fell betwixt us as I stood silent, at a loss for words whilst the two of them regarded me with keen, piercing gazes. The spell was broken, however, when one of the servers offered a glass of red wine to me. Before I could reply, Katriane accepted it and, with a gracious smile, presented it to me. I thanked her and, as it was not a large flagon, I downed its contents relatively swiftly. The whole of the time, I felt my hosts' eyes still riveted upon me as though drinking in my every move.

Seeing that my glass was nearly empty, Clotaire offered to refill it; however, after he took the goblet, he paused and instead set it down upon the nearby altar. Then he drew nearer to me as though about to whisper something in my ear. Spurred by some terrible instinct, I turned sharply and met his eyes. I believe then that I at last knew what was meant to happen. When I found my voice, I said:

"You told me that I was not obliged to become as you are."

"Only if you choose to deny me."

"I *do* deny you."

"Then do so without delay," he rejoined. "With one holy word, you shall have convinced me without a doubt of your intentions." His eyes still intent upon me, he took up the chalice from the altar and drank deeply of the remainder of the wine, awaiting my reply. Katriane as well watched me, her lips half-parted and her eyes relentlessly upon my own.

Cursed be that hour and still more cursed be my silence at that moment—for though I longed to utter the names of the saints and to summon from memory the most potent exorcisms at my command, I found myself utterly speechless. I do not know why this was so, for though I remembered with particular vividness the bitter hatred that Clotaire was capable of, I do not believe that it was any fear of incurring his wrath that rendered me silent. I *do* know that I shall never forgive myself for that moment of frailty—nay, though I live many years longer to become still more of a doddering old fool.

Clotaire saw in an instant my hesitation and I believe that a look of both relief and regret entered his eyes for a moment. Yet as I felt his inhumanly strong grasp upon my arm and readied myself for what I knew was to come, a cry rose up among those around us. Looking up, I saw that the edge of one of the hanging tapestries was being rapidly consumed by a lapping flame and that the fire was quickly spreading to the others. Amidst the chaos of the scattering people within that room, I saw Elaine bearing a torch and warding away those who attempted to come near her.

Clotaire flung me away from him, hastening towards Katriane who was shrinking away from the flames that now spanned that chamber, creeping along the wooden floorboards and spreading in all directions like a fiery flood. I struggled to reach Elaine's side and managed to catch hold of her hand, striving to reach the door. It was difficult to fight against the press of the throng on all sides—some were calling for water, others were attempting to smother the fire with cloaks and whatever else was available. All were fearful but none seemed willing to leave the chamber whilst Clotaire and his lady remained. I saw to my surprise that it was less a fear of the flames that seemed to possess the two spirits, but rather a fear of the tapestries' disintegration.

I realized all too quickly the reason behind this fear, for as one of the hangings crumbled into a formless pile of grey ashes, it revealed the stained glass image of the archangel Michael himself standing victorious over the fallen form of some evil spirit. The moonlit outlines of the window fell athwart the flaming floor and at sight of it, Katriane gave a stifled cry and hid her face against Clotaire's breast. A change had fallen over Clotaire as well, for his face had blanched to a fearful pallor and as he held Katriane his hands trembled piteously as though the insidious sickness that had possessed him in life had returned to reclaim him yet again.

"Father, please—we must leave!" Elaine began to pull me once again through the panicked crowd and towards the door. Just as we reached the threshold, one of the men close by caught sight of us and, seized with a sudden fury, raised a hand to strike my daughter. I managed to catch him just below the chin with my own fist, sending him crashing to the floor. Then we reached the wooden staircase and, though Elaine pulled me down after her, I could not forebear turning to look back into that fiery chamber. Nearly all of the tapestries had become little more than translucent, blackened curtains through which the holy images upon the stained glass windows, like shining sentinels, surrounded those within. Where the streaming, colored moonlight fell upon him, I saw revealed the ravaged, skeletal outlines of Clotaire's decaying form beneath the shroud as though the light filtered through those stained glass windows somehow revealed his true form, unadorned by the spectral glamour that rendered him, though dead, to have the appearance of a living man. Yet those eyes—those haunted, despairing eyes—remained the same and as I stood there, they happened to lift and rest upon me, and there was a look of suffering and reproach therein such as I have never beheld before. Then I heard a creak and felt the wooden stair upon which I stood sway ever so gently, and realized that the staircase was about to crumble.

Pulling Elaine along after me, I descended the staircase as swiftly as possible, feeling the hot breath of the flames at my back. Once we reached the foot of the stairs, we raced madly out of the chapel as a thunderous crash sounded somewhere behind us, for the fire had effectively eaten away the dry, wooden foundations of those stairs causing the entire staircase to collapse.

The courtyard was void of all but the flood of moonlight and silvery mist as well as the billowing smoke that poured forth from the chapel. There was no one about, the drawbridge remained lowered, and thus Elaine and I crossed out of that silent courtyard and departed forever from the Château de Conflans. Even then, we only ceased our flight at the coming of dawn when we had reached the road to Ximes and were at the summit of a hill overlooking the valley in which the château stood. We chanced to meet a passing group of knights bound for Ximes themselves and they kindly offered to accompany us in that direction.

Turning, we beheld the towering shape of the château in the distance, framed by the first rosy line of dawn at the horizon. The fire had died down to nothing, leaving but a thick, drifting smoke surrounding those secluded stone walls. I gazed on wordlessly, overcome by a great weariness, until one of the knights pointed and remarked, "Now that indeed is a rare sight."

My gaze turned to follow his pointing finger and at first I believed that I was looking upon a portion of the billowing cloud of smoke and fog that surrounded the château, so thick and white was the shifting shape that he pointed to. Only when they began to fly closer towards us, scattering close by upon the green meadow, did I see that it was a dense flock of doves. Yet I felt that there was something odd about their appearance and the manner in which they cocked their pale red eyes and seemed curiously unafraid of our presence.

"Their markings . . ." Elaine pointed. "There are two crimson marks upon each of their throats. Father—you do not think that they are—"

I believe I laughed then rather harshly, though more out of fear than amusement. "Clotaire has saved his children."

Elaine turned very white. "Then Clotaire and Katriane—are they yet alive?"

I watched as the doves ascended into the air, wheeling towards the battlements of the château, but did not reply; though I do not believe that Elaine realized it, my thoughts were a mixture of guilty hope and fearful denial. *Were* they yet alive?

The knights looked at us rather oddly, but said nothing. They were fortunately strangers and thus unacquainted with any knowledge of the Château de Conflans—an ignorance that I heartily envied. For my part, I turned my back to that valley and trudged on towards Ximes without another word.

I know of no tales that have passed out of the valley since my departure from that place so many years ago, but I can easily guess at a few. I imagine that a traveler, were he to take the wrong road out of Ximes, would find himself in a misty, desolate countryside overgrown with forest—a countryside where the mist is hot and dank as jungle steam and clings to his skin like some fevered, festering illness. If he continued onward, he would find a wooded valley and the stone ruins of a tall castle in its midst. Pigeons with pale feathers, red eyes, and curious crimson marks upon their throat would scatter as he passed into the shadowed, overgrown courtyard. Then, if he remained long enough or—still more foolishly—chose to pass the night, he would be met by two persons: a woman with steady, scintillant eyes and hair like that of a lioness, and a man with a mortal wound upon his breast and a look of long and insatiate despair. The end to the traveller's tale at this juncture would depend upon his own strength and decision. To my shame, I shall never forget that had Elaine not set fire to the tapestries within that chapel, my end would have been easy enough to guess at—and though I battled and overcame many malefic spirits and beings long afterwards, I have never dared to visit that part of Averoigne again. I do not believe that if I did, I should ever return.

Sir Jean-Claire de Vair ceased speaking, his eyes dimming once again as though too wearied to do more than fall into one of his usual restless sleeps. I felt terribly sorry for the poor old fellow, however, and felt that it would be wrong to say nothing at the close of his tale.

"No man is free of weakness to temptation," I murmured. "Praise be to the saints that you are free of this particular temptation so that it can do you no more harm."

"Yes," he replied. "Yes, François."

And as he spoke, he silently withdrew his hand and placed it on his lap under the table; yet not before I had caught a glimpse of a long, freshly-inflicted gash, thin and red, upon his palm—a gash that re-traced another, older scar that ran across his hand like a silver thread, as though it was the remnant of some knife wound inflicted many years earlier.

GUNS OF AVEROIGNE

by Cardinal Cox

Five King's Musketeers are riding hard
Through ancient thick oak forest around Ximes
A languid land conjured from fever dreams
Brave soldiers of the royal palace guard

Curious orders sent them so far south
Investigate tales of monsters on moors
So are diverted from religious wars
Hunting something big with ravening mouth

A scream, they stop then they turn through the trees
Maiden straddled by a gray wolf so large
Tight reins in hands and the guards pull-up dead

Some fumble as from scabbards foils come free
Training conquers their fears as one they charge
Two fire primed flintlock pistols at its head

Wounded the beast lumbers between the trees
The men check that the maiden is unharmed
She is not injured but still much alarmed
The troop discuss their plans, rise from their knees

Later on horseback they enter the town
Searching for a tavern in which to stay
Shadows lengthen as it is end of day
Bald priest scuttles past in flapping black gown

Next day they follow a clear bloody trail
Through forest to a low cottage alone
Inside, on a bed, they find a dying man

In slow broken whisper he tells his tale
"She is no maiden but an evil crone
She cursed me thus; kill the witch, if you can . . ."

Aghast, last night witch had the captain's bed
In that tavern by the town's market square
Folks say this truly a damned land where
Curses rather than holy prayers are said

Dead man they bury in a simple hole
Slowly the squad of four ride through the day
Wondering what they can to captain say
And if they might still somehow save his soul

Entering Ximes they find the black-clad priest
Force him to go with them to the low inn
Together they climb stairs to captain's room

With prayer and bullets they confront the beast
Turned into a snake-woman in her sin
Says priest, "Glad my sister goes to her tomb . . ."

Symposium of the Gargoyle

by Simon Whitechapel

Mais Reynard lui-même n'avait pas oublié les gargouilles. Souvent, en passant devant le superbe édifice de la cathédrale, il les contemplait avec une satisfaction secrète pour laquelle il aurait pu difficilement en attribuer ou en cerner les causes. Elles semblaient conserver pour lui une signification rare et mystique, indiquer un triomphe obscur mais plaisant.

— Le Sculpteur de gargouilles, *Clark Ashton Smith, translated by Patrick Rodrigue*

Évariste Laroche had been destined for some high professorship in a French or German academy, but was orphaned at the age of fifteen when the new bridge carrying passengers and freight over the Isoile collapsed into the river under the weight of an afternoon express. It was discovered that the contractor had swollen his already high profits by employing under-strength girders in the construction of the bridge, but the miscreant had fled Averoigne—and soon thereafter France—on receiving a warning by telegram from an anonymous confederate, and no damages for criminal neglect ever found their way to the young orphan.

He was forced to leave school and set his foot to the first rung of a career in accountancy, but the dust, gloom, and long hours of the office in which he worked, concomitant with the lingering grief of his parents' loss and dashing of his long-cherished hopes, undermined a never robust constitution, and by the age of seventeen he was chronically ill and forced to leave the firm. With the aid of his meagre savings and a small annuity bequeathed him by an aunt in Touraine who had been, until her death, his sole surviving relative, he did not wholly starve, but none of those who knew him expected him to see out his third decade. As his savings dwindled he was forced to seek out cheaper and cheaper accommodation, and he sometimes joked that though his rents were constantly falling, he himself was as constantly rising, inhabiting smaller and smaller rooms at the head of longer and longer stairs, until at last he was ensconced in a garret of a crumbling tenement owned by the notorious old miser Salfuyche (the maternal *grand-oncle*, though Évariste knew it not, of the contractor responsible for his parents' death).

Here, often confined to his bed for weeks by his worsening illness, Évariste occupied his mind by reading, drawing, and mathematics—once his best hope of academic distinction—until one day his friend Jean-Pierre brought him that for which he had saved for months. Jean-Pierre's was a worse misfortune, Évariste always insisted, than his own. Once an apprentice stone-carver, he had fallen from a height working to repair a flying buttress of the cathedral of Vyônes, and had never recovered full use of one arm or full possession of the wits shaken loose by the fall. He was Évariste's agent in the city during his worst illnesses, buying him food and making the rare purchases of books for which Évariste had managed to save. The long-saved-for object Jean-Pierre brought that never-to-be-forgotten day was old and much dinted but now infinitely precious to Évariste: a telescope with which he now spent many absorbing hours watching the birds of the cathedral of Vyônes, which his tenement window overlooked at two kilometres' distance, and the stars that by night descended in the western heavens.

And yet, though it drove the birds away, he liked to see the cathedral best when it rained and the gargoyles began to spout, discharging through their mouths the rain that filled and raced in the cathedral's gutters. Then it was that the gargoyles filled the role for which they were created, and he fancied sometimes, staring through his telescope, that the grins on their demonic faces grew wider, that their horns tilted more jauntily, their wings spread more exuberantly, quivering with scarce-restrained life, as though one day, in the very act of spouting, the gargoyles would leap from their stony vantage and swoop down through the rain-lashed air on the city over which they had so long presided, like that pair of the mediæval sculptor Blaise Reynard whose legend still circulated in Vyônes.

However, one gargoyle did not share in the general hilarity of the rain: *Le Saturnien*, the Saturnine One. All the others, in his hours of te-lescopy from his invalid's bed, Évariste had christened by name: Adramelech, Asmodée, Baphomet, Bélial, Belphégor, Lucifuge, Méphisto, Moloch, Samaël. But where their faces grinned with glee of wickedness, that of *Le Saturnien* scowled with unappeasable rancor; and where their horns were the jaunty curves of the goat, those of *Le Saturnien* were the oddly curling helices of some unclassifiable *bovidé*. Even the shadows seemed to lie heavier in *Le Saturnien*'s corner and the snow of winter to thaw slower in spring from his skull and shoulders. Évariste had spun a tale around him, imagining him no true gargoyle, but a *lithosarcique* (which is to say, stone-fleshed) prince of the planet for which he had been named, condemned to long centuries of exile on Earth for some crime of dark passion, and now endlessly brooding on his return and the vengeance he would wreak by shores of sullen-lapping acid or beneath crags of levin-scarred obsidian.

And indeed, when Évariste turned the musty pages of Yves Saint-Cizeau's *L'Architecture d'Averoigne à l'époque Gothique* or Adolphe Gailloux's *Histoire sommaire de la Cathédrale de Vyônes*—treasured volumes for whose purchase he had endured weeks of semi-starvation—he could find no trace of *Le Saturnien* on the lithographs of the cathedral, though Belphégor and Asmodée and the rest were clearly visible. Perhaps *Le Saturnien* had been overlooked by the artists; perhaps he had been added to the cathedral sometime in the past century, after the books had been published; perhaps Évariste's fantasies were true and the gargoyle had descended there of his own accord one night, wings still glistening with the rime of interplanetary flight.

But the mystery of the gargoyle's origins was by no means the sole enigma to attach to it: Évariste had also puzzled over what the gargoyle itself, or its sculptor, meant to convey by the disposition of its talons. Those of the left hand were curled shut save for the raised index, while those of the right formed the following curious gesture: the middle talon was folded to the palm and the index, third, and last were raised; and *Le Saturnien* either had no left thumb or had lost it to the nipping frost of an Averoigne winter. Since acquiring the telescope Évariste had sketched the gesture of the right hand many times in pencil or charcoal, and had tried to imitate it as many times with his own right hand, but he had always failed to adequately reproduce it. Either his middle-finger would not fold fully down or his ringfinger would not fully raise, and the manual tendons of gargoyles or Saturnians were, he had concluded, fashioned different to those of men.

Concomitant with his growing fascination with the gargoyle grew his fascination with the planet of its putative origins. When the cathedral and its environs grew too dark for survey and the birds that flocked there by day were at roost, he would turn the lens of his dinted telescope on the western sky above, seeking out in its season the white pearl of Saturn, strung on the invisible cord of the *écliptique*. The telescope was no precise instrument of science, for it had passed through a half- dozen hands before his and been the cheapest available in Vyônes, though almost beyond his means to purchase from the *mont-de-piété* in the quarter (owned through an intermediary, though again Évariste knew it not, by his landlord Salfuyche). Yet time and again his heart would catch in his throat to see the ring-girdled globe of Saturn floating minute and perfect against the black of the heavens. Was *Le Saturnien* indeed exiled thence or from a moon thereof, condemned for some nefandous crime under a darker sky, beneath a dimmer sun? Or had he committed no true wrong, but been a tyrannicide or rebel *manqué*, or victim of some dynastic plot he had escaped only by flight?

Ah, *peut-être*. If Évariste fell asleep musing thus, he would turn his telescope even more eagerly on the cathedral when he woke, hoping to find his hypotheses confirmed by seeing either that *Le Saturnien* had shifted position in the night, proving life lay hid beneath apparent stone, or that the gargoyle's talons now signaled in different and decipherable fashion. And one day, as he had long hoped, a change did indeed come to the gargoyle, though in no wise that he had foreseen. He turned his telescope on the cathedral to refresh his mind after a morning of geometrizing and a frugal lunch of bread, cheese, and sour red wine, and watched a dispute between two of the cathedral crows for a time before passing his lens over the line of gargoyles along the roof, saluting each *sotto voce* as his eye fell upon it.

"*Bonjour Belphégor, j'espère que tu as bien mangé . . . bonjour Moloch . . . et Asmodée, ça va? Je pense que tu es plus gros cet été . . . .*"

And so he came to *Le Saturnien*:

"*Bonjour, mon prin—*"

But what was this? The gargoyle was altered somehow amid its shadows . . . and then he saw the cause: the left horn was gone from the head, and not even a stump remained. There was a strange excitement in the sight, for the thought flashed upon him that the horn might be retrieved from where it now lay, for if it had fallen during the night who else in the city of Vyônes would know of its loss? He knew the spot directly beneath *Le Saturnien*'s perch well, having visited it often in the days before his illness came upon him. There was deep earth there, in which a sharp object falling from a height might bury itself with scarce a trace.

So it was that he barely possessed patience to wait out the hours until Jean-Pierre called on him again. Their friendship aside, Évariste's *sous* were highly valuable to the youth, for he had, of course, no pension from his cut-short apprenticeship, and work was hard to find even for the able-bodied in the Vyônes of that period, let alone for a half-cripple of uncertain wits.

That week, however, he had found a week's work assisting in the renovation of a house for a new-wed lawyer, and was visiting Évariste but once a day, in the evening, to bring him the next day's provisions or oil for his lamp. When his feet sounded at last on the stair, Évariste was bursting out the tale of what he had seen even before the door was fully open, and Jean-Pierre was simultaneously frowning and smiling, as he puzzled out the torrent of words and caught Évariste's excitement. When he understood the tale, he promised in his stammering *parole* that the next day, very early, before he began work for his employer, he would visit the cathedral and search the earth for the fallen horn, bringing it in the evening without fail should he find it there.

The next day stretched endless for Évariste, for he woke early and had many hours to fill before he learned whether Jean-Pierre had succeeded or failed in the search. Again and again he turned the telescope on the cathedral and the now-unicorn *Le Saturnien*, trying to count the spirals in the remaining horn. But the angle at which the horn protruded and the shadows of *Le Saturnien*'s corner defeated him now as always they had in the past, and he turned to sketching the gargoyle itself, neglecting the geometric proof that had been absorbing him but a day-and-a-half before.

Then at last the feet of Jean-Pierre were on the stair again, and were they hurrying? Yes, hurrying, for now the door burst open and the grin on the face of his friend told him the horn was found. Stammering worse than ever in his excitement, Jean-Pierre drew the thing from beneath his stained and patched *blouson de travail*. The horn was about fifty *centimètres* long, carved of an oddly unweathered stone, and

Évariste nodded his thanks as he took it eagerly, careless of the crusted earth that fell from it to his coverlet. Now he could count the spirals of the helix, murmuring them off under his breath. Yes, there were exactly thirteen from the base to the sharp tip, and was not the spiral the *mirabilis*, that which one of the Bernoullis—he forgot the name in his excitement—had had carved on his tomb?

But now he frowned a little, for the balance of the horn in his hands was somehow wrong.

"It displeases you, *m-mon p'tit?*" Jean-Pierre stammered, catching the frown.

"*Non, vieux ami*," Évariste reassured, shaking his head, "*mais il me semble* . . ."

And yes, as he scratched at the broken-off base, a skin of soft plaster yielded to his fingernail. The horn, or the lower part of it at least, was hollow. Flakes of plaster joined the earth lying on his coverlet as he broke the skin away and probed within the base. His fingers met resistance, and a moment later were drawing forth a tube—a rolled tube—of dark leather. It was stiff with age and as he began to unroll it he felt it crack beneath his fingers. He looked up.

"Jean-Pierre, my lamp, *s'il te plaît*."

When Jean-Pierre brought him the lamp, he sprinkled the leather with oil and massaged it in, softening the leather so that he could begin to unroll it again, little by little. It seemed many minutes before the square of leather lay open before him, held flat with a finger on opposite edges, so he could read the letters seared upon it who knew how long before with a tip of red-hot iron or steel:

```
V  B  C  T  I  D
V  C  S  A  E  I
N  D  M  V  V  O
N  V  M  S  N  L
C  E  T  V  S  E
M  V  N  F  D  C
```

ΟΙ ΑΡΙΘΜΟΙ ΑΡΧΟΥΣΙΝ
ΤΟ ΣΥΜΠΑΝ

"But what does it say, *mon p'tit?*" Jean-Pierre asked, craning his neck over the bed.

"Ah, I'm sorry, see for yourself, *vieux ami.*"

He turned the square so that Jean-Pierre could read what was written thereon, and he smiled ruefully at the look of disappointment on his friend's face.

"*C'-c'est de l'hébreu p-pour moi,*" Jean-Pierre stammered out.

Évariste laughed, releasing the edges of the square so that it rolled slowly into a tube again.

"Ah, I *wish* it were Hebrew, and unciphered. As it is, the Greek is all I understand, and it must be the key to the puzzle. 'Number governs all.' But what numbers do we have?"

He fell silent a moment.

"First six," he said slowly. "A six-by-six square. Thirty-six letters in all. And are we to include the letters of the *maxime Pythagoricienne?* No, I think not. It is not part of the square, and not in the Roman alphabet. Ah, *oui.*"

He unrolled the square again.

"Roman alphabet," he repeated, running his eyes over the square. "Yes, Roman. I believe the square is in Latin. The age and origin are right, and see: four E's, two I's, one each only of A and O, but seven V's. But how is it enciphered? *Code de César? Une scytale?* After all, the leather was *rolled . . . .*"

He shook his head slowly, falling silent again, then looked up at his friend with a smile.

"*Je suis bête,* Jean-Pierre. Number governs all. I must think of *Le Saturnien* also. Two horns that are now one horn . . . thirteen spirals of the fallen horn . . . one talon raised of the left hand . . . and . . . and what does he seek to convey by the talons of the right? Two talons raised, one lowered, one raised . . . . One thousand, one hundred, and one?"

Évariste nodded slowly, then reached for his pencil and a piece of the scrap paper he used for his calculations.

"You will learn *le secret, mon p'tit?*" Jean-Pierre said as his friend began to write, recreating the square of letters from memory.

Évariste glanced up for a moment, then looked back to his work, saying, "I will try. Ah, I will try."

When Jean-Pierre left him an hour later, he was absorbed in the work and barely acknowledged his friend's departure; and when Jean-Pierre returned to the garret the following evening, he found Évariste deeply asleep, still sitting upright in bed with his lap full of scribbled papers.

Jean-Pierre laid down the provisions he had brought and gently shook his friend's shoulder. Évariste sprang awake with a start.

"Ah, Jean-Pierre, *c'est toi*. I worked most of the night and could not hold off sleep during the day. But . . . *non*, he has collected it while I slept. Salfuyche's nephew," he went on, in response to Jean-Pierre's look of enquiry. "It is my day to pay rent. When I felt sleep overcoming me, I left the money on my table."

"B-but he w-will have seen *tes feuilles!*" Jean-Pierre said with concern.

"My papers? Ah, I see." Évariste looked down at the papers that filled his lap. "They would mean nothing to him. They mean little enough to me, alas. And . . . yes, I think they are all here, and the horn was safe beneath my pillow. See?"

He twisted himself to one side, lifting the horn forth from beneath his pillow, making two or three strokes through the air with it, like a sword.

"Such workmanship," he said. "Perhaps we can sell it, old friend, and earn a little that way, though I fear someone might reason that, save for those of the *narval* and *licorne*, horns come in twos, and so guess its ori—"

He broke off, suddenly frowning, then murmured, "Horns come in twos . . . Two. Two. That is it. Yes, that is it. *Le système binaire de* Leibniz. Not one thousand, one hundred, and one, but . . . one and four and eight. Thirteen. Thirteen, like the spirals of the horn. It has been staring me in the face all the while. The left hand signifies one and the right thirteen. One and thirteen, one *over* thirteen. *L'inverse de treize*, in the base of two, and yielding . . . ."

He started to push through the papers, searching for something.

"Jean-Pierre, please, my pencil. It has rolled to the floor."

Jean-Pierre retrieved it and handed it to his friend, who began to write rapidly, setting down a line of numbers, then a second, shorter line beneath it.

"*Oui, comme je pensais*, it is at a maximum. Look, Jean-Pierre. The *remainders* of the division."

He held the paper out for Jean-Pierre, who read with a shrug:

2 4 8 16 3 6 12 24 11 22 9 18 5 10 20 7 14 1

2 4 8 3 6 12 11 9 5 10 7 1

"Now," Évariste went on. "Two more lines."

Jean-Pierre watched as he repeated the second line of numbers twice, then began to add letters beneath them. When he was finished the paper looked like this:

```
1 2 4 8 3 6 12 11 9 5 10 7
V B C T I D V  C  S A E  I

1 2 4 8 3 6 12 11 9 5 10 7
N D M V V O N  V  M S N  L

1 2 4 8 3 6 12 11 9 5 10 7
C E T V S E M  V  N F D  C
```

"See? *Je crois que c'est une anagramme*, arranged according to the re-mainders of the reciprocal in the base of two. First and second remain where they are, but third goes to fourth, and fourth to eighth, and fifth to third and . . . ."

He wrote rapidly, murmuring the re-arrangements as he did so. Jean-Pierre, still understanding nothing of what he had been told, watched with a puzzled smile on his face that broadened uncertainly as Évariste looked up in triumph after he had completed the first line and a portion of the second.

"*Vois*, it works! It works! *C'est un message en latin!*"

Now the paper read:

```
1 2 4 8 3 6 12 11 9 5 10 7
V̶ B̶ C̶ T̶ I̶ D̶ V̶  C̶  S̶ A̶ E̶  I̶
V B I C A D I  T  S E C  V
```

```
1  2  4  8  3  6  12  11  9  5  10  7
N̶  D̶  M̶  V̶  V̶  O   N   V   M  S  N   L
N  D  V  M
```

```
1  2  4  8  3  6  12  11  9  5  10  7
C  E  T  V  S  E  M   V   N  F  D   C
```

He carried on, filling in the remainder of the second line and the whole of the third, then adding two more lines of letters, so that the paper looked like this:

```
1  2  4  8  3  6  12  11  9  5  10  7
V̶  B̶  C̶  T̶  I̶  D̶  V̶   C̶   S̶  A̶  E̶   I̶
V  B  I  C  A  D  I   T   S  E  C   V
```

```
1  2  4  8  3  6  12  11  9  5  10  7
N̶  D̶  M̶  V̶  V̶  O̶  N̶   V̶   M̶  S̶  N̶   L̶
N  D  V  M  S  O  L   V   M  N  V   N
```

```
1  2  4  8  3  6  12  11  9  5  10  7
C̶  E̶  T̶  V̶  S̶  E̶  M̶   V̶   N̶  F̶  D̶   C̶
C  E  S  T  F  E  C   V   N  D  V   M
```

VBI CADIT SECVNDVM
SOLVM NVNC EST FECVNDVM

"See, Jean-Pierre? See? A message, a message for us, from *Le Saturnien*! 'Where falls the second, the earth now is fecund.' It must mean the second horn. And look, see how bright the moon is tonight! Take my telescope—your eyes are sharper than mine. Find *Le Saturnien*, and tell me what you see."

Bewildered, still understanding little of what Évariste had said or done, Jean-Pierre took up the telescope and focused it through Évariste's open window on the cathedral.

"Yes, yes?" Évariste burst out impatiently. "What do you see?"

"*La d-deuxième c-corne de la g-gargouille*," stammered Jean-Pierre, "*elle est disp– disparue.*"

"I knew it! The second horn, the second horn has fallen, and there is a treasure waiting for us where it lies. *Vite, va,* go like the wind and see. But take your bag, to carry the thing, if it be possible."

Jean-Pierre lowered the telescope, shaking his head, and it was some moments before Évariste could fully explain the significance of the vanished second horn. Then Jean-Pierre was gone, his feet clattering *diminuendo* down the stairs. The hour that followed seemed like two, and time and again Évariste turned his telescope on the moon-bathed cathedral, straining his eye to see the now-hornless skull of *Le Saturnien*; but at last the feet were returning, *crescendo* up the stairs, and Jean-Pierre was bursting back into the room with his bag, panting with exertion and emotion. For a minute he could not speak, and then he began to stammer out his news.

"Salf–Salfuyche, *il est—il est m-mort!*"

"*Quoi?*"

"Salf–Salfuyche, he is dead!"

Gradually the tale came out: on arriving at the cathedral Jean-Pierre had discovered the old miser lying dead at the foot of the wall, transfixed by the second horn in the very act, it seemed, of delving in the earth for the treasure of which the paper had spoken.

"Then *his neveu* did see and understand my calculations and sketches while I slept!" Évariste cried. "Or at least understand their possible significance, and Salfuyche cracked a stolen copy of the square before us."

He shook his head and shrugged, with a rueful laugh.

"And now he has his reward. But we, do we have ours? What waited there, where the second horn fell?"

Jean-Pierre did not speak, but opened his bag and drew forth what it carried: a squat, lead-sealed bottle of dark glass, still crusted with earth. He handed it to Évariste.

"This was all you found? Well, it is a goodly weight, at least, but what does it contain?"

He shook the bottle and held it up to the lamp-light.

"Wine, old friend? A bottle of wine, centuries old? Is this our treasure? Then it must be of great value and . . . ."

But Jean-Pierre was shaking his head. "*Non. Nous buvons.*" He strode to Évariste's table and lifted the two cracked glasses in which the two of them had shared, in the past, so many indifferent vintages.

"No, old friend, do not be foolish. We cannot drink it, we must *sell* it. The bottle alone will be of great value, I believe, and the wine is surely long ago turned to purest v—"

Jean-Pierre did not argue, but plucked the bottle from Évariste's hand, tested the leaden seal for a moment with his fingers, grunted, and then broke the neck off with a single blow on the edge of the table. Now he began to pour two glasses of the wine and Évariste's startled protests ceased as the room filled with its scent, rich with spices to which he could put no name.

His eyes widened in wonder as Jean-Pierre turned back to him, lifting a filled glass toward him. The wine glittered dark purple in the light of his lamp, but there seemed to be extra colors therein on the threshold of vision, troubling his brain like the scent with memories from new-recalled dreams: shores of sullen-lapping green, crags of levin-scarred obsidian, the splendors of an uncloaked heavens, the searing cold of interplanetary flight.

He took the glass, hand shaking, so that wine spilled to the coverlet of his bed. Jean-Pierre watched him implacably.

"This... this is no earthly vintage, Jean-Pierre," Évariste said. "I fear to drink, and yet . . . ."

He shook his head, raised the glass to his lips, and drank; and Jean-Pierre, with a nod and grunt of satisfaction, followed suit.

The slaying of Salfuyche by a fallen gargoyle's horn, for reason of its bizarreness if not of the esteem in which the deceased was held in the city, occupied the front page of the *Tribune de Vyônes* for a week, and even found its way into the Parisian and foreign press; but the disappearance of Évariste Laroche and his friend Jean-Pierre Bracqueur earnt only a paragraph on an inner page of the *Tribune*, and no connection was ever drawn between the two events. If the second horn had been discovered in Évariste's deserted room, matters might have been different, but either the horn vanished with Évariste and Jean-Pierre, or Salfuyche's relatives seized it with his other possessions in lieu of notice and never drew, or never cared to draw, the attention of the police to its significance.

For certainly the old telescope reappeared in the stock of the *mont-de-piété* in a week or two, though if any future purchaser chanced to focus it on the cathedral and the gargoyles that decorated its roofs, he would have found that the cathedral authorities, with uncharacteristic despatch, had given *Le Saturnien* both two new horns and two new companions in his shadowed corner, and even refashioned his features to match the grins on theirs, as though the three were confederates in some soon-to-be-realized enterprise of high diabolic endeavor.

THE QUARRY

by Simon Whitechapel

> . . . *uvida*
> *Suspendisse potenti*
> *Vestimenta maris deo.*
> — Q. Horatii Flacci *Carmina* I v.

> "I have hung
> My dank and dripping weeds
> To the stern God of Sea."
> — Horace's *Odes* Book 1, 5 (Milton's translation)

After the *crise de nerfs* that had shattered his hopes of passing this year into the Ministry of the Interior, the student Gérard Dhuyne had been advised by his doctor to take six months of complete rest, and had come in search of it to Grémoire-en-Chaux, his dead parents' village in Averoigne. Twenty-three years before, his father and mother had been married in the black-stoned church of Saint André overlooking the river Isoile, but Gérard had few memories of his childhood in the place, which had ended when his father had, in his own phrase, "emigrated" to Paris.

"*Émigré*" was *le mot juste*, Gérard now realized, for the sleepy countryside of Averoigne seemed a world away from the gas-lit bustle and neurosis of Paris. Yet the sleep had a certain sinister quality to it, for the past lay thick here and even Christianity seemed a recent intruder. In Grémoire, after all, the church was the youngest building, and attendance there was sparse, though not for reasons of any socialistic free-thinking or atheism. The villagers were devout enough, but after a different fashion than that pleasing to *Mère l'Église*, for when Gérard took his morning and afternoon constitutionals he often came across offerings of flowers or fruit laid at one or another of the old stone circles on the hills that overlooked Grémoire. He did not disturb them, and indeed had the impulse to make an offering of his own, in thanksgiving for the slow but steady return of his health.

For was he not now able to walk as far as the old flooded quarry in the hills, and wake the next day with but a faint stiffness in his limbs? The quarry was one of his few memories from childhood in Averoigne, but perversely what he remembered had been entirely misleading. Where then its black cliffs had lain bare and its chilly waters lifeless, now plants and animals flourished: trees crowded the cliff-tops, ferns and creepers covered the cliffs, and its waters were full of lilies and rushes, at least in their shallower portions, and were hummed and cruised by a myriad insects: great dragonflies on patrol for prey and rivals, enamel-bright damselflies in blue, red, and green. Gérard had remarked the change to the village priest when, resting on the day after he first managed to walk to the quarry, he was looking over the church.

The priest had appeared silently at his elbow, startling him a little as he stood puzzling out the significance of a frieze based on some obscure passage of marine imagery in the Old Testament, and Gérard had sought for some topic to maintain the halting conversation that ensued.

"The old quarry, *mon père*, such a surprise to see it flourishing, for I remember as a child, in the company of my departed father, seeing it lie dead at all seasons of the year."

"Not so much of a surprise, *mon fils*," the priest had answered laconically. "*Voyez-vous, elle a été exorcisée.*"

Gérard had been startled again. It had been exorcised? The priest explained that his predecessor, *Père* Jean D'Aguîte of pious memory, had become convinced that the place lay under some diabolic interdiction—"A punishment, perhaps, for its having supplied stone for the construction of this very church," the priest murmured—and had sought permission from his bishop to perform the ceremony. His success was sufficient warrant for his suspicions, for the quarry had flourished thenceforward, though its waters retained much of their former chill and youngsters of the region were under strict instructions never to bathe therein, no matter what the temptation of summer heat, lest they be overtaken by fatal cramps.

"And so it is that they never do bathe therein, *mon fils*," the priest concluded.

"I should have thought that the warning might render the site perversely attractive to the rebellious young," Gérard had commented.

The priest shrugged.

"Perhaps *les jeunes* of Grémoire are too wise for rebellion, or perhaps there is some additional factor at work to render *la carrière* unattractive to them. But enough of that, I think. Might I ask whether you have seen our most excellent tapestries, donated by the Discalced Sisters of Sainte Priscille at Vyônes?"

He had then shown Gérard over the church and the student had looked at it with new eyes, now that he knew it was built of black stone from the quarry. Of course he should have realized it for himself, especially since the *décor* of the church primed the mind to make the connection: fish and underwater life of all and occasionally odd kinds were a strong motif therein. But no; he committed an anachronism there and passed too-harsh judgment on himself. The quarry had not, of course, been flooded when it supplied stone for the church in whenever-it-was it had been built. He had asked the priest the date of the church's construction, but he had pursed his lips and shrugged with peasant-like irony.

"Do you know, *mon fils*, I am ashamed to admit that I have forgotten? I shall look it up and send a note over to you. You are lodging with Madame Bressier, are you not?"

And later in the day the note had come in a fist more old-fashioned than he might have expected even in a backwater like Averoigne, telling him that the church had been built in 1756 and also that the phrase came from the *Livre de Job* XL, 20. Gérard was puzzled for a moment by the addendum, then remembered that he had asked about the origin of a Latin phrase beneath a stained-glass window— "Lucky to survive *la Révolution*," the priest had assured him—depicting some tumult, almost *impressionniste* in its vigor and lack of realism, of water and weed. The phrase had run AN EXTRAHERE POTERIS HAMO?, "Art thou able to draw out with a hook?", and the priest explained in the note that a word was missing between the EXTRAHERE and POTERIS; namely LEVIATHAN, *"un monstre aquatique dans la tradition juive"*.

Smiling a little at the quaintness of the priest's phraseology, Gérard scribbled a few words of thanks and dispatched them with the boy who had carried the note over—evidently, and unsurprisingly, some relation of Madame Bressier, for she had whisked him off to her kitchen and he emerged wiping crumbs from his lips. But as he took the note and turned to leave, Gérard halted him with a cry: "*Un moment,* please. Do you know of anyone in the village who makes rods for fishing?"

Of course the boy did, and Gérard had to cut short his enthusiastic advice as to the best fishing spots along the river Isoile, for he had quite another place in mind. The lifelessness of the old quarry had never been complete, he remembered now: there had been a blazing summer's day on which, hunting for butterflies with a net sewn by his mother on his tenth or eleventh birthday, he had paused by the quarry to enjoy its coolth and heard a heavy splash in mid-water, exciting ripples that reached him a minute or so later where he stood by the shore. No stone falling from the cliffs could have landed where the splash sounded, and he was sure also that he was alone at the quarry. Yes, there had been fish there before the exorcism and there were surely fish there now, grown greatly in size from their many years unmolested. Tomorrow he would buy a rod and try his luck. Such a soothing occupation, fishing—surely a final balm for his healing nerves.

The morrow dawned clear and hot, and Madame Bressier included a bottle of water in the lunch of bread, cheese and *pâté* she prepared for him, shaking her head when he told her he would find an abundance of water at the quarry.

"No, *monsieur*, I would not drink therefrom if I were you, and *hélas*, nor would I eat any creature you catch, if fish therein you must. No fisherman of Grémoire would set foot near the place, *monsieur*."

"*Mais elle a été exorcisée*," Gérard told her, smiling, to which she merely shrugged and crossed herself. Evidently prejudice against the quarry lingered even after the exorcism, and when Gérard left the house the thought crossed his mind to walk down to the Isoile instead and try his luck at one of the spots mentioned by the boy. But no; if the quarry had never been fished, think of what he might draw from it, if his cheap rod did not snap with the strain. Accordingly, he turned his steps resolutely towards the hills. He was glad of Madame Bressier's water before he arrived, however, for the sun struck fiercely at him as he followed the increasingly faint path to his destination. He paused a minute to drink in the shade of a stone circle, noting without surprise that a withered circlet of flowers laid on one of the stones had been renewed since he last passed that way.

When, finally, he arrived at the quarry, he sighed with relief, for its coolth seemed to flow out over him as it had that day in his childhood, and the green of its cliff- and water-vegetation was most refreshing to the eyes. He found a shaded spot on the shore facing the cliffs, baited his hook, and began to fish, casting his hook out among the lilies and the damselflies that stitched the air above them in blue, red, and green. But an hour later, when the shifting sun winkled him out, having sliced his shade completely away, he had caught nothing; and half-an-hour at a new spot proved no more fruitful. Perhaps the fish also found the heat oppressive, and sought the shade of the cliffs? He drew in his line, careful not to snag it on the lilies or other water-weed, and stood, craning his neck over the water, to scan the foot of the cliffs. *Là*, that looked an excellent spot: a tongue of rock whereon he could sit most comfortably, letting his line down into what looked the deepest and most shaded water of all. The water was clean of vegetation too, so he could fish without concern for snags.

And perhaps he could reach it without undue effort, if his hands and feet could recall their boyhood expertise in climbing. Had he ever climbed here? No, he thought, never. He had been here only three or four times in his boyhood, and remembered the place only for the strength of the impression it had made upon him. Indeed, he recalled now that the very thought of climbing on the naked rock of the cliffs had struck him with dread: not for the prospect of a fall in itself, but for the prospect of a fall into the water. He smiled as he carried his rod and lunch up from the shore to the cliff-top whence he would descend. He felt no dread now, for was not the place exorcised?

On the cliff-top he paused to spy his way down to the tongue of rock, and grunted with satisfaction as he heard a faint splash in the bare water near it and caught a pale glimmer as some *grand-père* of a fish sank back into the depths. They were there *plus sûrement*, waiting for his hook. He unpacked the bundle of food Madame Bressier had prepared for him, filling his pockets with its contents, then began his descent, hindered only by his fishing-rod, which he had to tediously lower and retrieve in stages, making careful each time that it was securely lodged, lest it fall and be lost. The plants that flourished on the cliffs were some help here, if not so much in his climbing, for he did not entirely trust the handholds they offered. And yet in five minutes he was safe on the tongue of rock, re-baiting his hook; and five minutes after that he was delightedly lifting his first fish from the water: a fine fat *tanche*.

"Well, *grand-père*," he said, having knocked the fish on the head and laid it aside on a shelf of rock, "let us see whether *grand-mère* will join you."

He turned back then to the water, and was about to cast his line again when a blur of white in the corner of his eye, down near the water, attracted his attention. He turned his head to see what it was and, with a sudden thumping in his chest, saw the left hand of a young woman lying flat on the rock at the water's margin. For a moment of horror that sealed the appearance of the hand permanently on his memory—its slimness and beauty, the elegance of the fingers, oddly unmarred by the incipient webbing at their base—he thought it was severed, then he saw the elegant wrist and part-forearm that descended from it to a body concealed in the water; and in the next moment, with a splash, the right hand joined it on the rock and both spread and gripped to lift the head and shoulders of their owner from the water. Gérard saw her face beneath the water as it rose, flashing white out of the darkness, and recognized its beauty even as he was disconcerted by a flash of green in the eyes that gazed upward, seemingly without seeing him.

But when the beautiful head was above water the eyes that met his and widened with surprise were brown as any peasant's of the region. The girl, who was evidently quite naked, arrested her egress from the water and spoke to him in an accent he did not recognize and that even obscured her meaning for a moment.

"*Ô, monsieur!, que faites-vous ici?*"

Still startled, he replied brusquely, "I fish, mademoiselle," and after a moment of chagrin joined in the laughter that chimed from her dripping lips. "But who are you, *mademoiselle?*" he said. "I thought I should have complete solitude here, even now that the quarry is exorcised."

"*Exorcisée, monsieur?* But, as you see, it retains *sa succube.*"

"*En verité sa naïade, mademoiselle,*" he returned gallantly; and she bowed her head in acknowledgment, then raised it to answer his original question.

"*Qui suis-je? Je suis Priscille, monsieur,*" she said, "daughter of the woodcutter Alexandre in the forest of Averoigne."

"Then you have come some way to swim," he said, restraining his curiosity at her evident education and intelligence. She shook her head, splattering him with cool droplets of water from her long black hair.

"*Non, monsieur.* An eave of the forest lies but half a league from here, and I walk very briskly."

"Do you come every day?" Gérard said, marveling, now that he was over his surprise, at the absurdity of the situation: the beautiful naked girl talking to him from the water of a flooded quarry.

"*En été*, yes, every day. I swim with my friends the fish, and rest here on the rock a while before I swim back."

"Then I have disturbed your routine, *mademoiselle*, for which I am heartily sorry."

Priscille gave a pretty shrug and prettier pout. "It is no matter. I can rest in the water as well as out, believe me."

"I did not see or hear you begin your swim, *mademoiselle*. Yet surely it commenced after my arrival."

"Oh, I enter the water over there." She nodded over her shoulder to a spot where the cliffs met the shore that faced them from the other side of the water. "There is a cave, *monsieur*, where I can leave my clothes, and I always enter the water most silently. I did not see you here in the shade, and would perhaps have turned back if I had."

"Then I am glad you did not see me," Gérard said. Priscille shrugged and pouted again, but said nothing. Casting about for something to resume the conversation, Gérard continued: "But from your accent you are not *averoignoise, mademoiselle?*"

"*C'est vrai, monsieur, ni française de rien.* My parents are Russian, of a dissenting sect driven out eight years ago, when I was a girl of but nine. Now my mother, *que Dieu ait son âme*, is dead and I live with and keep house for my father. It is a simple cottage, *monsieur*, but I would not exchange its hollyhocks and yellow roses for a palace."

But despite his prompting she would tell him little more of herself, and he was left unsatisfied when she shook her head to the last of his questions and informed him that she must swim to her cave and dress to return home.

"My father awaits me, *monsieur*, and he will fear that I have met with some misfortune if I do not return soon."

"I wonder that he allows his jewel to risk itself as it does," Gérard said with perhaps excessive gallantry; she shrugged and pouted for the last time and ducked abruptly beneath the water. Yet had not her left hand waved farewell to him as it entered the water last of all? Gérard got quickly to his feet and stared down into the depths into which she had disappeared. But no glimmer of white body interrupted their darkness, and after a minute he sat down again with a grunt of disappointment.

"Priscille," he said, sampling the word on his tongue. It was sweet, sweet as the girl herself, and he wondered if he should return the following day, to see if she would appear at the fishing-spot again. No, he thought that he should not, but on the day after that he would certainly return. Another splash from the water broke into his thoughts and he looked over at the spot Priscille had pointed out to him as concealing the cave. His heart beat a little faster at the thought he might see her slipping naked from the water, but perhaps she had already done so as he sat lost in his thoughts. Indeed, the heavy curtain of honeysuckle that hung from the cliff at that point would be a more-than-adequate shield for her modesty.

Suddenly overcome by hunger, he ate the food he had carried down with him and fished a further hour, his reveries on the girl interrupted only by his success with two further fat tench. He lined his pockets with fresh leaves torn from the cliff-face before slipping the fish therein and climbing back up the cliff, his rod left behind him. It would be quite safe here, he was sure, and it would be tedious to carry it up with him. Also, Priscille would be sure to see it if she returned tomorrow and would know that he intended to return himself. *Ergo*, if she was there when he returned the day after, he could conclude that she perhaps felt something of the attraction for him that he felt for her.

Two days later, having said nothing of his meeting with Priscille to the good but perhaps excessively loquacious Madame Bressier, he returned to the quarry, climbing down to his rod with his pockets full of food and sitting on the rock he had occupied before. As he picked up his rod, ready to bait its hook and cast, a laughing voice said from his left: "*Ah, c'est mon homme à la canne!*"

Startled, he almost dropped the rod.

"Priscille!" he said. The girl's head was propped coquettishly on her two hands as they rested on a shelf of rock three or so *mètres* away, holding her above the water as she watched him.

"*Mais oui, c'est moi!*"

With a splash, moving almost too fast for his eye to follow, she ducked into the water. He dropped the rod and was on his feet in an instant, running forward and staring down into the swirl of her departure. Where had she gone? But suddenly he turned and ran back to where he had been before: there was her left hand again, sliding silently from the water to wave to him from the spot it had emerged on the day he met her. Her right hand followed, and both went flat onto the rock, splaying to take her weight as she pushed her head and shoulders up to join them. Again, as he watched her face rise through the water, he had the impression that her open eyes flashed green, but there they were again above water, widening with mock surprise on his, brown and sparkling with laughter.

"*Bonjour, mon homme à la canne*," she said.

He sat down heavily, confused at the strength of the emotion he felt at seeing her again.

"*Bonjour, ma naïade*," he said. "Do you know of *monsieur le comte* and his portrait?"

She shrugged and pouted, and his heart contracted almost painfully in his breast. It was love, *par Dieu!*

"But are we so much out of the great circle," she asked, "we woodcutters' daughters of Averoigne?"

"You are no woodcutter's daughter, *ma naïade*."

"Do you seek to insult the honest trade of my father, *monsieur*? To say that a woodcutter such as he can raise no daughter well-versed in literature and current affairs?"

"I . . . I say no such thing," he stammered, unsure for a moment whether she spoke in jest or earnest. Her laughter broke the ambiguity, echoing weirdly over the water of the quarry.

"*Non, mon homme à la canne*, I am truly a woodcutter's daughter, I swear by the *bon Dieu*, but my father is no common woodcutter. It is a religious vocation with him, *monsieur*. He humbles himself for his own sins and the sins of his two nations, his natal Russia, his adopted France."

"And your sins, Priscille, does he humble himself for them?"

"But of course."

"I do not believe you. You are too beautiful to sin, and I—"

But her laughter interrupted him.

"Thou hast seen me first but two days before, *mon homme à la canne*, and already my poor beauty brings thee to blasphemy. Dost thou not know that a seemingly sweet rind may conceal a most poisonous flesh?"

"*De toi*," he returned, "I cannot believe it."

"*Mais vous blasphémez*," she said with a toss of her head that again splattered him with cool droplets of water from her hair. "I am a mortal maid, *mon homme à la canne*, and you must not say such things to me, lest the angels be listening and seek to punish us both."

"An angel *is* listening," he returned, and she snorted with anger.

"*Bah!* Cease your gallantries, *mon homme à la canne*, or I shall depart."

And she made as though to duck under the water.

"*Non! Excusez-moi, ma naï—mademoiselle*. I will speak no more of your beauty, nor provoke the wrath of heaven with the extravagance of my praise."

"*Bien.*"

She lifted herself back to her previous position, head, shoulders, and arms above water, breasts—*hélas!*—and body below it, pressed to the rock on which he sat.

"Let us speak of other things, *mon homme à la canne*. Tell me, how did Madame Bressier prepare the three fish that you carried away on Tuesday?"

He opened his mouth to reply, then grunted with surprise.

"But you had gone when I caught the latter two," he said, "and how do you know that I lodge with Madame Bressier?"

"Oh, as for that, it is common knowledge that our few visitors to Grémoire lodge with her. *Et les trois poissons*, that also is simple. I whispered to the fish of the quarry as I departed, telling them to sacrifice two of their number to the handsome youth who sat fishing."

"You think me handsome, then?"

"Ah, you twist my words. I described you so to the fish, *mon homme à la canne*. To them, certainly you are handsome. But"—with a secret momentary smile that told him she knew the answer even as she asked—"you have not said how Madame Bressier prepared your three fish."

"She did not prepare them at all, Priscille, as I think you know very well. She refused to cook them, and when I insisted that I should cook them for myself—"

She had been nodding smilingly to his words; now she interrupted him again: "When you insisted on cooking them for yourself, she gave you an old pot to boil them in, which she threw out that very evening."

"Yes. Exactly so. But again I must ask how you know these things."

She said nothing for a moment, merely reaching down with her left hand and scooping up a handful of water. She said something in a language he did not recognize, then turned her hand over and let the handful fall back.

"What was that you said?" he asked.

"Oh, it was a Russian proverb, *mon homme à la canne*. 'Ears are oft sharper below water than above.' "

"That was not like any Russian I have ever heard."

She tossed her head again, pointing her rounded chin at him, smooth and flawless as Grecian marble.

"And what do you expect? Am *I* like any girl you have ever met? 'Twas an old country dialect I used. The good folk of Moscow, St. Petersburg, they would understand it as little as you do, *mon homme à la canne*."

"I have a name, Priscille."

She smiled with an arch of her eyebrows. "Yes. That is true. But for now you are *mon homme à la canne*."

"What will you whisper to the fish today, when you depart and I begin to fish?"

"You shall have three, as before."

"Then that is good. Though simply cooked, the previous three were excellent eating. But are you not cruel, to order the fish to sacrifice themselves to me?"

"No. The quarry's waters grow crowded after many unmolested years and my subjects' quality of life correspondingly decreases. You do those remaining a service."

"Your subjects? But you are a woodcutter's daughter."

"And also a queen, *mon homme à la canne*. And their lives are mine to do with as I please."

"*Une reine?* Then who is your king?"

She pouted, glanced away from him, then looked up again into his eyes.

"As yet, I have no king."

"But you seek one?"

"*Peut-être.*"

"What can you offer him? *Régner sur des poissons?*"

"*Non. Pas seulement sur des poissons, sur les eaux tout entières.*"

"Ah, then you are queen not only of fish but, of all water, that you offer your king its shared dominion? But where then is your palace? Your throne?"

"Can you keep my secret?"

"But of course."

She nodded down at the water.

"My palace lies beneath, very deep, deeper than you can imagine. It is built of pearl, with a golden throne. But, alas, you have provoked my *nostalgie* by speaking of it, and I must return there."

And before he could move or speak, she ducked into the water with a fleeing wave of her left hand. He stood and stared down into the swirl of her departure, but no trace of her could be seen. He swore with disappointment and set to his fishing. In the first half-hour he caught two fish; before the end of the hour he had added a third; in the subsequent two hours he caught not one. She had spoken truly by chance or secret knowledge, and at last he drew in his line and prepared to climb the cliff above him. But he paused a moment, seeming to hear a whisper come to him over the water in promise that they would meet again: "*Au revoir, mon homme à la canne!*"

He left his rod behind as before, but it was not neglected two days. No, he returned to his fishing the following day, to discover Priscille waiting for him as she had before, head resting coquettishly on her two hands before she ducked and swam to emerge at her habitual spot. They talked for nearly an hour, first jestingly of her kingdom beneath the water, then of other topics, and again she knew how Madame Bressier had refused to cook his three fish and how he had boiled them for himself in the retrieved old pot.

"And how many shall I catch today, *ma reine de l'eau?*" he asked.

"Today but two, *mon homme à la canne.*"

"*Deux seulemente?*"

"*Oui.* For if you catch three, you will think that the quarry always yields that number and disregard my claim to power over the fish, and if you catch four, it will be too many for you to comfortably eat. Two will prove my power and leave you eager to return tomorrow to catch three again—*Mais non!*"

She interrupted herself, raising her left hand, shaking her head.

"*Non,*" she repeated. "I see in your eyes an incipient gallantry. You mean to tell me that three things will be caught today regardless—two fish and a heart. It is not true, *mon homme à la canne.* I caught your heart that first day, did I not? Ah, you admit it, and I am free to leave you. *Au revoir!*"

And with a duck and a swirl she was gone. He shrugged, smiling as he thought of how he would see her the following day, and then fished a half-hour to catch two fish, and then a further hour to convince himself that he would catch no more. On the following day he rose early to walk to Ximes, where, for a few francs, he bought a cheap but tasteful bracelet set with a silver fish, meaning it as a gift for Priscille. But when he reached the quarry and climbed down to the tongue of rock, she was not waiting for him; and four hours of fishing later, during which he caught three fish as she had predicted, she had not appeared. He left the bracelet on a rock with a note (*Pour la reine de l'eau de la parte de l'homme à la canne*), and climbed the cliff unhappily to return to his lodging with Madame Bressier. But when he returned the day after, the bracelet lay undisturbed, and in five hours of fishing he made no catch and saw no Priscille.

On the third day, at the end of a further unrewarded five hours of fishing, he climbed the cliff but did not return at once to his lodging in Grémoire. Instead, deeply worried by her failure to appear, he sought out the eave of the forest of Averoigne mentioned by Priscille, meaning to visit the cottage of her father and enquire after her welfare. Eave and cottage proved easy enough to find, but the hollyhocks and yellow roses of the latter had evidently grown thirty years or more untended: the place was a ruin, and when he entered it, stepping through an empty and sagging doorway, he found it gutted by time and the hands of passing *vagabonds.*

But as he turned to leave, wondering whether this could indeed be the cottage of which she had spoken, a regular shape in the trampled earthen floor caught his eye, and he bent to prise free what seemed to be a battered old picture, cheaply manufactured and with all its glass gone, but still faintly showing a Madonna and child. Ah, it was *une icone, une icone russe*, proof that some Russian exile had dwelt here. *Dwelt here long before*, he reminded himself, laying the icon carefully back to the floor. Priscille must have spun him a tale based on some long-gone Russian family who dwelt here. But where was she now? Where in truth did she dwell? He returned to his lodging in Grémoire and Madame Bressier nodded with satisfaction as he informed her that his day of fishing at the quarry had been fruitless yet again.

"My prayers for you were answered, *monsieur*," she said, "namely, that you should have no further luck there, and eat no more fish of its waters."

He shrugged ruefully, not caring to challenge her prejudice as he should have liked, for Priscille's sake.

"But tell me, Madame Bressier, is it not true that a family of Russians dwelt near the quarry in years past and that a daughter, perhaps, swam there once a day?"

"Russians? Near the quarry? I never did hear tell—ah, but a moment, *monsieur*. You recall to me . . . Yes, you are right, in my girlhood some old Russian did dwell there, but alone, I believe, working as a woodcutter. Leastways I never did hear of any daughter, or that anyone, Heaven forefend, swam in the quarry. Where did you hear of this, *monsieur?*"

"Idle talk in an inn, Madame Bressier."

He retired early to bed that night, but was unable to sleep for thought of Priscille. Surely, with her *"Au revoir"*, she had meant to see him again, and he grew sick and despairing by turns in contemplation of her possible present state: that she lay drowned at the bottom of the quarry or had merely tired of the game she played with him, and abandoned her swims until he left Averoigne. At dawn, hollow-headed with lack of sleep, he rose and silently dressed to walk to the quarry. Dew still covered the grass of the hills, and he caught glimpses of several foxes, slinking back to their lairs after a night's hunting. Arrived at the quarry, he paused atop the cliff and stared down into the water, which was darker than ever beneath him, submerged in lingering night. Then he climbed down to the tongue of rock and found, to his throat-tightening joy, that the bracelet had gone, though the note remained, still folded as though it had not been read.

He waited all day, refusing to fish and staring out fiercely over the water, demanding of it that it yield Priscille to him. It was as night approached that another significance of his demand occurred to him, and he shivered with dread and disgust. If she had drowned three days before, then perhaps today her body would rise, foully bloated, shimmering with decay. He felt sure now that the necklace had been dislodged from its rock by some animal and fallen into the water, or been seized by *une pie*. He had watched *les hirondelles* swooping on insect-hunt over the water during that day, unmoved in his grief by their speed and grace, and perhaps *les pies* came here too, at times. Oh, but it was useless; if he did not climb for home now he would have to stay all night, and he could not rid himself now of the image of Priscille's corpse rising to the surface in foul corruption.

But as he turned to set hand to the cliff, it came—a whisper over the water: *"Gérard! Viens, Gérard!"* He spun where he stood, straining his eyes into the gathering dusk. It had been Priscille, her voice, whispering to him, calling him by name as she had never done before.

"Priscille!" he shouted in reply. *"Où es tu?"*

The whisper came again: *"Gérard! Viens, Gérard!"* And was that the glimmer of a pale face and outstretched hands on the shore opposite him? Was Priscille there in a dark dress, holding out her hands to him, calling him by name? He turned back to the cliff, meaning to climb it and race around to her, but the whisper came again: *"Non, Gérard! Nage à moi!"*—"No, Gérard! Swim to me!"

He turned and stared desperately at the shore, trying to make out if a figure truly stood there, holding out its hands to him, shaking its head in impatient urgency. Oh, here the whisper came again: *"Gérard, mon amour! Viens! Nage à moi!"*—"My love". She had called him "my love"! He began to strip for the swim across the quarry, hopping on his left foot, then his right as he dragged his boots off before wrenching down his trousers, tearing his shirt off, splattering the rock with stray buttons. Now, finally, he could slip into the water and swim to her. The water was cool, welcoming, and he laughed for joy as he kicked off from the rock and began to swim with strong, fluent strokes. A moment later, beneath the water, a slim left hand closed lovingly over his ankle to draw him irresistibly under.

Many thanks to Philippe Gindre for correcting and improving the French of this story.

THE GARGOYLES OF NOTRE-DAME

by Matthew Baugh

"I feel a spiritual presence," Gianetti Annunciata said. "It is drawing closer."

Vallières glanced around the circular table which held a crystal ball, a lit candle, and a stack of tarot cards. To the distinguished, white-haired man's left sat Madame Beaudin, a plump, matronly woman who held his hand. Next to her was her attorney, Monsieur Moubray, then her companion, Mademoiselle Denault, followed by the tall, turbaned figure of Sâr Dubnotal, a Frenchman with a reputation in Paris society for laying ghosts and solving mysteries with his psychic abilities. Finally, at Vallières' right hand was the medium, a beautiful Italian woman with a wealth of dark hair.

"Is it Raymond?" Madame Beaudin asked. She sounded so eager that Vallières' heart went out to her. He had no use for spiritualists and it was difficult for him to watch his employer's clients defrauded by such charlatans. Then again, it was difficult for him to see them de-frauded by Favraux, his employer, but that was a necessary evil. The man, who only called himself Vallières, had spent a lot of time and ef-fort infiltrating Favraux's financial empire. One day, very soon, he would use all that he had learned, and the corrupt banker's many vic-tims would be avenged. But that was still in the future. For now, he was playing a role, and that meant accompanying a wealthy client to this absurd ritual.

A white mist began to gather over the table.

Ectoplasm, Vallières thought. Without seeming to, his keen eyes searched for the source of the mysterious substance. He was surprised when he couldn't find it; Annunciata and her cohort must be excep-tionally skilled.

"Celeste," the medium said. Her voice had changed to the deep and cultured tones of a Frenchman with the trace of a Gascon accent. The gray-haired man marveled at her talent for mimicry.

"Raymond; it is you!"

"Why have you summoned me?" the medium asked.

"I . . . I have to ask you a question. The bank has come to me with some investments. It will cost forty-thousand francs, our whole savings, but Monsieur Favraux has guaranteed me that there will be a great profit. Isn't that so, Monsieur Vallières?"

The gray-haired man fought to keep from grimacing. He knew that his employer's investment opportunity was a sham, and had been glad when she had asked to consult some friends before signing away her money. He had been disappointed to learn that the chief person she wanted to consult was her late husband. Unable to say much without giving himself away, he simply nodded his head.

"The banker's secretary?" Annunciata asked in the man's voice. "No, you are deceived."

Vallières' eyebrows drew together. He was not what he seemed to be, but there was no way for the medium to know that. He remained silent, trusting that this was part of the ruse on the widow.

"What do you mean?" Madame Beaudin asked with a confused expression.

"No matter," Annunciata said. "Celeste, you must not invest a cent in Favraux's schemes. Not now or ever."

The woman gasped and Vallières felt the tension in his muscles relax a bit. A glance at the lawyer showed that he was also relieved to hear those words.

"But . . . why, Raymond?" the widow said.

"You asked and I have answered. That is all I can say."

"Very well, my dear," she said, gathering her courage. "Now there are some other . . ."

"No!" boomed the bass voice from the pretty woman's mouth. "I answered one question because I loved you in life and love you still. But I have passed beyond the concerns of this world, and you must accept that."

"You . . . you're leaving me?"

"Use your own wits and the advice of those you can trust, Celeste. Do not call me again by this medium or another for I will not come."

The widow sank into her chair, looking stunned. As she did, Annunciata's gaze shifted to the Sâr and she spoke. The voice was harsher this time and more guttural. Gone were all traces of Gascony. The new voice sounded vaguely German.

"El Tebib!" she growled, "if you wish to find me, you must go to the holy place where the grotesques gather. Tonight, as the midnight hour strikes," she said. "You must face your foeman's wrath and lust."

Sâr Dubnotal's bearded face reflected surprise, then anger. He rose and faced the medium with one palm thrust toward her.

"Enough!" he said in a low voice. "By Mitra and thrice-great Viritrilbia, I command you to release her!"

The deep voice growled and a cold breeze swept through the room, scattering papers and extinguishing the candle.

The medium spoke and it was Monsieur Beaudin's voice again. "You must not go alone," she cried. "There is another who must accompany . . . ."

The sentence ended in a cry of pain, this time in the woman's own voice. The wind stopped and the tarot cards shot into the air and scattered through the room. A pair of the cards fell onto the back of Vallières' hand.

In the dimness that followed, the gray-haired man found the gaslights and turned them up. In their glow, he looked bewildered while Madame Beaudin and her companion huddled together in fear; Sâr Dubnotal supported a very pale Gianetti Annunciata. Vallières noticed that he had unconsciously held onto the tarot cards and glanced at them. One was The Magician, and the other Justice.

He hesitated a moment, shocked, then tucked the cards into his jacket and moved back to the others.

"Forgive me, my friends," the Sâr said, as he helped Gianetti to her feet. "A powerful force has interfered with our séance; fortunately, the danger to you is over. Please, go home now for I must tend to Mademoiselle Annunciata as well as . . . other business."

The group was distraught and confused, except for Vallières who, gently but inexorably, led the others out of Sâr Dubnotal's apartment and into the Avenue de l'Opéra. But as the doors closed, the gaze he cast behind him was anything but gentle. Something was happening here, and he would be back to discover what it was.

It was half past eleven when Sâr Dubnotal stepped out of his building and into a waiting taxi. Down the block, the man who had been Vallières was instantly alert. No one looking at him now would have recognized the kindly old man. A white wig and makeup had been stripped away to reveal a charismatic, youthful face partly obscured by the collar of his long cloak and the shadows of his wide-brimmed hat. The kind-looking older man had resumed his Identity as Judex, the mysterious avenging figure who haunted the underworld. He sat behind the wheel of a powerful modern sedan, which slipped out after the taxi into the moonlit streets of Paris.

He followed without headlights and at a distance; traffic this time of night was almost non-existent, and he didn't want the Sâr to know he was being followed. He used parallel streets when he could, and hung back when it became clear where his quarry was going.

He waited until the taxi had crossed the Pont d'Arcole onto the Île de la Cité before he followed. He saw Dubnotal disembark onto the steps of the Notre-Dame Cathedral and dismiss the cab. As he watched, another man stepped from the shadows to greet Dubnotal, a priest in a black cassock and a red sash. The two shook hands and spoke in voices too low for Judex to understand. After a moment, they walked to the entrance of the South Tower. The priest unlocked the door and the two men entered.

As the door closed, Judex was already in motion. Moving silently and almost invisibly under the cover of night, he reached the door quickly. He checked to make certain he wasn't being observed, then quietly opened the portal and slipped inside. He could hear the two men's footsteps clanging on the narrow spiral stair as they ascended the 387 steps to the top.

The man in black followed and his footfalls made only the faintest whisper of noise. When he reached the top, he paused, listening to the two men who had stepped onto the tower's narrow walkway.

". . . and you are certain this is the place that was meant?" came a voice. It sounded like a man past the prime of life and somewhat out of breath. Judex assumed it must be the clergyman.

"Where else?" replied a voice he recognized as the Sâr's. It was deep and resonant, and not the least winded. "The message said 'the holy place where the grotesques gather.' I knew at once that it had to be the Cathedral and its Galerie des Chimères."

"I do not understand," the priest replied.

"I have an enemy who I have been pursuing for months," Dubnotal said. "He has challenged me to come here tonight."

"My son, I owe you a great debt, but I cannot allow your fight to enter this holy place."

"It is not my choice, Monsieur l'abbé. Herr Doctor Von Meyer does not respect sanctity of any kind. Whatever he is planning, it would happen tonight whether I had come or not."

"If that is true, then I can only pray you are able to stop him."

"Thank you," Dubnotal said. "Fortunately, I will not face him alone."

"I don't know what I can do to help," the priest said.

"Thank you," Monsieur l'abbé," the Sâr replied. "But there will be another to help me. Perhaps he is already here."

He glanced around, and Judex withdrew deeper into the darkness. His fingers brushed the handle of one of the Steyr automatic pistols he carried. His brow furrowed as he wondered who this man was and what sort of game he was playing.

"Is there anything different here?" the turbaned man continued. "Anything unusual?"

"Only these," the priest said, gesturing at a pair of hideous statues. One had the head of a tiger and the wings of an eagle, the other had a satyr's face and bat wings. Beyond that, Judex couldn't make them out.

"New gargoyles?"

"Actually, they're chimerae," the priest said. "We have them on loan from the cathedral in Vyônes. There have been several attacks by vandals recently, and even an attempt to steal these statues. The bishop thought it best to bring them here for temporary safekeeping."

"Very sensible," Sâr Dubnotal said. "If you don't mind, father, I'd like to be alone to commune with your gargoyles and chimerae for a while."

"I do not understand."

"I believe my enemy will strike at me tonight. If that happens, I don't want you to be in harm's way."

"But, what about you?"

"I've taken steps to protect myself," the Sâr replied. "Come back at dawn. If I am successful, I will be able to tell you much more."

The priest hesitated, then nodded. "Very well. I don't like this, but I do trust you, my friend. May Our Lady and all the saints and angels watch over you tonight."

When the priest had gone, Sâr Dubnotal took a long look around the interior of the tower. "He's gone," he called. "You may as well come out; I know you're here."

Judex didn't believe that the man could have seen him, but he saw no reason to remain concealed. He stepped from the shadows, his long cloak folded around him.

"Ah!" the Sâr said, a thin smile forming on his lips. "You are a stealthy one. But are you one of the Herr Doctor's agents, or the one Gianetti predicted?"

Judex raised his left hand. With a stage magician's flourish, he made the tarot card seem to appear in his hand. Then he tossed it to land face up near the mystic's feet so the word Justice could easily be read.

"That tells me what you are," Dubnotal said, raising an eyebrow. "I still don't know *who* you are."

"I call myself Judex."

Judging by his expression, Sâr Dubnotal was hoping for more of an answer, but Judex wasn't inclined to give him one. The man in black relied on knowing more than his enemies—more even then his potential allies. He liked having enough information to be the master of the situation. Mysterious people and unexpected happenings, like the séance, were a frustration and always a potential source of danger.

"Very well, Monsieur Judex," Dubnotal said. "Did you hear what I said to the abbé?"

"That a rival magician with a German name sent a message to draw you here and strike at you? I heard that."

"You sound skeptical, my friend," the mystic said.

"I don't hold with mummery and hocus pocus," Judex replied. "I may not know how you managed everything at the séance . . ."

"So you were there!" Dubnotal's eyes narrowed in thought, then opened wide. "Of course! You were the old man, Vallières. That is an impressive disguise, Monsieur."

Judex kept his face blank with effort. The man's shrewd deductions had rattled him more than he wanted to show.

"If you're going to continue this guessing game, I'll be on my way." Judex turned to go.

"Please," Dubnotal said. There was something in his voice that made Judex pause—a trace of vulnerability in his confident façade. He turned back to face the mystic.

"Stand vigil with me until midnight," he said. "If something happens, I will need your help."

"And if nothing happens?"

"Then you have my word that I will never trouble you again."

Judex nodded. "Until midnight."

"Thank you, Monsieur," Dubnotal said. "Then it is time to prepare."

He took a piece of chalk from his pocket and began to draw patterns on the floor of the tower.

"Come into the circle," he said.

"What is it?" Judex said.

"A form of protection," Dubnotal replied. "It will shield us against any magical attack."

"Thank you, but I'll see to my own safety," Judex said. He drew back into the shadows and watched as the Sâr continued his drawing. First, he made a large circle, then at each of the points of the compass he wrote something in Hebrew. Halfway between each set of words he drew a five-pointed star, then a smaller circle within the first. He drew four more Hebrew letters at the cardinal points and finally two interlocked triangles, forming a six-pointed star, with himself in the center.

"What do you do if you need to counter-attack?" Judex asked. He found himself both amused and vaguely troubled by the mystic's preparations. He seemed so sincere about his mummery.

"I have this," Dubnotal replied. Reaching into his jacket, he produced a short, straight dagger with a three-edged blade and a hideous, demonic face on the pommel.

"This is a Tibetan phurba," the mystic said. "It should suffice against anything my enemy can send at me."

Hearing footsteps on the spiral stair, Judex faded back into the shadows. A few moments later the door opened and a tall, dour looking man in the dark cloak of a sacristan emerged, followed by three younger assistants. The sacristan nodded curtly to Sâr Dubnotal and led the group to the platform where the four bells in the tower hadn't been rung since before the days of Quasimodo. They took their seats and began working a system of foot-pedals to get the huge bells ringing. Judex glanced across to the South tower where the massive Bourdon Emmanuel hung silent. The colossal bell was only rung on high holy days.

The clamor of the bells was deafening but mercifully brief. As the twelfth stroke rang out and then began to fade away, Judex heard a new sound—the scrape of stone on stone. He turned to the two grotesques and saw something that chilled him to the core. The two hideous statues from Vyônes were moving. Their eyes were lit with a hellish glow and their limbs had gone from stony immobility to fluid, animal grace.

The sacristan crossed himself and his helpers froze in horror as the monsters moved toward Sâr Dubnotal. They reached the edge of the circle and stopped as if they had encountered a wall. Inside his ring of protection the mystic raised his strange dagger and began to chant something in some language Judex didn't recognize.

The cat-headed gargoyle opened its mouth in a silent roar. It bared terrible fangs at Dubnotal and swung a taloned paw. The claws struck sparks of blue flame as they encountered the invisible barrier and failed to reach their target. Judex noted that the creature's other hand was missing, apparently broken off sometime in the past.

The second grotesque, which he now clearly saw to be a bat-winged satyr with the upper torso of a leering, horned man and the lower body shaped like the hindquarters of a goat, didn't waste any effort on the barrier. It turned toward the cringing bell-ringers and began to stalk them.

"Stay back!" Judex shouted as he drew his pistols and emerged from the shadows. He fired both weapons and the bullets struck the monster's torso side-by-side.

Surprised, the gargoyle stepped backward and clutched its chest. Then it moved its hands and a triumphant leer lit its face. The bullets had barely made a mark on the solid granite of its body.

"Run!" Judex yelled to the terrified men. "Get to the stair; I'll hold this thing here!"

He fired as he spoke, this time striking the creature in the forehead. Again, the damage was negligible, but the shot managed to focus the gargoyle's attention on him. He lost track of the ringers and Sâr Dubnotal's fight as it sprang at him. Judex dodged by the narrowest of margins.

As the creature turned on him again, Judex shot it point blank in one glowing eye. He heard the bullet ricochet away with a whine as the gargoyle's clawed hand caught the front of his shirt. With frightening ease, it picked him off his feet and tossed him away. The force of the throw carried Judex out of the tower into the open space, two-hundred feet above the ground. His back struck something solid and he lost his grip on one of the pistols. He grabbed frantically and his hands caught something. With a start he realized that he was hanging from a gargoyle, one of the Cathedral's many hideous waterspouts. With a surge of effort, he managed to pull himself atop it and lay there, gasping.

The monster didn't give him a moment to rest. It lunged at him. Judex had managed to hold onto one of his pistols and fired once at point blank range to no effect. As the thing's stone fingers encircled his throat, he grasped its wrist and heaved backward, thrusting his foot into its midsection as he did. The improvised throw worked; using his leg as a lever he thrust the monster up and over. Judex struggled for a moment to keep from joining his foe in its plunge into space. A moment later he rose and looked down.

"Impossible," he whispered.

The gargoyle hadn't struck the ground. Somehow—defying physics and common sense—its outspread wings had caught air, and it glided beneath him like a monstrous bat. It swung away from the tower and gained altitude.

Judex knew that, if the gargoyle gained the tower again, his chances of beating it were next to nothing. Taking careful aim he fired all his remaining bullets in quick succession. The first punched a hole in the monster's wing. Like the rest of the monster's body, the membrane was stone—or stone-like flesh—but here it was thin enough to puncture. The second and third bullets also made holes from which fine cracks extended. When the fourth shot struck, a large chunk split away and the gargoyle's flight became erratic. The final bullets fairly shattered the wing, sending the monster down to the cobbles with a shattering impact.

He stared down on the broken remains of the monster for a moment, then clambered back into the tower. The ringers were gone, he saw, and Dubnotal still stood in his protective circle, though he was too busy dodging to do anything else. Apparently, the cat-headed gargoyle was helpless to pass the barrier, but nothing prevented him from tearing up boards, metal rods, and loose pieces of stonework and using them as missiles.

"Judex, look out!" the Sâr cried. It was an unnecessary warning and one that cost the mystic dearly. The monster hurled a chunk of rock the size of a big man's fist. The projectile caught the Sâr in the torso and sent him reeling out of the circle, the phurba falling from his grip. The monster's lips pulled back from its fangs in a snarl of pleasure, and it stalked toward him.

Reflexively, Judex raised his pistol before remembering it was empty. The gargoyle had turned its back on him in its single-minded desire to kill Sâr Dubnotal and he used that. Racing after the monster he leaped on its back, locking his legs around its waist and one arm around its neck. He used the other to hammer at its head with the pistol.

The creature staggered, but quickly recovered. It was immensely strong and his weight impaired it no more than a housecat's would have slowed himself. Worse, his hammering blows with the pistol barely scratched its head. The gargoyle flexed its wings, crushing him between them. Judex gasped in pain, but tightened his grip. Then the creature reached back, over its head. He felt the talons pierce his cloak and clothing to tear into the flesh of his back as it gripped him. Then the thing pulled him loose with frightening ease and slammed him down.

Ignoring his pain, the man in black tried to roll away, but the monster was too fast. It placed a knee in his belly, crushing the wind out of him. The monster's talons dug into his chest muscles as it pinned him to the tower floor. Judex struck at it with the pistol and managed to break off one of the thing's fingers, but it swung the stump of its other arm, smashing the weapon out of his grasp. The cat's head lowered, fangs bared, and Judex thrust up both hands in a futile attempt to hold it back.

As the mouth opened, ready to tear out his throat, Judex heard chanting from behind the creature. Sâr Dubnotal had risen and held the phurba in his hands as he murmured strange words. As the jaws descended on his throat, he saw the Sâr let go of the ritual knife. Amazingly, it did not fall but hovered for a moment before shooting toward the gargoyle's back. He heard the rasp of iron against stone, then the monster reared back, its face a mask of pain and rage. It toppled to the side, as stiff and unmoving as stone should be.

As Judex rose, he saw Dubnotal kneel by the fallen gargoyle to inspect it. The handle of the phurba projected from the monster's back, between its shoulder-blades.

"Is it . . . dead?" he asked.

"Yes," Dubnotal replied. "At least, as much as that word can be applied to a creature like this. I should have recognized these gargoyles sooner. They were the work of a stonecutter named Blaise Reynard. Legend says that his wrath and lust were so great that they somehow animated the creatures, and that neither magic nor the protection of holy symbols was any use against them. It is as I feared, my enemy has discovered the ancient magic of Averoigne and will be almost impossible to stop."

Judex shuddered and took a deep breath to steady himself. He had seen things this night that he didn't want to believe but, having seen, he couldn't turn his back on them. Evil such as this couldn't go unchecked, even if it meant delaying his own plans of vengeance.

"You saved my life, Sorcerer," he said.

"No more than you saved mine, my mysterious friend."

"If you need me again, will you be able to reach me?"

"I will." Dubnotal turned his attention back to the gargoyle for a moment. "The authorities will come soon," he said. "I will stay to deal with them, and to see to the final disposal of the gargoyles, but it may be best if you are gone when they arrive."

But when he looked up, Judex had already disappeared.

THE RETURN OF THE COLOSSUS

by Brian McNaughton

The situation was looked upon by the more superstitious as a veritable omening of the world's end.
—Clark Ashton Smith: "The Colossus of Ylourgne."

In the spring of 1916, to his intense chagrin, Lt. Cyril Fairchild of the Royal Welch Fusiliers was seconded to an experimental warfare unit and despatched on what seemed a fool's errand to the untroubled province of Averoigne.

Cyril was a very young man who looked younger, with the azure eyes and flaxen locks of a Botticelli angel. His men, who had attained their stunted trollhood in the shadows of lowering coal-tips, at first sniggered over the unspeakable uses to which such a lovely lad might be put in the pits. The blood that pinkened Cyril's downy cheeks and rose-petal lips, however, flowed undiluted from the veins of Hengest and Horsa; and in his first action, a trench-raid of medieval intimacy, he proved himself a very devil.

Whatever credit his daring earned him with his men was immediately squandered when he drew his Webley to keep them from bayoneting prisoners. His chivalry was rewarded with the nickname "Little Hansel," combining the slanders that he was a fairy-tale youth, too good to be true, and possibly an agent of the Kaiser. Cyril could sense the indictment in the whispered asides or sober expressions of the other ranks. "They are basically decent chaps, and the gamest lot you would ever want beside you in a scrap," he noted in one of his frequent letters to his fiancée, Penelope Delapoer, "but lack a proper appreciation of their place in the natural order."

He had been looking forward to a big show brewing near the Somme for a chance to redeem himself when orders whisked him to a chateau in the rear, where a don-in-uniform confused him with hints, questions, tags from Horace and readings in decayed Latin from a moldy book. A steel engraving in this book, of a piece with its depictions of gryphons and mermaids, showed a giant that was fabled to have ravaged Averoigne in bygone times. As one convinced that all

legends conceal more than a grain of truth (the war may have distracted him from a quest for relics of the historical Cinderella), the unlikely
officer actually believed this bollocks.

Cyril wondered if his detested nickname had not recommended
him for this mission. "As we have no Jack-the-Giant-Killers among
our less indispensable subs, this is clearly a task for Little Hansel," he
could almost hear Major Brashley telling the brigadier.

"Your men dig, don't they?" the don-in-uniform asked. Cyril was
accompanied by a vexing trio, Privates Powell and Thomas and Corporal Jenkins, who insisted on viewing their respite from punishing the
Hun as a lark. He answered, thinking of trenches and latrines, "Assid-
uously, Sir."

"Good, good. It's underground, or so this Father Nathaire tells
us." He studied a letter but did not share its specifics. "Miners, they
may be the thing, so send for as many more as you need. But first go to
St. Azédarac, talk to this padre, and see what you can dig up." He gave
a series of asthmatic whinnies, as if that were a rich joke.

St. Azédarac was a toybox whose cone-topped towers and crenel-
ated walls had yet to suffer from the tantrums of the adolescent century. The girls in starched linen and wooden clogs, the mustached wid-
ows in perpetual mourning, even the dray-horses that steamed in a
prickling mist seemed to be waiting patiently for Albrecht Dürer to
come and sketch them. Plucked from a world of mud and noise, Cyril
found the green radiance of the surrounding hills, the bleating of lambs
and the restive clanking of cowbells almost balefully alien to a modern
sensibility. Jenkins and Thomas and Powell sensed this, too, for the
archaic swagger they adopted in the cobbled streets suggested harque-
busiers on leave from the Religious Wars, who would not be trifled
with by civilian ghosts.

Father Nathaire suited his parish. His bulging eyes and translucent
skin were those of an Inquisitor who had denied himself all in the dogged extraction of Truth. Expecting a steep descent into the dark hall of
his rectory, Cyril nearly sprawled flat, for the priest's large and waxy
face gleamed below the twisted shoulders of a child-sized body that a
black cassock rendered nearly invisible.

The four young men were nevertheless forced to stretch their legs
to keep up with his remorseless scuttle up the steep hill overlooking

the town. When they paused gratefully for red wine, crusty bread and a local cheese that Cyril found sublime—but, "This cheese smells like my feet," Thomas muttered—the priest said, "The Colossus was the work of Satan. To use it against his more evil creations is no more than just."

"The Boche, you mean?"

"As a splendid beginning."

"What, er, is it?" asked Cyril, who still didn't entirely believe his orders.

"A man, perhaps, a giant man, assembled and animated by sorcery—"

A nasty Welsh noise erupted from the throat of Corporal Jenkins, who then hastily begged the priest's indulgence.

"—or by a science that is still mercifully beyond our understanding," Father Nathaire continued, not pausing in his recitation even as he made an absolving sign at the corporal.

Cyril wondered at the priest's offhandedness and at Jenkins's apparent release from guilt. If the awful power of God, whom he had learned not to believe in as a student at Christ Church, could be invoked and dispensed so casually, this would be a greater miracle than any clockwork scarecrow from the Dark Ages.

Their destination was not the ruin of a Cistercian abbey that crowned the hill, as Cyril had speculated, but a deep ravine athwart the upward path. The stream that carved it had long ago been diverted, and the gap was filled almost to its rim at one point with the debris of an ancient rockslide. Father Nathaire hiked up his soutaine and descended onto boulders balanced like jackstraws with the indifference of a spider. Uncertain whether to follow but unwilling to solicit advice, the lieutenant cast a blank look at the corporal, who cast it back with practiced ease. Deciding to press on, he was pleasantly surprised to hear the men picking their way down after him.

When it seemed that further descent was impossible, the priest ducked through a narrow fissure and disappeared into the heart of the pile. Cyril switched on his electric torch and followed into a descending tunnel of relatively recent construction.

Their guide bobbed onward with the aplomb of Dante's Virgil, nor did the Englishman feel any discomfort beyond that of damp and cobwebs, but the three miners' sons were most uneasy. Much muttering echoed in the tunnel before Cyril put a stop to it.

"I thought you lads would be used to this sort of thing," he chided.

"Not this sort of thing, no, Sir," said Jenkins. "Yon lintel, look you, the bleeders didn't know what they was about when they stuck it there. And it looks like . . . ."

"Rats, Sir," said Powell when the corporal hesitated, "bloody great—your pardon, Father—buggering rats."

"Spiders, Sir," said Thomas, "as big as my Grammy Evans's Sunday dinner-plates, with—"

"—it was dug from the inside out," Jenkins concluded in a mutter, as if reluctant to advance this queer opinion.

They were right about the rats, at least, which followed them down to a cavern so large that it drank the torchlight. The floor sloped to a vast pit on whose very lip the priest stood rubbing his hands as debonairly as a fly. Lacking his assurance of a glorious afterlife, perhaps, the Britons all but hugged the floor as they inched to his side.

"It was said that the component parts of the Colossus rebelled against their bondage, forcing it to lie down and decompose." Smirking into the abyss, the priest added, "But that, as you see, was not so."

Cyril peered over the rim into what looked like a mass grave from the Middle Ages, a compacted hill of cadavers that had been twisted into a mare's-nest of intertwined limbs. The pile was domed at the center, sloping down to black emptiness at the sides, and a cool breeze flowed steadily from the depths. It carried a scent of rot that seemed remarkably strong after the demi-millennium the bodies must have lain here.

"No rats?" Cyril said, for he saw little evidence of verminous damage. Eyes, flat and dull as common stones, reflected the light of his torch. Some of the bodies were no more than leather and bones, but a few looked alarmingly fleshy. To make a symmetrical dome, they had been packed every whichway; buttocks and pudenda thrust at him in a mockery of temptation, a frozen image of an orgy in Hell.

He shivered off this unhealthful fancy and repeated his question. Father Nathaire shrugged and waved a hand at the shadows, no longer pinpricked with red eyes.

"They are French rats. They know what is good for their livers, if not their souls."

"Bloody hell," said Jenkins, and Cyril at the same time noticed a change in the atmosphere. The breeze from the pit had stopped, and now it resumed in the opposite direction. The downward flow of air was accompanied by a long-drawn stridulation, as of a sarcophagus being furtively dragged across a stone floor.

Jenkins said, "It's breathing, Sir. Snoring."

"*It?* What do you mean, *it?* There's nothing here, just old bones…"

Cyril had extended his torch over the edge to descry the limits of the pile. His voice faltered as he tried to comprehend what he saw. The central dome, vast as that of St. Paul's, which rose almost to the top of the pit, did not limit the charnel. It rose high above a lateral field of corpses that had been tamped down just as tightly. He discerned a pattern, a monstrous architecture of interwoven bodies.

"Good Lord! It's a head. And those, down there—"

"Yes, those are his shoulders. But there is more, much more."

The direction of the air-current changed again. His men looked sick, but Cyril doubted that the recurrence of the vile odor was entirely to blame. "It's a trick of the ventilation, that's all," he told them briskly. "Look alive, then, we have to inspect the damned thing."

Cyril accepted the fact that men are expendable, subalterns slightly less so. He held no foolish illusions about giving orders he himself wouldn't execute. But he could see that they believed he was acting from some such romantic notion when he ordered them to secure a rope and tie a harness around his chest, and he was willing to take credit for it. So much for their bloody Little *Hansel!*

In fact he perceived no danger, and his curiosity was uncontainable. No weapon lay here, nothing at all in the line of "experimental warfare," but a morbid wonder did, a macabre creation of medieval zealots to rival any Wonder of the Ancient World. If by some odd chance the Pyramids had gone undiscovered until the present, he who found them would achieve immortality; and Cyril stood in that man's boots. The war seemed suddenly far away. More closely glowed a peacetime world where he would present measurements and considered speculations to the Royal Society.

"You'll want a gas-mask, Sir," Jenkins said.

"He'll want a canary," said Powell. "A canary, Sir, that's your one sure defense against mephitic exhalations."

"Take this," Father Nathaire said, offering a wooden cross.

It was no standard crucifix, but the image of a martyr who had been nailed upside down, his feet spread on the crossbar in a most undignified way and his face wearing an expression, either through indifferent craftsmanship or Gallic whimsy, that looked sardonic. As he stuffed the fetish into his blouse, Cyril suppressed a smile at the absurdity of taking a tiny image of a dead man to a mountain of real ones. Although he would never have carried the one nor visited the other, he felt this was rather like importing a naughty postcard into a Paris brothel.

Instructing the men to play out the rope slowly and, should he give two sharp jerks, to haul him up at once, he descended gingerly over the forehead and brow-ridge. He feared the old bones might collapse to powder under his boots, and where would such vandalism put him in the eye of posterity? To his relief, the cadavers were as solid and firmly fixed in place as stone blocks. That they might be stone, and this a conventional sculpture, briefly dismayed him, but a closer look gave reassurance. Black, brown, yellow, some shockingly fresh and white, they were very real corpses whose various degrees of decomposition had been arrested. No sculpture could have duplicated in all their infinite gradations the effects of mould and decay, of insect damage and rodent predation, on so many twisted limbs and staring faces.

"Are you all right, Sir?"

"Yes, yes," Cyril said, but cursed a trifle shrilly as his cap tumbled away and his hair riffled in the downward draft, the indrawn "breath" of the abyss, when he stood perched on a hillock that comprised the bridge of a vulturish nose; a nose that was not unlike Father Nathaire's. The four figures at the rim of the pit—three of them bending forward in earnest concern, but the clergyman displaying the aloof serenity of a maniac—seemed very far above him, and an infinity of darkness extended below.

He shone his torch down over the twin shields of the breasts, each large as a wall of the British Museum, but its beam dispersed before it could reveal them fully. On the floor of some immeasurably remote Avernus, could the giant be flouting the laws of physics by standing on two feet? Of course this was only a Gargantuan bust, but he couldn't shake the conviction that a descent with a longer rope would reveal a complete anatomy.

"How many thousands—tens of thousands—bloody millions of corpses?" he muttered, and he cut short a giggle of grisly impropriety.

That question could be solved by a mathematical formula, yet to be devised. *Why* remained a mystery, though not beyond the scope of all conjecture. The Black Death had killed every third person in Europe. The world had suffered nothing like it since; its dread light still flickers when we bless one who sneezes.

The survivors would have had all the material they needed for this Colossus. Infected by the vision of some mad artist, some Arcimboldo of necrophilia, they had assembled it in terror and desperation. The subject, the sum of all the specific men and women, was an abstraction: Man. No immortal hero flaunting marble thews at the heavens, just a heap of decayed meat, this image of its makers was fittingly buried in a forgotten pit.

He thought the artificers would have been forced to use a finer material for the closed eyelids, but he saw that these had also been fashioned from corpses. Except for a few grotesqueries that mocked the human form in the marbled pattern, they had been stamped or rolled so flat as to lose their shape. Unflattened fingers extended from the edge to suggest lashes.

When he took a step back for a better look, these lashes twitched. The eyelids then lifted like the curtains of an infernal stage.

As a foeman armed with a Mauser automatic against his trench-knife, met suddenly face-to-face in a disputed worm-hole, had not made him do, Cyril screamed. He didn't know whether to reach for his revolver or the crucifix, and in his confusion he forgot to signal before he tripped over his boots and fell into the abyss.

"Have a care, Sir!" called Powell, who thought, or who affected to think, that his fall had been an exuberant leap, that his cry had expressed high spirits. An attempt to validate this interpretation kept Cyril silent even when the harness bit cruelly into his armpits and he was bounced upside down at the end of the rope. Before he could right himself he swung against the lower lip of the monster and halfway into its intolerably moist mouth. Disgust mingled with terror in the thin sound that squeezed through his gritted teeth.

"Darkness visible," he muttered as he slipped and slid in a vain effort to escape the wet underlip, "darkness visible," nor could he at first say why.

Scores of crowded faces had composed the irises of those terrible eyes. Each face had been turned towards him. Each human eye—even the blind milky ones, even the blank sockets, but, most frightfully of all, the ones that glittered with awareness—had focused on him. In the center of these clustered faces had stared the pupils, made of no human material, made of an indescribable *nothing*. That was it! Milton's description of Hell's illumination, "not light, but darkness visible," described those pupils. He knew that he could never again enjoy Milton, for he had looked into Hell.

His future reading pleasures were a moot point, however, for the lips had now closed on him and squeezed him in a slimy, airless embrace. They worked at him, rolled him; at any moment he would know the touch of the teeth, huge slabs of calcified flesh that he had not dared to look at closely on his way in. He tried to kick, he tried to draw his pistol, but he couldn't move. His eyes felt ready to burst like tormenting boils.

And then, with a contemptuous flick of its tongue, the Colossus spat him out.

No one had witnessed his panic; he had done most of his screaming inside his head. Physically incapable of speech after he was hauled from the pit, he made no answer to questions about the soggy state of his uniform, and his silence was taken for the calm reflection of a man whose thoughts could never be distracted by mere terror. His quiet monotone, wrung dry of all feeling, and his banal words, the only ones he could at length form, enhanced this image of casual heroism: "I rather suspect we've found it."

The men turned whiter even than Father Nathaire's normal shade, and for an instant it seemed they might bolt, but Jenkins managed to laugh, "God help Fritz," and then they all laughed, none louder than Cyril.

Lying under canvas that night, he was plagued by dreams of an elusive but consistent flavor. When at last he woke fully, after a lifetime of startled outcries and sickly delusions of waking, he fancied that he had dreamed of London, but that belief faltered under scrutiny. The locations he remembered could not be matched with Belgravia or Piccadilly or other places he knew: these were foreign scenes, but in the context of the dream so familiar that he had taken scant notice of them.

The real likeness to the greatest of cities lay in the innumerable multitude of innominate humanity that had babbled about him. It was as if he had spent the night pushing through crowds whose every stranger had been determined to detain him and confide in him matters of vital importance. Whatever they had told him, he had understood little, for they had spoken in dream-French.

Not only had he not understood, he hadn't wanted to. He woke with the impression that all those importunate strangers had earnestly desired to talk about the sort of things one didn't talk about: to speak passionately of failed hopes, lost loves, secret sins and lonely obsessions. Embarrassment compounded his confusion until he abandoned politeness and fought his way forward in a near frenzy to be left alone.

Of all those thousands, he recalled only a scholar's drone, a bully's strut, a girl's glimmering eyes, a hag's incongruously mellifluous voice. All these and more flashed brightly for a moment before fading and flaking into ashes from which they could never again be retrieved.

But a soldier in a war has no time to brood on his dreams, and he was soon mired in the details of exploiting his discovery. He hoped to organize the local civilians, but Father Nathaire advised him that no native would go near the place. "It gives them nightmares," the dwarf explained with a smile no more knowing than usual.

The only telephone in town ornamented the priest's study, where Cyril wasted the morning trying to cajole or threaten a line to the experimental warfare people through a succession of operators as ephemeral and cryptic as the spirits of his dream. Failing miserably, he tried to reach the government in Paris to demand men and equipment.

Although he managed to worm his way to a very junior clerk in a department of public works, he had only begun to recite his list of requisites before being dismissed as a prankster. Shortly after this functionary had sputtered his denunciation of English drolleries and rung off, the phone went completely dead. Cyril believed that the government had thus flicked him off like a flea, but the priest averred that such interruptions were common; and that they often lasted for weeks.

Cyril returned to the site in late afternoon, mulling over impracticable schemes for sending the news by carrier pigeon or heliograph. He mused aloud to Powell that they would need a crane, disassembled at some dockyard and carried hundreds of miles overland, to lift the rocks and the thing beneath them. In the absence of any lorry or railway wagon big enough to hold it, the monster might be hoisted by balloons—it was dashed inconvenient that England had no proper Zepps—and lofted to the front when the wind was right.

"You'll live in history like the builders of your Stonehenge, Sir," the Welshman rhapsodized with what Cyril suspected only later of having been irony.

"It's alive, then, isn't it?" Jenkins said. He added a corollary inevitable to any non-com: "Why not get it to march, Sir?"

Cyril thought this ridiculous; he suspected that Jenkins did, too. The fearful tension they hadn't dared admit was released in unmilitary hilarity when Cyril agreed to have a go at it. They raced one another down the precipitous rockpile and into the menacing tunnel like schoolboys on holiday, and not even the enormous cavern, nor the smell and sound of the monster's breath, could sober them.

"Right, then, you sodding excuse for a giant!" Jenkins shouted into the pit. "On your feet, you horrible little man! Alley-oop, Alphonse!"

The vast sound of breathing neither faltered nor quickened. In the silence that followed the last echoes of these commands, it seemed newly ominous.

"Give it a dose of your French, Sir," Thomas suggested, and the timidity of his whisper confirmed the sudden death of everyone's jolly mood.

Why not? *"Venez ici, Monsieur Colosse! La Patrie vous require."*

Nothing happened: nothing, at least, that the others sensed. But from the darkness of the cavern Cyril saw and heard the folk from his dream returning, beseeching, a host of Ancient Mariners who ached to unburden themselves.

This time he identified their language as Old French, their dress as medieval, and a superstitious man would have further recognized them as the ghosts that still haunted their curious grave. But Cyril knew them for hallucinations brought on by exertion in bad air, no more real than Alice's vexatious playing-cards, and he dealt with them as firmly.

"Stop it!" he cried, "Go away!" and he was obeyed. And obeyed, too, far beyond his intention, when some impulse led him to employ a Biblical turn of phrase: "Colossus, come forth!"

The Colossus raised its arms from the pit and pressed its palms to the ceiling of the cavern, a precarious heap of interdependent boulders, lifting it "like Mr. Lloyd George doffing his silk hat," Powell later said, but it was more like a circus strongman hoisting some heterogeneous weight. The bulging of muscles gave the component parts of the monster an illusory life as hundreds of legs stretched, arms unfolded and sightless heads rolled loosely. Corpses slipped everywhere like swimmers—or, more precisely, like drifting corpses caught in an irresistible sluiceway—to arrive at new positions in the overall fabric. Limbs or heads popped out and flopped here and there, but they marred the outline of the rippling muscles no more than hairs on the arms of a man.

For the first time in centuries the sun, bloodied by its setting and hazed by a storm of dust, burst into the abyss. The rats ran shrieking, a whirlwind of bats exploded, the four men screamed unashamedly and tried to crawl into one another's arms as boulders fell around them like hailstones, only to bounce and fall again. The Colossus hurled aside the rubbish to trigger an avalanche that went unnoticed by all but those in the valley below.

Cyril had expected a roar of Miltonic magnitude to accompany the thing's efforts, but the sound it made, though loud enough for Satan, was less evil than eerie: the sighs and groans of a multitudinous choir in the reverberant loft of its throat.

When the dust had settled and the boulders come to rest, when the men had sheepishly disengaged their tangled limbs and stilled their chattering teeth, they found themselves standing in the shadow of a foot whose arch seemed high and wide as the great door of Westminster Abbey. Far, far above them, the face of the Colossus was turned toward the crimson ball of the sun with a look of resignation and distaste.

"The men were wondering if you mightn't christen it," Cyril told Father Nathaire when he joined them on the hill at twilight.

"Christen it?" He seemed scandalized. "One does not baptize the dead."

"Like a ship, look you," Jenkins said. "With a bottle of champagne, Padre. Where's the harm in that?"

The priest surveyed it, requiring him to lean back so far that he stumbled and might have fallen if Cyril hadn't taken his arm. With exasperating literal-mindedness, he said, "It is not a ship."

"They want to name it after me, Padre," Thomas boasted, and Jenkins dealt him a surreptitious kick. Cyril ignored this. He knew very well why the men called it "Big John Thomas." He had overheard Powell suggesting that it would play hell with the victory parade down the Champs Elysee if the Colossus were suddenly inflamed by the wanton display of its only suitable mate (aside from a lady called Jane Ellis, of Rhondda), the Arc de Triomphe.

"In exceptional circumstances, however," the priest said, "those who are about to die may be received into the bosom of the Church."

Just then the sky blackened and the earliest stars blinked out. The shape of the monster changed like a black cloud; it took Cyril a moment to grasp that it was lowering itself to one knee. He assumed the priest's offer had been directed at the giant. Was it signaling acceptance? No: its intent became obvious as it laid its hand, palm upward, on the ground near them.

"For England and St. George!" Cyril meant to shout, but the words stuck in his throat as he bounded into the palm and urged the men onward with a wave of his pistol. Slowly, laboriously, retching and grimacing, they followed.

The priest raised his hand as if to bless them at last, but Cyril was struck by the odd fancy that this was a gesture of command. The Colossus rose at that very moment, like a child with a handful of toy soldiers. He peered over the edge to see Father Nathaire vanish into the shadow of the foot, although it seemed in the uncertain light that he vanished like a burrowing worm into the foot itself.

Cyril gave no orders, but the Colossus turned its face to the northeast and strode forward with a steadily-increasing velocity that soon grew alarming to the men perched on its shoulder. Its feet pounded the earth like a great hollow drum as it devoured leagues of field and forest. The splintering crashes that rose from the darkness were trees underfoot, Cyril told himself, though sometimes a chorus of thin cries suggested that they were trampling buildings. A bridge collapsed beneath them. Water boiling to its waist, the Colossus pressed on without missing a step.

Terror gave way to exhilaration. It was impossible to share his impressions with the others in the blasting wind of their passage, but he believed he heard the men laughing; and sometimes it seemed that other voices joined in the laughter. Their speed increased even more when, beyond the horizon, Cyril saw what he would once have called heat-lightning. That phrase belonged to a scarcely remembered world of fireflies in the green gloom of summer evenings, when such tinpot charades as thunder and lightning had seemed awesome.

He heard even louder thuds than those of the mighty feet.

Brigadier Sir Rolf Hunt-Barker, Bart., seemed not fully appreciative of the wonder that Cyril had brought him, due to his apparent state of elevated confusion. But the lieutenant was unwilling to fault the mental condition of a superior officer who had been deprived the fealty of twenty-two thousand men before lunchtime that day, all of them marching with full field packs and in measured cadence up to the muzzles of the German guns, or as close to them as their individual fortunes had permitted.

It would be impossible to maintain secrecy for long. The Colossus had arrived before dawn, and that afternoon a Fokker *Eindecker* had determinedly buzzed the rear area where it lay under camouflage tarpaulins. Sir Rolf decreed that it should attack the enemy trenches shortly after nightfall. He rejected Cyril's pleas that its way be paved with an artillery barrage.

"Surprise the sods, that's half the battle," the brigadier said. "One track minds, that's the Huns' weakness. Ever listen to their bloody awful Wagner, on and on and on for eight hours at a stretch without one tune you can whistle? Throw a surprise at Fritz and he's like a schoolgirl with a thumb on her button, he lapses into coma and lets you have your way. 'This vass not in the battle-plan, Herr General.' Haw! Beer and music, that's all they're good for, and they can keep their music. We'll beat their swords into ploughshares for them, and we'll do it with their thick skulls. Surprise!"

The brigadier wanted the Colossus to carry a howitzer, but the difficulty of converting a field-piece to a side-arm, to say nothing of training the irregular conscript to use it, soon became obvious. In the end a Lewis gun was strapped to its shoulder, which Cyril could man while traveling behind like a Red Indian's papoose. Five knapsacks of grenades would ride on the monster's back beside him, to be distributed at his discretion.

The only other equipment Sir Rolf allowed, indeed insisted upon, was a pair of Union Jacks draped fore and aft on the giant's loins for modesty and "to make sure Fritz knows who's stamping his kraut-crammed jowls into the mud."

The French, who might have been said to own the Colossus, were too late in advancing their vehement objections to this.

Cyril thought that Sir Rolf had relented and he was getting some artillery support, however minimal, when he heard the distinctive *crump!* of a mortar behind him. Then the star-shell burst overhead. Within minutes it was joined by a leisurely descent of parachute flares like Pentecostal tongues in the enormous night. The brigadier had wanted Fritz to see what was coming for him, and he did, but instead of lapsing into coma he woke in a chaos of whistles, sirens and bugles and opened up with a dozen machine-guns and a thousand rifles.

"Mind you don't muck up our wire," the brigadier had said, but in the stark light of wafting flares Cyril saw that the Colossus dragged hundreds of yards of it from his ankles, along with its attendant stakes and entangled soldiery: as if a plucky detachment of today's dead had joined the medieval corpses to march against the arch-foe of Western Civilization. This image was spoiled when he noted that the march was more like a madhouse quadrille, a flopping, rolling and continual shedding of loose parts and individuals, along with a sporadic recruitment of bloated things that the draglines wrenched out of the mud.

"I gave as good as I got," Cyril said aloud as he composed a letter to Penelope to keep his mind at one remove from his descent into Hell, but that was untrue. He could give only a sputtering cackle of small-caliber bullets while getting the massed firepower of an army that had long been pining for one big target. The giant thrummed and creaked like a ship battered by wind and wave. A rain of bone fragments rattled on Cyril's helmet as the vast ear above him was whittled away.

A whole German division saw his pathetic gun as the likeliest aim-ing-point on the monster. He released the grips and slid below the shoulder, where he found himself pressed against a woman: as dead as anything could be, but writhing in a mockery of passion as part of the muscles that swung the ponderous arms in time to the stride of the Colossus. He wrenched his mind from thoughts that made him unworthy of Penelope and surveyed the mud behind him, where he noticed for the first time that his chaps were cheering him on.

The foe brought larger weapons into play. The Teutonic delight in skipping shells off the ground and counting on air-borne concussion to do all the damage seemed less efficient than would have been direct aim at the solar plexus. Their method had little effect on the inexorable legs and feet. But as each scorching wind roared against its chest from exploding shells, Cyril grew more aware of a stench of roasting carrion. As the heat was transferred through the shoulders, the bodies around him began noticeably to soften, to weep and bleed unspeakable fluids.

"Turn back!" he screamed, not thinking what this would mean to his own position vis-à-vis the enemy, but only of the knights and scholars and lovers and laborers of his dream, who were being punched to pieces by the steel chisel-point of a universal fusillade. "They're killing you!" In sardonic response, the mouth of a nearby corpse flapped suddenly open as its liquefaction quickened.

Unwilling to cringe at the rear any longer, he heaved himself back to the shoulder, his boots now sinking like one climbing a muddy slope. He seized the gun and opened fire on the Hun trenches, shaking the weapon and screaming as if to lend the piffling spray of lead the force of his outrage. The gun jammed. He tore open the nearest sack of grenades. Before he could grasp one he found himself tumbling helplessly through a world of white light.

For a short while, he sensed the presence of countless companions.

"Bloody fucking hell," said Private Thomas, who witnessed the direct hit to the chest of the Colossus from the questionable safety of a firing-step. He had wagered heavily that Little Hansel would win the war single-handed, and he saw the sudden blossoming of the monster into a cloud of tumbling bodies and wafting flags as a symbol of three months' pay strewn to the winds.

"It was a lucky shot," Powell said with false sympathy. "Our Colossus should have taken a round from Big Bertha in the belly without so much as rescheduling his bowel movements."

"Shut your bloody holes and look sharp for the attack!" Jenkins shouted.

"Our attack, he probably means," Thomas groaned, and he was dead right.

No part of the Colossus remained intact, no giant leg or foot to prove that it had walked the waterish waste, only corpses. Rain fell all that night, mingled with occasional showers of high-explosive shells and sleet-storms of machine-gun fire. The dead rose from their graves to be rearranged and reburied. The landscape was smudged out and redrawn again, the soup of mud and men and steel replenished and stirred yet again, until no one could have said with any certainty which were the new corpses and which the old.

THE MUSE OF AVEROIGNE

by Ron Hilger & Henry J. Vester III

My name is Philip Hastane, and several years ago I had the distinct pleasure of touring many of the great historic castles of central France. I had never before been abroad, and the impact of these magnificent bastions of medieval history upon me was both profound and disturbing; in particular, the one that forms the basis of the following story. As a part-time fiction writer and journalist for my small hometown newspaper *The Auburn Journal*, I had never experienced anything like the ancient grandeur and sense of culture contained within these old stone fortresses. Most impressive of all was the Château of La Frênaie, located deep within the primeval forest of Averoigne, beyond the river Isoile from the cathedral city of Vyônes.

The tour guide of this venerable and well-preserved château seemed especially proud of the many fine tapestries which adorned the great hall, and one in particular, the largest and most intricately wrought, he described in great detail.

"This tapestry, or arras," my guide explained, "is ancient beyond all reckoning, and no Châtelaine in living memory has been able to tell how or when it came to be hanging here in the great hall of La Frênaie. Having been expanded and repaired on numerous occasions over the centuries, the loving embroidery of long-forgotten ladies shines forth through the ages like a glorious beacon of Grace and Beauty not to be found in modern times. The stitching is faded and torn in many places with the passage of time and the effects of dust and the moth. But the very fibers of the weave are saturated with the radiant memories of timeless medieval mornings and endless golden afternoons, centuries of wondrous events recorded and passed down to future generations. Some of the many scenes woven hereon reflect a beautiful and magical history of La Frênaie, as in the central image, which details the hunting of the Unicorn. Others depict savage horrors and blasphemous evils that stalked the ancient midnight forest to the bane of many a medieval traveler, as depicted by the fire-spewing serpents, Satyrs, and other bestial creatures leering here and there from amidst the foliage." Here he paused and gave me an odd, appraising sort of look, motioned me closer and lowered his voice before continuing.

"It has been passed down in whispered tradition from one generation to the next, that many ages ago a spirit or Muse was imprisoned within this tapestry by an omnipotent wizard. This Muse is said to be of an age with the land itself, and that she had already taken a thousand variant forms by the time the first Roman footprint was pressed into the soil of this region of arcane mystery known as Averoigne. Her name and nature and history are not known, although many have been the profitless speculations regarding her. The wizened scholar of mystic lore discerns her secrets no better than does the ignorant rag-picker. It is widely believed that the Muse will, on infrequent occasions, reveal some of the tales encrypted in the tapestry's colored threads. But this wonder can only occur when she perceives a soul less entrenched than its fellows in the tawdry affairs of this earthly life. Such a soul as this she may entice with glimpses of rare visions, accounts of fabulous deeds, and revelations of horrific magicks in days gone by.

"Could it be, my friend, that you possess such a soul as this? Do you feel sometimes an alien in a land not your own? A stranger out of place in the present age? Perhaps you are one of those to whom the forest, at night, sings that ancient song never heard in the city, or for whom the passing clouds paint pictures never seen on any artist's canvas. Does your soul hunger for things which your heart cannot define, and does it know beyond question that magick—true magick—lies just beyond the limits of your mortal senses? If these things are true, then come, stand before this tattered and faded mural of an elder world. Gaze upon it with your inward eyes, and know with absolute certainty that the centuries may be rolled back as easily as a scroll, and recalled as surely and vividly as a childhood memory.

"See, over here, a small château in a forest clearing. The path which leads to the door is bordered with overgrown brambles. The stitching is so minute, so precise, that the branches seem to emerge from the arras, the very leaves seem almost to rustle in the breeze. You inhale, and a scent of moist forest air and rich loamy soil fills your awareness. A light wind tosses your hair, and you hear footsteps approaching along the path." As I gazed in fascination upon the arras, an intense wave of vertigo swept over me. I began to sway towards the tapestry, which seemed to ripple and swirl and expand to receive me.

The full moon rose above the treetops, pouring down its silver curse upon the small château. The footsteps faltered, then paused at the edge of the forest surrounding the rustic structure. Feral eyes appraised the isolated dwelling, observing the pungent grey smoke rising from the chimney, the yellow light of a single lamp escaping through the windows and from underneath the door. The watcher sniffed the night smells and clenched a crystal vial tightly in his hairy paw.

The memories rose unbidden in his mind as they often did when he viewed the château. Memories of a time before the ravenous curse of lycanthropy consumed his mortal Soul and left him a shadowy creature of the night forest. He had built the château himself and lived there with his beautiful young bride for many happy years . . . he thought perhaps there were children as well. But then his memories became confused with hunger and the rending of soft white flesh with his iron claws and the spurting of hot blood beneath his tearing fangs. He had roamed the night forest for years, and had slain every man, woman, and child within an ever-widening circle like lethal ripples spreading outward from some malignant core of evil. Yet no matter how far he roamed, he always returned to stare into the window of the château in hope of glimpsing the woman who still dwelt within. He did not know why she still remained, he only knew she was a constant annoying distraction. Never could he bring himself to kill her, nor could he leave her, though he had tried to do both on several occasions. Tonight, however, he had other aspirations. He held the vial aloft and peered at its contents. The philtre was the color of moonbeams tainted with blood, his own blood, infected with the curse of the werewolf. Tonight she would join him or he would slay her.

He was not hungry. He had feasted earlier that evening after ambushing a pair of travelers along the forest road. Dropping down upon them from the trees, he had ripped the throat from the first before the other was even aware of him. The second screamed briefly before his head was nearly separated from his shoulders, effectively silencing his scream.

No, *this* kill was not to satisfy hunger, but to appease his rage and frustration; he must either have the woman, or kill her and be free of her forever.

Somewhere above him an owl screeched. As if this were a signal, he suddenly moved forward, crossing the distance to the door in a few leaps and bounds. The stout oaken door yielded immediately beneath his blows and he sprang into the château. The woman stood frozen in the middle of the room. She saw the vial he held extended towards her and the wild light burning in his eyes. Her own eyes gleamed in response as she said evenly, "So. You have finally come for me."

A lupine throat is ill-constructed for human speech, nor had the wolf-creature attempted to speak even once during the past four ensanguined years. But he tried now, and the result sounded to the woman's ears like the reluctant, tortured grinding of a great millstone.

"Drink," the wolf-thing commanded. "Drink, or die!"

"This evil-looking potion must be the handiwork of the witch Amalthea. How many of her enemies did you have to slay as payment for this philtre, I wonder?" she said, accepting the vial.

"Drink!" the monster rasped again, its eyes now furiously ablaze with anticipation. The woman crossed the small room and seated herself on a stool near the hearth, holding the vial before her so that the flames cast spears of crimson light through the liquid within.

"Become a werewolf . . . a loup-garou," she murmured to herself. "Consider the alternative. Death! But consider the possibilities . . . ."

She thought bitterly of how the village priest had pronounced her and the children accursed after he learned that her husband had become a werewolf. She remembered how, when the fever had struck the children, she had begged the priest, the doctor, the townspeople for the mercy of their aid, and had been cruelly rebuffed, pelted with stones, and driven out of the village. She remembered burying her dead children, and the three tortuous, desperately lonely years which followed her terrible loss. As she thought on these things, a slow, grim smile came to her face, which had known no smile for three long years. Turning, she looked full into the savage countenance of the monster that was her husband, and pulled the stopper from the crystal vial.

When I regained my senses, I was still examining the tapestry's little château in the forest clearing, and my guide was still lecturing as if unaware of my dizzy spell.

"Notice the two tiny wolves running through the forest. Reach out your hand M'sieur, and feel with your fingertips the intricate needlework. If you close your eyes, you can almost hear them howling." Apparently mistaking my dazed countenance for one of awestruck appreciation, he continued his discourse.

"Step this way M'sieur, so that we may better view the central image of the Unicorn hunt. This depiction of the Unicorn is unique, for it is the only known tapestry in all of France to color the mythic animal black instead of white. The horn is rich, gleaming ivory with five ridges running the length of the horn, spiraling out to its tip. Notice the detail of the hunters with all their colorful garments and assorted weapons, the regal bearing of the Lord of La Frênaie and his courtiers, the noble grace and strength of the beast."

As I viewed the described scene, I gradually became aware of the sound of muffled voices, apparently from a room directly behind the tapestry. I leaned forward slightly in an effort to better distinguish the words and realized with a sudden chill that the figures engaged in the Unicorn hunt were subtly beginning to move, and the sound of far-off conversation was emanating from the arras itself!

Piedro de La Frênaie pursued the trail of the Black Unicorn on the heels of his frantically baying pack of hounds, eager for another glimpse of his elusive prey. The bolt from his arbalest had struck the beast in the shoulder, he was certain, but the dogs tracked the beast into a sudden bank of thick, white mist. Reining in his majestic stallion, he briefly considered this unexpected development. Such fog banks were not uncommon at this early hour in the forest, but it seemed uncanny that it should suddenly appear at this exact time and place, perfectly obscuring any trail, and baffling his pursuit. Piedro looked behind to see if others followed the trail behind him, but he could not distinguish anything beyond a dozen yards or so. He could, however, clearly hear the furious baying of the hounds echoing through the forest ahead. The mysterious fog could not distract the hounds from the scent, so the hunt was still on!

"Françios, Gaspard, follow me! The dogs still have the scent!" He shouted to the two men he thought closest behind, and spurred his mount forward once again to the chase. As he followed the hounds as quickly as he dared through the obscuring mist, he recalled some of the ancient legends concerning the Unicorn. The most common tales concerning Unicorns dealt with pure and gentle maidens unexpectedly meeting a white Unicorn in some private forest glade. There the Unicorn would reveal secrets of the maiden's future, usually disclosing the identity of the maiden's one true love, as well as the methods by which she could first meet, then capture the young gallant's heart. The least often repeated stories told of the enigmatic Black Unicorn. It was whispered that the ivory horn of this extraordinarily rare beast would grant immortality to the fortunate knight who could slay the noble beast and remove the talisman from its dead body. The Black Unicorn had never before been seen in Piedro's or his father's lifetime, and Piedro considered it his destiny to slay the beast, take hold of its horn, and learn the truth of the matter.

On and on through the dank, misty forest he rode, following the ceaseless baying of the hounds. Finally, the noise grew louder and seemed to have become stationary, which could only mean the beast had fallen, weakened at last by loss of blood, or perhaps cornered by the dogs. But as he drew closer he realized the dogs had stopped barking, which struck him as being extremely odd. With growing trepidation he advanced into the silent, fog-shrouded forest until at last he discerned a dark mass on the ground before him.

Slowly he approached. The Black Unicorn was lying on its side, apparently dead, or nearly so.

"At last!" he gloated to himself. "The horn is mine!"

Preparing to dispatch the beast with his sword, he began to dismount. Suddenly, the Unicorn opened its eyes and screamed a horrid, unearthly cry unlike anything he had ever heard. Its eyes lit with a wild fiery light like twin windows opening into Hell. His mount whinnied in fear and reared up in terror, throwing Piedro violently from its back. The yard-long ivory horn rose to meet him as he fell, impaling him through the heart and emerging in a great gout of blood from his back.

With his last strength, the master of La Frênaie grasped the horn in his hands as his destiny was fulfilled.

I staggered forward, clutching my chest. My heart felt as if pierced by a shaft of white-hot metal. My guide turned and supported me as I slumped forward.

"M'sieur!" he cried in alarm. "What is wrong?"

"My heart" I managed to gasp before I lost consciousness altogether.

When I awoke, I felt disoriented and ill. I was lying on a sofa in the entry hall of La Frênaie, my guide peering down at me with an expression of concern and cautious relief.

"How do you feel, M'sieur?" he asked, helping me to a sitting position. "You gave us quite a scare, we were just about to call for the doctor."

"I'm a little weak and shaken, but I don't think it's a heart attack, or anything serious. I'm sure I'll be all right in a minute." I could not explain why I felt this way, so after I had recovered, I simply smiled and thanked him for his kindness.

I left shortly thereafter and returned to California, cutting short my vacation. The impressions I received from the tapestry had confused my memory, and somewhat muddled my thinking. The visions seemed so real, as if I had actually experienced them myself. It seemed too bizarre to be explained by an over-active imagination, or by a nervous breakdown of some sort. Perhaps it was merely the power of suggestion?

Slowly, I became myself again after falling back into my old routine. Occasionally I still have disturbing dreams in which I return to medieval Averoigne, and do battle with mythical monsters that stalk me relentlessly through its haunted castles and darkling forests, leaving me exhausted and ill. My friends believe these spells are related to insomnia and migraine headaches. But the thing I cannot explain and which I pray is never discovered is the five-pointed spiral scar upon the left side of my chest and the smaller corresponding scar on my back, just beneath my left shoulder blade.

And sometimes, when the moon is full, I lie awake as bloodthirsty urges pulse through my veins and I savagely yearn to quit this modern world and rejoin my mate across the wide waters in Averoigne. The guide of La Frênaie made reference to those Souls who feel born out of their time, who see and feel things that others do not. He made it sound like a wonderful thing at the time; a blessing to those fortunate few. I can assure you that he was mistaken. For me, at least, it has been more like a curse.

Esprit D'Averoigne

by Paul Toffaleti

Hearthside lady is woven in a tapestry of threads.
On a wall inside a stone-cold fortress she clings,
telling tales of primitive hardships, frailty, and survival.
Midst time-faded order of fiber, colors and outlines,
last of a hundred-year generation in righteous battle
to halt English invaders and their stronghold designs,
she and her company do claim this aerie perch:
Wild hewn rock above bridgeless, unforgiving torrent.

Night watch and fireside vigil, word, gesture and quiet wait:
in fabric of art doth she evade the threat of fear and death
which lurk beyond the river bends . . .

I reach to the symboled wall, to that everlasting youthful soul,
When the snows have melted and the current ebbed for passage,
I too will descend and cross and tread the other bank.

THE FELL FÊTE

by Manuel Arenas

And she went away from me and moved through the fair,
And fondly I watched her move here and move there.
And then she went homeward, just one star awake
Like the swan in the evening moves over the lake.

Last night she came to me, my dead love came in,
So softly she came that her feet made no din.
And she laid her hand on me and this she did say,
"Oh, it will not be long, love, till our wedding day."

— *She Moved Through the Fair*, Traditional Irish ballad

Anacleto awoke hot and bothered from his troubled sleep, rubbed his reddened, sleep-deprived eyes and blinked to refocus. Despite the chill of the autumn temperatures outside his room at the Inn of Haute Espérance, he felt uncomfortably warm and sweaty. He had just awakened from a nightmare where he was being smothered by a dark shadow which pressed upon his chest and sucked the vitality from his immobile body. The sensation was alternately erotic and terrifying. As waves of divine agony rippled through his supine form, he felt the smothering umbra engulf his face as the darkness took the silhouetted form of a woman murmuring, "Oh, it will not be long, love . . ." Waking with a gasp, he muttered an inaudible oath under his breath and hyperventilated. That girl!—that damned fairy girl!—he couldn't get her out of his mind. Every time he shut his eyes she was there, waiting for him; slender, sultry, and white as a ghost, with auburn hair and absinthian eyes of an albescent green. In fact, he wouldn't have been surprised if she also had a bit of the *green fairy* in her blood somewhere.

When he first saw her earlier that evening in a claret-colored velvet dress, looking like a lady from an anachronistic role playing troupe, gliding through the stalls at a local bleu cheese festival in La Frênaie, he thought of the Irish folk ballad "She Moved through the Fair". He stared at her so intently that he didn't realize at first that she was staring back. Startled and not a little embarrassed, he snapped out of his amative trance and quickly looked away. She laughed, a sound which reverberated like a knell, still dissipating in his ears when she suddenly appeared at his side. She addressed him in a language he was not familiar with, but which sounded to him a bit like what he knew of Catalan. He answered in his best French and she laughed again, then responded in kind, saying, "Ah, you are not from these parts, I can tell. Your French is passable, but your accent is a bit off. I assume that you are either Italian or Spanish, from the southern parts no doubt, with your dark, handsome looks. I daresay you have a touch of Moorish blood in you, *n'est-ce pas?*"

"I am Spanish," he replied, "from *Andalucía*; my name is Anacleto, may I know yours?"

"No, you may not—ahahaha!" Again, that eldritch laughter, then she continued, "What are you doing so far away from home?"

"I am a student of Brichester University, in England. It used to have copies of the rare tomes essential for my studies but, after a religious zealot burned several priceless grimoires in the early oughts, access has become very limited to them. I wondered if I could do some of my own original research, so I decided to take a week away from my tiny dormitory, and from writing my thesis about the prevalence of sorcery and diabolism in the *Moyen Âge,* to visit France and travel through the region of Averoigne to see the various historical sites in person, and to delve into the local lore first hand."

"Oh? And what have you found, *mon cher?*"

"Well, yesterday I found some rare accounts of the Bishop Azédarac of Ximes which do not paint him in such a saintly light as he is historically remembered."

"Azédarac? The blackguard—I forbid you to speak of him again in my presence!"

"Surely you jest," Anacleto scoffed. "You speak as if you have some personal gripe with him, but the Bishop Azédarac's haloed cranium has been dust for almost a millennia by now! Additionally, I have been looking into the legends of Sieur Hugh du Malinbois and his chatelaine, who were notorious sorcerers and also rumored to have been vampires."

At this last intelligence, she became all of a sudden very serious, and in the intermittent lambency of the flickering flambeaus from the nearby fair stalls her pallid visage became rutilant and her eyes trembled as if they would burst from their sockets. Grabbing his face gruffly, she then kissed him deeply and passionately with her red, fulsome lips, and in a sepulchral voice that echoed of incantations in midnight realms she intoned, "I have been watching you, I have chosen you, and so now you are mine. When I call for you, you shall hear me wherever you are, stop whatever you are doing; then, listen for the piper and he will lead you to me."

Her message delivered, she cooled back to her colorless, comely self, pinched his cheek and said, "Now, my studious little Spaniard, you have been kissed by a fairy. *Au revoir, mon bel Espagnol!*" Smiling, but still maintaining eye contact, she stepped back toward the woods and disappeared into shadow, leaving Anacleto stunned and speechless.

What nonsense, he thought now as he paced his room in the darkness; he was a fool to even give her proclamations any credence, much the less allow them to upset him so. His friends back home at Brichester would laugh at his gullibility and make much sport of his having fallen under the spell of some eccentric country girl. He also needed to return to sleep *tout de suite* if he was ever going to be able to wake up at a reasonable hour to visit the Abbey of Périgon and seek permission to access their great library of rare tomes and precious manuscripts for his research on the weird legends behind the ruin of the Château des Faussesflammes.

Perhaps if he let a little of that autumnal airflow into his stuffy room, he would sleep a little easier. Taking a nip from a bottle of the local vintage on his nightstand to calm his nerves, he threw open the latticed casement windows of his little room and inhaled deeply of the chill nocturnal breeze. In the rush of the current, he could smell the fragrance of the forest flora which grew just below his windowsill followed sharply by a noxious odor of mixed dampness and decay, accompanied by a strange music carried in on the wind from the sparsely-litten road through the forest.

Soon afterward he noticed a light appear in an open window in a small cottage across the way. A moment later, the front door burst open and a young well-formed woman walked out into the weird nocturne in her nightgown and disappeared into the forest. In the room adjacent to his own, the windows flew open and the innkeeper's son climbed down an ivied trellis in his undergarments and headed toward the forest. Between the gnarled, pedunculated branches of the ancient oaks Anacleto could see silhouettes of other young men and women, arms outstretched, feeling their way in the darkness whilst deeper shadows flit and flew around them.

Watching the grotesque farce play out from the vantage point in his room, he felt a persistent urge to join in. Realizing that it must be some form of dark enchantment at work, he reached for the crucifix which he wore about his neck, and for a moment felt that he could re-sist the pull. Gaining confidence, he began reciting some protective prayers he had learned as a boy from his devoutly Catholic *abuelita*— but all to no avail, once he espied the emergent shade of the Black Pip-er.

Rising into view, his shadow grew long onto the road, snuffing all light in its path. Even at a distance, Anacleto could feel the Piper's marmoreal gaze upon him. His reptilian eyes were mesmerizing, and lacking in emotion as much as in color. Like a translucent creature that lives in the deep lightless recesses of a great cavern, not even the rose-ate hue of underlying capillaries, so prevalent in albinism, was present. On his narrow crown he wore a tri-horned jester's cap with miniature bells that tolled woefully as he pranced and capered. His straight white hair hung like a pall on his knobby shoulders, which were clad, as was the rest of his lanky frame, in a costume that at first glance appeared to be of a solid black color. However, as Anacletos eyes were drawn to the person of the Piper, he could discern a piebald pattern of diamonds alternating in degrees of blackness, the darker of which was a shade so profound that it drew its observer, almost magnetically, into its nigrescent depth. Indeed, Anacleto felt that were it not for the inter-mittent interruption of the lighter shade, one might be sucked into the atramentous void of the darker. The Piper's long, skinny arms jutted out from his body like the pepipalps of a whip spider, and in his pallid hands he bore a bone flute on which he played his mournful tune.

Accompanying the Piper were a band of familiars with shadowy miens and red slit-like eyes. Anacleto could barely perceive them ca-vorting in the periphery of his purview, but in his ears he heard the sound of their caliginous concert: it began with drumming—a dry, flat sound of derma-bound drums, swelling in a crescendo, pounding like the pulse of some cthonic beast rising from its subterranean lair. Then came the bombards and the bagpipes, dissonantly skirling and twisting their way through the air in a *sonneurs de couple,* transmogrifying into a banshee's wail, to summon the fey souls. Like Hamelin rats, they were drawn by the strain, stirred to rise from their beds and walk, falling into file upon meeting their spellbound brethren on the darkened roads, marching. They came from miles around, on forgotten roads, from nearby towns, like gossamer strands, that all lead to the center of a spider's web, and Anacleto could do nothing but yank the crucifix from his throat, vault over the window sill, and fall in line, following the Black Piper and his band of phantom minstrels.

This particular web came in the shape of a quaint, yet forgotten hamlet within the bosky region of Averoigne, which is reputed to be the home of many a *bête noire.* On the outskirts of the settlement the marchers were corralled by the Black Piper and his ghostly band, who led them in a cortège to the gates of the secluded *Hameu de Malinbois.* Hidden deep within the center of the forest, this settlement consisted of thirteen small, simple domiciles and a sprawling cemetery. There were no farms, nor was any trade plied therein, but the denizens appropriated whatever they needed from the nearby towns—and what they needed had just arrived in single file, led by the Black Piper and his darksome coterie.

Greeting them at the gates were a bevy of beautiful, pale-faced beings with livid smiles and hungry eyes. Foremost among them was Anacleto's fairy girl, who greeted him with open arms and a hearty salutation of, *"Bonsoir mon bel Espagnol!"* The enchanted walkers, recognizing their own sweethearts, rushed into their respective embraces as the Piper and his band struck up a lively tune. The couples reeled around a great brazier to the music and laughed the way young lovers do. After the dancing was done, the guests were treated to a feast of exquisite foods, which they washed down with many bottles of the hearty regional wine. Buzzing from the rich food and the heady drink, the paramours broke off into darkened corners, where they giggled and sighed in delight.

It was at this point that Anacleto's lady-friend spoke to him in confidence. "My name is Ambrosine du Malinbois. Yes, I am of the family whose reputation you are trying so hard to besmirch. I cannot allow you to do this. We have lived in this hamlet for centuries hidden from the prying eyes of outsiders who would do us harm, like they did to my grandsire and his chatelaine. And why? Because of superstition and ignorance! Yes, we have taken lives, but what are the lives of a dozen dullards to the life of even one adept? We don't waste our time consuming the idiot entertainments of the masses, we use our protracted existences to probe the secrets of the Universe which your clergy and academics fear and guard so niggardly.

"I was told to watch you and see what your intentions were, and to stop you if you learned too much about our hamlet, but you seemed harmless enough, and you are so beautiful *mon amoureux sombre*, I could not allow them to hurt you. I pleaded with them to spare you and they condescended to permit me to bring you here to the fête. Now our future, if there is to be one, is in the hands of the Dark One."

Anacleto, incredulous, sputtered, "W-wait, what?! What do you mean by all of this?" Grabbing her arm firmly, he continued in a desperate tone, "Amb-Ambrosine, what is going on here? What dark enchantment is being woven here? How is it that my will ebbs at every cacophonic note that is spawned by that demon's pipe? Ambrosine, if you truly love me as you say, please let me go from this accursed place!"

"No my love, it is too late for that, there is no escaping your fate. You must either stay with me or go with Moribond, and that decision belongs to neither you nor me. Hush now my love, do not weep, I have made oblations to the Dark One and have asked permission to claim you as my helpmate. We shall learn his verdict soon with the distribution of the soul cakes."

On cue, a dissonant trill interrupted the lull in the festivities, quickly arresting the attention of those present, in particular Anacleto, who flinched at the sound. It was the Black Piper again, his long, arachnid limbs moving in hypnotic time to his infernal air. Once everyone had settled down and turned their enchanted gazes to his soulless countenance, he stopped playing and stretched out his lanky arm toward a large elevated wooden stage with a podium, lit on either side by cressets, where stood a hooded figure, clad in black. White lissome hands sprouted from the sleeves of the robe and pulled back the hood to reveal a startling creature; a female, who, like the Piper, seemed to bear no coloring or pigmentation on her person. She bore the appearance of an ivory statue which, like Pygmalion's Galatea, had come to life. The one distinguishing feature in her alabaster mien was the presence of a black stain on her lips that cascaded from her bottom labium stopping about halfway to her chin. She surveyed the hushed ensemble with an unsettling glance, then addressed the crowd in a voice which bore none of the charm of Anacleto's companion, yet all of the wyrd. Her voice was feminine, yet deep and hollow, and her tongue, like her lips, was black. The words she spoke appeared to be for the benefit of the denizens of the hamlet alone, and not their guests, for it was in a language which only they seemed to understand, and it was not any language Anacleto had heard before, not even the Occitan dialect used by his strange new friend when she first addressed him. The woman opened a musty tome laid out before her on the podium. Turning the brittle pages to a particular passage, she set her translucent eyes to the page and began to read aloud its contents. Although he could not understand the specifics of her words, he feared their import when he recognized the name of a certain fearsome entity, Iog-Sotôt, being invoked, to which the assembly responded likewise. Then she read another passage wherein she invoked a name he had only just heard Ambrosine mention moments before: "Moribond", the French word for being at the brink of death. Closing the book, she nodded to the Piper who, signaling his band to join in, played a tune which might have been considered jaunty, were it not for the minor key.

"What did she say? And who is this Moribond?" Anacleto asked his companion.

"She was reading from the *Livre d'Eibon*, a passage which speaks of Iog-Sotôt, the soul eater, and Moribond, the sheaveman who collects the souls for Iog-Sotôt's consumption. Yearly, during the autumn equinox, we pay tribute to Him with the sacrifice of twelve young souls, one for each month of the year. A thirteenth soul, selected by a game of chance, is granted life eternal with the coven to replace the fallen and the adepts who have moved on to higher levels of consciousness to become like the gods themselves. I can say no more, I am fearful for the outcome."

Ambrosine and the pale hosts left their guests to select a single cake each to bring to their paramours, with great ceremony and anticipation, from a tray which seemingly materialized from the shadows, but Anacleto could swear he saw the incandescent eyes of the shadowy servitor that proffered the tray. The young men and women, still clad in whatever they were wearing when they were summoned, accepted the cakes with some trepidation but with no real will to refuse. They were encouraged to consume the cakes; some were hesitant, but complied after minimal coaxing, and all finding the little loaves to be quite tasty, gobbled them up right away. All save for Anacleto that is, who found a little faceless figurine made of a nigrous translucent mineral in his cake.

Noting this, Ambrosine grabbed his hand and raised it up triumphantly as she shouted enthusiastically in her lilting Francophone tones, *"My beautiful Spaniard and I have won!"* At which the others solemnly kissed their paramours and stepped back to ascend the steps to the podium stage and into a circle of chalk inscribed in blood with arcane symbols and names like "Azètot" and "Sodoqua" and sprinkled with rock salt, wherein stood the white woman with the black tongue. Ambrosine elatedly kissed Anacleto, then led him up the steps of the stage to the circle and told him tenderly, but firmly, as one speaks to a cherished child, "Look away my love, and do not look back or move a muscle until I tell you to do so."

Perceiving the gravity of her instruction, Anacleto closed his teary eyes tightly and turned his face away from his compeers. The dry beating of the drums reprised their mesmerizing rhythm and the Black Piper led the other winds in a dirgeful tune as the denizens of the *hameau* began chanting a word, the name "Moribond . . . Moribond . . . Moribond . . . ."

At the center of the boneyard stood a large tumulus, or burial mound, set with two massive limestone doors, decorated with the usual *memento mori* imagery of death's heads and winged hourglasses amidst an array of cabalistic symbols, from which now came a rumbling that jostled the doors forcefully as a dark brume escaped between the crevices like over-brimming pots. Bursting with a crack of doom, the doors flew open and vomited a noxious vapor from the newly revealed aperture, which billowed into the cemetery and was carried on a foul wind to Anacleto's nostrils, causing him to wince and gag, yet he made sure to keep his eyes closed tightly. A thunderous clopping rose from within the tumulus of colossal hooves clacking on a stair as two red points appeared within the mephitis, followed by the muzzle, crest, and body of a gargantuan draught horse, the coat of which absorbed rather than reflected the dappled moonlight struggling in vain to break through the shadowy lacework of the gnarled and knotted trees, which stretched their bare withered branches outward like writhing souls in Purgatory, seeking succor and deliverance.

The steed was of the same superlatively-black color as the darker diamonds on the Piper's raiment from its poll to its feathers, the only other color present being the red of its eyes, which glowed with an infernal luminescence. As the beast emerged from the fog its rider came into view, and the fey guests stared in awe at his grim countenance, as the white woman at the podium bellowed in an archaic, yet to the learned Anacleto, still recognizable French dialect, "With the countenance of Iog-Sotôt there are no limits to our unyielding quest for knowledge, and there are no secrets we cannot discover. Our quest may lead us through darker domains than the one we presently inhabit, but we are vesperal beings, so our sight is not hampered by the mirk, and the trained adept may see beyond this world into the benighted Vale of Pnath where sightless ghouls revel in a charnel banquet as the resultant ossuary tumbles and shifts at the burrowing of cyclopean worms. Night-gaunts carry the offal from our sacrifice to these ghouls for their funereal feasts, snatched from the chaff threshed by He Who Sheafs, Moribond, the Harvester of Souls, and Iog-Sotôt is appeased for another year. Come Moribond, accept our sacrifice for your master!"

The rider, Moribond, was an animated skeleton of gigantic proportions. Around his dull pate flew a ring of unnaturally large inky flies with red peering eyes, which orbited his skull like infernal satellites, their crimson compound eyes watching in all directions and continuously relaying their observations though stridulation back to the ever-absorbing consciousness of Iog-Sotôt—a behavior uncommon in flies, but these were hardly common flies. In his teeth Moribond clenched a sole chrysanthemum, which drooped from his jaw like a predator carrying his senseless prey. He had minimal gear, just a saddle, a bag and a holster in which he kept a massive scythe, all made of black leather. Beneath his saddle was a black cloth emblazoned with a white chrysanthemum. Coming to a halt, he regarded the relinquished lovers, all of whom where hypnotized by his stultifying gaze, which swirled constantly with thanatotic images that he projected into the minds of his prey. Alighting from his perch, he pulled the flower from his teeth and tossed it with a derisive bow to the podium. Returning his attention to the task at hand, he raised his scythe and in a quick movement mowed through the sacrificial offerings in "one fell swoop", as per the idiom, sending a profuse spray of blood into the crowd at the podium, most of whom did not flinch. Anacleto dared not move, nor open his eyes. Momentarily setting his scythe aside, Moribond stared intently at the quivering carcasses, which bled copiously in their dying spasms. Projecting a dark ray from his murky eye sockets, he spied the glittering souls of his victims as they were exposed in his caliginous glare, then swiping a phantom manus through the lot, he collected them all in a supernatural grasp, after which he bound them in a black ribbon and stuffed them in his saddle bag. Blowing a repellent kiss to the white lady, he mounted his melanistic steed and slowly trotted back to the tumulus and the charnel underworld from whence he came. The citizens of the *Hameau de Malinbois* did not stir, however, as the ritual was not yet done. The noisome atmosphere was soon stirred by the noiseless flapping of coriaceous wings. Faceless, rawboned devils the color of midnight flew out from the tumulus to retrieve the remnants of the sacrifices, which they bore to the lightless Vale of Pnath. As the last of the creatures dove into the murk of the burial mound, the inhabitants of the hamlet exhaled in relief and flew to lap up the gory residue of their belated guests.

As Anacleto stood, aghast, the splash of his compeer's warm blood still dripping from his face, Ambrosine laid her lily-white hand on his shivering shoulder and, licking the blood from his cheek, she cooed and whispered in his ear in Franco-tinged English, "Oh, it will not be long love, till our wedding day."

BOUFONOULA

by DJ Tyrer

Jonathan had persuaded his parents to fund his trip to France on the grounds it would be educational, but it seemed the only things he had learnt so far was that the GCSE-level French he hadn't thought about in a decade wasn't sufficient preparation for actually speaking with a native, and that phrase books could only get you so far.

Right now, he was somewhere in south-central France. South-central was the best he could locate himself as he was completely lost. The rental car's satnav wasn't working and road signs and map reading most definitely hadn't been on the GCSE test.

"I should've stayed in Paris," he told the dashboard. At least in Paris you could find plenty of English speakers and a good time. Out here in the towns and villages, all he had managed to find so far were surly monoglots and suspicious gendarmes. Had he known which way to point his car, he would've turned around and gone back.

It was starting to get dark and, despite the signs apparently pointing to various villages with names that seemed unpronounceable even for France, Jonathan had just been driving down country lanes between fields and forests for the past few hours. If he couldn't find a place to stay, he would have to park on the verge and sleep in the car. The darkness encroached relentlessly upon the countryside with only a sliver of moon to offset its grasp.

Then, down a narrow side-lane, he spotted a farmhouse.

It was a long shot, he knew: most of the provincial French people he had met so far seemed to loathe foreigners. If he were lucky, perhaps they would just gouge him on the price rather than turn him away.

He turned onto the farm track and drove carefully up to it, the branches of the trees on either side scraping at the sides and roof of his car.

The beams of his headlights raking across the front of the farmhouse must have alerted whoever was inside to his arrival as, a moment later, the front door opened. A figure appeared in the orange rectangle of light and looked out towards him; a woman, going by the outline of a dress. At least he couldn't see any sign of a shotgun in her hands.

A little nervously, Jonathan stepped out of the car.

In the darkness, something made a sound somewhere between a cough, a croak and a bark.

The Frenchwoman fired off a rapid string of sounds he couldn't even comprehend as words, let alone translate.

"Uh, parlez-vous Anglais?" he asked, fumbling for his phrasebook in case he needed to ask for a room in French.

"Anglais? Oui—I mean, yes. I speak your language, even though it is as barbarous a tongue as Français."

"Sorry?"

"This is Averoigne—long before the French came here, we spoke Averoinhat and, for some of us, it remains our cradle tongue."

"Oh."

"But, you didn't drive out to discuss language and history, did you? How is it I may serve you?"

Jonathan barely managed to stifle a grin at the flowery language: although her face was shadowed and her mouth was seemingly wider than he liked, she appeared to be an attractive young woman, giving the offer quite the wrong connotations.

"Um, I wondered if you had a room I might rent? I need a place to stay tonight."

"To rent? No. To stay in? Yes. It is not our custom to charge our guests for rent and it would be nice to have a guest here; this is a remote and lonely country and I am all on my own." She twitched a smile that made him wonder if the wording of her previous offer had been deliberate. "Would you like to come in?"

"Yes, thank you." He switched off the car engine, grabbed his backpack and followed her inside.

There was a faint smell of damp and age to the house, but otherwise it was a pleasant and welcoming place of dark beams and white-plastered walls with a blazing log fire in the stone-flagged kitchen into which she led him.

"Something to eat?" she asked him. "I have some soup and bread fresh baked today."

"That would be great. Thank you."

"Wine or coffee to drink?"

"Uh, coffee, please."

The woman doled out the soup, buttered some bread and poured him a coffee and a cup for herself. Watching her, he decided she *was* attractive, despite her wide, thin-lipped mouth. Her hair was long and a shiny black, as if she had just stepped out of the shower, and was perfectly offset by her pale skin. She had on a simple tabard-style dress of eggshell blue.

"Mmm, this is good," he said taking a bite of the bread dipped in the soup. "Thank you. Oh, my name's Jonathan, by the way."

"They call me Boufonoula," she said, spelling it for him.

"That sounds more Irish than French to me."

"It is Averoinhat."

"What does it mean?"

She laughed pleasantly. "Oh, nothing special."

He finished the meal while she sipped at her coffee and they chatted about all the inconsequential things, like the weather, that two strangers chat about when uncertain what to say.

"Now," she said when they had finished their coffee, "I could show you to the guest bedroom. But, I would recommend the master bedroom: it is better appointed and I think you might find the company congenial."

"Well, when you put the offer like that," he grinned, "how could I refuse? I think I'll opt for the master bedroom."

She grinned in turn. "Very good. Follow me."

Boufonoula took his hand and led him to a large bedroom dominated by a spacious four-poster bed.

Smiling her wide, thin smile, she slipped out of her dress with a litheness that made him think of a cat.

She slid her slim, pale body into the bed and beckoned him to join her. He needed no further persuasion.

The morning sun woke Jonathan with a pleasant caress. Half-opening his eyes, he yawned and stretched; he patted the space beside him, but Boufonoula wasn't there. He opened his eyes and sat up. There was a white cat curled up at the end of the bed, but no sign of her.

Assuming she was making breakfast, he headed downstairs, but the kitchen was empty. But, there was a note and a pot of coffee. He poured himself a cup and sat down to read what she had written; absently, he patted the cat as he did so while it rubbed against his leg.

I'll see you tonight, he read, *should you choose to stay. If not, then farewell. Help yourself to whatever you want. I hope you choose to stay. B.*

Jonathan rubbed his nose for a moment and the cat jumped up onto the table and meowed at him.

"I guess she has the farm to tend to," he told it. "Well, I think I'll stay for a while. What do you say?"

It meowed as if in approval and he laughed.

"Right, time for breakfast."

When she reappeared that evening, Boufonoula smiled widely to see Jonathan had chosen to remain. Supper was provided and, then, they retreated upstairs to the four-poster bed and spent the night in one another's arms.

But, come morning, she was gone by the time he was woken by the cat pacing about on the bed.

"Where does she go?" he asked it, scratching its ear.

Okay, so there was farm work to do, but did she never return to the farmhouse during the day? And, yes, farm work started early and ended late, but no kiss goodbye? No mention in her note of what she was doing? There was nothing specific, but something about it all made him suspicious.

"I'm being silly, aren't I?" he asked the cat and it meowed as if in agreement on the point. "But, still . . ."

Unlike the previous day, he chose not to lounge about, relaxing and doing nothing, but instead took a look around the farmhouse, the cat trailing after him. The building had two floors with a cellar and the occasional attic space accessed like cupboards high up the wall, but was long and low. There was barely a single straight surface in the place: the long dark beams were curved or undulating, as if they were branches that had barely been shaped, while the plaster walls seemed to bulge without consistency.

As she had said, she lived alone: the other three bedrooms were all dusty from disuse. The cellar was about an inch deep in water, and things—frogs, perhaps—sploshed about in the darkness. Otherwise, the house was nothing special. To the front was a small gravel-strewn yard where his car was parked, with an empty stable block across from the house, while to the rear an herb garden was bounded by trees.

But the library was special. Although his French was abysmal and his Latin almost non-existent, Jonathan could make out certain titles, such as ones that seemed to be *The Discovery of Lycanthropy* and *Lycanthropy in Averoigne*, and various words that seemed to imply demonology and witchcraft. Then there were those antique tomes that seemed infused with import by their age and which had strange, potent-sounding titles such as *Necronomicon* and *Krypticon*.

At first sight, he thought they, like the furniture of the house, must pre-date Boufonoula, having been inherited with the in-built shelving that held them. Indeed, they probably were. Yet, like the furniture, it was clear that, inherited or not, she made use of them, for they were free of dust and, looking inside a couple, he saw they were annotated in what he recognized as her hand.

Certain vague, niggly thoughts suddenly coalesced under the influence of those titles and Jonathan found himself thinking something that just couldn't be true.

He looked down at the cat. The cat looked up at him.

It couldn't be true. It was madness. And, yet . . .

Just as he expected, that evening, the cat slipped away and, a short while later, Boufonoula appeared. He asked her about the animal.

"The cat? I suppose she goes out to hunt her prey. Speaking of which, supper . . ."

Then, sex. But, while she had been cooking, Jonathan had set the alarm on his phone so that he would wake before sunrise.

The vibration of the phone beneath his pillow woke him as planned and, through bleary eyes, he saw a figure slipping from the room. Jonathan quickly rose and dressed, then quietly descended the stairs.

There was no sign of her in the hall or in the kitchen, but, when he looked out the window, he spotted a figure at the far end of the herb garden disappearing down a trail between the trees.

Jonathan dashed outside and followed her.

The trail led through what seemed to be a forest, then reached a marshy clearing with a pond and a grotto. Several abnormally-large toads crept about the banks of the pond and seemed to eye him suspiciously.

There was no sign of Boufonoula, human or cat, but, then, he thought he saw movement in the darkness of the grotto and he called her name.

A figure emerged from the shadows, but it wasn't her. Where Boufonoula had been young and attractive and slim, this woman was squat and broad, aged and ugly. Yet, there was a resemblance and, for a moment, he imagined it must be her mother. Except she was wearing the same dress that Boufanoula always wore . . . .

"You . . . ." He couldn't believe it. The transforming into a cat seemed scarcely more ridiculous.

She laughed, a sound that was like a horrible, phlegmy cough. "Oh dear, my secret's out. Yes, this is me, my beloved…"

"It can't be . . . ."

"Oh, but it can. My mother was a witch and my father was a near-formless child of her master. They lay together here in this grotto in worship of my grandfather and here I was born. Six centuries have passed. Lovers come and go, but none can love me in this, my true form. Oh, they rut wildly with me by night, but when the light of day reveals me to them, their ardor sags . . . .

"Do you still yearn for me, Jonathan?" She slipped off the dress to reveal her corpulent, grey-green form, like a toad stood upon its hind legs.

Jonathan was glad he hadn't breakfasted as watery vomit filled his mouth. He spat it out.

"Apparently not." She sighed, a horrible noise, then dropped to all fours, seeming to become more and more like a wide-mouthed, sleepy-eyed toad as he watched.

"I will have you in me," she said, her voice barely human, "as lover or lunch."

He turned and ran for the trail with the obscene thing that had once been his lover not far behind.

Jonathan had never believed in ghosts or witches or demons or werewolves, but he had seen plenty of horror movies and he was certain werewolves could be killed by silver bullets. Of course, they were supposed to change in moonlight, but surely a were-toad was much the same? And the silver, it didn't have to be a bullet, did it? They also used silver knives . . .

There was silver cutlery in the farmhouse kitchen.

He burst from the woods and trampled mint and thyme without regard. Running into the kitchen, he yanked a drawer out onto the floor, spilling its contents.

The toad-thing appeared in the doorway.

Jonathan seized a knife and backed away.

It lumbered up onto the kitchen table and leered at him.

He stabbed it with the knife.

"Aah!" it cried, then it laughed its horrible coughing laugh. "Foolish boy: silver is of the moon and night time, and the night is my grandfather's province. Now, gold, the metal of the sun . . . But, now, you die . . ."

It leapt clumsily at him, but he was already running out the door into the hall, heading for the front door, desperate to get outside. If he could make it to his car, he might just make it.

Boufonoula was just behind him as he slammed the front door open and exploded out into the yard. He fumbled in his pocket for the car keys—they weren't there!

He stumbled to a halt, gravel skittering underfoot.

There was a horrible laugh behind him.

"Lost your keys?" it asked in a voice thick with mucus. "Oh dear...."

Could he make it to the road?

He began to run . . . .

MOTHER OF TOADS

by DJ Tyrer

Conflict in his breast
A war rages between his lust
And a surging wave of disgust
For the witch's lover now has seen
His lover's grotesque shape
After a night akin to rape
And, though in a most amorous tone
She calls to him by name
His feelings never can be the same
For though she can shift her form
To svelte from bulky load
He knows she is always a grotesque toad

A Honeymoon in Averoigne

by Trevor O. Childers

The sun sank low into the hills, washing the walled city of Vyônes in crimson and shadow. Along its narrow old cobblestone streets, a couple walked, hand in hand, towards the Campanile Hotel. The streetlights flickered on as the last vestiges of dusk faded into night, and the two leaned in close. The old city watched the pair as they walked back to their hotel.

They were strangers to the land, but eagerly accepted by it. Freshly married and still wanting to experience everything together, the couple had come to the obscure region of Averoigne for their honeymoon. The woman, Stephanie, had been enchanted by the tales of intrigue and the bizarre. Her husband, Greg, was happy to oblige her.

Stephanie stood by the window, splitting her gaze between the view and the map in her hands. The lights of the city glimmered, tiny bright dots in a sea of darkness. The view afforded them a good sight of the cathedral only a few streets away. It sat like a monolithic centerpiece; its black stone darker than the night's shade around it. Despite the warmth of the hotel room, she could feel the chill in the air.

"What are you looking at?"

"I heard about an old abbey south of here," Stephanie said, "The guy in the bar said the view was beautiful."

"I bet he did," Greg said, wrapping his arms around her. "How far out?"

"If we take the car here . . . take this trail . . ." she calculated out loud, "that's about . . . there and back . . . . By the scenic route, it'd take a full day."

"I do love scenic routes," he said, kissing her neck.

"Oh, I *know* you do," she said with a laugh.

"Enough maps for tonight." He spun her around and pulled her in close. The map fell from her hands as they kissed. Cloaked in the safety of the walled city, they spent the night in a passionate embrace.

The next day, they embarked on their outing. They drove down the road to St. Zénobie and parked at the trail head. The air was chilly and damp as they hiked on; smoky fog drifted through the towering trees. The still-rising sun was a white blotch behind the distant clouds. For hours, they trod upon the thin whispers of trails, weaving through trees, over hills, and across small streams. Finally, they reached the ruined abbey.

It sat abandoned, a bulwark of mortar and stone against the hungry forest. A small road, nothing more than a patchwork of cobblestones and weeds, ran from the woodland trail to the dilapidated porch before the large wooden doors. It was a husk of its bygone self: its now-broken walls and columns a skeleton of a once-impressive structure.

"What did you say the name of this place was?" Greg asked.

"Périgon," his wife replied as she led him forward. "It was home to—"

"Monks?" he asked as she paused to take in a breath. She shot him an impish look and he grinned back at her.

"Benedictine Monks. They didn't do the whole starvation and poverty thing. Practically hedonists by dark age standards."

"What happened to them?"

"The Revolution." A pause as the implication flew over her husband. "They were Catholic."

"Right . . . ."

"They actually lived out here for quite a while before the new Republic came and took it. They cared more about removing the monks than taking the building, though. It was seventeen ninety-nine or eight, I think."

"How do you know all this?"

"Internet," she said curtly.

Greg laughed as she approached the door. "C'mon."

An old dog's head knocker, its features worn and ring stolen by time, grew out of the door. It seemed to glare and snarl at them—a dare to trespass any further. Pushed back, the wooden door revealed a darkened entryway beyond. Sunlight poured in from the door, revealing cobwebs, rubble, and dust. Through the abbey's narthex, the beam of light shot through the broken ceiling and spilled over a pillar. The door's echo gave way to the silence that had long held dominion over the place.

The entryway extended into a long church, marked by neglect, and dowsed in shadows. The two lovers walked in slowly, careful not to disturb the immemorial stasis of the place. Their footsteps, the rustling of their packs, and even their breath seemed to echo in the hallowed halls.

"It's beautiful," Stephanie said, her gaze pinned to some distant point in the chapel.

"Yeah, I guess. In a creepy sort of way. Certainly worthy of a photo."

His phone clicked as he took a picture and the hall echoed the sound back. It was like an audible shudder at the man's boldness, for those that would care to notice.

"Look at the dust." Stephanie pulled Greg's arm and pointed down to darkness. "The way it moves in the light. It's like . . . like it's dancing."

They moved through the decrepit monastery like field mice, timidly checking each corner for danger and wonder. They peered over rubble where passages were inaccessible and slid through where they could. Wherever they went, though, however beautiful the sights were, they always felt like trespassers.

In the center of the cloister, now overgrown after centuries of neglect, a large tree stood triumphantly taller than the ruined walls surrounding it. The light streaming into the square gave an eerie, otherworldly feel to the scene.

"That," Greg remarked, "is a big tree."

"Yeah, wow," Stephanie said, more than a little awestruck. "It must have grown here after the monastery was abandoned."

She walked forward into the creeping nature that had grown out of the cloister. The tree looked ancient. She circled around and found a black gouge running down the other side where lightning had struck some time ago. She reached out and touched it. She could feel—

"Looks like the perfect spot for lunch," Greg said, breaking her trance.

They broke out their lunch and ate in the luminescence of the reclaimed cloister. They had brought trail mix, tuna salad, beef jerky, and energy bars; everything they knew they would need for a meal on the trail. And because it was their honeymoon and because they were in France, they had also brought along some wine in a metal bottle.

"So, what's the ghost story with this place?"

"What do you mean?" Stephanie asked, gazing thoughtfully at the tree.

"Everyplace we've been here has some kind of spooky story or whatever, and you've been eating them up since before we got married. So, what's with this place? Gargoyles? Werewolves? Wait . . . kinky nuns?"

"Ha! I'd have really loved that . . . . No, I can't remember the story . . . just that there were Benedictine monks here, and they had a really big library. Oh, and they grew a lot of vegetables and stuff in their garden."

"Riveting," he said with mock enthusiasm. "At least it's more believable than that story about the giant zombie."

"I'll see what else I can find," she said with a wry smile, finally tearing her gaze from the tree. She pulled out her phone and began typing. "Damn, signal is weak out here. Let's see...."

"I wonder why no one came out here to turn this place into a museum or whatever."

"Probably because it's so remote." She made a frustrated noise as the loading page stalled.

"Then why'd they live so far out here?"

"Probably because it's so remote," she repeated, a teasing smile spreading across her face.

"Just seems like a waste. This place must have been something special back in the day. Then again," he looked up at the preeminent tree, "this is something else altogether."

"Yeah," she said, joining in his gazing. "Oh, it finally loaded. Wow, so there's actually a lot of stories about monks *from* the abbey, but . . . . Okay, here we go. So, there's an old story about monks here that got really drunk off some wine. I guess they made it here? Anyway, one of them made out with this statue they found of Venus—"

"The Greek lady?"

"Roman, actually. The Roman Goddess of love."

"Wait, I thought that was Italy."

"They invaded France. Before it was France. Remem— Did you even pay attention in school? Anyway, this monk was making out with a statue. It fell over and crushed him to death."

"Now that's some unsafe s—"

"No!" she said with mock severity. "Don't you dare finish that one."

"Awww. Fine. So, that's it?"

"Not entirely. The Monks said that when they found their dead brother, the statue had changed position. Like, its arms and legs and head; it was in a different pose." She scrolled down. "Ha, wow! They couldn't even get him out, so they just buried them both in the vegetable garden and started a new one on the other side of the abbey. Wow...."

"Must have been some statue. So, wait . . . it's still here?"

"No. No, no, no, no, no. We're not digging up some naked statue with a skeleton under it. Not on my honeymoon!"

When they finished their picnic, they packed up and explored the place. They took selfies and pictures of the ruins, and even managed to send some of them to their friends. They looked through some more of the ruin's nooks and crannies, picking out some choice souvenirs to remember the place by.

By the time they were done, it was somewhat past midday. They never liked checking the time when they were hiking; they knew nature kept its own. While they had visited the ruin, a part of the sky had grown dark with the clouds of an oncoming storm.

"We'd better head back before that storm rolls in," Stephanie said.

Greg walked over with a stout new walking stick in hand. It was a layered mix of light browns and grays, straight but for a few knots and a curve at the top. That curve had been carved into a chicken's head, holding within its beak a leather cord with wooden beads. Despite its age and resting place, it seemed as fresh as the day of its making.

"Found a souvenir?"

"Yeah, it's hornbeam, strong. Good condition, too. Besides, no one else is going to use it."

With a smirk and a shake of her head, she walked off, leading them to the rough trail they had taken to the abandoned abbey. As they returned to the tangled forest, the last pure rays of sun disappeared behind dark and angry clouds. The fog from earlier still hung in clumps, and the hazy light from the clouds made them almost iridescent.

Slowly, the sounds of the forest dropped away as the mist began to grow thick around the pair. Insects failed to buzz, owls to hoot, and the wind ceased its rustling through the trees. They walked over a stone-still stream, the long dead leaves and alabaster haze of the foggy remnants obscuring the now-darkened trees around them. Moths fluttered away from them and spiders cautiously surveyed their passing over increasingly rotting leaves and wicked thorns. Even their steps were muted by the darker forest floor.

Eventually they stopped to take a break. They each looked around as they sipped water, not eager to rest long with the oncoming downpour chasing them.

"Does it feel . . . different to you?" Stephanie asked, feeling the weight of their drastically changed atmosphere.

"What? Nah, it's just the clouds," Greg replied dismissively as he peered over the map. "Makes it all seem darker. Like that time in Colorado."

"Did you get us lost?" she asked, turning to look at him. "Like that time in Colorado?"

"No," he said, the confused sweep of his gaze betraying his answer. "No, of course not. It's . . . it's this way."

They walked on through the forest. The increasingly hostile bramble, obscured directions, and otherworldliness of their environment began to take its toll. Panic planted its seeds in their hearts as distant thunder curled around them and barely apparent shadows danced in the distance. Every story they had heard during their time in Averoigne slowly crept back into their minds and, privately, they wondered how true those stories really were.

When they finally found a path, they followed it eagerly, plodding through a stagnant, slightly luminous stream as their pace quickened. They emerged from the forest into a clearing next to where the dead stream pooled into a tarn. The last vestiges of light were just enough to reveal what awaited the lost couple.

Before them rose an edifice that stood brazenly despite its age, a crumbling ruin of a castle that defied the world. The yawning gray walls, though pocked with invading trees and vines, stood starkly against the darkened world around it, like a vast hoary block that spread outwards against the darkening sky. It was empty, devoid of sound, light, or ancient marking, and yet commanded the attention of the world. The two stood before the bastion, an unseen dread piercing their hearts as they gazed upon its terrible glory.

"Whe—" Greg swallowed and regained himself. "Where did this come from?"

"Wow . . . . It must have been hidden in the trees," Stephanie said.

"We, uh, we need to get to the car, though." A roll of thunder punctuated his urgency.

But Stephanie walked forward, transfixed by the ancient castle, and her husband trailed behind, halfway to panic. The sepulchral thing stared back at her as they approached.

"Stephanie!"

"We're further away from the car," she said, slowly turning back to her husband. "We've gotten closer to the mountain, see? We're not going to make it back before this storm hits."

Greg felt a drop plip on his ear as she finished speaking, and another fell on his jacket as she continued up to the gates. Reluctantly, he followed.

At once, the absent wind returned in force, and the world swirled around them. Branches cracked and dead leaves danced as the rain fell, and the couple broke into a run. Lightning spread across the sky, and a boom filled their ears a split-second later. It sounded almost like laughter.

The dark shadows of the barbican embraced them just as the rain came down in earnest. A chill wind howled through the tunnel, bringing in icy rain. Thorns had crept into what was left of the forward post, offering no barbless wall to lean against. They looked across the lowered drawbridge and saw a window in the keep, illuminated with light from a lone flame.

Wordlessly, they both sprinted through the rain, past the nature-ruined portcullis, and into the castle proper. They barely dodged the tangling vines and choking weeds as they weaved through the courtyard. By the time they reached the doors to the keep, they were both soaked and cut.

What little light there was streamed into the hall as the door groaned open. A bright flash of lightning lit the sequestered chamber for an instant before a rumbling boom again filled the air. The light vanished as the doors slammed shut, and the wind dropped to a distant eerie whistle in the unlit room.

"Wh-what is this place?" Greg asked, panting as he fumbled through his pack. The room echoed with the sounds of his blind groping for a flashlight.

"I-I don't know, I . . . I think this is . . . Faussesflammes," Stephanie said, equally out of breath. "It's, like, a château people tell ghost stories about."

"Great." He finally pulled out a glow stick. "We're spending a night in a haunted castle." With a crack, artificial crimson light filled the room. The stone walls sported remnants of tapestries, weapon mounts, and fine stonework. Ashen smudges hung around strange cressets affixed to the wall. A lone fireplace sat in the distance, wicked gargoyles emerging from the wall to hold it aloft. Cobwebs and rubble scattered and clung to the place, and the teasing light of a still flame was visible from around the corner. The place seemed almost coolly angry that anyone would dare disturb its slumber.

"You gotta admit," Stephanie said with a grin, "it's kinda sexy."

Wind whistled through the cracks in the stonework as the two surveyed the chamber. It was like something out of an old Universal Studios movie—an obvious set that felt all too real. Stephanie gently brushed the walls with her fingertips as she regained her breath.

"So, uh," Greg finished panting with two large breaths, "what are some of the stories here?"

"Weird stuff. A knight or nobleman lived here, but he was also an evil sorcerer or something. And there were other things, like people who summoned demons, I think. Things lived around here, too. Goblins, snake people—"

"Werewolves," Greg said without question.

"—werewolves, goat people, ghosts. Even vampires."

"What, like, French Dracula?" he asked, then in an atrocious accent, "I wan-to suck you' bloo'!"

"Okay, Bela Le Gosi . . . ." She smiled. "It's weird, though. No one could ever tell me where the place was. It was just . . . around here."

"Well, we found it and it looks like we're stuck in it." He peered around the eerily-lit room as thunder reverberated through the stone. "We should find someplace else in here to camp."

She turned away from the leering gargoyle and beamed an over-eager smile. "There was a light up in one of the towers. Maybe some-one else is here, too."

Greg nodded as more thunder rolled outside. They grabbed their packs and headed up the stairs.

Through the château, their crimson glow stick led the way down twisting, oddly-angled halls, tight corners, and dead ends. Despite the crumbling exterior and a thick coating of cobwebs and dust, the châ-teau's insides showed little signs of age. The doors, stonework, furni-ture, and trappings were all strangely preserved underneath all the usual signs of ancient neglect.

Vague lights were teasingly visible from just around every corner, hinting at well-lit torches just around the bend. But each turn revealed only a darkened hallway beyond. The strange metal cressets that stood bolted to the walls were cold and empty. The couple called out, politely at first before turning to harsh demands, but no answer ever came to them. As they stalked the fleeting lights, the wind continued to cackle and shadows danced just beyond their sight.

They found many rooms with varying furnishings, but no true light or sign of recent habitation. Eventually, they stopped in a lavish bed-room and put their packs down. The storm raged strangely through the large glass windows, simultaneously up close and at a distance.

"It's almost beautiful," Stephanie said, walking up to the dingy glass.

"Yeah, almost," Greg said, pulling out their gear.

Whenever they went hiking, even for just a day, they brought all they might need to spend a night in the woods. Extra food, a sleeping bag, a small tent, medical supplies, tools, and even a flare gun.

"Any of those stories mention weird lights?" he asked.

"Not that I can remember, no. But the name does mean 'false flames'. Maybe it's just some trick of the architecture?"

"Some trick." Greg started unpacking the food and sleeping bags. "Anything you can remember besides just 'weird stuff'?"

"Uh, let's see. . . ." Stephanie walked back to the bed, dust flying up as she sat on the blankets. "There's only one big one. There was a troubadour named . . . Gerard, and he came across the place after get-ting lost in the woods because of an evil enchantment. He got—"

"Wait," he said as he joined his wife on the bed and handed her some food, "if he knew it was some evil spell, why didn't he just leave?"

"He tried to, but he kept on coming back to the same place. Anyway, the knight, Malinbois or something, was waiting for him and invited him to dinner. There was also a girl, Florence I think, and her servants that wer—No, Fleurette! Her name was Fleurette. They were all held captive and locked in their rooms after dinner. And in the middle of the night, the knight and his wife went into the rooms and drank their blood!"

"Buh-laahhh!" Greg did his French Dracula again, eliciting a giggle.

"But Gerard knew something was up, so he pretended to be asleep and waited for the knight to come back. When he did, Gerard and Fleurette's manservant attacked and beat him back with the walking stick. He chased the two vampires off and waited until daylight, found their crypt, and killed them."

"And saved the girl?"

"Pretty much. That's the only real story; the rest were just rumors about what lived here."

"Yeah, you said ghosts, goats, werewolves, demons, and lizards?"

"And witches, yeah. But what creepy castle doesn't have ghosts, and what place *here* doesn't have werewolves?" She thirstily drank from her water bottle. "There were stories about a satyr, though."

"Like the Greek thing?"

"Yeah, but that's kind of all over the region. There was a story about a snake-lady. She would lure people to the château in their dreams and they'd never be seen again."

Lightning flashed in concert with a boom of thunder, punctuating her tale. The two looked out at the rainy haze beyond.

"I've got a bad feeling about this place," Greg said soberly. "The storm, getting lost, those lights, this . . . place. I don't like it."

"Well, there goes my idea," she said, playfully nudging him.

"What?"

"I was going to explore the place." She stood up and finished the snack bar as she walked to the doorway. "I mean, it *is* a château, and a pretty nice one, considering. We should have some fun while we're here. Who else can say they did something like this on their honeymoon?"

Thunder rumbled in the distance as he stood and walked over to her. She had *that* smile on her face, and *that* put a smirk on his. He put his hands on her arms, folded tightly to her chest.

"Okay," he surrendered, "but let's change into some dry clothes first."

Their spare clothes were *mostly* dry—certainly more so than their current attire. They set up their sleeping bags on the large bed, its bedding and blankets still intact and even comfy. When they were ready to set out, the storm had only increased in strength. Greg grabbed a small pack with some food, chalk, and a compass. Stephanie grabbed her camera and thoroughly captured their quarters.

The stonework shuddered with the thunder as they traveled down the still and unfamiliar halls of the château.

Stephanie peered into each room they came across. Some were empty, some furnished, but each was in the same eerily preserved state; untouched by ruin under the telltale signs of age. She snapped pictures and selfies, and tried sending some to friends, but the poor signal in the abbey was non-existent inside the stone fortress.

Meanwhile, Greg paced down the hallways trying to catch the Barmecidal flames. Though it was now past dusk beyond the dark storm clouds, the halls were mysteriously illuminated. Not just by the ephemeral hints of light around the corners, but as if some unseen torch lit each hall from the cressets. The illumination was vague at best, keeping the perceived world in a state between light and dark. It was enough to make out details and enough for shadows to grow.

Eventually, the two came to a covered terrace that encircled a small courtyard. The rain still pulsed steadily, but they could make out most of the other side. The courtyard's stony surface had mostly given way to choking weeds, but in the middle stood a statued fountain of a knight, crumbled and gripped by thick vines.

"I think it's letting up," Stephanie said after a distant rumble.

Then the shattering crash of lighting sounded as white-purple veins spread across the sky.

"Or not," she corrected herself.

"Look." Greg pointed.

Through the rain, the outline of large windows was visible. From inside shone the same traces of light as from the empty corridors, but somehow brighter.

The rain intensified as they made their way cautiously around the dilapidated knight. After the confined maze of the castle's interior, the open space of the courtyard made them both wary. The rain obscured much of the courtyard's opposite terrace. Though neither had seen any sign of habitation in the château, save the light, they couldn't help but wonder who or what could be hiding in the obscurity of rain and stone.

Before the approaching couple were two large doors, made of wood and bound by rusted iron. Together, they pushed one door open and proceeded inside.

They emerged into a vaguely-lit dining hall dominated on one end by a large, long-unused fireplace and a lengthy wooden table in its center. There was a soft sound amidst the still silence, slowly working its way forward.

"Wow," Stephanie said in awe. "Should have eaten dinner in here."

As they neared the table, an aroma drifted to meet them, one of freshly cooked meat and baked bread, of exotic spices and earthy wine. The curious scent embraced them, and the hunger staved off by their makeshift meal began to grow. The strange half-light revealed to them the table already set for two, and awaiting them was an array of fruits and vegetables, steaming baguettes, a pot of boiling stew, ancient wine already in glasses, and a large roasted hog with an apple in its mouth.

The far-off whisper turned to music as the lights grew. The room remained indistinct, but the high ceiling was just as visible as the trace of wall at the far end. The music, from a period as old as the château, filled the room and echoed, hauntingly imperfect and beautiful, from the high ceiling.

"Well, that's just weird," Greg said.

"Yeah . . . . Hey, are you . . . are you hungry?"

"Very. But . . . ."

"Yeah . . . ."

The couple backed away from the scene slowly, reaching for one another. They had heard the stories of this land and, despite fascination, had shaken them off. It was old superstition, local flavor and nothing more. But here they were in the Château Faussesflammes, a meal prepared for them with music, and an impenetrable storm outside.

As they backed away, they felt a tug deep inside them. Their hunger grew with their increasingly ragged breaths and each step became more difficult than the last.

Finally, they exited to the terrace, rain still pouring down in the center, and pulled the massive door closed. The knight was barely visible, choked by ivy and a severed sword arm lying in the mud.

Both still felt the pull of the ghostly hall behind them, the desire to stay inside, to eat and drink and dance and love to the phantasmal orchestra and spectral flames. Sluggishly, the two lovers turned to look at one another and saw on each other a look of automated lust, a primal mask with dull and vacant eyes.

They moved closer to one another and felt a need to embrace. Blood rushing through their veins was all they could hear, and they felt a sharp longing for all that the château promised. They kissed, roughly, as some primitive part of them took control. They fumbled at removing their packs and pushing on the door, awkwardly unable to decide which to do first.

The straps of Greg's pack slipped off his shoulders, but the larger one around his waist was still tightly clasped. The weight pulled at him just enough for his feet to slip on the rain-slick stonework.

He hit the ground hard and yelped in pain. Stephanie stopped her mad scrabble at once and knelt beside her husband. As she helped him up, they both felt the haunting tug creep back into their hearts.

"We need to leave," Stephanie said. Greg only nodded.

They walked back to their commandeered room at a brisk pace. Around them, they each thought they heard hisses from the shadows. The low-lit flames from the corners seemed hostile now, as if they were heralding some monster behind the corner.

But no shadows moved against them, no creatures revealed themselves, and they returned to their chambers without incident. In lieu of a proper lock, they braced the door with a chair and the hornbeam staff. Greg began pulling out a map, a compass, and lamps. Lightning flashed, filling the room with blinding light and a rumble soon after.

"Greg, we can't go out in this weather."

"Well, we can't stay here, either!"

She walked over and knelt to look at him, worry as plain in her eyes as the panic was in his.

"Everything is okay," she whispered. "It's just an old castle. Who knows what we saw? But we're fine now, here. Together..."

He nodded. Both of them knew how dangerous it was to go out in a storm like this. Together, they walked over to the bed and spent the night in their annexed room.

Stephanie awoke slowly, unaware of how much time had passed. The rain outside had ceased, but darkness still draped the outside. She moaned contently as she reached over to Greg but felt only the cold fabric of the sleeping bag.

The realization beat in her chest like a drum, and she shot up to frantically look around the room. She found nothing, only the fraction of the room illuminated by the light. The darkness outside seemed to increasingly spill in from the window and the ever-present silence added to the racing of her heart.

"Greg," she worked up the courage to call out. "Where are you, hun?"

No answer came, spurring her to rise from the bed. She donned her clothes and grabbed the flashlight, but her search of their occupied quarters revealed only their gear. She reached the door and discovered the makeshift barricade had been laid aside.

Outside, the hallways were still lit with the same Barmecidal flames as earlier. She called out, several times, but no reply came. She went back inside the room and packed up their belongings, making sure everything was ready to go when she found him. To the chorus of her ragged, nervous breath, she grabbed the hornbeam staff and pack before she entered the dark corridor.

Stalking down the halls, Stephanie kept calling out for her husband. She used chalk to mark her way through the labyrinthine keep. While before she found the whistling wind and pounding rain to be unsettling, she now discovered that the still silence was even more unnerving. It was a silence that begged to be heard, and if focused on for too long would reveal the whispering sound of sliding coils. As she continued her desperate search, Stephanie found herself calling out not to find Greg but to escape that pervasive silence, and she muttered his name like a mantra between her desperate cries.

Eventually, she found herself back in the courtyard, the still-lit dining hall across the way. She walked across the open courtyard, stonework broken by overgrowth, and looked up. Above her was blackness; a vast and featureless dark sky.

Transfixed by the black sky, she walked straight into the statue's plinth and staggered back. The vines that had grown over the stone horse and rider looked vicious up close, like tightly bound black-green wire. Circling the figure, she saw how the vines had worked their way into the cracked stonework. One thick strand had wrapped itself around the knight's neck before disappearing into the cracked helmet.

Walking backwards from the ruined effigy, Stephanie tripped over the knight's fallen sword and tumbled to the ground. The pack on her back hit first with a dull, wet thud and she found herself anchored by its new bulk. She released the straps that tethered her and rose, spinning around to face the high, lit hall.

Music played from inside, a seductive hint of a harpsichord, flutes, and drums. She picked up the hornbeam staff and pocketed the flare gun and flashlight before she approached the heavy wooden doors. With effort, she thrust them open and charged into the empty but lively chamber. The aromatic feast was still arrayed down the long table, the music and lights were projected from some unknown source. Greg, alone and wearing an elegant frock coat, danced before an empty fireplace.

"Greg!" Stephanie yelled as she ran over to him. "Greg, what are you doing?"

As she approached, he put an end to his phantom waltz and looked at her, his eyes as blank and dull as before. The coat he wore was loose and ill-fitted, but still pristine under cobwebs and dust.

"Stephanie," he said with hollow excitement, "you made it!"

He reached out and kissed her. Again, she found herself surrendering to lust and falling into him for a moment. She could stay here with him for the rest of her li—

A split second of clarity bought her enough time to stop what she was doing and move away.

"Stop. Greg, please," she said, fending him off as he pursued.

She looked at him as he reached out, his expression simultaneously offended and blank. She grabbed his shoulders and shook him as much as she would dare. The creeping tug in her mind begged her to stop.

He blinked slowly and his senses returned. He looked around, not confused by where he was, but why he was there. He quickly and awkwardly shed the old frock coat, then looked around.

"I . . . I heard a sound. I went to check it out. I can't explain why, I just . . . I had to follow it. I found this jacket and I . . . ."

"Honey . . . the rain's gone. We need to leave."

He nodded as he tossed the coat and followed Stephanie out hand in hand. The music around them grew louder and discordant as they ran to the open doors and out into the weed-choked courtyard. They passed Stephanie's discarded pack and ran back into the serpentine halls.

While the shadow-swaddled corridors of Château Faussesflammes were mysterious and beckoning before, they now held a lethal promise that stalked the two fleeing lovers. Indiscernible sounds wove themselves in between footfalls and panting breaths; sounds that made them question if all they had heard before was really just the wind. The poor illumination provided by the castle grew dimmer as they raced towards the keep's entrance. Both could feel a preternatural presence bearing down on them as they ran, ready to swallow them up if they stopped.

Then the spectral lights vanished as quickly as they turned a corner. After a cacophony of shallow breaths, Greg grabbed the flashlight from Stephanie's pocket and its white beam pierced the encroaching blackness. But the shadows, like a rolling black fog, pushed back against their desperate beam. The darkness grew with the whispers. Soon, the luminous lance was rendered inert and they were adrift in a sea of conspiring darkness, tethered only to each other by their white-knuckle grips. Grabbing hold of the hornbeam staff, Stephanie swept the ground before them and they pressed on.

The malicious whispers, now like the scraping of sandpaper on metal, surrounded them as they made their way forward. Creeping into the couple's minds, those phantom voices touched their very souls with dread and ecstasy, fear and desire.

Only because of that primal part of them, the one that instilled their bodies with an instinctual need to escape peril, did they keep moving. But another part of them wanted to stay, motivated by fear and want muddled together like black ink in water. They only half-remembered the way out, their innocent arrival seeming more like days ago than mere hours.

The stout hornbeam staff felt sluggish in Stephanie's hands as she swept it before their feet. Any sound of it hitting the floor in front of them was drowned out by the creeping whispers and she was left to navigate by the feel of wood striking stone.

She froze in place as she felt a tug on the staff, and Greg crashed into her. She relaxed her grip and the hornbeam drifted on its own. Then came a wrench that nearly took it away. Seized with panic, Stephanie pulled out the flare gun and fired it off into the yawning black.

The darkness retreated in a wash of milky crimson, revealing an impossibly wide space unbound by walls, floors, or ceilings. The shadows bordering the flare's light rippled with shapes half-familiar to the two. Wolves and goats, serpents and toads, and forms of men all reached out at them, hands and claws growing closer as the scarlet burned away. Fear and wonder took them completely, and they found themselves transfixed and waiting.

In the same moment, they squeezed one another's hands. Stephanie breathed in deep, steeling herself for the blind flight, and felt Greg press a kiss against her knuckles.

They ran forward, staff swinging wildly to no effect. Threatening whispers accompanied tearing grasps as the shadows crashed down on them and drowned out all feeling.

Stephanie hit something hard, her body rebounding off it. She moved her hand over the obstacle with torpid clumsiness and eventually recognized the door. She cried out to no avail, unable to overcome the whispers around her and was awarded with the choking taste of ash. She threw herself at the door once, twice, three times; uncaring of the abuse she put her body through.

Finally, the door burst open and Stephanie spilled out into the ruined bailey, accompanied by a piercing and unnatural scream. The impenetrable, all-consuming blackness that was the sky above pushed down as shadows quickly spewed forth.

"Come on!" Stephanie yelled as she bolted towards the portcullis. The hazardous sprint seemed interminable as she dodged weeds, bramble, and broken stonework. Her body screamed with pain and fear as her mind was still half-anchored to the ancient construct.

Ragged and breathless, with tears and sweat streaming down, she crossed the barbican's threshold.

At once, the black sky was gone, replaced with the blinding light of the midday sun. Birds twittered in the distance and a gentle breeze created the all-too familiar and comforting sound of rustling leaves. This pleasant new environment turned breaths of exhaustion into fits of laughter.

Stephanie turned back and looked at the château, a crumbling ruin that was much less than it was before.

"Doesn't look so bad now," she said, a smile creeping across her face.

When no response came, panic seized her. She looked around and called out for Greg, but he was nowhere to be found. Her breath caught in her throat. She thought of all the times she had been so enthralled by those stories, thinking them just that.

Her jaw quivered as her gaze was drawn back to the massive bulwark of the castle. The immemorial château looked sinister again, almost sneering. It mocked her loss, another victory over foreign interlopers.

Captive breath burning inside, her despair turned to rage. She gripped the hornbeam staff, now an old and faithful friend, and exhaled.

Slowly, she walked back towards the Château Faussesflammes.

To Klarkash-Ton, Lord of Averoigne

by H.P. Lovecraft

A time-black tower against dim banks of cloud;
Around its base the pathless pressing wood.
Shadow and silence, moss and mould, enshroud
Grey, age fell'd slabs that once as cromlechs stood,
No fall of foot, no song of bird awakes
The lethal aisles of sempiternal night
Tho' oft with stir of wings the dense air shakes
As in the towre there glows a pallid light.

For here, apart, dwells one whose hands have wrought
Strange eidola that chill the world with fear;
Whose graven runes in tones of dread have taught
What things beyond the star-gulfs lurk and leer.
Dark Lord of Averiogne—whose windows stare
On pits of dream no other gaze could bear!

ABOUT THE AUTHORS

Manuel Arenas currently resides in Phoenix, Arizona where he pens his Gothic fantasies and dark ditties sheltered behind heavy curtains, as he shuns the oppressive orb which glares down on him from the cloudless, dust filled desert sky. His work has appeared in various genre publications, most notably in the poetry journal *Spectral Realms*. For more info, visit his blog at mannysbookofshadows.wordpress.com.

Matthew Baugh is the author of more than forty published short stories dealing with monsters, pirates, gunslingers, robots, elder horrors, dinosaurs, and whatever else strikes his fancy. His favorite authors include Umberto Eco, Robert E. Howard, R.A. MacAvoy, Raymond Chandler, and Alexandre Dumas. When not writing stories he is an ordained minister serving a church in Manhattan Beach, CA. Matthew's most difficult challenge is always writing about himself in the third person for the "about the authors" section.

Trevor O. Childers is a Vendor Management Specialist at Fidelity National Agency Solutions by day and a writer of horror, science fiction, and fantasy until the next morning. He writes from his home and sometimes from the local coffee shop. He lives in Plano, Texas with his girlfriend Kendall and their cat Luna. He attended the Virginia Military Institute where he earned a Bachelor of Arts in English with a Concentration in Writing. While there, he served as a tutor at the writing center, an Editor for *New Horizons*, the school's undergraduate research journal, and the Editor-in-Chief of *Sounding Brass*, the school's prose and poetry journal. This is his fifth publication, having been previously published in *Lovecraftiana* Magazine, *Swords Against Cthulhu III: A New Dark Age*, and *Sounding Brass*.

Dan Clore is an avant-garde freelance writer and scholar of horror & weird fantasy with an excellent (albeit occasionally baffling) sense of humor. He's published articles in *Lovecraft Studies*, *Studies in Weird Fiction*, and numerous other journals and critical anthologies, as well as authoring *Weird Words: A Lovecraftian Lexicon*. His fiction is collected in the volume *The Unspeakable and Others*.

James Chambers is an award-winning author of horror, crime, fantasy, and science fiction who received the Bram Stoker Award® for the graphic novel, *Kolchak the Night Stalker: The Forgotten Lore of Edgar Allan Poe* and is a three-time Bram Stoker Award nominee. He is the author of the collections *On the Night Border*, described by *Booklist* as "a haunting exploration of the space where the real world and nightmares collide," and *Resurrection House* as well as the *Corpse Fauna* novella series and the dark urban fantasy novella, *Three Chords of Chaos*. *Publisher's Weekly* gave his Lovecraftian collection, *The Engines of Sacrifice*, a starred review and called it "...chillingly evocative." His website is: www.jameschambersonline.com.

Keith Chapman was an editor and contributor for various fiction publications in London in the 1960s, such as *Edgar Wallace Mystery Magazine*, before shifting to New Zealand where he spent nearly 35 years in newspaper and magazine journalism. "I've written fiction under several names in many genres besides fantasy: Western, adventure, supernatural, mystery, war, romance, whatever ... novels, comic book scripts, and short stories. In fact, I can say that since leaving school I've never earned a dollar other than from written words." In the 1990s Keith began writing the Chap O'Keefe Western novels and later edited the Black Horse Extra online magazine for six years. As well as standalone titles, the O'Keefe Westerns include the adventures of an ex-Pinkerton detective, Joshua Dillard, and the exploits of the engaging Miss Lilian Goodnight, a feisty heroine better known as Misfit Lil. Chap O'Keefe books were published in the series Black Horse Westerns (alongside reissues of such classic authors as Ernest Haycox, Max Brand, William Colt MacDonald, and Les Savage, Jr.) and Ulverscroft's Linford Western Library and Dales Westerns. Many of the O'Keefe Westerns are now available as eBooks.

Cardinal Cox first encountered the works of CAS in tatty Panther collections. Now in his fifties, his work has been printed in the small press for around thirty-five years. When a schoolboy he worked in holidays on archaeological sites. Amongst the posts he has held he has been a Poet-in-Residence of a Victorian cemetery (for three years) and the Dracula Society (for two years). Out of the latter he was commissioned to write a one-man "spooken-word" show (High Stakes) that he toured around, including a performance at Worldcon 75 in Helsinki, Finland.

Ashley Dioses is a writer of dark fantasy, horror, and weird poetry from southern California. Her debut collection of dark traditional poetry, *Diary of a Sorceress*, was released from Hippocampus Press in 2017. Her second collection of early works, *The Withering*, is forthcoming from Gehenna and Hinnom Books. Her poetry has appeared in *Weird Fiction Review*, *Spectral Realms*, *Weirdbook* Magazine, and elsewhere. Her poem "Carathis," appeared in Ellen Datlow's full recommended Best Horror of the Year Volume Seven list. She has also appeared in the *Horror Writers Association Poetry Showcase 2016* for her poem "Ghoul Mistress." She is currently an Active Member in the HWA and a member of the SFPA. Aside from writing, her other passions include martial arts and delving into esoteric and occult studies. She blogs at fiendlover.blogspot.com.

Garnett Elliott lives and works in Tucson, Arizona. Nominated for a Derringer award, he has had previous work published in *Alfred Hitchcock's Mystery Magazine*, *Beneath Ceaseless Skies*, and numerous online magazines. He wrote several volumes of *The Drifter Detective* series, available from Beat to a Pulp publishing. More recently, he has published the role-playing games *Neonpunk Crysis*, *Blood Sundown*, and *Red Venus* with Filigree Forge, all available at DriveThru RPG.

Wade German is the author of two collections of poetry, *The Ladies of the Everlasting Lichen and Other Relics* (Mount Abraxas Press, 2019) and *Dreams from a Black Nebula* (Hippocampus Press, 2014). His poems have appeared in numerous journals and anthologies such as *Dreams and Nightmares*, *Fungi*, *Spectral Realms*, *Weird Fiction Review*, *Anno Klarkash-Ton* (*Rainfall Books, 2017*) and *Best of Black Wings* (PS Publishing, 2019).

Colin Harker is a scholar, author, and screenwriter of horror, with a particular predilection for the Gothic. Two of her stories have been performed by the award-winning NoSleep Podcast and her published works have appeared in anthologies such as *The Book of Blasphemous Words* and *Dreams of Desolation.* The haunting tales of Clark Ashton

Smith have exerted a profound influence on her writing since she first began reading him as a teenager and the realm of Averoigne in particular, with its scheming sorcerers and sympathetic vampires, has always held a special place in her heart.

Ron Hilger is a Northern California native who has organized such Clark Ashton Smith related events as "The CAS Centennial Conference" in 1993 and "The CAS Plaque Dedication" in 2002. Hilger has also edited *The Averoigne Chronicles* (for Centipede Press), *Red World of Polaris* (with Scott Connors for Night Shade Books, 2003), and *Star Changes* (with Scott Connors for Darkside Press, 2005.) Together, Ron Hilger and Scott Connors edited the five-volume set, *The Collected Fantasies of Clark Ashton Smith* and *The Miscellaneous Writings of Clark Ashton Smith* for Night Shade Books, which have come to be regarded as the definitive versions of Smith's stories. He is already at work on his next project, *The Hyperborean Mythos.*

Aaron Hollingsworth is a Missourian of mostly Western European decent, with a touch of mountain goat and catfish. He has always been a storyteller, whether he was playing with action figures as a child, writing bad poetry as a teen, composing depressing love songs or GMing tabletop role-playing games in his twenties, or indie-publishing fiction in his thirties. His goal as a writer is to write "about the impossible in the best way possible". While his influences are many, his discovery of Clark Ashton Smith was like finding the Holy Grail; something elusive that cannot be grasped for long, but an impossible level of artistry still worth striving for. Aaron Hollingsworth lives in Kansas City, and is the author of such works as the *Four Winds - One Storm* series, *The Broken Bards of Paris*, *The Apothecary of Mantua*, *The Steel Tales* series, as well as numerous RPG books. He invites the curious to visit his website at: aaronhollingsworth.com and to like his Facebook page: Aaron Hollingsworth-Writer.

If **H.P. Lovecraft** is someone you've never heard of, hang your head in shame.

The late **Brian McNaughton** was a reporter for the *Newark Evening News* during the day, while at the night writing fantasy-horror stories that mixed sex, satire, and black humor. Altogether he published about two hundred short stories in magazines and several books. *The Throne of Bones*, a collection of horror-fantasy stories about ghouls set in an opulent, decadent world reminiscent of Clark Ashton Smith, won the 1998 World Fantasy Award for best collection, and was nominated for the Bram Stoker Award for Best Fiction Collection. Most of his work has been re-published by Wildside Press, including the short story collections *Nasty Stories* and *Even More Nasty Stories*.

Michael Minnis was born and raised in Michigan. He read his first Clark Ashton Smith story, *The Colossus of Ylourgne,* at age 15. Mike's stories have appeared in *Dead but Dreaming, Eldritch Blue, Rehearsals for Oblivion, Horrors Beyond, Reves d'Ulthar, Lost Worlds of Space and Time,* and *Your Poisoned Dreams.* Michael's work was also compiled in the collections *Anencephalous* and *The Girl Who Walked in Circles.* In 2008, Mike received an Honorable Mention in Datlow and Windling's 16th Edition of *The Year's Best Fantasy and Horror* for his short story *Salt Air, Dead but Dreaming.* Michael recently wrote and published a children's and young adult book, *Three Paws: Sophia and Her Story of Triumph.* Michael is an avid student of the Civil War and World War II. His novels include *The Last Confederate Freak Show* and *The Peoples' Hare.* Michael lives in Highland, MI.

Glenn A. Rahman, in the 1970s and 80s, was a frequent per-computer era contributor to the semi-pro scene, such as *Fantasy Crosswinds, Eldritch Tales,* and *Crypt of Cthulhu.* His first professional publication came with the release of the fantasy board game *Divine Right*, published by TSR, Inc. in 1979. This was followed by *Knights of Camelot* (1980, TSR), the *Trojan War* (1980, Metagaming), and *Down with the King* (1980, Avalon Hill). During this time, Glenn Rahman and his brother Philip (founder of the still-extant Fedogan and Bremer book company, specializing in Cthulhu Mythos and supernaturally-themed literature) created a two-part article for *Sorcerer's Apprentice,* the *Lovecraft Variant* and the *Monsters of the Cthulhu Mythos* which amounted to the first successful transference of H.P. Lovecraft's style of supernatural literature into a modern role-playing format. In addition, Mr. Rahman has continued to publish board gaming and fantasy role-playing articles and supplements widely. His first book-length fictional work was serialized in *Dragon Magazine* (beginning in 1980), entitled *The Minarian Legends*, which keyed off his original *Divine Right* universe. In 1989, Mr. Rahman's HPL-inspired novel *Heir of Darkness* was released from New Infinities Productions, Inc., followed in 2001 when Sidecar Books of Minneapolis, MN published his *Gardens of Lucullus*, a Cthulhu Mythos novel in collaboration with Richard L. Tierney. Currently, a new edition of *Divine Right* is slated for release in 2020, to be followed soon by a second original board game, *Scarlet Empire*.

David Reid Ross is an amateur historian with a lifelong interest in the "Late Antique" era in Europe and the Near East. He has written two books covering the early development of Islam: "House of War" and "Throne of Glass". "The Cult of the Singing Flame" is his first fiction story, originally posted (somewhat chaotically) to fanfiction.net 2017. He also writes code; "TIMPIST" is a rendition of a TRS-80 game into C#, which can be had from CodeProject.com. He would like to dedicate this story to the memory of Robert E. Howard.

Edward Stasheff is wanted in thirteen states for armchair anarchy, contributing to the delinquency of everyone, and criminally bad jokes. He runs Pickman's Press, a publisher of Lovecrafian Horror, Weird Fiction, and Dark Fantasy, starting in 2018 with *Corporate Cthulhu: Mythos Tales of Bureaucratic Nightmare*. He has a short story appearing in Elm Books' new steampunk mystery anthology *Death in the Age of Steam*. Despite his growing notoriety and infamy, he remains a big nerd.

Richard Tierney was born in north central Iowa. Beginning in his teens, he has been both a fan and scholar of H.P. Lovecraft, Robert E. Howard, Clark Ashton Smith and other great names from the pulp fiction era. In 1961, he earned a degree in entomological science (Iowa State College) and served for many years with the U.S. Forest Service in the West of the United States and Alaska. An archaeological tourist by instinct, he has traveled widely, especially in Mexico, Central, and South America. Many of the ideas and images that he has employed in his stories have been inspired by his extensive travels. In the literary field, Mr. Tierney has frequently been both an editor and a writer of adventure fiction, mainly in the realm of dark fantasy. He has coauthored the *Red Sonja* series for Ace Books (early 1980's) and created the popular hero-adventurer, Simon of Gitta, a fictionalized version of Simon Magus. His hardcover works include *Collected Poems* (1983, Arkham House), *The House of the Toad* (1993, Fedogan and Bremer) and *The Drums of Chaos* (2008, Mythos Books.)

DJ Tyrer is the person behind Atlantean Publishing and has been widely published in anthologies and magazines around the world, such as *Chilling Horror Short Stories* (Flame Tree), *The Mad Visions of al-Hazred*, *The Idolators of Cthulhu* and *Miskatonic Dreams* (all Alban Lake), *What Dwells Below* (Sirens Call), and *Steampunk Cthulhu* (Chaosium), and issues of *Sirens Call, Cyaegha, Ravenwood Quarterly*, and *Weirdbook*, as well as having a Yellow Mythos novella available in paperback and on the Kindle, *The Yellow House* (Dunhams Manor) and a comic horror e-novelette with Smith and Lovecraftian elements, *A Trip to the Middle of the World*, available from Alban Lake through Infinite Realms Bookstore. Check out his website at djtyrer.blogspot.co.uk, or follow him on Twitter @djtyrer.

Henry J. Vester III spent his larval stage in southern California, feasting on the works of Edgar Rice Burroughs, Arthur Conan Doyle, H.P. Lovecraft, Robert E. Howard, and Sax Rohmer. His amazed discovery of the works of Clark Ashton Smith added new and unguessed dimensions to his life from that time forward. Vester has contributed tales, articles, and poetry to *Fungi, Chronicles of the Cthulhu Codex, Eldritch Tales*, and others, and has appeared in the Chaosium volumes *The Innsmouth Cycle* and *The Tsathoggua Cycle*. He has been a Guest Reader at the H.P. Lovecraft Film Festival in Portland, Oregon, and has contributed material to *The Eldritch Dark* website, which honors the life and work of Clark Ashton Smith. Now retired from his career as a family therapist, Vester continues to elude both the FBI and the Brotherhood of the Silver Claw, and makes his home in the high desert country of southern Oregon.

Simon Whitechapel has been a keyly committed core component of the Klarkash-Ton Kommunity ever since he bought a battered Panther paperback of *Genius Loci* on Tardebigge Market in 1987. He thinks that the world's most powerful drugs are H_2O, math and language, and that Clark Ashton Smith is therefore one of the greatest pharmacologists who ever lived. He blogs at OverlordoftheUberFeral.com, and his CAS tributes are available at http://lulu.com/sortilege.

More Books from Pickman's Press

THE AVEROIGNE ARCHIVES

For the first time in paperback or ebook, all of Clark Ashton Smith's weird tales of Averoigne—the sinister, monster-haunted province of medieval France—are collected into one volume. Were-wolves and satyrs stalk the dark forests, witches and necromancers lurk in the swamps, and gargoyles and giants terror-ize the cathedral city of Vyônes.

CORPORATE CTHULHU

Just like the Great Old Ones, corpora-tions are powerful but unseen entities we have no control over, yet subtly manipu-late our lives and our world—and we don't even realize it. Who needs a Cthulhu Cult when you've got Cthulhu, Inc.? Endure twenty-five Mythos tales of bureaucratic nightmare, but remember: it's nothing personal—just business.

Paperbacks available from Amazon, Barnes & Noble, and Lulu.

eBooks available from Amazon, Barnes & Noble, Google Play, Apple iBooks, Kobo eBookstore, Drive Thru Fiction, and Lulu.

www.ingramcontent.com/pod-product-compliance
Lightning Source LLC
Chambersburg PA
CBHW071741110726
47908CB00006B/1663